*A Historic Odyssey & Civil War Love Story*

This captivating, true love story describes in vivid detail the life and times of a Civil War Union captain, William Hunter, who catches the heart of a lovely Confederate widow smuggler. Their fiery, dramatic romance unfolds against the odds of war and personal pain.

Hunter, an officer of the United States Colored Troops, finds peace and understanding with his troops in the beautiful but beleaguered city of Natchez, Mississippi—the area where his ancestors were once slaveholders.

Hunter Hall weaves the dark thread of African American history throughout. Following Black history's haunting path through slavery, emancipation and participation as key players in the drama of their own liberation and attainment of their God-given right to stand as free men and women.

Paralleling the lives of many immigrants, the Hunter family arrives on this continent during the Colonial period. They are involved in the politics of the nation as it grows by helping to found the state of Mississippi and having a voice in the Senate in Washington, D.C.

Follow the family as it moves from postwar Illinois to abundant Iowa then to turbulent Kansas and eventually to Nebraska.

The mysterious, dramatic closure of the story will linger in your memory.

# Hunter Hall

*A Historic Odyssey & Civil War Love Story*

Amy Sadle

This is a work of fiction. Names, characters, places and incidents are either a matter of historical record or a product of the author's imagination or are used fictiously.

For information address Amy Sadle, Box H, Syracuse, NE 68446.


First Edition.

*Designed by Nora Tallmon*

Library of Congress Control Number 2003113582

ISBN 0-9743819-7-7

# Dedication

This book is dedicated to Drucilla Inez Hunter Sadle, a strong, loving and wise mother-in-law. It is a book I know she would enjoy.

# Table of Contents

# Prologue

Many people have been assets and resources in the six-year adventure of putting this narrative together. Of greatest support has been my husband who has traveled and worked with me to trace his great grandfathers' story.

The inspirations of some divine nature were overwhelming; it was as though my mother-in-law stood beside me in this project.

Frequently I invented a scenario, only to find that it was a fact. I have acknowledged the experts, scholars and friends who have aided me at the conclusion of the novel. These are advisors who shared family legends, expertise, designed, proofed and edited the volume.

The premise I began with was a personal vision that no instance in History or life appears without the fiber and threads that have created it. No person exists without divine design. The quilt of past, present, and future is formed from unique fragments that are tied by the tiny, momentous stitches of ancestry and events. Every family in this nation has a comparative dramatic history to this family and the comrades of William Hugh Hunter.

Sarah Drucilla Scothorne Hunter was also a product of the times and many interwoven lives. In her honor I am attempting to give a historic, but fictionalized story of the strong Southern women of Natchez. They suffered personally in every case and endured an unbelievable thirteen years of occupation by the Union.

When we began to research genealogy many years ago we had no idea that my husband's great-grandfather was the officer of Black troops in the Civil War. The chains of history rattled, later a friend stood with us on a windy night at Forks of the Road and pointed to a nearby location.

This location, Monmouth Plantation, was where Captain Hunter was assigned daily duty, and a place that needed to be part of the story. Important to the story also was an adjacent historic slave market called Forks of the Road. The story of the Black soldiers needed to be expanded to include the Americans who came involuntary yet have added so much to our unified history and culture.

This book is based on the genealogy of William Hunter, many diaries and documents of the Civil War. It is true to history in most cases, but it has been dramatized to help the reader find empathy with the suffering and courage of the three peoples who met here 1863-1866 during the active war.

Each culture carried the dignity and pride in their peoples' contributions to the building of a nation despite the differing positions each took in the War of Brothers. The Southerners, the Northern Soldiers and the Colored Freedmen lived an uneasy truce in this beautiful setting, which is one of the great historic cities of our Nation. In the occupation of Natchez each group kept looking over their shoulders at past mistakes and shuddered at what the uncertain future would bring to them.

In this book the history of the Hunters is told from the 1600s until the 21st century. The figure of William Hunter and the lovely Confederate widow whom he married are the centerpiece. This real love story is of such a dramatic nature that it shines as a classic story of the Civil War. The footnotes indicate specific persons, quotes and resources. In the general all efforts have been made for possible fictional accuracy to the period or genealogical fact. The majority of the characters, unless documented, have historic basis only and are not real persons.

# Chapter 1
# Bones

Arising from the mist of the past, the story of the Hunter family begins with their immigration to the New World.

Packed like a pickled herring in a barrel, Mary perched uncomfortably on her right side on the very edge of the bed. Her left hand crossed her body and clutched the stitching of the rough, shuck filled mattress while her right arm was scrolled in front of her neck grasping the corner of the feather tick that covered the three of them.

Henry lay pressed against her back, snoring in quiet bursts, his breath warmed the back of her neck below her bed cap. His heavy leg thrown across her thigh both pinned and protected her from falling from the risky posture that she was impelled to adopt to stay covered and in the bed. She was sure she had lain this way for over an hour. The solid ache in her back and shoulder was increasing, as was her body's natural demand.

With increasing discomfort, she knew she must get up. Simultaneously, rolling backward and using an even firm pressure to move Henry away, she pushed his thigh off her own, allowing his leg to drop like a dead tree limb behind her. Draping her legs over the edge of the high bed she dropped to the rough, cold floor. The March moon was full and a thin light muffled its entry though the leaded panes of the second floor window of the inn. Hands on hips, she stood, paused and squinted at the bed. With some irritation she found it was just as she expected.

There was an empty space between her husband Henry and her 12-year-old son. Will was sprawled and lying on his back, mouth wide open. When she returned to the bed, her choice of position would be to climb between them or to attempt to move Henry back toward Will, thus giving her enough room to lie down again. Neither choice was appealing, but the chill in the room and her own need to sleep in this bed were desperate. This bed may be the last privacy she might enjoy for several months. The impetus could not be denied. Somehow, in the night, with her restless mood, the small decision of where to sleep seemed a real dilemma.

The rough wooden floor under her feet had a coolness that almost felt moist. Mary stepped to the foot of the simple bed, and bent to feel near the bed leg. Her hand touched cold china, she reached to the right until she found a handle, then pulling the chamber pot out well beyond the bed leg she removed the lid, laying it quickly and quietly on the floor. The acrid, unpleasant odor of waste filled her nostrils. Catching up her heavy nightdress she hurried to relieve herself, rose and gingerly replaced the lid with a soft clink. She slid the pot back under the rope-hung bed.

She looked at the bed, loathe to disturb her men folk. Quietly, Mary moved to the single window. It was high enough that she had to stretch to peek out. No lights were visible in the Edinburgh street twenty feet below. Only moonlit reflections rewarded her efforts. The view of street showed no life of any kind.

She had resolutely held her eyes closed to pretend to be sleeping for a very long time. Tension and dread had made it hard to relax. It seemed that she might never have slumbered at all. Since she had a sensation of waking, she must have been asleep prior to recognizing her discomfort and the risk of falling from the bed. Her breath now formed a mist that fogged the window and she turned away, uncertain of the time. No hint of sky color or street activity answered her internal query.

Sighing, she shivered slightly and quickly moved back to the side of the bed she had escaped. Lifting the feather tick she put her cold palm on her husband's warm nightshirt, pushed and whispered, "Henry, I must get into bed and need that you move." Miraculously, he made a grunting noise, rolled over, wrestled into his son's space and settled. Her husband began to snore once more. Mary crawled into the high bed and pulled the ticking over her nose. The familiar fragrance of her husband and the warmth of her own breath was comforting. Lying flat on her back, entirely settled, was a great blessing. She repeated a silent prayer, then tried to relax so that she too could find sleep.

A foggy dimness of light seeped through the window. The morning sky's color, strained by her eyelashes, eased itself into her consciousness. When she finally crawled back into the world through the pale warm cloud of sleep, it was to the morning noises of the man and boy. Grunts, coughing, clearing of throats, the creak of leather and the splash of water in the washbowl finally made this ominous morning a reality. Modestly, Mary turned on her side, her back toward the men, giving them privacy to prepare for the day.

The sounds of their morning rituals were familiar and filled her heart with loving security and pride. Will, his anticipation a bubbling ebullition, whispered short questions to his father. They were the questions of an innocent boy.

"What if they sail without us?"

The calm, steady reply came, "They will nay."

"Are there other boys on the ship?"

"I could nay say," Henry answered.

"How long until we go to the dock?" The boy whispered in mock caution.

This elicited only a grunt from his father who, by the sound, was splashing his face at the basin. A door creaked and Henry quickly and sternly responded, "You must wait for me before you go down, lad." The door creaked as it closed again. A few minutes more and the sounds informed their mother and wife that they had left the room, allowing Mary privacy for her own morning grooming. The woman sat up and wrapped herself in the ticking. She snuggled deeper into the warmth it still held and was loath to leave it.

Viewed through the heavy glass panes she evaluated a hint of reflected pink and gold in the still dark sky. In her sleepy warmth it was hard to move, not only because she was physically comfortable but also because she dreaded what lay ahead.

After their former neighbors, the MacClains, finally reached the Colonies, they had written a painful account of their own tumultuous ship journey, with deaths, violence and illness. Mary read slowly, so Henry had read their letter aloud to her. Their advice was stern about the preparations the Hunters must make for their own voyage. There were plans to be made for both their health and for their safety. Unfaltering, her husband read in his deep voice, a voice which she usually found comforting.

As he read, she had averted her eyes from his face and watched his dark, collar-length, burly beard. It moved up and down—his white teeth visible between full lips—those teeth were sometimes lost from sight as he spoke. It was as though she could only concentrate on his lips and beard instead of the words and distance. Pensively he then sat silent, the letter lay limp in hands dropped to his lap on top of the parchment.

Finally, her eyes left his mouth to fall upon his supine hands. For the first time since he had begun reading, she looked into his eyes. The crinkles at the outer edges of his eyes that always appeared when he smiled or laughed were gone. Her husband's facial skin was sagging and the walnut brown of his eyes seemed fogged, showing none of the golden reflections she loved.

Henry's eyes were large, blank and empty, just as they were today and as they had been ever since he had read the letter. His eyes were now only hollow and distracted. Since the letter came, he had also been quieter and more meditative, seeming to live only inside his own thoughts.

Upon leaving this bed, an unknown world awaited her and her family. Between the New World and any hope of a good life lay the dirty, dark horror of the passage across the great Atlantic Ocean in March. The voyage was a danger not only for her, but Henry, Will and the fragile shards of what her life had been in Scotland. Now, who and what she had been was gone. It was ended, like a door slammed in a gust of wind.

Once she had been a bride, full of dreams. Later, she became a young mother full of awe for the child at her breast. Her life had been full, warm and satisfying. Then four years ago the argument of James the Second and the persecution of his followers, appeared in their region like a cloud of ominous bees.

Jacobite supporters were in opposition to the crown and the succession of the Prince and Princess of Orange, which decided the ascendancy to the throne. Their Presbyterian neighbors felt, as did they, that the House of Stuart and James had been the proper rulers. The gossip that first warned them of the coming risks had now became a reality, one they all called the Jacobite Persecution. This danger had become a shadow over all she held valuable. The innocent optimism of those early years of her life were now obscured by increasing fear and numbing astonishment at what was happening around them and to their neighbors.

Henry and she were fortunate, compared to many. Close family or friends had been executed, imprisoned, beaten, and all they owned was stolen or burned. Some had been sold as servants to the plantations in the Colonies.

Her family's political sentiments were widely known and the Hunter family was in danger. Mary's last hope was that they would be able to escape Scotland before the malevolence devoured them, also.

Four days ago, with the wind whipping her cloak and ripping at her bonnet, she had opened the door of their cottage for the last time. Stepping through that door was haunting, for all her family owned was gone except the curtains she had woven and a single straight-backed chair, sitting in front of the cold fireplace, in the center of the great room. It was the first cold hearth in the fifteen years since she came from her Father's house, bringing with her a coal from his hearth to spark the warmth of her own first married fire in her new home. Her own life had been richly satisfying in Henry Hunter's simple, stone cottage.

Mary's childhood had been a happy one. Her father was a prosperous farmer, with high standards and single-minded authority. Da was seldom directly involved in the rearing of his two girls, yet his stocky frame, when it became a solid post holding a scowling face, was terrifying enough to bring the girls into obedience. His gruff and abrupt admonishments shriveled their self-confidence. Any implied threat of discipline became their inspiration to polite, quiet obedience.

He was seldom inside the neat three-room stone house during the day, except in the winter when the crops were harvested and the animals penned in the stone corrals near the cottage. Then, he spent long hours before the light of the fire reading either to himself or to the family while the wind whistled and groaned outside. His library of ten books was magical to his daughters, no matter how many times they heard them read in his rich voice. The reading was a great comfort on long days and nights when they were indoors. Never idle, along with Mum, they spun, carded, wove or knitted. Mary still imagined she could hear the whir of the small flax wheel whenever she read or heard a story that she had first heard as a child.

He was such a serious man, yet there had been a place of magic in him she glimpsed only a few times. Sometimes, when he read with a thick brogue the adventures of King Arthur or the Lady of the Lake his voice sped with expectancy and excitement; his eyes reflected his unconscious absorption.

One occasion she had seen the dreaminess in her Da, had been the rare time the two of them had shared an entire day alone. Business took them by cart to visit another clan. Since there would be a girl at the farm who was also eleven, her Father had asked her to accompany him. They rose early and rode in the rocking, jolting cart for many hours.

Planning to eat the cheese and bread they had brought, he stopped the cart and tethered the pony to a bush. Looking around, he declared solemnly, "'Tis there, my girl," and nodded toward the barren top of a hill where massive rectangular stones seemed oddly out of place. They climbed up toward the rocks, eventually finding an overgrown path. She watched the rough ground, selecting each step and finally, upon cresting the hill, looked around. The view was dramatic and she could see many miles across the barrens. When she turned, her father had a strange expression, it seemed reverent or even fearful. Da was silently looking about the place they stood.

Mary turned in a slow circle and saw on each side there were huge rocks set roughly in a circular pattern. Several were lying on the ground. In the center of the circle was a heap of smaller stones. Balancing against each other were two exceptionally large, slab-like pieces of white stone. This place of stones was so unusual and unnatural. There was almost a sense of this place being built for some reason. Even at eleven, she knew these monoliths were far too large to have been easily moved to this place. *Could nature do this? If man, what manner of man? Why?*

Tucking her skirt about her, she sat on the ground in a clear spot. As he noticed the child's movement, her Da came to her side and joined her on the ground. Breaking bread and cheese, he silently passed them to her. They quietly ate while the sun warmed them.

All the while this solemn man looked about and finally he spoke. "Tis one of the places where we all began, there was magic here and secrets, until the end of time it will still be mysterious." *What a strange thing to say*. She thought of the contradiction of his behavior, as her stern and hard working father spoke of some strange magic. Mary sat quiet and wondering.

When her father finally rose to leave, he walked over to the huge white structure in the middle and, although he stayed a step back, he leaned and reached out to touch one of the surfaces. "Lass, have I told you? These stones were already all about on the land when my people came here in 1080 following David the First.[1] When we arrived in these lovely, heath covered hills, these stones already stood. Some people, long gone or secretly living among us, formed these circles for the practice of religion or magic. This spot is older than time and holds secrets untold.

Slowly, he began back down the hill on the overgrown path. She followed him at a distance. Looking at her feet, she gave a shrill squeal. Quickly, her father moved to her and looked down. Lying on packed earth was a partially burned, white-bleached, human skull almost overgrown with moss. Two hollows, where eyes had lain, stared up at the girl's. Da lay a hand on each of her shoulders and comforted her. "This place is old, older than Scotland. Many things, good and bad, have happened here. No matter what lies here now it will do you no harm. The past does no damage for it is the past that has made all of us. Beware, fear stops those who lack the courage to make history."

That moment had allowed her to see a bit of the dreamer and mystic in her father and she wondered if he had once been too timid to "make history."

*Why would one choose to "make history?"* Just living was quite enough for a twelve year old girl.

They made their way down the hill toward the pony and cart waiting by the road.

Her mother, now four years dead a from appendicitis, had been a joyous, beautiful sausage of a woman who laughed and sang at her work. She kept her two daughters, Mary and Ellen, busy from dawn to dusk, saying it kept them from temptation. As a child Mary had often wondered what temptation was? After her own son, Will, was born she understood temptation. It was the daring, challenge and exploration of a little boy. Since her twin brothers had died of the pox three years before her older sister Ellen was born, Mary had only known the way of little girls who were more easily held within bounds.

Scottish boys are not unique. Boyhood's are universal. Running, screaming and rock throwing must come from Mother's milk that has curdled. Lads come with a love of dirt that has no reverence for injury or ruined and torn clothing. Their defensive independence is to shove, tug or pummel.

Until he was four, her son, Will, pulled at the pups' ears with no fear of their teeth. He tried to walk as far as possible on top of the stone fences before he fell, as he always did. It was years before he learned to fall without injury. He would wallow in the center of a flock of sheep with no fear of the protective ewes. Because of this, he was forbidden and protected from the pigsty, which became Mary's task to oversee.

Now, at twelve years of age, after church he would disappear as his parents visited with friends, only to return with his clothing almost shredded on his body, and his straight dark hair standing on end. His dark blue eyes were always sparkling, albeit through blackened eyelids. In her heart, she secretly called him "little temptation." Yet, once, while he was still small, she had used the term aloud and Henry had chastised her. The phrase became one of many secrets that she held inside herself.

Her sister, Ellen, was two years older and always, even now, stood four inches above Mary's five feet. As they grew to womanhood, Mary took secret pride in her own fullness of breast and roundness of shape. Ellen was built like a reed. This characteristic seemed the only way she had ever bested her older sister. It wasn't that she disliked Ellen, rather she always felt left behind the older girl. It made her ready to compare, defy or run to keep up with her sister.

There was an incident when Ellen was being courted and Mary was fourteen. In imitation and jealousy of her sister, Mary had openly flirted at church, winking, flipping her skirt and staring at the neighbor boy who sat across the aisle in his family pew. Her Mum scowled, took her roughly by the elbow out of the congregation and walked her the one mile home from the church. They had moved at a fast clip down the road. When they arrived at home, Mum slapped her face and followed this with as stern a tongue-lashing as she had ever received. It had crushed her, and each Sunday thereafter she stared fixedly at the toes of her shoes throughout the services.

In their youth, Ellen and she had seldom fought openly. Usually, they only threw under-the-breath, insulting retorts at each other. When their parents were not looking, they shot darting, eye-rolling glances between themselves.

When they were eight and ten they were sent, each with two wooden pails, to the well house for water to rinse the laundry. Ellen filled her pails first and set them in the center of the doorway where they blocked the passage. Mary was very careful but on the way out the girl had an impulse and she purposely shoved one bucket with her foot and it tipped over. Hands on her hips, Ellen demanded that her sister "just go fill it again for me, you clumsy lass!"

"'Twas your own error to leave it there to block my way!" came the retort. Ellen stepped forward, leaned down and placed her nose so close to her sister's face that she could feel the other's breath on her cheeks.

"Just you do it!" Ellen snapped, stamping her foot.

The temptation was too much; Mary sat her pails down, put her palms flat on her sister's middle and pushed. Ellen staggered back like an ice skater losing balance, tripped over her remaining pail of water and fell backward into the puddle it had created.

The view of her supine sister was so funny and the excitement of the bettering her was too much. Mary began to laugh. Rolling over, a mass of muddy stockings, skirts and petticoats, Ellen got to her feet and ran headlong to butt her younger sister's middle. She pushed Mary backward until the girl fell onto her bottom. Then grabbing a pail that held some water Ellen dumped it atop her sister's head. With a pause she stared at her sodden sister. She then gasped, almost in surprise at what she had done. It was as though she could not understand what had occurred.

As her eyes widened the older girl panted, "What will Mum say?"

A moment of silence sliced the sodden scene and then Mary began to giggle. "Dear Mother, we are wet."

Ellen snickered and began a chuckle that, like their mother's, began deep in her belly and rolled upward to burst through a wide mouth. Collapsing in tears and rolling with laughter they gasped out other clever answers.

"It is raining in the well house!"

"Mum, we have no idea!" whispered Mary in a choking voice. On and on went the insanity.

It was a full twenty minutes before they were in self-control. Then realization struck of the disorder they were involved in. They smoothed and shook clothing. They wiped at their hair. Refilling their pails, they hurried to deliver the water, with the fantasy that they could make up for lost time and their frightful appearance. As they neared the house a curtain dropped and Mary was sure she saw her Mum's shadow.

They delivered their pails with eyes downcast and rushed around the back of the cottage. Plopping down on the ground they sat with their backs against the cool, rough stone of the house. Strangely, Mum said nothing. *Could it be possible there would be no scolding or punishment?* As soon as possible they changed their garments for fresh ones, rinsed their clothing and presented the soiled ones to their mother for laundry.

As Mum completed the laundry they went to their regular task of spreading the damp clothes on bushes and fences to dry. Without being asked, they stirred the supper stew, which was simmering in an iron pot that was hanging on a hinged iron rod just out of the direct fire.

That spring evening Da returned at dusk. Their father told the two hired lads goodnight at the gate and saw them start striding down the road. The sisters rushed to set the plates at the table. As the family ate the girls were quiet, finding much of interest on their plates. As soon as they finished eating, both rose politely and hurried to the small room where they shared a cot and after neatly hanging their clothing on pegs they pulled sleep gowns over their heads and took turns combing out each other's hair. While working at this chore they could hear their mother's whisper in the great room and their eyes locked in horror.

After about ten minutes they heard Da's voice outside the door. "My daughters, I would speak with you." Pushing Mary ahead of her, Ellen opened the door of their tiny sleeping room and crossed to where Da sat in a tall, ladder-backed chair. They stood wide-eyed in front of him, unconsciously placing themselves just out of his arm's reach.

He solemnly began by slowly moving his direct, intense gaze from one to the other. "If young ladies deport themselves like gutter waifs, no man will seek them in marriage. It is a shame to a family to have daughters of such a personality that no one wants them as a wife. It is time to begin earnestly deporting yourselves as gracefully and womanly as possible. Be ever aware that you carry the pride of your name and that of your clan. You must be so sweet and gentle as to attract kind husbands rather than scoundrels who will beat you. To that end, each night I will begin to teach you to cipher, read and write." Their punishment was a reward. Few women had such skills, not even their own Mother.

Ellen had been quicker than Mary at reading, but Mary found her own best talent was with numbers. They both practiced their new skills as often as possible for it was somehow thrilling to feel that they were becoming more wise and powerful. Dictated by their father's preoccupation with the fields, fences and animals, the teaching was not regular. Still many evenings, the three of them bent by candlelight at their studies. Their mother smiled with pride, but could be no aid to her daughters.

For the next five years the lessons had continued until Ellen left to be married. For a year a bright young fellow from a village twenty miles away had courted her once a month on Sundays. They had sat demurely in the great room laughing, teasing or visiting. Sometimes they walked near the house but never out of sight. When Ellen was sixteen, after the first bans were announced, Mary rounded a corner of the house and found the couple much too close. He had placed his hand on the small of Ellen's back. Shocked and embarrassed the sight also left Mary feeling jealous and curious.

Her sister's marriage was frightening to Mary. Ellen was a pretty and shy bride. That morning of the wedding before they went to the church, as Mary plaited flowers into the braids piled onto Ellen's head, the girl bride pulled Mary's face down, kissed her and whispered, "Sister, I am frightened." The two of them clung together and wept.

After the wedding and a feast with friends and neighbors, the couple prepared to leave for their new home. Her new brother-in-law, was a sturdy twenty-four-year-old who owned a large, fine flock of sheep and a small cottage. The man had loaded a two-wheeled pony cart. Ellen's possessions were placed in the back, with gifts from the wedding and her dowry linens. Four head of sheep that had belonged to her father were tethered to the cart on long ropes and stood grazing near by. Demurely, Ellen held her light summer skirts so as to prevent them from catching a gust of wind. Her straw bonnet was tied on her head, hiding her face as she was helped into the cart beside her new husband. Mary and she looked deeply into each other's eyes with tears rolling down their cheeks. The young man climbed into the cart beside his bride, glanced back to the packed cart then snapped the reins. Down the road they slowly went with the sheep following. The cart rolled to the clopping rhythm of the ponies' hooves which made a drum roll in the dust and swayed as they passed over rocks. Bleating, the sheep reluctantly were forced to slowly tag behind.

Ellen never looked back. After touching her eyes with her apron, Mum went into the house behind Da. Mary watched for half an hour as the cart went up the three hills and down the three glens. As the cart finally topped the last rise it was only a speck. Her sister appeared to just drop off the end of the earth. She leaned on the gate for a long time staring. That night she cried herself to sleep.

Every two or three months her sister and new husband came briefly to visit. In that first year, her parents and she had visited the newlyweds twice when the farm allowed them to be away. It was such a joy to see each other. The sisters always sneaked away to whisper and giggle. When Mary asked how it was to be married, her sister simply blushed and looked away. There was the closeness still and loneliness for each other. Yet, Ellen was becoming a different person. Within a year, she was with child, so the visits grew farther apart. The couple birthed a strong son and Ellen took on a new, more confident role as a seventeen-year-old mother, full of responsibility. No matter how much the sisters loved and missed each other, the strange differences between them were growing more real.

It was a surprise when, on rare occasions during visits, Ellen, a twinkle in her eye, said Henry Hunter had asked about her sister. Mary had no idea who this man was, but it appeared that at her sister's wedding the groom's twenty-year-old, university friend had noticed and admired her. Now, on rare occasions, when the two men were together, Ellen reported that Mr. Hunter inquired about the small, shapely, brunette girl he had seen at the wedding.

In secret, Mary's romantic fantasies bloomed about this unknown, young man. At night she tried piling her hair high on her head in different ways, walking back and forth across the cramped, rough, candle-lit room. She practiced swishing her skirts without showing her ankles. Sometimes she even practiced kissing by pressing her lips against the cold surface of her own image in her hand mirror. Yet, any real picture of the mysterious man, named Henry Hunter, remained a blank.

When it began, her courtship had been exciting. To be desired, admired and pursued was heady. During the spring after her nephew was born, Henry had written her father a note inquiring if it would be appropriate that he visit to speak of an important matter. When her Father finished reading the letter, he looked at the sealing wax on the back, then the letter. "I do not know this Mr. Hunter," he vacantly told his wife.

Mum then asked that he read the letter aloud, and as he read a smile grew across her face like a sunset lighting the barrens. With a soft voice the older woman answered her husband, "'Twas the young man who came from Edinburgh for Ellen's wedding."

With great surprise Mary's father leaned forward toward his wife. "Is he a farmer?" he inquired. "What would he be about with me?" A stranger approaching this quiet private man was an unsettling break in his rhythm of his life.

The woman simply smiled and tilting her head to one side, she looked Mary in the face to see if the girl had some idea of the true purpose of the letter. The fire in her daughter's face was blistering and red. The knitting needle the girl was holding in her right hand fell to the floor. The situation was so surprising and embarrassing. Mary simply picked up the lost needle, stabbed both needles through the rough, cream colored ball of yarn and went to her room.

Even curiosity about what her parents would say could not hold her in the great room now that she realized her mother knew about Mr. Hunter. *How could Ellen have told her?* How embarrassing!

It was such a momentous thing that was happening. The possibility of a courtship was both exciting and overwhelming. Yet, a modest reserve kept her from returning to the room to ask what her Father's answer was, or what her Mother knew of Mr. Hunter's interest in her. Mary tried vainly to sleep the night the letter was read, or the nights after. She spent even more time gazing into her mirror evaluating her features and any small blemishes. The teenager propped the mirror against a wall checking her shapely body. Almost haunted in her distraction, she became a sixteen-year-old dreamer walking in her sleep. Her mother had to demand her attention again and again.

Three weeks later her Mum was cooking and Mary was beating the paddle in the butter churn. Wiping her hands on a small rag of worn linen, her mother came to the table and took a seat near her. "Lass, tomorrow morning Mr. Hunter will be coming to talk with your father. I believe he is coming to see if he can have our permission to court you. I understand he is of our own clan, the Hunters of your grandfather, thus we know of his family. You will want to talk to your father once you have some idea of how welcome you are to this courtship. Your sister says he is a fine and educated man, that he is honest and decent. Although not well to do, he has a fine start in life as a farmer and a church presbyter."

"Mum," the girl whispered, "I do not even remember him, what if I am frightened or do not like him?" Mary was horrified that the man might be ugly, dumb or coarse.

Reaching to touch her arm, the Mother comforted her daughter, "Your father is a wise man and cares for you. He will make a good decision, but it will help if you can tell him how you feel about the courtship and this man. I do nay know if the decision will be made right away."

After supper that night Mary was overwhelmed, anxious and slept only when finally grasped by exhaustion and pulled into nervous nightmares.

The day arrived when this mysterious man was expected. It was softly warm with whispering gusts of wind. As the time approached Mary lingered in the yard until, in the distance, she saw a rider approaching. Then she rushed into the house. Breathless, she whispered to her Mother "I think Mr. Hunter is coming," and scurried into her room.

There she tidied her hair, replacing a tiny bit of heather that she had threaded above her left ear. She pinched her cheeks and lips then broke a tiny bit of cinnamon stick she had been saving. She chewed the spice to sweeten her breath. Then she sat stiffly on the bed, waiting. The girl's stomach was knotted and her hands were sweaty and trembling.

After a long time she heard the approaching beat of horse's hooves. Then, there was the creak of leather and the grinding of stones at the fence gate. Almost immediately Mary heard the door of the cottage groan and the small stones on the path crunched under her Father's boots.

"Good day ta ye. Mr. Henry Hunter, be ye?" Her Da's voice was warm, strong and friendly. She heard her father offer to get some water for the horse and the two men could be heard speaking softly as they rounded the house toward the well house.

When it seemed the men were at the rear of the cottage, Mary realized that she could peek out the window. She rushed past her Mum who was rocking and knitting near the front door. Standing well back, the nervous lass strained her neck around to look through the window while keeping her own person out of view.

It was not possible to hear them but now she saw Henry for the first time. Broad shoulders supported a head covered by thick, wavy, dark brown hair. A scarf of Hunter clan, green plaid, with a tiny red and white thread run through, was wrapped around his neck. One loose end of the scarf was thrown over his shoulder. She studied his trim build. Mary checked his height against her father and found him some several inches taller. His hips were narrow and buttocks tight, yet there was roundness to his thighs indicating taunt muscling.

Then, to her horror, the young man turned toward the house as he lifted the water pail toward his horse and she was sure his eyes fastened on hers. Mary's heart thudded in her chest. She rushed to a chair in the corner of the main room that was as far from the window as possible. The maiden seated herself and arranged her skirts demurely. She pasted on the calm, disinterested face she had practiced all week. In her embarrassment, it was much harder to do so now.

The men's voices were soft blurs as they settled the horse. They moved slowly toward the cottage, she heard her father proudly describing the boundaries of his farm. They crunched across the small rocks toward the cottage. The sun at their back cast long shadows through the open door and they finally walked into their own shadow patterns that lay on the floor before them. Mr. Hunter became flesh and blood. Da and the young man walked directly to her Mother who was then introduced to the gentleman.

Then they both turned, "Mary," Father spoke gently in her direction, nodding his head in encouragement. The girl rose, stood straight and slowly walked to the men. "This is my daughter, Mary."

For the first time she saw his clean-shaven features, he had a small nose and dark eyes. There was a small cleft in his strong chin. "How do you do?" he smiled as he greeted her. His voice was gentle, slow and warm enough to wrap herself into it.

The girl bobbed her head and extended her hand. Henry reached out and softly but firmly embraced her hand without shaking it. He held her small hand in his while looking into her face with his own walnut eyes, "I am glad to be seeing you again, Mary."

Those eyes melted something inside her. Even more moving was when Henry held her hand so long, firmly and warmly. The embarrassment inside her left and she felt calm and safe, as she would ever after in his presence.

When they were married six months later, Henry Hunter had received as her dowry a small bag of gold pieces. She never knew how many. There was also a fat brown and white cow tied to the fence. The cow had been her Father's. The beast had large, beautiful, brown lashed eyes. It was large in the belly where a calf grew.

In his wagon there was the lashed bundle of a bed ticking that her

Mum and her Da's sisters had sewn. The tick was stuffed with goose down which they had gathered, saved and stuffed into the covering during the courtship. There was also a small wooden chest of things she herself had lovingly made for her first home. Mary had three bundles of clothing. There was a strong wooden box that was filled with hay. Inside it lay a beautiful, blue and white, Chinese tea set that had been a wedding gift from her sister, Ellen. Mary and Henry's new life lay before them and any fear they felt was swallowed in their tentative optimism.

This morning in the room on the second story of the inn, Mary's memory reviewed the first time she had seen the tiny stone cottage where Henry delivered her. The large main room had an addition he had built for his bride. The new room had been completely empty except for a lovely, carved bed with a high headboard that had been her wedding gift from her husband. This bed was where she first lay with Henry as they learned together the secrets of marriage. That bed was where she had struggled three days, only to birth a beautiful, stillborn daughter. It was the bed where she and her husband fought, she cried, then both forgave the other. In its secret warmth they laughed and teased and played. It was also in this bed that Will had been born.

Four days ago she had viewed that small, now empty bedroom, for the last time. The bed had been sold to a neighbor. She had walked stiffly from their room and bravely moved across the great room to the door to leave. That day, as she left the house forever, she felt that by pulling the heavy door shut the ghosts of her life would be trapped so no one else could steal them. Instead, straightening her back, she had strode across the great room and out, leaving the door open like her personal statement, "The Hunters are gone forever!"

At the inn this morning, she secretly relived her farewell visit to the cottage. Her mind's eye once again saw the emptiness of their cottage and she mentally looked into each corner. When her aching heart remembered the tall closet which Henry had given her five years ago, tears rolled down her cheeks. He had traded, saved and worked with the woodcarver to make her the closet. It had a graceful arch on the top with carving on the cornice and legs. Henry had wiped and waxed until the wood glowed in the evening firelight. With pride she had placed it to one side of the great room so that all their visitors could see it as they entered. The closet had been full of their clothing; the drawers held the linen, clean and fresh, packed with heather and sage. Mary remembered the wagon she had recently watched rolling down the road to another's home with the treasured closet nested in hay.

She mentally numbered each of her treasures on the wall shelf by the entry door. There she had placed her delicate, blue, china teapot, creamer with sugar bowl and six cups and saucers. There was a small brass statue of a dog that had been her Da's. On a bit of tatted lace her Mum had made, lay the heather she had carried on her wedding day, the plant was now dried and faded to a pale grey. Beside the bouquet was a Bible that was Henry's. These few things were now tucked into her luggage.

The last thing her family did as they prepared to leave for Edinburgh was to stop and tell Ellen good-bye. The sisters lied to themselves, saying somehow they would see each other again. As Mary looked at her tall nephew and the two baby nieces, she knew that there would be a day she would not even recognize them if she saw them on the street. How she appreciated her brother- in- law, for he was so sound and solid. She had no fears for the welfare of Ellen or her family. The two women only felt the crushing pain of loss and her departure. They cried and clung to each other. Once they were on the road again, she realized she had grit her teeth so hard to keep from sobbing out loud that her teeth and jaws hurt.

She stiffened in the bed at the inn. Mary threw back the goose-down tick, and she chastised herself, "There is no need to look back. I must not be afraid of the future, or at the least must pretend that I am brave."

It was all gone, the furniture, linens, dishes and kettles sold to those who would never know or care what her things had meant to her. The price had been generous, for all their neighbors wanted to help them begin a new life.

Counting each precious item in her memory, as one selecting flowers for a vase, she said a mental good-bye to each possession. Yet, the blessing of selling their possessions and the cottage had made this passage possible. The profit even offered a bit more comfort because they would sail in a shared stateroom on the ship instead of a berth in the bowels below the waterline. The money their goods raised gave them a small, new beginning and it was one that might save their lives.

Swallowing, she braced, and with her teeth firmly set, she moved to roll from the high bed and put her feet onto the floor. Against one wall of the tiny inn room her leather hatbox lay next to a soft valise with her outer clothing. The other goods they had chosen to take to the New World were already at the dock in the care of a street urchin they had hired to watch them by sleeping on the pile overnight. Two parcels were all she would have for these next months as the ship rolled toward the colonies and the unknown. If only she could be optimistic. The isolation from her father,

her sister, other family and friends was acutely painful. The omniscient, mysterious future was paralyzing in its black enormity.

After using the chamber pot, she got the hatbox and placed it on the bed. From a place on the floor near the headboard she retrieved her shoes. Climbing back onto the bed she pulled the quilt back over her lap as she began the process of putting shoes on her cold feet. She opened the box and taking out the rolled, heavy stockings she put them on, one at a time, and rolled the garters up to secure them. She put her shoes on.

Since her feet were warmer, Mary could now bear standing. Once again, she slipped from the bed, reaching into the box, she removed several items, including some folded garments that were nested into her winter hat. She carefully lay her pantaloons on the bed and unrolled them. A smooth, blue patterned teacup and two saucers were delicately removed from inside the undergarment. She lay these on the bed. Next, her bodice was removed from the box and similar treasures were released in the same manner.

Giving the pantaloons a shake and turning them the right direction she carefully stepped into them and pulled the lacing at the waist tightly. Untying the neckline of her nightgown and gathering it up she pulled it over her head, slipping out. She lay it on the bed. Mary threw the bodice across her back, pulled it together at the front and laced it. As quickly as possible, she wrestled into the petticoat that had hung on the bedpost, but the coolness of the fabric offered little immediate comfort.

Her simple woolen dress also hung on the bedpost. She reached, pulling the skirt wide, and dove into it, wriggling until it slid over her shoulders and onto her body. She did not button it but moved it about until it formed to her shape before she fixed it. Then she removed her nightcap and smoothed her hands across the braids she had so carefully plaited last night. The rich brown ropes were piled high on her head, looping in and under themselves in a circlet pattern.

She went to her toilet. Last evening, in this strange place, she luxuriated in a complete bath. Henry, in his kindness, had brought the hot water up and given her a long hour to soap, scrub her body and wash her hair. It would be several months before she could bath and wash her hair again. When he and Will had returned she was fresh in her nightgown and was thoughtfully combing her hair dry. Henry helped her find her hair part, being tall he could easily center it like a white thread dividing her skull.

Her husband quietly smoked a pipe, sitting in the only chair in the room, watching as she combed and braided with her experienced hands. She had intensely watched his face as she worked. The man's expression was quiet but somehow empty. They had not spoken of their feelings, so she did not know his and remained quiet. Her own fears and sorrow could only add to his personal dilemma.

He had repeated the details the MacClains had included in their letter, saying she had to know. That had been two weeks ago when they knew they must leave. They must leave everything and everyone they knew and loved. It was that night they gave up hope and acknowledged the unspoken desperation and fear they had been living with. Henry had simply said, "We best be going, it is time." So they prepared. If they did not leave they might be driven out or become prisoners.

This morning, the cold water would do for her toilet. Mary took the basin the men had used to the window. She sat it on the floor as she loosened the window latch, then she hoisted the basin of water, called a warning to the street and threw the water out the window. Returning to the sideboard, she took the corner of the rough, linen towel the inn provided and wiped a bit of hair away from the basin where Henry had trimmed his beard. There was a partial pitcher of water that she used to refill the basin. From her box, rolled in a rag, she took out a bar of the fragrant soap she had made last fall when they butchered. She had a secret, modest pride in her soap. It was smoother and more fragrant than any soap the other Jacobean wives made. She always took great pains to rub fragrant herbs into the batter and grind the talc to the smoothest texture.

After that she poured a bit of clean water into the china basin from a pitcher on the washstand. She performed her bath like a ceremony or ritual. Using another corner of the linen she dampened it, and using the soap she washed, in her usual order, her face, then reaching into her dress, her underarms, finally she lifted her skirts and cleansed her private parts through the slit in her pantaloons. With the third corner she rinsed each of her parts in the same sequence and then using the center of the towel she dried. Now she splashed some water onto her hand and wiping it to the other, she smoothed her braids, the hair near her face and the nape of her neck. "How I miss the mirror that hung next to my cupboard," she carped. "'Tis enough," Mary scolded herself.

Buttoning and smoothing her dress, she returned to the bed where she rolled the nightcap around a teacup, then layering a saucer, she began to roll them into her nightdress. The dark bonnet she would be wearing was laid aside. Finally, she nested the garments into the inverted form of her crisp, summer bonnet having replaced everything into the box, she fixed the lid and strapped it tightly with the leather that bound it.

Mary nervously turned, checking the room. She secured her dress, touching the small, bone buttons on the slate, colored dress. She checked them from her waist, across her breasts and up to the silk band at the high neck. She gripped the fabric at either side of the skirt and giving a chuck of a tug she pulled and straightened the garment. Standing more erect, like a dignified lady, she now felt more like a proper Presbyterian elder's wife. Filled with the pretense of confidence, she plastered a dignified mask onto her face.

Mary marched defiantly to the door. Releasing the leather latch, she reached for the hand-smoothed wood of the door grip and pulled the heavy, groaning door open. This allowed her to cross into the narrow, dark hall. The door creaked shut and she gave it a firm shove to affix it. Hearing a noise at her left, she furtively searched in the dim gloom and two doors down she saw the large form of a man with a bundle near his feet. He seemed preoccupied with looking through the open door into his room and was illuminated slightly by the reflection from the inside. Slightly turning his head toward her, he nodded then returned to his prior inspection of his own room.

The feigned courage she had worn melted and in her chest the lump of her heart speeded. As fast as a cat caught in the light of a lantern, she turned on her heel in the other direction and stepped toward the soft sounds and odors of the inn's great room. On tiptoe, she began to descend down the narrow steps, then halfway down, remembered the courage she was pretending she possessed. Any alarm she allowed to surface from her breast or a worried expression on her countenance would raise concern in Henry and Will. If they were to sense her dark panic it would worry them. Pausing, she again tugged at her dress and checked her buttons, stood straight and tried to gracefully continue her descent.

The steep, narrow stairs ended in a blank wall and she turned to the left, remembering her path because of the two prior days they had lodged and eaten at this inn. The previous day's meals had been plentiful, but simple. There had been soups with little meat and too much water and heavy bread lacking enough salt and lard. One meal had been pork, which was over roasted until the outer crust was tough as baked, horse flesh. She knew what the breakfast would be and as she entered the room she glanced at the rough, wooden benches and tables and knew she was right, oatmeal mush.

The first odor that filled her nostrils was that of grog. One of the five people at breakfast, a sour faced, well-dressed man was using grog to wash his meal down. Drinking in the morning was distasteful to her, but apprehensively she knew before this ordeal was over her repugnance for this would be far out of balance with the experiences that lay before her. Will and Henry looked up smiling from where they sat with the huge fireplace warming and lighting their backs. A very heavy woman wearing a knitted shawl and a chambray, flowered bonnet was on the opposite side of the trestle table. Beside her was a white-haired boy of three or four. She was feeding him, oblivious of the yellow mucus running out his nose and down his upper lip.

Mary nodded in her best 'demure wife' way, showing the face she always wore in public. Then, carefully pulling her skirts, she squeezed between the board and bench, and gently seated herself.

"Mary," Henry greeted her. Will straightened some, raising his face from a crouched posture over his wooden bowl. He smiled widely hoping he would not receive a reproving glance from her for his ravenous attitude as he ate his breakfast. When he was not chastised, the boy returned to eating, only a bit more slowly as he sat up straight.

Rising, her husband went to a large, iron pot suspended by a rod just out of the fire so as to not burn the oatmeal, while still keeping the mixture hot. Taking a wooden bowl from the mantel, he shook it and wiped his hand inside. With a ladle from inside the pot, he dipped two servings into the bowl, then tenderly placed it in front of her. Going to a metal kettle sitting in the hearth, he tipped and poured steamy hot water into a wooden mug that he had found on a simple side table. This was also placed before his wife as he compassionately looked down on her chestnut, braided head.

Looking toward the stairs he saw a tall, shy man and a half-grown boy enter the room. After laying bundles in the corner the poorly dressed pair proceeded quickly across the room toward the table where the man sat who was drinking grog.

Mary reached for the crackled, golden, pottery pitcher on the table and poured thick cream into both the water and the glistening, grey mixture in the bowl before her. The heat and fragrance of the oatmeal was comforting and the cream was sweet to her tongue as she began to delicately eat.

*If the ship is late,* she told herself, *we may not eat again until tomorrow.* She pretended to be hungry, although her knotted stomach threatened to make her retch. Nodding her ascent to her family with a smile, although she felt quite full after finishing the first bowl, and she allowed Henry to serve her again. Will, of course, was not pretending hunger and followed with his third serving of the steaming breakfast adding extra cream.

She wrapped her hands around her mug to warm them. The heat from the fireplace and the warm food in her stomach did give her some comfort. Taking the warm water and cream to her nose, she inhaled the sweetness and began to sip it slowly. The breakfast took about half an hour and when the door opened to allow a man in a swallow tail coat to enter, she saw behind him a misty, grey sky loosing its last touch of color.

"Tide waits on no one," Henry declared in a firm voice, rose and went to a large man who was the innkeeper. This man was observing his house from a dim corner. Henry settled the bill, then went into the street to find a cart. Will and she stood and went toward the stairs. When they arrived in their room, they quickly lay the goose down ticking flat and, with each of them on opposite sides of the bed, the mother and son began to roll it as tightly as possible. Will held it down, laying across the bed and on top of the roll, as Mary found the thongs they had dropped in a corner and she tied it tightly in four places making a long, bound roll of the whole thing. They lay all the things they would be taking on the bed alongside the ticking.

Next, they walked the room, checking dim corners and under the bed for mislaid possessions.

Each put on their hat and coat. The chill had started to leave the room and with the breakfast warmth still lingering, the coat Will wore and Mary's cloak felt too heavy. Since clothing not worn would have to be carried, and outside they would need coats, they just endured the discomfort.

Each took turns at privacy, after a brief time knocked lightly and returned to the room. Mary lay the tick across the boy's shoulders and fastened lashings under each of his arms. He picked up her valise in one hand and his bundle under his other arm, then stepped sideways through the doorway and preceded toward the stairs. Mary rinsed her face. Using a cup she rinsed her mouth and spat into the basin, then picking up her hatbox, she followed Will.

Halfway down the stairs she passed Henry on his way up. Lightly, her husband lay a hand on her arm. "The driver is waiting, he wears a red cap and has a spotted pony." She made her way down, across the great room without looking up and pushed through the heavy, rough door that opened to the street.

The moment she stepped out onto the narrow curb that bordered the inn she was awed at the street and its confusion. *How could this be the street she had viewed in the middle of the night?* Now it was crowded with carts, horses' hooves were clattering on worn paving stones and riders were trying to wind between bulky, horse drawn liveries. There were a smattering of carriages moving through the street, these had curtains drawn at the windows to close out the dirt and noise.

The old roadway was wide but people, horses, vehicles and stray dogs were all dashing about raising rough calls. Street urchins yelled at each other, pedestrians dressed in rags and wound about in frayed scarves were everywhere. At either gutter, a brown, thick, smelly substance was flowing in a slow, western direction carrying small shards of unknown debris toward the docks.

Mary had been to Edinburgh a number of times before but never in this neighborhood, which was closer to the harbor. It all seemed so rough and dirty even though she knew that farther to the West were neighborhoods that were much worse. Those were streets no one would choose to visit. When she had come to the city before it was to visit shops full of exciting goods that had arrived from all over the world. Twice, she had visited the immense, dramatic cathedral. There had been picnics in beautiful parks and dining in lovely places. Her family had several times visited friends of Henry and three times stayed in an inn more frequented by ladies of her class. This part of Edinburgh was just too overwhelming. Perhaps, this is why Henry had left Will and she in the inn for two days while he made the arrangements.

Her son, wearing his strange, huge, white tick collar, had a knit cap pulled over his forehead. With his bundle and her valise in either hand, he came to her side. She looked up and down the street, several buildings away, she saw a red capped driver and a small, two wheeled cart. "Will, ask that driver if it is Mr. Hunter's cart," she instructed, nodding her head in that direction. He hurried away, dodging and turning to pass people on the curb. Stopping, he looked up at the man and she watched them speak. Then, Will lifted first her valise, and next his own bundle, into the bed of the cart and came back to his mother.

As he had been taught, he took her elbow and walked beside her down the street until they stood beside the transport. The driver nodded "Ya like up?" "No thank you, I will wait for Mr. Hunter," she replied. He turned forward to study the street over the rump of his bony, patchy, tan pony.

It was hard not to stare, she tried to be discreet as she inventoried the hubbub of the street. On the other side of the dirty street she saw the couple from the inn who had the runny nosed boy. The family of three was walking rapidly down the curb carrying several bundles.

Mary watched a carriage pass which was more elegant than any she had ever seen, even the driver, with a long whip, was dressed to the teeth and had shiny black boots. A boy about Will's age walked by whistling and carrying a wooden box balanced on his head. She heard a sound behind her of an opening door and a man's voice bidding farewell to someone. Then, Mary smelled the fragrance of baking bread which enveloped her briefly. The pleasant odor was a contrast to the nearby surroundings.

As preoccupied as she was, she didn't become aware of Henry until he spoke. "We'll be off now, Lassie," he murmured tenderly at her back. He reached up to place the rest of the luggage he was carrying into the cart and Will scurried up after it. Her hatbox was carefully lifted and placed inside the cart. Bending down, Henry opened his hand, she stepped one foot into it and with a small bounce, grasping the front of the cart and the hand the driver offered, she gained her seat beside him in the front of the vehicle. She released her husband's hand to gather and place her skirts. Overlapping her cloak, she tucked it about her ankles. Henry seated himself on the tailgate of the small wagon beside Will and called to the driver, "We are ready now."

The driver raised the reigns, clucked then they began a slow, bumpy, inauspicious course toward the docks. Uneven cobbles swayed the cart, and it proceeded slowly so as not to meet any mishap with other traffic. The two men behind attempted to avoid becoming soiled as they crossed puddles or a drain. At each wet hazard they raised their legs horizontally above the street. Henry kept nervously glancing over his shoulder toward Mary and the meager bags that held their possessions.

To the woman, it was as though she were passing through a dark, strange forest. Every sound, smell and sight seemed to have portent. Her senses were taunt and she tried to interpret, integrate and record everything around her. Mary's heartbeat was rapid and her breath came shorter than usual. The trip took almost an hour, much of it in the dock area because several times they waited in queue at intersections as someone or something crossed their path.

Like the street in front of the inn, the harbor scene left her weak and in awe. She heard cursing in a most vulgar manner all about her. The fragrances of wet wood, mold and the sea were almost overwhelmed with fish odor and other rotting pungency. When sailors moved too close to the cart, sweat and body stench overcame her. Over this whole scenario rolled a putrid vegetable smell that caused her to hold a perfumed handkerchief to her nose.

When they neared the portside they proceeded slowly with Henry jumping off several times to ask directions. In a haphazard line along docks and wharves were moored ships of all sizes and nature. Each vessel had varying degrees of activity aboard.

At last, she saw a pile of trunks and crates on the dock that she recognized as their own. A poorly dressed, young boy of large stature was perched precariously on the top of the stack, one knee balancing his chin. His features were coarse and his curly, dark hair was matted. The clothing he wore was tattered and one leg of his trousers was shredded to the knee exposing another pair of differently colored pants beneath.

Jumping from the back of the cart, Henry went quickly up to the trunks and the boy sat straight at attention. Words were passed and the lad jumped down to speak more directly to her husband. In a few seconds the cart was directed to the stack of luggage where Will, Henry and the boy unloaded the cases that were in the cart onto the pile that lay on the dock. Henry came around and holding Mary by the waist helped her jump down from the cart seat. Her husband paid the driver and dismissed him.

Twice he slowly circled the mound that held all of their worldly possessions. He carefully counted each box and trunk and checked their condition. The street urchin stood quietly, his eyes on the ground until the accounting was done. Reaching well within his waistcoat under his cloak, Henry withdrew a pouch that had been tucked inside his trousers, took some coins out and put them into the hand which had been thrust at him. The boy looked carefully, then made a tight fist of the coins and looking about like a furtive, wild animal, he made a dash across the dock and up a narrow alley as though a thousand devils were after him. Perhaps in this wild place, where many acted like animals, devils well might be after him.

Henry loosed the bonds holding the feather tick about Will's shoulders and lay it atop the pile of luggage. Coming to Mary, he lay his arm across her shoulder and gave her a hug. "Now my girl, we are on our way. You will want to sit, for it will be a long time before we are loaded, the tide is many hours away." He turned one way, then the other, ascertaining which ship at the dock was the one they had passage on. He strode toward it with Will at his heels. Turning to the boy, the father said something and his son stopped dead as the Father moved toward a large ship with four masts, not too far away. Will watched, then turned toward Mary and came back to stand by her as she sat solidly on a small trunk.

For about an hour she sat trying not to fidget, but did loosen the ties on her bonnet and squirmed her toes about in her shoes. Trying to be modest, she studied all that was in her periphery and did not respond to strange noises behind her. Will had no such restraint. He jumped, paced and bobbed; never leaving but a few steps from her side yet rounding their bivouac continually. A very unhealthy, yellow dog with dirty hair came close several times and the boy stomped and yelled to drive it away.

Ships had seemed so romantic as she had watched them on the ocean but never before had she been this close to one. The size of some of them was surprising and how high those not yet loaded rode in the water made them appear like kites bobbing in the sky. There were also many small skiffs and rowboats like children's toys in among the ships.

For some time she watched a couple fishermen unloading their catch into woven or wooden boxes and baskets. The fishermen carried them down the dock to where she could see long open sheds. When the wind was from the ocean it was pleasant and cooling, but when it swirled the other direction rancid dock smells were overpowering. Once a rude voice behind her commented, "the lady might be lost" with a loud guffaw. Will stood stiffly in front of her glaring over her head at the source of the coarse voice.

Finally, she saw Henry as he walked back down the swaying gangway and stepped onto the dock. With relief she stood to await him. "We will move our things to the ship now."

He took her valise and hatbox with one arm, while he hoisted a small trunk onto his other shoulder. They both went straight to the berth he had just left, leaving Will with the boxes. When they were near the ship he sat his burden down and told her to wait and keep watch on the luggage. It took a dozen trips for the man and boy to carry the rest of the things. Then, leaving Will a single large trunk, Henry boarded the ship. Her husband eventually returned with two very big men who carried the trunk up the gangway and sat it down on the deck. Will and Henry carried a number of the other trunks and boxes up the gangway to add to the Hunter stack of goods on the ship's deck that would be stowed below by the ship's crew. All that remained with them were the tick and the things that they would have in the cabin on the voyage.

This first leg of the trip would take them to Liverpool, England. There they would transfer their goods and board the *Mary and Elizabeth*. The lengthy trip to the New World would be completed from this second port.*

"We will be a long time on water, let us stay here in the fresh air a while longer," Henry said. Mary saw the man and boy from the next room at the inn approaching them. She also recognized the heavy lady with the runny nosed child, they were now accompanied by a man. The boy looked at her shyly in recognition. In this chaos of strangers any familiar face was a comfort.

Will's excitement was growing. He was asking an uninterrupted string of questions and speaking rapidly. Becoming ever more adventurous, he had to be called back to his parents several times.

When the sun indicated it was nearly noon. Henry left briefly to return with some fresh water, bread and cheese. Mary opened her tightly packed valise, after feeling inside for a while, she came out with a small handful of shriveled, dried apples which they divided. The MacClains had warned that they should bring the fruit. The trip caused so much illness and fruit seemed to help.

The boy with the runny nose stared at the fruit. Everything in her spirit wanted to share hers, but she knew that if her family was to survive each mouthful was valuable. Each decision she made would be important for her loved ones from now on. So, she turned her back, hiding the morsel in her hand as she chewed. She knew that they would be staying in a cramped room with ten others, but most of the other passengers would be below in the dark, dank hold. They would be crushed into crowded wooden bunks. The blessing of the cabin had been paid for with her possessions and the cottage. Now, her fear and awareness of this strange, fearful ocean voyage made any small comfort, even a dried apple, a talisman to grasp.

Mary was alarmed when she heard a scream near her. This violent shout shook her. Turning she saw a fist thrown, a man flew backward and stumbling he fell, with a hairy-faced sailor towering above him. The sailor swore an oath, kicked the fallen man in the ribs and swaggered down the dock, sure of his supremacy. The battle went almost without notice, and was apparently a normal occurrence. More people were making their way back and forth on the swaying gangway of the ship that they would soon be boarding.

From the corner of her eye she saw the mongrel yellow cur again. He was traversing back and forth among the people on the dock, occasionally appearing to lap something from the wharf. Hypnotized, she watched as he gradually worked his way closer.

**The exact time or means of migration to Virginia is unknown but this was the way many Jacobites left Scotland in the 1600s.*

Just then, from a distance, a pack of three other wild dogs came racing and snarling. The lead dog was carrying something in its mouth. As the ménage passed the cur, the drama was electric. The yellow dog bust like lightening and dashed to close the distance between himself and the lead dog. Yellow threw himself at the racing pack and became part of a viscous ball of snarling, biting fur which rolled and tumbled.

Flying from this mass, a bloody bone slid to land at her feet. In horror, Mary stared down transfixed by the iridescent sinew and bone. She recalled the skull she had discovered as a child on the trip with her father. Henry quickly stepped over and kicked the bone well away from his wife. Somehow, the dirty yellow dog broke free, clamped his jaws around the bone. With saliva foaming and dripping, he dashed off, leaving the others still fighting.

The violence, the blood and the stark bone left Mary's pulse pounding. Haunted memories flooded her. Her father had said, "Fear stops those who can make History." All that she could feel at the time was fear.

## Chapter 2
# New Lives

Mary sat before the tall window, looking through the patterned whirlpool of poured glass. The ripples resembled those created by an insect walking magically across the surface of a quiet pool. The heavy, grey green drapes had been drawn back and were held in place by a braided, wine colored cord. She was resting in a fine, carved mahogany armchair with the upholstery generously padded to make it more comfortable for her frail body.

Her old eyes slowly inventoried the spacious room where she sat. Each piece of furniture held a memory. Full of reverie, she stared at a large cabinet, which was a duplication of the cupboard she had left behind in Scotland so many years ago. In her mind's eye it was the same piece. It reminded her of how she missed Henry.

On the mantel of the fireplace sat a bleeding, blue and white china tea set. These pieces included the old-fashioned handleless cups, saucers, a svelte sugar bowl and a round-bodied teapot. This set reminded her of her beloved sister who had died many years ago. Dwelling on the china, the elderly lady could almost hear her sister's laughter and was warm in her love, once more.

Near the door was a ceiling high bookcase. She could not read the titles from where she sat. This was a library of impressive size. Many of the books had been ordered from Europe. The size or color of each reminded her of old friends and memories she had found in the pages. Most of all they were the legacy of her father and she recalled his words, that it was the past that has made us all and his admonition to have the courage to make history.

Outside the warm April sun made dark patterns on the lawn near the house. The oak tree she and Henry had planted over forty years ago now shaded the whole front porch and patterned the grass with randomly shaped, cooling shadows. The white stones that lined the walkway were variably grey in shadow or sparkling white in full sun. Her eyes followed the path to the public road. Mary studied the coachmen, carts and many Negroes standing by carriages tied to the fence and hitching posts. Several hundred guests were strolling beyond the house on the front meadow.

It was 1699 in Nansemond County, in southeast Virginia. Across the road, on the broad green carpet of grass, a very long row of trestles were covered with platters of food, pitchers, baskets, bowls and dishes of all sizes. These vessels brimmed with food. The linen cloths covering the boards were pulsing with the lazy whisper of a wind. The guests were slowly moving about in bowing, bobbing groups, like flocks of sparrows, as they visited. Small children near the tables were sneaking bites of food and darting away, as her house slaves shooed them off.

The wide front entrance door of the house was open to the warmth, so the sound of voices and distant fiddle music seeped into the house like the babble of water. Soon her Grandson William would be coming for her. She was the matriarch of the host family, so the festivities would not begin until she appeared. This stately public reverence for her was pleasing.

She looked down at her hand on the polished, carved arm of the chair. Her white skin was transparent like oiled paper, here and there were brown blotches that the lace at her wrists almost hid. A beautiful ring, loose now that her body was shrinking, caught the light and the garnet setting looked like drops of glistening blood.

Mary reached to feel for loose hair at the nape of her neck below the tatted lace cap that covered her fine, thin cobweb of white hair. She found the hair was tightly pulled up and altogether smooth. The elegant, old lady unconsciously checked the buttons on her bodice.

Across the lawn, under a tree she saw William positioning a small rocking chair under a spreading tree, checking the balance, and squinting toward the sun to see the direction of the light. William Junior was very handsome. Like his father, he had warm brown hair, was darkly tanned and tall. He held himself well, with an easy but erect posture. The Nansemond, Virginia neighbors liked and admired him. His life had been easier than his Father's, but he too had labored to add to the estate and oversee the farming. The thirty-year-old planter was good at managing the production of rice, indigo, tobacco, and at overseeing the slaves.

She had no doubt that her grandson and primary heir would be elected to the House of Burgess in the upcoming election. This was the purpose of today's picnic. Parties for the county landowners were the courtship of voters in an attempt to win their votes—for only they voted. Only major landowners were even considered as candidates. No other candidate would be able to entertain as the Hunters could. This party would last into the middle of the night after dancing and a late supper. Then slaves would help load the last reveler into his carriage for the ride home. Only a few dozen visitors would be staying over for the night. It was many years since Mary had been required to take responsibility for guests. Her daughter-in-law, Nell, who was Henry's wife, and William Junior's wife, Sarah, offered guests an easy and comfortable hospitality. There were ten household servants who would care for visitors.

As the younger William headed across the road and toward the long walkway to the house, his father, Will the elder, crossed the road toward him. They stopped to speak with each other for a while. It seemed less than the twenty years it had been since she looked from the house to see her husband, Henry, and his son, Will, talking this way. Now, Mary watched Will and William Junior.

The younger man was taller and wore dark, rich blue trousers tucked into his riding boots. The other was heavier and white of hair and beard. Her elderly son wore a wide-sleeved, white shirt with a black string-tie. Each man seemed cheerful but gave a strong impression in their posture. As they spoke they turned several times checking the guests, the carriages and looking toward the cookhouse.

Henry, the younger grandson, approached to join them. They motioned authoritatively to Tilly, a hopsack shift, clad slave who, when summoned, ran to them. They gave her some instruction that sent the small almond colored girl scurrying back toward the rear of the house. Then the younger William turned and again strode in the direction of the house.

The house servant, Tilly, was the granddaughter of Thomas, the first slave Henry and she bought. Her ties to Mary's family always recalled the early years. Those first three years, after they had arrived in Virginia, had been so hard. The English Crown had granted them fifty acres per family member. This 150 acres was increased by their own means to another hundred.

In the beginning, their land was boggy and sullen; resisting crops, encouraging insects, molds, blights and sun blistering. They tried to build, clear and plant for themselves on the acres the Crown had allowed them. Even with the three of them, it was miserable. There were few successes other than the vegetables, a milk cow and pigs for their own providence. They were left with next to nothing else at the end of the year.

The emigrant family had nothing except a dank shack and low rations to show for their efforts. Henry would sit on the doorstep, quietly smoking his pipe each night, looking at the land. After the first pitiful harvest of some corn and tobacco, he took to rising early and walking the land. Seemingly, he was memorizing each acre and each tree. After each walk he would take a stick and draw and cipher in the dirt in front of the cabin. Her Henry seemed to be seeking a plan or solution.

The three Hunters were very isolated. One tinker, a few travelers—maybe only ten—had passed by the first year. One man, who stayed with them overnight every few months, was known only as Wallow, a name he seemed to have given himself. He wore tallow soaked, deer hide clothing and moccasins. What little they knew of the Indians they learned from him, but it was information that helped calm their fears. There was little danger here, only an uncomfortable wariness.

In the evenings, Wallow would smoke his pipe, telling hunting stories and of wild adventures. These stories they found hard to believe. Yet, the break in monotony made his visits welcome and his hate of the Crown stirred them, even though they remained silent, fearing to trust him completely with their own misgivings and resentments.

Once a year, they could afford to order goods from England that might take a year to arrive. They sent for cheese, books, shoes, hats, fabric and most important seed for crops and the garden. There was no church near enough to go to worship and they could only pray and read the Bible at the family table on Sundays.

Isolation increased the problems when illness presented itself. There was no doctor they could summon. The family had learned to bleed and to purge to relieve some conditions. Simple tobacco was sometime eaten when they were congested. They grew may apple, ginseng and witch hazel. Poultices and steam were sometimes their only relief. [2]

The nearest neighbor was twenty miles north and that first eight months they saw them only twice. They were the Calendars, a couple with four small children. This family had been in Northern Virginia for four years, and then three years ago, had moved further South. The land they owned sat higher than their own. They raised tobacco and their own food with much more success than did the Hunters. With nine slaves the Calendars were also able to produce a good market crop.

Even with the tariffs, this family was slowly becoming well to do by producing for export. Tobacco was a shilling a pound – equal to a week's work in England by a laborer. The large crops they produced meant that in a matter of time the family would be prosperous

The first visit to the Calendars had come after Edward Calendar had ridden to the house on his way toward Charleston on business. He accepted their meager hospitality and spent the night. Upon his departure he had asked Henry if they would come to visit his family in a month, when they would be celebrating the harvest.

The depressive situation and loneliness had been a rock to which Mary's heart was tied. Trying not to let Henry know how she felt, she daydreamed of the visit; of wearing a nice dress, talking to another woman and laughing. Laughter was in short supply in their home. When she was alone in the cabin dwelling on the upcoming visit, she would go to her trunk and begin to prepare for this momentous trip.

Her summer dress was nice but when she tried it on she found she had lost a great deal of weight, so she went to her sewing basket to get a needle and thread to take the gown in. She then tried on the dress again, finding it now fit much better. She removed some tatted lace from a handkerchief and stitched it onto her straw hat. After twisting to see herself in the mirror she took off the hat. Digging in her trunk, she found a bit of blue ribbon to add to the lace and allowed some of it to trail down the back. The decoration of her straw hat pleased her.

Each time she play-acted with her wardrobe, she returned it carefully folded to the top of the other clothing in her trunk before Will or Henry returned. Undergarments and her best sleep shift were now laundered, folded, and wrapped in paper. Mary placed small bags with spicy pine needles into the trunk. These were a poor substitute for the lavender and heather of Scotland.

She mentally selected and rejected a hundred recipes for food to be taken as a gift. This was either because they were not special enough or she lacked some ingredient. Finally, she settled on ginger cakes, as hers were so light and special. The ginger she had hoarded was a rare treat. She took some of her precious sugar and finding currants prepared some jam that she placed in a spice tin. Just before they left she would bake the ginger cakes, then bind it all in a hand-woven, linen cloth from Scotland and tie it with another bit of ribbon that in-turn held some dried berries that were still on the stem.

This simple, but exciting, plan for going to visit another woman filled her days and gave her some hope to hold to her lonely breast.

It was no surprise that she was completely prepared and dressed just before dawn on the appointed day. She heard the men preparing the cart where she and Henry would ride. Will would be riding on his saddle horse. The night before, she had heard Henry call and she went outside to hold a lantern while he moved a log and rock at the rear of the house. This area he dug up, and filled with a heavy, canvas bag, holding their valuables. The dirt was replaced, and a log and the rock put in their original position.

Three times since they had lived here, large groups of Indians had passed by, stopping to stare at their home before they moved on. Twice this year, strangers other than Wallow had come to eat and sleep before going on their way. This country was always full of threat of the danger. They had decided to hide what they had to live on for these next years. Henry filled the pouch he wore inside his trousers with gold, some jewelry and coins, but left the rest buried. Should disaster happen at home or on the trip, they would not be wiped out.

There was no blush of color to the sky as they climbed into the cart. Mary pulled a woolen shawl about her because of the chill of the pinewoods. A thick mist, which smelled of the dying smoke from the cabin, mixed with the musty richness of damp soil and decaying vegetation. The cart pulled slowly into the murk along the public path that passed near their cabin.

It was an hour before there was full light and another hour before they began to talk to each other. Mary broke the silence, as her excitement built, "De ye think we might find a cow? You thought it might be good to have another?"

Henry cleared his throat, then responded with some optimism. "Well, my girl, perhaps we can find a one that is with calf."

"Cheese would be good, and beef now and then would be a fine thing," Will enthusiastically added.

With sudden excitement, their son added, "A horse might be nice."

"Nay," his father chided, "we have two horses and a mule that we feed now." Chuckling, he said, "I do not favor horse meat." They all laughed.

Yes, the trip was lovely as they talked, and even laughed, on that day.

When they arrived at the Calendars in the late evening, all three were dusty and weary yet more relaxed than they had been for a very long time. Since the Calendar house was in a long low valley, they had seen the lights in the pitch dark for almost an hour before they arrived. The group of travelers came to a stop near the house. The front the door flew open and Edward stepped out.

Their home was not a cabin but a square house of hewn wood and it had a porch. To Mary it seemed wonderful. The small, high windows were open to the air, with the curtains pulled back. When Henry helped her down, she was stiff. She reached up for her linen bundle. Her husband held it toward her and she took it in her hands. Feeling humble, worried now that the gift might be too small or perhaps not fine enough, Mary looked uncertainly at the object in her hands.

Will dismounted and took his Mother's hatbox carefully, with one arm he encircled her elbow to help her onto the porch. A tall, blond woman, just a little younger than herself, appeared at the elbow of the portly man in the doorway. From her poignant smile Mary instantly realized that this woman was as starved for female company as she. Edward reached for Mary's elbow, which Will relinquished, and she was ushered into the house.

"Mrs. Hunter, this is my wife Cynthia," Edward Calendar introduced the women as they shook hands.

"The children are sleeping," he indicated three small pallets near a fireplace where a low fire glowed with coals like ruby and ebony. The two Hunter men entered and introductions continued.

Neither woman could take her eyes off the other, in a pause Mary stepped toward the hostess to offer the linen wrapped food. Cynthia clutched it to her chest like a cask of gold and moistness filled her eyes. "Oh, how lovely," the woman of the house whispered. With almost no glance at the bundle itself, the giving ceremony was the hunger-filling act between the young women.

The guests were ushered to a long, polished trestle table and took seats on the benches. Tankards of beer were offered to the men. The women took cold milk that Edward had retrieved from the well house. Cynthia proudly removed a cloth from a plate in the middle of the table. With a knife that lay beside the plate, she sliced a spice cake. As she watched, Mary sensed that this woman had prepared for this exceptional event, just as she had.

Walking to the end of the great room, being careful not to trip on boots and saddles which lay along the wall, the hostess opened a lovely sideboard. This furniture was somewhat out of character with the rough in interior of the house. Inside the cabinet, Mary glimpsed the other woman's treasures. She reached above the daily-use, carved, wooden bowls. From a small stack she lady selected five white, china saucers that she brought to the table where she served the spice cake to all.

With the food, came several hours of visiting until the tallow candles burned to nubs. The ladies went out for a walk and upon their return the men went out to smoke a bit. While the men were outside, Cynthia lit a new tallow candle in a pewter candlestick, and led Mary into one of the two bedrooms that opened from the gathering room.

This room had no window and there were pegs on the wall with garments hanging on them. Self-consciously, Mary untied her bonnet. Reaching and carefully taking it from her, the other woman admired it, and hung it by the ties on an empty peg. The hatbox sat just inside the door where Will had deposited it.

Cynthia pointed at a fat, floor pallet covered with a bright fabric cover. "Oh, how lovely," Mary gasped, as she bent to touch it. With pride, her new friend blushed, "I made it last winter."

"How do you do that?" Mary questioned, almost breathless at its beauty.

"It is a quilt. My family sewed pieces of material we saved into a solid piece using patterns. It is very warm. This pattern is simple," Cynthia replied modestly. "Some of the other women do the most wonderful things with quilts."

Mary felt a thrill—a new friend and this thing of beauty to sleep under—tomorrow she must examine it and ask more about how it was made.

Awkwardly, Cynthia stepped toward the door to leave but seemed unable to cross the threshold. Mary stared, took a quick step to the other woman and they embraced each other tightly for a long moment, the fragrance of the other's hair and body was like perfume.

That visit was a beginning in many ways. It was their first important Colonial friendship. The Hunters would have these friends for a lifetime. It was also an introduction to a different way of life in this new land. Mary hoped that the Hunters would someday live as well as the Calendars.

The visit was also a close-up introduction to something their own family had small experience with…slavery. The next day, Edward took the three of them behind the house. They went to two tiny, cabins where he loudly and firmly demanded the people within come outside.

The host proudly lined up the nine slaves he owned for his new friend's inspection. Mary stared at a woman who was lighter in color than the rest and quite skinny. There were two children belonging to the younger woman, a boy of perhaps eight and a girl of about five years. The women wore on their heads old scarves that had once had color but were now only rags, and the children were each dressed in a single garments like a shirt that were incredibly soiled and torn. The five men were between twenty and forty years, and all stood, soundlessly staring at the ground. That is with the exception, a very tall, slender Black man who, in the contrary, stared with no emotion at some imaginary point well above their heads. This man had raised black patterns on his skin, which were like the tattoos of the sailors, but quite unique in pattern. The four other men had tattered shirts and torn trousers, while the tall one was bare to the waist in an immodest manner that was somewhat embarrassing to Mary and she averted her eyes. Even in the early morning the Black men's sweat and odor bit at her nostrils. None of the people looked anyone in the eye. It was embarrassing for Mary to be expected to stand and stare at these unique human beings.

Henry stood, remaining respectfully quiet, as Edward spoke of the virtues of his slaves and their contribution to his prosperity. He firmly demanded the slaves turn around so the guests could see their bodies. It wasn't that her family was naive. They had known a few people who had household slaves or servants in Scotland; not all of these were Negroes. Upon their landing in the Colonies, they had seen many slaves in the New World. There were many working in the fields as they traveled to their new home. William and Mary just had never been this close to any Black people or been asked to consider them in this particular way.

The visit at Calendar's lasted two days, and it was glorious. The women talked, shared recipes, laughter and stories about their children. After they were comfortable, they even shared a few fears and secrets. The men looked at crops and animals. Edward took her men folk up the road to visit a man who had a cow that would be coming in fresh soon. Henry struck a deal to come back and purchase her. This meant they could return to visit again in a few months and that was exciting.

On the trip home, Will shared his ever-present enthusiasm, "We need slaves. That could mean we would have enough help to get everything done. We could clear more land."

Henry seemed hesitant, and spoke slowly and solemnly, "That is a lot of people to feed and care for. We would need another cabin. I do not know a thing about Negroes or how to work with them. It is rather frightening."

This particular conversation went on for hours. Something in Mary was restless and uncomfortable as the men talked. Sometimes, one line of reasoning seemed to be wise, and then the other seemed to be the better choice.

All those dark eyes of the slaves staring at the ground was unsettling. They had looked well fed and when they had come into the house, bringing water or cleaning vegetables, it had been tempting to think of having similar help with her own chores. She thought of the books her Father had read. Many of them referred to slaves and servants throughout history but the books never went into any detail. Some of these had been captives of war or debtors coming from many distant nations and peoples. Even the Bible described them, instructing slaves in proper behavior.

It was still a shock to see human beings that were owned by someone and think of owning people yourself. Perhaps, it was even a dangerous position. Slavery was so very strange, and yet quite prevalent in this new homeland.

The decision that came from what the Hunters considered on that trip came to fruition the following spring when Henry went to Charleston. He and Will came home with two bound men. They had curly, dark hair and were thick-bodied Welshmen. They did not stare at the ground when in the presence of the family. Both had thick calluses at their ankles from chains. They came with small bundles of clothing and possessions.

Alarmed, Mary had pulled Henry aside and asked who they were. The men had been chained as criminals and sent to the colonies by the Crown. Henry made inquiries to their bondsman, who had informed her husband that they were brothers who had fought against the King. This was their punishment, banishment to the Colonies. Henry paid for their passage in return for their bonding promise. In Charleston, slaves were much more expensive than bondsmen. Henry had reasoned that their help was not as compromising as slave ownership.

In return for having their passage paid, the indentured men were required to work for four years and were provided with board and food only. Upon fulfilling the time, then they would become free and able to make their own way in the New World.

David and Samuel James became a new part of their family that day. Mary was now free to work more in her home, helping outside only when they planted and harvested. She continued to care for the vegetable garden, churned, sewed and dried or preserved food. She could now concentrate on laundry, candles, food, weaving and making their home more livable.

David and Samuel helped Henry to take trees down and build their own dirt floor cabin. While they were at this task a dream came true. Mary got a plank floor for her one room cabin and they installed the real luxury, a single window—with glass—that Henry had carefully brought from Charleston.

Working from dawn to dusk, the four men built, cleared, ditched the water and cared for the crops. This year might even see some profit from tobacco, corn, cheese and two calves. The brothers took pride in their work. They were strong and healthy, as were their appetites.

The problem with this new labor was that these men were also independent of spirit. They tended to be less than interested in the prosperity of their bondholder. When they disappeared they might be found fishing, although they did share the catch, which was welcome addition to the table. They tended to argue with each other at the top of their lungs and several times even had fistfights. On some occasions the Welshmen got in touch with a quantity of alcohol and became drunk.

One of these drunken events was at a time when Henry was depending on them and he was furious. He grabbed a tree branch, shucked the leaves and proceeded to thrash the unconscious drunks. David leapt up and raised a fist to Henry. The man held it upraised, his red face, dripping sweat. He then lowered his fist with a sullen sneer on his face.

The first time Wallow stopped after their arrival the conversation at the table had seemed to billow into a high-energy, bombastic event. The brothers began recounting numerous stories until they became so ribald that Mary went outside to stand in a grove of jack pine until they quieted.

Many of the stories at the table were exiting to Will and he asked unending questions of Wallow and the James brothers. Her son was beginning to experience his adulthood. Adventure was a growing hunger that stemmed from his own response to isolation, increasing self-confidence and young, male energy.

During this time, Henry sold some land he felt was not productive enough. They now had the young couple who had purchased the land for neighbors. The Hunters then purchased several hundred more acres adjoining their own land. This land expansion would begin the increase of their holdings for the next hundred years.

Late in the third year of indenture, the James brothers and Henry all knew the time had come to find slaves. This plantation simply needed more labor and soon the Welshmen would be leaving. After their time in the Colonies, Henry and Mary had become more comfortable with the Negroes their acquaintances owned.

Finally, Henry and Will went with Edward to the Charleston slave market. This city was 12,000 and one of the largest in the colonies. Edward's experience was supportive as they examined teeth, muscles, and feet, and then bartered and harangued for their first slave. Newly off the ship, this broad-chested short Black man appeared to be around twenty-five years old.

After some discussion, her husband asked Mary to name the man and she called him Thomas. With terror in his eyes, he would crouch above his food bolting it down. Sensing his terror, the family decided not to use food to reward his completion of tasks or to withhold it as punishment, for it seemed too cruel. Instead they would give him a penny coin or a handkerchief when his work was outstanding. They gave the man a smile and a pat on the shoulder when his efforts succeeded. Henry would pantomime his instructions. The family began to teach a few simple words to the man. Ever wary and conscious of stories he had heard of runaways and violence, Henry never let Thomas out of sight and locked him in his windowless cabin each night, no matter the temperature.

Gradually, Thomas began to communicate. He was strong and often did wise things like forming temporary corrals out of saplings or creating whistles from tree limbs. His touch with both animals and children was gentle. When things needed to be built he had a native, intuitive wisdom. His wide smile and glittering eyes said he took pride in these tasks. Eventually, the Hunters began to put more trust in him, allowing him to fish and snare small game. After many years, they taught him how to use the gun and bring down deer or small game. Thomas had a sure eye with a target.

Occasionally, Mary would find the young man leaning on a tree murmuring something she could not understand and staring passionately toward the East. One time, he struggled to make her understand and asked how far it was to his home. It took a great deal of marks in the dirt and broken language to tell him of the great distance. At the end of the exchange he shook his head and strode away. His emotions were well hidden under a solemn, blank expression. The woman felt his pain and accepted the agony he felt as similar to her own losses in Scotland. Thomas' existence here was sealed even though he also longed for his home, as they did. Somehow, sharing with Henry these observations of Thomas did not seem appropriate. Any experiences Henry or Will might have that paralleled her own were never brought up in conversation. Perhaps, the men also felt the empathy and guilt that Mary secretly carried.

That year, their slave could understand that the James brothers would be leaving and 'Massa Hunta' would be buying more slaves. Timidly he knocked on the door one night, and in very broken language, told them he was lonely and he would work very hard if he could have a wife. On a trip to the Calendars with his owners, Thomas had found he could communicate a bit with one of the slaves there. Looking back, Mary sensed a small bit of the great loneliness the man must have felt for his own land and people. He had no language, a strange lifestyle and he ate new foods which were often repugnant to him. This man, who had become her friend, had suffered a loss of all he held dear.

Little by little the Negro was beginning to understand the Colonial system and language. The next trip to Charleston that Henry made he came home with four new slaves walking behind his horse, their ankles were tied to each other with rope. In the group was a teenage boy, a thirty-year-old, coal Black man who spoke English, a very tall, lighter woman and a narrow-faced, ebony girl of sixteen whom they named Nana. Nana would bear seven children by Thomas for the Hunters. Four of these children would live to adulthood. Now, the Hunters were slave owners, and the cycle of slave and land purchase had begun to accelerate in the common pattern of the Colonies in the Americas.

One circumstance of living in isolation so many years with Thomas as their property, was that he became a trusted member of the family. His contributions had been many. It was rare that there were misunderstandings, for he would always follow Henry's demands. The most threatening demeanor he exhibited was a clouding of his eyes or rarely seen glowering looks as he left after chastisement.

Unfortunately, not all the servants and field hands that had been purchased over the years were so easy to oversee. One valuable worker they owned had run away, never to be found. In this case, they suspected that the young man was hiding close by for a long time because of his ties with his fellows at their plantation. For theft or damage, or direct disobedience the discipline used was to be locked in a slave cabin alone for a period of time. It was rare that there were more serious problems, but these Henry responded to by removing food for several days.

Over the years at least three field workers were sold when they became impossible to control. After a few years, as planter slave owners they found that married couples with children were the most productive and content. The Hunter family also found that gifts and rewards usually brought a response of obedience.

There was ever yet an uneasiness that Mary felt, just behind the existence of slave ownership. Thomas, in the comfort and pleasure of raising his own family, and growing familiarity with her family, became ever more open with Mary. This was awkward and seemed to her, almost a betrayal of Henry, no matter the respect and appreciation she had grown to feel for Thomas.

In snippets, very slowly, the Black man shared parts of his African life with Mary. Some of the customs were very strange to the Scottish woman. His broken vocabulary often had no common word to name things or events. Many of the things he had shared over the years made no sense to his owner's wife. Once, in pantomime, he showed her some strange, stomping dance where he jumped, waved and thrust his arms in abandon. Thomas tried to explain the purpose but she had been bewildered.

Mary had wished she did not understand the day when, with his hands, he formed the shape of a woman, showing her the height by laying his hand on his own chest. Then, smiling, he acted out the nursing of a baby in the imaginary woman's arms. Proudly, he then held up two fingers. That day, at that moment, a pain constricted her throat. She turned abruptly and walked away. She knew what this story had meant, and she did not want to think of it.

Mary shuddered to think of how much, or how little, this personal knowledge about Thomas would upset her husband. *Would he punish Thomas or be angry with her?* The best thing, she decided, would be to avoid such contact and keep any information that the two had previously shared a private secret.

Several years after her Black friend had attempted to tell her about his lost wife and children, he had made the most shocking exposure of all to her. This haunting communication crossed Mary's mind many times thereafter.

On a business and personal trip, she, Henry, Will and his new bride, Sarah, took Thomas and another strong servant to the coast, north of Charleston. They made camps on the beach, on a warm, moonlit night. Will and Sarah retired early, tired from the trip. Henry and the other servant had seen tracks during the day and left to find game, hopefully a resting deer. For a long time, Thomas sat near a tree, alertly protecting the camp. Eventually, he walked toward the water and stood in the reflected shine at tidemark on the wet beach.

The scene was bright in the full moon. Mary Hunter looked at his strong body silhouetted against the rolling ebb and flow of the ocean. The sound of the water surrounded her. Then, above the sound of the sea, she heard a song of wail followed by murmurs. This song, repeated over and over, was almost the same pattern as the water's rhythm. The plaintive music touched her curiosity and its obvious pain aroused her sympathy.

The lady stood, shaking the sand from her skirts onto the blanket where she had been sitting. Slowly, she moved down the beach, approaching behind her fellow traveler. When she was about ten yards away, she stopped and listened intently to the mournful song that continued for many minutes. Woven into the tones were pain and loss that needed no translation. Mary watched the dark shape and when the song ended Thomas turned. She saw, reflected in the man's eyes, a luminous moistness. Finally, he turned and walked past her returning to the fireside.

Mary remained near the water looking at the silver, rolling Atlantic for at least fifteen minutes. Turning toward the campsite, she observed that the man was scratching into the sand with a long, narrow firebrand. Taking a seat on a log near him, she continued to watch the obscure scratching which the man took great pains to design. Now and then, he paused to erase, wiping a mark away then creating a new one more carefully.

"What is this Thomas?" she softly asked.

Looking up, he paused, then strongly answered, "Ship, it a ship."

Looking for a sail and masts the images seemed unrecognizable. She could see no resemblance.

"Ship I come by," the man stated simply, calmly and firmly.

Then he began his story. "Near my hut and village is another people. They send for my people to help them. Many of my people go to the big water where the other people live." Pausing, he waved the pointed, blackened stick toward the East across the water.

"What we see when we come to the big water is ship close by the sand. The other tribe's chief point to ship. He say many of his people be on ship. We need to bring them back to the village."

Thomas was once more quiet for minutes. His voice was husky as he returned to the story, "We all know slave ships. It is good to be afraid, no one comes back from there. They have guns that eats you like a animal." Looking Mary in eye he clarified, "call cannon."

His mistress nodded slightly and made no indication for him to stop the story. "The chief say for many days wonderful things lay on the sand. The ship and strange men are far out in the water. His whole village takes the things from the sand. One day, many canoe on the beach. Many good things are in the canoe. The women, the babies and some hunters go to the boat. White men from the ship then run from the trees and take the people. They hold the people and put chains on them, hit them and drag them to the canoes. Many from the villagers die when fire sticks eat them," Looking up he shares, "guns," and once more Mary nods. "Some run away and hide," he continued the story.

"The hunters and my village men want to return the people stolen by the canoes. The people all be on ship now. We watch and talk. The canoe comes many times but the people do not go to the canoe. One day, three big canoes come out of water to sand. When the strange soldiers go into the trees we attack. The battle is hard. Many people die by the big knives and firesticks. I fight strong and am running by the water to catch a white man. Someone hit me on my head and back of legs and I sleep. When I open my eyes I am in the dark. A chain be on my leg and arm. I feel the moving of water under me. Many of my people are with me. We talk quiet. Many women cry with no noise. For many days we lay there on the wet wood. Each day we all go to top of ship in the chains. We feed on meat and fruit of our own land. All our people look hard at the sand and the trees. We hope for escape. We try to plan but see no plan. After a long time we leave the place we live and go on the water. It is many nights when we come to a new place. It has no sand. This place has great houses made of rocks."

Thomas paused for a long time, staring at the water in the moonlight. Then the tragic story continued.

"We stay on ship many days by this place. Then many canoes come and bring many, many people of a tribe we not know. We do not know their words. Now, so many be on the wood floor inside the ship we cannot lay to sleep at night. We do not like to be here. We are afraid and we do not like this new tribe. Already, many be sick, they vomit and cry out. Some begin to die. Many who have been hurt begin to swell and the sores stink bad. This is both my people and the other too."

"See Ms. Mary," the man pointed his stick at the strange drawing in the sand. "Each mark is people." Looking at the hundreds of marks in horror, she stared for a long time. Mary realized the amazing number of people. She remembered her own Atlantic crossing, and the cramped quarters below deck. She had always tried not to imagine how the Black people who arrived on these shores came to be here. *Yes*, she really had known, just not understood it so starkly.

When his mistress raised her eyes so did Thomas and they both stared at the moonlit ocean. The man bent and swept the marks away using the stick that he had used to create them. Without turning, keeping his eyes on the horizon, he continued his story, "Many not come here. Many die on water—no food, no air. They close the door and no air comes in. As we cannot breath, many kill each other to save breath. When we get food the tribes kill each other to take more food. Those with wounds and sores just rot and die. Some do not die but go to sleep and not wake. These people sing all the time the quiet song of death. Some women hold their children and jump into the ocean, the chains that tie them pull many others into the water with them. The men on the ship hit and cut some people who fight with the other. The two tribes hate each other." The man sharply focused on the horizon in silence. Then he flatly mumbled, "I never see my village again."

From that day Mary wished she had never heard the story or felt this pain in a person who played such a large part in her life. Henry never heard the tragic tale, nor did Will. Mary would sometimes plead the case for their slaves. Her understanding of the hard lives they lived in Virginia and knowing how they or their family had arrived here gave her a heart wrenching and haunting pity. Her men folk only felt that she was being compassionate. Thomas and she never spoke in this way again.

As her grandson William came into the room Mary heard the footfalls, but never took her eyes from the small brown girl across the road at the picnic. Quietly, Mary looked at Tilly and saw in her the resemblance of her grandfather, Thomas. The girl's family was so woven into their own. *What a strange relationship?* It was one that was accepted, but built on needs and power. The dependency fell both ways for Thomas' and the Hunters. There were relationships, but these were out of kilter, no matter the emotional, personal impact.

The sun would be warm at the picnic and the day would tire her. It seemed that now everything tired Mary. Yet, she still wished to be in the middle of all events, and it was of great importance to her to help her grandson achieve success in the election. Actually, she would also be helping Henry, her other grandson, for it had been agreed upon that William would appoint his brother sheriff, once he was in office. She also loved parties and seeing neighbors. Mary was vainly pleased with the attention she knew she would receive. The old matriarch's sense of success was deep and she was full of pride.

She heard the familiar creak of the porch floorboards then a firm step moving through the hall and into the sitting room. Bending down the young man kissed her forehead. "Grandmother, how does it feel to know that your boy will soon be in the House of Burgess. When you came on that ship and touched the land did you know how much would someday belong to you, your son and now your grandson? It is a fine day for the Hunters. We have truly written our name on the land."

When she looked up, a flush of joy filled her. Could any child be this wonderful, bright or handsome? How she loved each of her grandsons, each was as special as when she first lay eyes on them in the arms of their mothers.

The smile on her lips widened, "Pride will bring ye to humility, young man." She laughingly chastened, although pride almost burst her own chest.

Leaning over the tiny bird of a woman, he kissed her forehead with soft warm lips. "We will greet our guests now, come Grandmother."

Gently, her took her elbow and helped her up. Mary stopped a moment to arrange her skirts, check her buttons and pat her hair once more. Firmly holding the young man's arm, they crossed the room, moved down the hall and across the threshold. The porch was full of visitors, they stopped a moment to speak with various neighbors and to be introduced to some people. After so many years, these guests were grandchildren of her own friends. The walkway was open, they slowly and carefully proceeded down the way and across the road.

For years of slaves had moved rocks and weeds from the front acres of the house. The lawn was now wide and smooth with tall grass which produced the musk of greenness. On the lawn were more county folks to be greeted, so the lady and young man moved slowly, stopping frequently.

It was only a short while before, leaning a bit, Mary whispered, "I am tired."

The pair then went directly, but carefully, to a rocking chair under one tree. Tilly was just positioning a small table beside the chair and a houseboy was covering it with a cloth and placing a small china pitcher of water and a drinking glass on it. The young boy then stood behind the chair, ready to wait on the old lady, and if needed to shoo flies or fan her. He wore a torn linsy woolie shirt that had belonged to someone a couple sizes larger than himself. Above his bare feet were pants that were too short and shredded to the knee to free his calves. William seated his grandmother very carefully.

Her grandson went out onto the lawn, near the tables. His wife, Sarah, came from the crowd and took his arm. Moving to the center of the crowd, and nodding to the Bishop who was a longtime family friend, William clapped his hands. Slowly, the murmuring quieted.

"My friends and neighbors, I thank you for your presence at Hunter Hall. I'm sure no finer group of low-country folk have ever been gathered. I hope none more hungry." Soft laughter and applause followed his cheerful greeting.

"I envision our visits today will unite us in the interest of Nansamond, and that you will well consider selecting me to represent you in Williamsburg. The Hunters have prospered, here in Tidewater, but all the neighborhood needs to grow and increase our markets. We need to pursue fair tariffs and keep our ports open. I hope I will be able to defend our interests in Burgess. Thank you and please speak with me on any issue that is of importance to you. Be full of good cheer as we all share this day. Enjoy any small hospitality we offer at Hunter Hall. Now, the Bishop will give blessing."

After a brief, but solemn word of prayer given by the clergyman, William filled a plate and took it to his grandmother where she sat under the tree. According to community position, the rest of the guests took their plates and proceeded along the trestle to fill dishes. They were assisted or served with the help of household servants which included some extra Negro women who had been brought from the fields.

Mary nibbled at her food as the many guests found places on the grass to sit and eat. Many of the men leaned on trees or sat on the back of wagons. Some guests retreated to the wide porch at the front of the house. The fiddle player on the porch was joined by a large, beautiful, brunette flutist, and merry music undulated across the beautiful scene. With a light motion of her hand, the old lady had the slave boy move her plate away and pass her a water glass. The water was still cool from the well house.

The ladies on the lawn were dressed in their best dresses. Their faces were protected from the sun by bonnets. As she looked about her, Mary studied how the other ladies were wearing their hair and what style of dresses seemed to be popular. Her own simple loose fitting bodice and skirt were of excellent quality, but by no means new. Really, it was her curiosity rather than any real interest in fashion that inspired her gaze.

The children running about and laughing were, as always, a joy to see. She watched warmed by their energy. They sounded like playful pups or fox kittens. For a moment, in the distance, she saw several of her own great-grandchildren racing in some kind of game of catch. They squealed and laughed as they were caught. Near her, there was a tall tree with a bench underneath. It was here, William's wife, Sarah, was sitting. Several other ladies were with her and they were all speaking softly.

William Junior was somewhere at her back for she recognized his clear voice. She eavesdropped on his conversation. The group of men were discussing events at the House of Burgess in Williamsburg. Burgess had freedom to vote and therefore was the only real power held by the Colonials. The men were comparing the appointment of various judges and justices that had been made by the British governor. These appointments were made with the approval of the House of Burgess.

The intense conversation by the planters compared the sheriffs appointed by Burgess. Virginia was a small place and prominent families were known by all. Ongoing was the discussion of more representation for their interests in the Colonies, especially Virginia.

The major conversation context pivoted about the debate on the ruling, only six years ago, which limited each county to two members of Burgess, with a change at least every seven years. This change of representatives would be her grandson William's opportunity. The pay would only be fifteen shillings a day and travel costs. Pay was not the incentive, the power would be immense within their own county. William would appoint his brother for Henry would make a fine sheriff. He might even be able to appoint more of his family to public service.

After she had eaten and was slowly rocking, Mary was covered by a foggy dreaminess. The voices of the men made a rumbling rhythm. Her head finally rolled to one side and the lady—warm, content and full—fell asleep. In a dreaming memory, she saw herself as a young woman. Memories filtered into her dream. It was as though she were once again in that ship on the vicious Atlantic during early spring. In her arms was the dirty-nosed boy from the inn, whose cold had left him almost unable to breathe and gasping for life. Beside her, the child's mother smothered her face in her apron and sobbed.

They were sitting in a murky dark, except for a swinging lamp hung in the center of the low passenger hold. From the hold's perimeter, dozens of grey faces stared hollowly at her and the young boy. She sat upon a thin tick stooped under a low bunk. The child's sweaty forehead smelled of dirt and vomit. Mary saw herself fumble into her pocket to draw out a fragrant, leathery piece of shriveled apple. Biting off small bits, she slowly chewed them. She then carefully placed bits of sweet moistness into the dying child's mouth. There was a faint smile on the pale face as he painfully swallowed the tiny morsels, and he coughed deeply between accepting each bite.

When the apple slices were gone, she continued to rock and hold the child while the mother wept. Mary finally felt a shudder and the complete limpness of the child that told her it was over. There would be another canvas bag burial at sea. Like a rock dropping into the ocean, the bags floated for just a moment in the ship's wake after being slid into the water. Then, the bodies quickly disappeared below.

As though blown away by the wind, the scene of the child's death was gone. There was now a memory of a sharp pain in her own belly. She lay, curled in a ball in the dark. She was weeping and gasping. Her body was being thrown about and only by rolling in a ball could she keep her own head from being slammed repeatedly into the floor. There was an awful slipperiness under her, and the smell of waste and vomit seemed to cover her like the slimy surface of a slug. In her hand was the sharp fragment of a fragile blue and white china cup. Her fingers felt the broken piece with no fear of cutting herself. *How could more pain or blood be worse than this existence?*

It had been at least two days since the storm began, and all on the ship were all ordered to stay in the cabin or below. Most of the people in the cabin were lashed to walls so that they would not be thrown about. Children were held in their parents tired, aching arms and passed back and forth for relief. This cup shattering, when it fell from her valise to break, seemed to be the end of everything for her. Homesickness, fear, the amputated hand of the sailor who became caught in the rigging…Mary remembered it all, including the man who fell overboard with no one able to get a rope to him. There was so much the sickness on the ship as it rolled up and down watery mountains. The broken cup symbolized so much more. It was her total loss of hope.

Again, blackness that was like a deep abyss covered the old woman in her rotating dream, and any immediate pain the previous dream had awakened was numbed. In this newest dream, she was enveloped by the sound of nothingness. Then there was the old memory of the clop, clop, clop of hooves. A vision of soft morning light slowly pierced the darkness. In the moment of awakening to the new scene, she had smelled the familiar fragrance of her own dear Henry. It was the odor of leather, dust and the musk of his own body. Her eyes had flown open as he nudged her by shrugging his shoulder where her weary head had rested.

Sitting upright, Mary had been disoriented by the bright light that at first blurred her sight. With effort, she focused on the landscape. From the location on the road she looked to the East and saw the slicing, dark blue line of ocean. In the month since they landed, their group of three had slept by the road, at inns or in the rustic cabins where they had been invited to stay with other Colonists. Now, they were finally in tidewater Virginia in the Suffolk area. Tonight, at least, the bed, on the ground south of here, would be resting on their own land.

Having experienced so much on shipboard had forever changed Mary. No longer would she accept fear or oppression. A fire burned in her heart to fight, win and conquer. The tenderness of a young girl had been replaced by the strength and determination of full womanhood. Even within her family, she felt more of a partnership with Henry and capable of anything demanded of her. Her dear Da's admonishment on fear of the future, had become her credo.

Henry halted the horses and wagon when the family reached the bay's edge. He leaned back toward the baggage and barrels in the cart where the adolescent boy slept. He shook Will's boot to wake his son. Then the man quietly pointed ahead toward a lighter blue area of water where the it undulated among yellow-green grasses. Tears of joy and relief fell from each person's eyes. Moisture sliced down Mary's dusty cheeks leaving glistening paths. There was no sound except for the murmur of ocean on the out tide and the call of a gull. That was a language of life and hope to the tired matron. The road worn group sat studying the view and the expanse of land running from the ocean westward for almost a mile. Then the area Henry pointed to was more inland.

This dream memory gradually faded and another took its place. In the next vision, the woman who was her looked at her own feet. There, instead of the cart or road was a green mound, with azalea surrounding it on one side. Her dear Henry was seated on the mound, his back against an inscribed piece of marble tombstone. He was handsome and much younger than when she had buried him. Just as it was when he came every night now, he smiled again and held out his hand.

Suddenly, the frail old lady felt her head jerk and realized she had dozed off. She had been full of food, warm in the sun, and lulled by pleasant sights and sounds. She simply had laid her head back on the chair and fallen asleep. The Black child was still at her side. He had been assigned to see that she did not fall from her chair when she slept.

When her eyes widened she saw that Sarah had left her seat under the tree and was coming toward her. "Grandmother Hunter, would you like to visit with anyone? I will find them and bring them to you."

"Yes, I would like to meet young Mrs. Norsworthy. Her husband, George, will be at Burgess with William Junior. I do not think I have met her. Thank you, my dear." Mary studied Sarah as she turned and slowly scanned the crowd. Natural, dark-blond hair fell in waves and soft curls from under a straw hat. The woman displayed strength in her carriage that showed spirit and dignity.

Not seeing Mrs. Norsworthy, the granddaughter-in-law excused herself from William's grandmother and went toward the area where the majority of the guests were standing and visiting. In about ten minutes she slowly wandered back with a tiny dark woman at her side. The lady had a full skirt of grey and a blouse of a fine, white lawn tucked into the tiny waist of the skirt. She was wearing a straw bonnet that shaded her face. When she approached her thickly lashed, dark eyes glittered from the hat's shadow and the tiny mouth rolled into a bright smile.

Sarah introduced the woman, "Mrs. George Norsworthy and this is William's grandmother, the Widow Hunter."

The women, who had newly met, looked deeply into each other's eyes. The younger woman had heard of Mrs. Hunter and did not underestimate her power, albeit her age. This well respected woman had great wisdom and insight into the history, families and politics of early Virginia.

Polite questions were asked about the younger woman's family. Did she have children? Who were her neighbors? Yet all the time there was a sense of the friendly, old lady taking her measure and gleaning any information that might help her grandson when he went to Williamsburg. It was widely known that in her earlier days, her men folk talked with this Scottish lady about all the plans and decisions on this farm, which she and her husband had begun to build over fifty years ago.

Mary had early learned, that she was good not only with the bookkeeping but also in decision making. She played a major role in the Hunters' prosperity. Her genteel, yet wily, presence at meetings usually led to success. Such a reputation was to the chagrin of many males, who felt it was not proper for a woman to be in her position.

Finally, Mary offered the younger women water and sent the slave boy for another cool pitcher and some fresh glasses. While they waited for the racing, Black child to return, the conversation lulled. Smiling past the women standing by her, Mary caught the eye of another woman and with a slight wave of her hand invited this lady over to speak with her. This woman, approaching, had been her neighbor for twenty years. They were quite glad to see each other and the two old friends started to recite a litany of family, funerals and health matters.

The younger women stood patiently until the water was delivered. Finally, Mary said, "I know you want to have a chance to visit, do not let me hold you." With a courteous smile and twinkling eyes, Mary acknowledged the visitor standing by Sarah, "So good to meet you, Mrs. Norsworthy." The younger woman deferred with a parting nod.

"Thank you, Sarah," Mary beamed at her granddaughter-in-law. The young wives of George Norsworthy and William Hunter smiled politely at the matriarch and walked away, leaving the older matrons to visit. The wives of Burgess stepped closely side-by-side, "Your husband's grandmother is respected by everyone." Mrs. Norsworthy smiled with assurance at her assessment of the Grand Dame.

"Yes, she is quite exemplary. It will be a sad day when Mary Hunter is gone from Hunter Hall." Sarah replied casually with politeness, unaware of the portent.

In less than a month, that very event came to pass. Mary would reach back to Henry when he held his hand out to her from his graveyard seat. The house was quiet for several days as Mary lay pale and sleepy, with a deep rattling sound in her chest. After a small cold that did not linger, Mary had been left with fullness in her chest and took to bed.

Sarah had been quietly, less present in the home for she was in her third month with child. Nell was in charge of the care of the old lady during her final illness. In less than a week, Mary Hunter was laid to rest beside her husband in the small azalea enclosed area of the family burying ground.

In early June, George Norsworthy and William Hunter, Junior began the 150-mile trip to Williamsburg. The small village of Williamsburg possessed a college and there were 1,500 people as permanent residents. Two times a year that population swelled when Burgess convened during "public times." [2]

The companions rode through the tall jack pines along the sandy trail on the northwest side of the bay. To reach the ferry was a ride of several days from where they had begun. Unless they intended to follow the whole shore of the bay, they planned to camp at the ferry mooring that night so they could cross the bay to Williamsburg in the morning. Virginia and June are made for each other. The weather allowed them warmth, the ocean perfumed their path and optimism was their commander and leader.

George was in his second year in the House and more than willing to fill the younger man in on the gossip. He informed his colleague of the personalities they would be encountering in the Capitol. These men were more than on a duty journey. They were on the road to success and power. The House of Burgess was a list of Virginia's leading planters. To be invited, then elected, meant a major personal step upward. This was where Colonial leaders were born.

England might control the politics but it was the biannual House of Burgess that decided the price and quality of tobacco. They set taxes, controlled education, Indian relations and religion. It was they who appointed county servants who, in turn, held local power in their hands. Their's was a democracy made up of aristocratic names that would someday lead to the presidency for a number of families. [2]

The land started to rise above the bay and from there each could look back toward the lovely farm country and the small, Virginia villages nesting just inland from the water's edge. William reined his long legged, brown mare in and paused to look over the scene. Dismounting with a creak of leather, William stared at the ocean and some unseen, far point in the northeast.

As he looked across the water, he somberly wondered what Scotland was like. The story of his ancestor's journey to the Colonies was, to him, the greatest adventure he could imagine. He turned to look back the direction of the farm he had left, knowing that the new baby would be born by the time he returned. This new child would join two older siblings.

June meetings often did not end until fall. With the harvest and a new child being born, William knew he would secretly be very homesick.

His fears were only personal for the farm was in the able hands of his brother, Henry, who was strong and competent. His family and the plantation were in good order.

It was now with pride and excitement that the two of them once again mounted, and moved northward. They were ready to represent the Colonists of their region. Secretly, each man harbored a desire to try to escape English control and become more independent. They passionately desired less European financial control and less responsibility toward the Crown. Both hoped Colonists could be released from the chaffing indignity of being forced to serve in the militia. Yet, each man knew it wise to be very discreet and wait. Someday, perhaps soon, the Colonists would have more say in the commerce and welfare of their land.

The scene was peaceful and lovely. Two straight-backed, prosperously dressed, young men trotting along on well-formed steeds. Their rolls of clothing were tied behind their saddles, and both had a small valise fixed on either side of their mounts. Any goods they needed beyond those they carried could be obtained in Williamsburg.

Running behind each gentleman were their servants. These adolescents were keeping pace like shadows of their owners and masters. Bouncing shoes were tied about their necks as they ran barefoot. Each boy carried a bundle of 'proper' clothing tied onto his back. These younger men also felt some pride, anticipation of travel and a potential for adventure. The Hunter slave had never had shoes before. The shoes were a sign of dignity, no matter how uncomfortable they felt on sixteen-year-old feet.

This boy stole looks toward the east where the ocean appeared to fall of the face of the earth. With pride the servant smiled to himself. He knew the ocean did not end at the horizon. His own grandfather had come from that direction. He had lived long, far days away before he was brought to this continent. The boy proudly was called Young Thomas.

He also smiled because he secretly knew numbers and could write his name. Perhaps, in this place he was going, he could also learn to read, if the master felt it would make him a better man's servant. If not, Young Thomas might just learn to read anyway, just very carefully.

Chapter 3

# Vicksburg

The United States had seen major changes in the three generations of history since Mary Hunter's death in Virginia. There had been unbelievable land expansion into areas of the New World that the colonists had not known existed. The colonies had become a single nation. The Revolution had accomplished the goal of breaking from England, but how painful the cost to many families that revolution had been! Death, suffering and loss followed the battles. Almost all American families and communities were touched in some manner.

There had not always been clear loyalties during the American Revolution. The political scene had been fraught with economic and social problems. Throughout the war many of the citizens still had continued to hold loyalties across the sea.

Now, almost 200 years later Private William Hugh Hunter, a descendent of Henry and Mary Hunter, sits on a dark hill in Mississippi. It is the summer of 1863. He is on a battlefield that divides the same nation even more than the American Revolution had divided people a hundred years earlier. This time the separation is even more painful than was the chasm created by the war for liberty. This is a war to divide or unify the same nation. It is a war between stubborn and defensive brothers. Ultimately the result of this conflagration will also define the rights of the former Africans who now reside on this continent.

My post at the Battle of Vicksburg is with a small detachment of Fifteenth Illinois sharpshooters. The is over three hundred feet from the main road between John Allen Street and Georgia Salient Works. This location is on the far south and west perimeter of the combat. Not far from here is a large entrenchment of Confederate soldiers, mostly from Alabama and Georgia. These soldiers flank and protect the southern part of a north south road. The majority of my own regiment is north and east of our location.

Tonight the tree bark cuts into my back and I forcibly squirm from side to side allowing the texture of the wood to scratch my weary shoulders through the rough, woolen, sack fabric of my uniform. On this late June night, the earth is damp on my trouser seat, although the scrap of gum blanket I sit on is folded double. My behind is uncomfortably clammy and cold. *William Hunter, it is like you are sitting on a dead fish,* I think with disgust.

This week I've survived several instantaneous, drenching rainsqualls and now on the night watch there is a moldering brownness to the air. Thankfully it is too early in the summer for the worst of the insects such as I had suffered as I previously followed the war into the Deep South.

It is well after ten at night so there is a lull in the battle sounds. By this time there are usually only the occasional night sounds of a random horse or soldier of my own company that is bivouacked at my back to the east, in the shallow gully. Occasional distant rifle fire echoes like a drum-roll from the largest area of battlefield that is located on the hills to the east of Vicksburg, Mississippi.

This city rests anxiously on a two hundred-foot bluff above a horseshoe bend in the Mississippi River. There are battles daily that surround the town. Miles of combat lines of Union and Confederate soldiers cut across the landscape like open abscesses. Mostly to the east and north of me, major battles are being fought in bloody, loud repetition day after day. The city has been under continual bombardment for over a month now. From the water of the great Mississippi, the Union Navy keeps aiming and shooting four miles toward the city with an irregular, but blistering barrage.

This is a conflict of continual, face to face violence, with the battle lines frequently less than three hundred feet from each other. The major body of my own regiment, the Fifteenth Illinois volunteers, is a short distance northeast of my own post. That regiment has soundlessly built rifle pits at night. The men have also dug deep trenches by placing cotton bales before them, shoving them along for protection. The enemy, at not more than ten rods, did not discover these pits until morning. The short distance means that the rebels can catch grenades or our canisters and hurl them back at us before they explode.[3]

At any one time, as many as ten battles are fought while hundreds of locations defend the space each holds. The major battles always slow at night, becoming just single deadly shot from a sharpshooter, a shower of canister, or an occasional bomb explosion in the city of Vicksburg. There is an overpowering, fog-like quiet right now.

Often at night, in this battle, the Billy Yanks call across the lines to the Johnny Rebs to pass news, send taunting insults, or sometimes arrange the trade of goods. The gossip of the troops is passed among them in the dark. Sometimes, the opposing troops even join the other in song.

A rebel will call out in the dark, "Been marching behind you boys. What makes your folks leave us so many good clothes and fine blankets?"

From across the lines comes the Union answer, "We obey the injunction to clothe the naked and feed the hungry."

The rebels then call out, "When is Grant going to march into Vicksburg?"

The answers would be sharp and clear, "When you get your last mule and dog eat up."

With a bitter barb a Yank might call from a different location, "Haven't you Rebs got a new general—General Starvation?"

The rebel reply would be shouted with derision, "Have you Yanks all got nigger wives yet?" [4]

Some of the more poignant nighttime conversations at this battle are those of the Missouri troops. Missouri has supplied the battle of Vicksburg forty-two units, fifteen of these are Confederate and twenty-seven are Union regiments. These men of two different armies often share hometowns and sometimes, even share families. When a Missouri soldier, of either army dies, both sides often mourn together. [5]

My own outpost is under an order of silence but usually the other voices and distant songs of the evening will waft down the valley in the dark. But not tonight—it is very quiet. The nightly, wary truce always seems eerie and restless to me. Even the insect noises seem loud in the darkness. The strong moonlight tonight will most likely mean this should be a quiet watch till morning. Probably, no one will attempt to cross the meadow or road on this southern perimeter of the knoll where I am perched.

Locked in the heavy silence, it seems like I am in a casket with the lid closed. I am shielded by thick, low bushes in front of me. Trees hide each of us seven sharpshooters at the posts where we are stationed. One soldier to the north of me is snuggled in a fork of a large, low tree. With a companion, I am twenty feet beyond this man on a narrow, dirt road near Hall's Ferry Road. The ferry road, near here, runs from the city of Vicksburg toward the river. Where I sit is above the smaller road to the north end of the area that we are assigned to defend. There were two other sentries watching the front perimeter. Two of our men also sit just beyond the gully and camp. These men scrutinize eastward toward the gully.

As I peer southward, I study the moonlit, open area below me. The road we protect is cut through steep, Loess clay banks. The pathway has been worn into the Vicksburg hills by continual use and natural drainage. When this small road comes out of the gully, it winds two miles southwest to the great river and the port. The port is now held immobile by the Union troops. It is active with our soldiers, supplies and boats.

The Union Sanitary Commission's Admiral Porter is anchored near by. His unit oversees the wounded. Volunteer nurses, doctors and soldiers accomplish this.

My sharpshooters unit has been called more regularly in the last weeks to enter combat in attack actions. Now, with both the armies entrenched, attack from the front is less frequent. Yet, sharpshooters are still most effective. When we are called, our line charges, men running four feet apart, firing as quickly as we can load. Each of us have been chosen for our skill with the rifle, and our ability to quickly reload. Many of us carry weapons brought from home for we are most sure with these. I take great pride in the fact I have been thus selected, and I feel confidence in my own skill.

One of the highlights of this battlefield for the Union sharpshooters, was an attack at what is called Garrott's Line. The Georgia and Alabama boys held a north/south line located north of us. Their position lies between our post and the old Mississippi. On June 17, not many days ago, our men hit Colonel Isham W. Garrott's Alabama troops' position.

We hit them hard and Colonel Garrott died there. The effectiveness of sharpshooters was proven again. Quick, accurate, precision firing is direct. It's knife point direction takes a toll of the enemy, when employed. We had no casualties in this action, but took several in addition to that of the Colonel.*

During the day at our guard posts, there are always a few people who arrive without proper Union passes to proceed on the road. Some civilians still live within the battlefield. These citizens live precariously in the middle of chaos. They are stopped and searched, often arrested, or sometimes detained as spies if we were suspicious of them.

Union troops furtively move up and down the road each day in varying frequency and numbers. Yet, what few travelers do come on road during the day, disappear as the curfew is enforced. There is minimal military movement to the river or back at night.

A couple times, usually at night, riflemen have shot at the other men or me while we were on guardposts. This risk fuels a cautious wariness among the night watch. For this reason we move to random watch assignments each night.

About a week ago one of my fellows on night watch had called the warning, "Who goes?" Then, hearing no reply, he had shot toward the source of the noise. Our men all roused and rushed with caution to the perimeter trees that the soldier had targeted. There lay a young Confederate, lung shot, his lips spattering with bloody spittle and gasping his last breaths.

**The real battle record of William Hunter's Sharpshooters is unknown.*

In his leather dispatch bag was a desperate note to Confederate General Johnston, from General Pemberton pleading for reinforcement, support and supplies for his army. General Johnston was elsewhere making plans he thought were more strategic. We already knew the enemy was hungry, tired and desperate. This is not news to the Yankees.

Urgently, each man in my own army wants to endure and defeat these separatists. Yet compassion, war weariness, and brotherhood sometimes color the drama of the whole battlefield. In this circumstance of close proximity, many Union soldiers feel an increased a sense of brotherhood with the Rebs. A good shot across the lines or a defeat on the field can rouse both our anger and pride. A look into the dead face of a scrawny boy, who is too young to die, or a man old enough to be our father, hammers another nail into all the troops' hearts. Still on both sides, to a man, is the shared passionate hate of this war.

I think to myself, *three years, Dear God, it has to end.* The Southerners are slowly being beaten by a lack of weapons, and food. Yet here, as in many recent conflicts, their battle success rate is often superior to our own. These men truly fight with their whole hearts.

On the south and east coasts, Confederates are successfully and regularly running the blockade the Union has put in place on the open water. Thus, despite our armies desire to stop the flow of weapons and goods, they still slowly leak these materials into the hands of the Rebel army. Strong leaders, like General Robert E. Lee and General Nathan B. Forrest, have many effective counterparts in the Confederacy.

The prideful lack of the cooperation of a few Southern officers has been a deficit of the Confederate leadership from the beginning. Independent to a fault, too often a Confederate commander has seen a new opportunity and does not accomplish the assigned and agreed upon rendezvous with other troops. Vicksburg is a vivid example of this, with the decision of Johnston to not bring relief to Pemberton.

I like this location I guard tonight. I have been stationed here before. It is at the crest of a hill with a tree at my back so it is more secure. I am less visible at this spot, while the overlook is more open for viewing perimeters. Here it is possible to escape enduring the strain of squatting all night without the support of trees or fences to lean on. Jed, who is on duty with me, is leaning on the backside of this same large tree. He is also peering a different direction through a spiky growth of volunteer trees.

We are both Illinois men but we had not become familiar until Vicksburg. Twenty-five of us were assigned from our various infantry companies to this sharpshooter post. We guard only this perimeter. Our Illinois soldiers are under the command of General Hurlburt, with one assigned officer, Captain George Stearnes. We are used, most of the time, as scouts and skirmishers.

We have been in this siege for over a month. On the 29th of March the massed Union army had begun the one hundred and eighty-mile march—not arriving at our destination at Vicksburg until May 20th. The army had first been ferried across the "Big Muddy" far to the north, then marched down the Louisiana side to the boats. At great peril, Admiral Porter arrived with all manner of boats to ferry us from the Louisiana side in a winding and difficult journey. We crossed back across the river to Mississippi, south of Vicksburg at Grand Gulf, and then proceeded by river to Bruinsburg.

The massed army marched westward toward Jackson, Mississippi with almost 60,000 men. General Grant ordered us to preserve rations by foraging on the march. Each evening's light was created by fires made of fence posts, on which we cooked our stolen suppers. We lived off the land in fine fettle.

Soon after, with General James B. McPhearson and General McCleran and in command of 20,000 men, we were engaged in the battle of Fort Gibson. The casualties we sustained there were 790. We inflicted 850 casualties on the enemy. The Rebels retreated and we marched on in a huge circle, joining thousands more as we made our way westward to arrive eventually to the back door of Vicksburg.

On the route, before we could reach Jackson, Mississippi, we were once more forced to battle. The Battle of Raymond was again a rout by us.

Upon knowledge of our success, the contraband swarmed upon us for refuge. These thousands of contraband were the free men, women and children of Color. Following emancipation in January, many slaves left their owner's bonds. These homeless, wandering people were everywhere and they followed our army. Freedom achieved—they found they had no homes, occupation or safety, and looked to our army to protect them.[10]

We departed, on May 13. Moving through the drizzle and muck, the huge army marched on toward the city of Jackson, Mississippi arriving on May 14. The battle at this important city, which is east of Vicksburg, was again a success for the Union Army. We had only light casualties but inflicted 845 casualties on our enemy. General Grant commanded the burning and destruction of many public buildings and all resources within the city that might supply the Confederates.

As our great army looped back westward toward the goal of Vicksburg, General Sherman saw to the final destruction of the railways from Jackson. The Vicksburg line could have been a vital supply line for the Rebels.

Upon knowledge of our rear approach to Vicksburg, General Pemberton departed that city, leaving only 10,000 soldiers to protect it. He had marched to meet us with 23,000 men. We were 32,000 strong. When the armies met on May 15, it was in overwhelming heat at Champion Hill, just east of Vicksburg. The four-hour clash was desperate and bloody. This time our soldiers who died were 6,200.

Seeing the wisdom of protecting Vicksburg, and under orders from Confederate President Jefferson Davis, Pemberton then withdrew and retreated back to the small city which he commanded.

Upon our pursuit and in our approach to the beleaguered city, we again met resistance by the Rebels at Big Black River. The soldiers in grey, by necessity, were forced to escape across the river with many of them drowning. Our casualties were light at Black River but one of note was Fred Grant, the son of General Grant. The twelve-year-old was only slightly wounded. The boy was his father's orderly and was with him at all times, even in battle.

The first wave of our army arrived at our goal in Vicksburg on May 18. That night, we lit the sky by burning civilian homes within our lines. My own regiment, the Fifteenth Illinois, arrived and took position on May 20.[7]

The immediate reception of our total army's arrival in the city became the first major battle upon this field. The next day, the twenty-first, the Union army was put on full, military rations. On the twenty-second, we perpetrated a major assault. The intensity and duration of this first full battle continued with no break until a truce on the evening of the twenty-fifth.

Those that fell dead and wounded lay between the lines for those three days of violent fighting. The stench of death was as strong as that of the smoke and weaponry. There was dreadful pleading by the wounded of both armies, who lay bleeding and thirsty, crying for aid as the shots flew over them. Many died helplessly during the ensuing battle. When the truce was called on the twenty-fifth, the burial parties only covered the bodies lightly with earth where they lay. Burial in this continual strife has required much, so often we have only dug trenches for mass graves.

Strangely, during that first truce, we all crossed lines to the enemy to visit or play cards. Perhaps, it was then we first realized the brotherhood of soldiers—our fellow countrymen. We all were common men for the most part, living this hell and knowing tonight might be our last waking sleep.

Now, there is a whispering from the other side of the tree, I hear a voice that sounds like the buzz of a katydid's song. Jed's voice hisses, slicing the otherwise dead silence. "Ever go to Springfield?"

I am apprehensive of any discussion on guard post. Yet, after a patient pause, I reply with a short, purring answer. "Nope, I started once with a wagon of corn but decided to go to Chicago instead." Ten minutes of silence ensue as though Jed's question had only been a reassurance that each of us we were not alone.

"Hear something down where the road curves?" Jed murmured with intensity. We both strained, pulses suddenly racing, and our ears keened by alarmed alertness. As we stared, a small forest animal quickly waddled across the road and into the grass where we were focused. Both of us exhaled, relaxed, and once more, sat back against the tree, resuming silence.

For the next hour I filled my mind with the mental wanderings of a bored soldier. This evening my mind rolled like the pages of a book being flipped. For a while, I mulled various vistas of my home in Carroll County, Illinois. Then I envisioned the seventy-five acre farm I wanted to purchase north of Mt. Carroll, in Wysox Township Township. It is open acres lying in a broad band from the road toward the north. The land undulates in soft rises and falls of earth. In my mind, I can feel the sun, and the mule reigns in my hand as I plow.

The property I dream about is near Father's house. My father owns three hundred and twenty acres straddling two county lines. He raises fine horses, pigs and plants a variety of crops. The farm I want is also only four miles from where an older brother, Henry Clay, and his family live. Henry Clay operates a foundry and mill on a tree-grown creek. He is a clever and resourceful person, whose company I enjoy.

The proximity to him and my Father makes the property I dream of purchasing ever more enhancing. I imagine how we will all help each other at harvest. There would also be strong hands to aid in clearing trees from my own land. Our greater family will be able to gather frequently for holidays and meals.

In my mind, there is already a house sitting on my land. The dwelling is near the road on the southern boundary. The building rests on the brow of a low hill. Sometimes, I imagine the house to be small and cozy. Sometimes, in my mind, it is very grand like the lovely houses we have seen here in the South.

There is always a woman in the house, one I sense or hear calling me to supper. In my dreaming, I see a shadow of her shape at an imaginary window. This mysterious woman is lovely. I am sure of that, and she has long hair. In my dreams, she has never turned, so I cannot see her face. The shadows hold no color, just a form created by the wistful loneliness in my heart.

I almost ache to once more be safe, clean, well fed and in control of my own life. Prior 1861 and my enlistment in this war, I had always been more attracted to adventure than quiet comfort, or settling down with a wife. There had been some bold flirtations with girls in my youth and a few inept, shy kisses when I was younger, in Illinois. Most of the time, I was very busy and quite strict in my life values and goals. Most of my energy went into helping my father with his endeavors. I simply was not very predisposed to seek women in a serious way.

One neighbor girl was free with her affections. Many of my fellows were known to visit her secretly and as often as they could sneak away. I was allured with the passionate possibility of sexual adventure, but resisted out of cowardice. With embarrassment, I remember the one time I had arranged a rendezvous with this frivolous girl, then did not keep the appointment.

Prior to enlisting, I had made a brief trip to Pikes Peak. I left with a small group of adventuresome, young men in 1860. We had returned to Illinois in 1861. The west was demanding, and it was difficult to succeed there. The life was full of risk, more from the greedy miners than the Indians. That adventure had proved to be a grand challenge, but of no lasting benefit or opportunity to our small troop. Only one of the men had remained in the West, the rest of us returned, much the wiser. On our arrival back in Illinois, the threat of war had set our county on fire. Soon, my comrades and I had enlisted.

On that brief trip out west, I had visited a prostitute. Men with whom I associated preformed this endeavor as often as the opportunity allowed. To the rough men in the mining company, prostitution was a normal event, such as dining at another table or walking down a strange street. To me the single experience at a house of ill repute had been disgusting. The woman was none too clean. She was sullen, and slovenly in speech. The act was quick and cold. She was far too repugnant to caress, kiss, or even to be held in my arms.

The imaginary woman I put into my imaginary house is warm, sweet and decent. She was not like the childish, foolish, town girls I had previously accompanied to dances. She is, most certainly, not like the fallen woman in Colorado. My manhood will be perfect with her, and our passion will grow. I dream I will father children, mostly sons.

We would live in the bosom of my larger, nearby family. Occasionally, my brothers and sisters who have moved away from Mt. Carroll, will come from Iowa to visit my wife and I. My brothers, who are also at war, will have returned safely, as I will have. Sometimes, we will travel to see them, accompanied by my own happy family.

Sitting on this damp hillside surrounded by an enemy intent on killing me, a pang of pain strikes me—the horror of my dying and never having a real life, home or wife. *How can I survive the war and not loose hope?* I tell myself, with defensive embarrassment at my own naivete, *If I do not dream, I may see no tomorrow.* With a deep sigh of resignation, I stare into the darkness.

Still in reverie, my mind slips to a new topic. Last week, a soldier from Indiana had received a letter with a long newspaper clipping. The article clearly indicated the disdain of American voters for the newly implemented enlistment of Negroes in the Army. My own beliefs were compatible with the justice of this, but it would remain to be seen what end this would bring. I was just not sure at all. Fresh troops would be a God's send. *How would they perform?*, I asked myself.

The news article also reviewed the various opinions of the Eastern populace. It seemed the masses of the labor force were quite opposed to the enlistment of former slaves. This mood appears to be especially strong among the new emigrant Irish and Germans. These immigrants are holding desperately onto their own jobs. They feel frantic at the thought of a Black tide of labor arriving in the North after the war. The immigrants fear these free men will be willing to work for less pay, and force them out of their jobs. For the Coloreds to have veteran status would further make these immigrant people even more at risk.

Last week, when I delivered a dispatch to the command post, I read a treatise. The pamphlet was authored by a free, Negro abolitionist who spoke around the nation with great elegance. This man, William Frederic Douglas, had reassured the North that few freed slaves would immigrate to the north for a number of reasons. The South, with its familiarity had been their home for generations, also, the people had little information or understanding of life and occupations in the North. The means to make such a move were usually beyond them. In January of 1863, the Emancipation Proclamation had not, in fact, been followed by such mass movements.

Frederic Douglas continued with a powerfully, persuasive statement. His personal plea was to enlist them in this battle where their welfare was at such risk. "Once, let the Black man get upon his person the brass letters 'U.S.,' let him get an eagle on his buttons and a musket on his shoulder and bullets in his pockets and there is no power on earth which can deny that he has earned the right to citizenship in the United States." This in spite of the promises they had received when enlisting during the Revolutionary War. [7]

Domination by Northern industry and trade are as deeply offensive to the South as the exploitation of the Southern Black is to the North. The bullying and threats of the other has wounded pride on both sides. There are also other vital economic elements that are strong underlying factors for the secession. Such economic issues are part of a competitive jealousy between the North and the South.

The South feels offence at the belligerence of the Federal government in making all decisions for them. Often the decisions are to the detriment of the self-control of their own interests. Southern legislators, like then Senator Jefferson Davis, have been debating and fighting in Washington D.C. for years to defend the dignity and independence of the block of Southern states.

That news article I read had raised long, loud arguments among several of the soldiers around the fire. The whole conversation had been upsetting to me. The ire of my fellow soldiers made me restless. *Did I really know what I believe? Am I really ready to kill and die for the issues?* There were things worth the battle. *This nation could not be split, no, at any cost!* I deeply hated slavery. *This horror must end!* Yet the interwoven politics are so complex and tricky, that it is not just a single, clear issue.

The arguing soldiers balanced the added fresh troop strength by the possibility of more Blacks enlisting. Black soldiers are a frequent topic with the troops here and one that divides opinions. Now these very Union soldiers of Color are involved in this war, and philosophies need more solidarity to unify our efforts and morale. There is no solidarity; each of us is of a different mind

On June 7, the Confederate attack at Milliken's Bend had been a strong trial under fire by Black troops. Their bravery in thwarting the 3,000 troops of Richard Taylor's command was a thrilling event for the Union. The battle was hand to hand, and one of the more violent battles of the war. Subsequently, many of our officers and soldiers were reexamining the arming of Colored troops.

From the beginning of this War of Rebellion, Black men have served. They are used, as in the Navy, as drivers, and for general labor, such as digging graves or to attend the officers. In fact among the enemy, most Southern officers were accompanied into war by a Colored servant. These Coloreds have even fought in battles beside their masters. This fact was now of some comment, since only Southern slaves have been freed by the Emancipation Act, not those in Northern states.

When the topic of Colored enlistment comes up in conversation, a number of men still resent the idea of Black men wearing "their" uniform. Many question the aptitude and intelligence of these people. If the question of Black soldiers is controversial, that of Colored officers is an even hotter topic of debate. We hear of David Cooke, who was with the Ninety-second Illinois, and is an excellent soldier, and he is a Colored officer.

*Slavery?* I ask myself. Now that is a big topic. It is one that supposedly has been decided. Yet, emancipation has also created different problems. Just look at the contraband tribes wandering all over the country.

How soldiers feel about slavery varies from soldier to soldier. Most of the men in my regiment had seen few Negroes before the war. We have passed many slaves as we marched through the South. Yet, most Northern soldiers have little personal contact with Negroes. Now, as the free contrabands follow us everywhere. we stare at them, uncomfortably, and feel helpless with sympathy.

News articles, churches, abolitionists or political speeches have often formed soldiers' personal opinions about going to war, freeing the slaves or even interpreting which events that proceeded had eventually caused the war. There was no true overall consensus among the Yankees. *Was the cause of the war secession or abolition?*

In Wysox Township, my home, abolition was not a question it was a deep commitment. Our entire neighborhood was part of the Underground Railroad. We might not have Colored neighbors, but we had taken a stand. Many an escaping slave was hidden in a home or barn. Then they were moved to the next secret "station." Usually, they were hidden under vegetables in a wagon, as they moved on toward Canada.

Smiling to myself in the dark quiet, I swatted at a mosquito that was intent on landing on my cheek. It was with pride I knew that concerning slavery I was firmly standing for something that was very important. Why, when the call came for enlistment in Wysox Township, so many neighborhood men came forward that some had to wait for the next call to enlist. I was, if not the first, one of the first from Carroll County to enlist.[8]

Since I had been motionless for several hours now, my body aches. Standing, I prop my rifle against the tree, stretch, take my canteen out to drink some unpleasant water from it. I lean around the tree to peek at Jed. He looks up, in the moonlight his white teeth marking a silent smile. I settle again.

The press of the North is often a source of dissention for the soldiers. It criticizes our commanders, and helps set them against each other. Lincoln is criticized, vilified and ridiculed at every turn. So many officers, like McClernand, who have political interests and want the war to enhance their appeal for election after the war. The political goals sometimes set officers at odds, like roosters preening.

The reporters were always with us and attended all the battles. They risk all to report from the field. The pain is that, despite the many that are clear thinking, others put their own careers and political slants into their reporting. The result is dissention, confusion, disloyalty and sometimes misinformation.

Now, in the dark, as I mull the previous campfire conversations about the war. Louis whispers an observation, in this dark night from his tree fork position near Jed and I. "Will, I been thinkin' if nigras are goin' fightn' that is a lot of soldiers for us. You think they be good soldiers?"

From the other side of the tree a long silence ensued, then Jed answered, "Louis you be tetched to even give it a thought. The Rebs can't win, we're too strong, and our own Illinois General Grant will teach them a thing or two. We don' need no niggers."

"I think darky soldiers would scare the South for fear of reprisal. Damn sure they do not want them enlisted in the army," Louis replied, adding his special viewpoint.

"In Vicksburg, the shelling has broken most of the windows, and blown buildings apart. Women and children have fled the town, and are camped in the countryside around about here. They say citizens in town are living in caves they built; when the bombs come, all the neighbors rush inside and hide in fear. The blockade-runners can't get them no mail, no food. The Reb soldiers goin' to lose. They are only hangin' on, and the civilians in Vicksburg are as good as done already," Jed whispers once more.

There was the sound of crunching leaves and grass, and we fall dead silent; the whispers cut short, our breath held in fear. Our officer, Captain George Stearnes, had probably caught us talking on watch—a very serious infraction. He stands forty feet away, and we saw his shadowy gray form under a tree. The moon casts a faint glint on his buttons. He clears his throat but says nothing, a reminder to tend to their duties in silence. With relief, we hope the talk had not been heard and that we might not be punished. A watch was vital. To sleep during watch is treason; a soldier can be executed. Our infraction is no mean thing.

The next hours are quiet. Then Jed lit his pipe, against all orders. Holding his cupped hand around it to hide the flame and coals, he begins to puff. The rich, smoky fragrance blends with the damp, earth smells. I lean around the trunk and see the warm glow of his face as he draws on the pipe. It betrays us. His defiance of officers, and arrogance is a real character flaw. I dread watches with him. I made a soft "humpf" to show my disapproval, and go back on alert.

I am feeling cozy and far too relaxed so I wiggle my toes in my boots. Then I clench and unclench my fists repeatedly to stay awake and alert. Laying the gun down, I stand and stiffly move my body in a rocking manner; shifting weight repeatedly to bring circulation back into my stiff legs. After retrieving my Enfield, I slowly walk the perimeter, stop, listen and stare into the moonlit night; looking toward the other designated sentry posts. Most can be made out slightly visible but in one case I feel a sentry to the north is far too visible.

Returning to my assigned position, I squat, remove my kepi cap and scratch through my thick, curling hair. The grit of dirt and sand fills my nails but the sharpness leaves a pleasant tingle on my scalp. I have now worn this same uniform for almost two months. Early in the long march to arrive here, I had an opportunity to bath and wash my clothing in a river in Louisiana.

I shake out the gum blanket, refold it, then sit again, moving until my back is once more comfortable against the tree. I fasten the top button of my sack coat; for it is cooler now than it had been earlier on watch. Checking the moon, I judge that soon the watch will be over and we can go back to camp, crawl into our tents and sleep until called to "stand to."

I feel a certain tension. Most surprise attacks occur a half-hour before dusk or dawn, and are usually on the perimeters. We were a definite boundary on the southern end of the battlefield. This of all times is the most important time to be alert.

## Chapter 4
# Soldiers' Life

Finally, the watch accomplished, I hear the soft approach of footsteps accompanied by three short whistles, so I go to alert. Three of my comrades are crawling out of the ravine to relieve Jed, Louis and I. I felt relieved it is not Captain Stearnes again. If we had been caught talking last night, we are going to be reprimanded. I still have apprehension about this infraction.

With a silent nod, I pick up my gum blanket, and began to pick my way down the gully, fighting through the tangled foliage of the knoll. Moving toward the tent site, I go to find water for I have drained my canteen in the night.

Finding the water bucket, I remove the lid and using a metal ladle that hangs inside, I take three long drinks of the tepid, metallic flavored liquid. I replaced the ladle and secure the lid. My weapon held at a causal angle, I wander to my small, two-man tent and place the weapon inside with my cap. Then I spread the gum blanket to lie on.

Dropping to my knees, I crawl inside, roll over and come to a seated position to remove my boots, and pull my rank smelling feet out of them. My feet are long and narrow, just barely covered by tattered, knit stockings. These are damp with sweat, leather oils and dirt. Every joint in my body aches as this discomfort grows steadily. I know arthritis is swelling every joint. Lying back to pillow my head with one arm, I roll to my side and pull a blanket over my soiled body. Just as the first delicate hue begins in the east I close my eyes.

I mull events a while as I try to doze off. This evening, before my watch, my fellows had passed a tattered scrap of paper back and forth. It was reportedly a copy of a wire. The report announced that a large number of Southern troops were converging in south central Pennsylvania right now. The huge Southern army, under Lee, was moving steadily toward Washington with large numbers and must be stopped. A major battle seemed to be impending there.

A chill ran down my back as I heard the announcement read. The two strongest armies meeting somewhere out in the east would be a major clash. Could this event be the "Great Battle" to end the war? To hide my emotions, I removed my cap and ran my fingers through my hair, all the while staring at my feet. It made me short of breath to hope that there might actually be an end of this war.

My mind raced, as I stared at my boots. The siege here at Vicksburg on the western front had to conclude soon. This brutal fight could not go on at this pace much longer. A victory here would be a most important one for the Union Army. Beating the Rebs at Vicksburg could change the balance of strength. Our army would then control the Mississippi clear to the ocean.

I sighed and gave thought to this new day. With better light for battle each morning, we would soon be serenaded by the rolling explosions as the daily war resumed on the eastern battlefield—some three miles away.

Like everyday in the last three and half years, military breakfast would be served. It would be acrid, thick coffee and greasy, salt bacon with hard tack to soak in the coffee. Sometimes there were pancakes at lunch, with hominy or an occasional potato. Meals were commonly beans, or perhaps an infrequent stew. For variety there was pillaged bounty when the opportunity had occurred. This had been our diet since '61.

When families came to visit, or came for their wounded or dead, they would bring food such as several dozen hens, other fresh produce, or baked goods. This bounty was a real treat for us. Most of us hated the menu and complained continually. We even made insulting poems and songs about the fare. At first, here at Vicksburg, they had fed us chicken and sweet potatoes until, in denial of our repugnance of the standard menu, the men had rebelled demanding to be returned to the normal nasty fare.[9]

My military career as a private for these years has been a life of "stand at attention, walk a hundred miles, clean weapons, launder and bath in streams, sleep on the ground." The army has built corduroy roads over swamps and muddy roads by dropping trees to create a solid ground. Or we have waded ankle, or a few times knee, deep in the muck. We have forded rivers on the engineer's bridges, or held our shot and weapons above our heads and waded through slick, icy brooks and rivers. Sometimes, with so many of us moving together, we create an even more impossible roadway. Impossible that is, when our day's march would find an impassible obstacle and we had to turn around and retrace our steps over a path our own feet had made even more treacherous.

Then there would be sudden attacks, short, violent battles, or the Shiloh's, Champion Hills and other battles, that drenched us in death and terror. This is how I have lived from the snows of Missouri in makeshift lean-tos, to the heat and bugs of the South. Life with rats, lice, ticks, leeches and bed bugs has been almost like having pets. It has been repeated day after day, until the cycle becomes hypnotic.

Part of me itches to break this tense boredom of war; mentally it is mostly like slow strangulation, overshadowed by a wary tension that never leaves. This hyperawareness saves all our lives from hidden marksmen, attacks or sudden death. Sometimes, survival is only by bare luck. The soldiers rush forward with staccato anticipation of a major battle. We have moved toward an action until we came to a dead stop as our movement has turned out to be in vain. We have often found only a small action or there was not a conflict at all, for the enemy had moved on or our information was misleading.

My own Company K has implemented numerous skirmishes. We also fought at Shiloh, where nine men from Carroll County fell or were wounded. Soon after that battle, we marched to the Hatachie River where we met 25,000 Confederates. There we lost over four hundred men. The smell of the dead was carried on our clothing and numbed our brains. A part of me is in a war fog, which goes on, with no end in sight.[10]

I joined the Union army in Illinois on March 21 of 1861. We mustered on May 24, in Freeport, Illinois, a town north of our home. There we became the Fifteenth Volunteer Infantry Regiment. After gathering at Freeport, we had several days of heated politicking and the election of officers and non-coms. Next, we were moved south by steamer and marched to St. Charles, Hannibal and Jefferson Barracks in Missouri. After that, our regiment covered the retreat of the battle of Wilson's Creek, Missouri. That year, our regiment suffered a hard winter quarters in Otterville, Missouri. Eventually, the Fifteenth Regiment moved into Tennessee, marching, fighting and marching again.[10]

I learned early that a persistent companion of war is illness. There were violent deaths from battle but the silent and massive loss of men to disease was continual. Most limp on, carrying their pain in brave silence. Diarrhea and dysentery were frequent and common illnesses. When possible, the more seriously ill were moved to locations that have U.S. Sanitary Commission hospitals. These included soldiers with tuberculosis, small pox or venereal disease. Poor water, no true latrines and badly prepared food keeps us on the edge of illness at all times.

Among the camp followers are a number of evangelists, for we are sober now—void of bravado. Many a soldier has had a campfire conversion. We sing continually, sometimes quite familiar tunes and sometimes those with ribald humor. Our band has been at our side always, and various musicians also lead us in marching. Each man clings to humor, song, faith or dreams to maintain their sanity.

It was around a year later during the first week of April '62, when, fast on the heels of the battle of Corinth, we marched with Hurlburt's division to Shiloh, Tennessee. Our band was playing as we marched, we were all in high spirits. The location was a sleepy church in the countryside. The weather was beautiful and the verdant blooming flowers were unusually fragrant. We were singing as we marched and camped near the church.

There, early in the morning, our army met Generals Beauregard and Johnston who led 50,000 brave Confederate troops. The rebels arrived so suddenly that a number of our boys were shot in their sleep. The reports said our force was around 30,000. [3]

Benjamin Prentiss' division held a low-lying position that was eventually called the Hornet's Nest by the Southerners. This is where I fought with the Fifteenth those two days. We had suffered a light rain all day. In the beginning of the battle, there were several retreats that included as many as 10,000 Union soldiers. General McClernand and General Sherman suffered severe loses. General Grant had not appeared on the field on the first morning, having been somewhat unprepared for the attack.

The Fifty-third Ohio that supported our right flank, retreated never having fired a shot, leaving us in the Hornet's Nest exposed on that flank. In desperation, we closed ranks while facing the enemy on both the front and flank, while pinned in the low spot. With some disorientation, we rallied and fought on. Several times, briefly, other regiments joined us in small forces. Terrified horses and mules would run across the battle area, often dragging armament. On leaving the field that night in a driving rain storm, the officers of the Sixth found the remains of my own regiment at the landing, 550 bedraggled survivors that is.

That night the Union Officer General Buell arrived with 20,000 fresh reinforcements, saving the Union from total defeat. The second day, the Illinois troops were selected to make a charge. The valiant Fourteenth Illinois arrived and stood stalwart at our left side. On April 7, General Grant appeared on the field at the Hornet's Nest and personally led that charge. All the soldiers cheered as he rode at our front from the Hornets' Nest toward the enemy. [3]

It was the defining battle and by mid-afternoon Southern battalions began to withdraw toward Corinth. We were too weary to pursue. In those two days of battle 100,000 men engaged. There were 23,741 casualties—killed, wounded or missing—at Shiloh Church, in addition to those captured. At the Hornet's Nest, the Fifteenth lost two-hundred and fifty and we inflicted a total of 2,000 casualties on the Confederates. [10]

More horses were killed on the field than in any other battle in history. The carcasses littered the whole scene.

With no memory of going to sleep, this morning I finally relax and slide away from consciousness and am suddenly lost in a black nothingness. Nothing, that was, until "it" returns. "It" is a reoccurring nightmare that I live again and again.

In this nightmare that haunts me, the Fifteenth Illinois still stands at the hollow of the Hornet's Nest, to the right is the fleeing Ohio. All over the field there is the sudden silence from one sector or another, signifying the surrender or flight of more Federals. Our commanders close the ranks and, with unbeatable odds, we fight on, stumbling across dying or wounded comrades while we load our guns.

We move forward to better positions. The Fourteenth Illinois joins us, giving us renewed courage. Then General Grant leads us with our bayonets fixed in a charge. With a final burst of energy, relief and the pride of fighting well, our regiment sees the fleeing Rebels. The fellow Fourteenth Illinois troops were heroic, our saviors and our brothers. [3]

The Fourteenth and Fifteenth Illinois had fought side by side against amazing obstacles at the Hornet's Nest and were bonded eternally that April at Shiloh. We would forever form a brotherhood that General Grant acknowledged until the end of the war, even to the day they marched side by side in Washington in victory. Trust, respect, gratitude and courage became the golden-forged bond between two regiments that has seldom been matched in military history. [10]

The battle had roared on for hours, then like a sputtering candle, the battle sounds became sparse and spasmodic. When I paused for a furtive look, there were no standing Rebs anywhere near. Empty, with wrenching pain surging throughout my body, I looked blankly across the field. The roaring in my ears echoed after two days of screams, rifle shot and cannon roar. I heard a noise like a waterfall. In that pounding silence I was, in fact, deaf to all but the boldest noise.

With an overpowering feeling of great distance, I stared vacantly from my viewpoint on the hill. My watery eyes saw the surroundings on that ravaged location. Shreds of bloody bodies, dismembered limbs and decapitated heads lay all over the mounds of blue and grey forms. Lost weapons and equipment were scattered about. I was suddenly swept by disorientation since Rebel hands no longer held the weapons, the armory appeared to be like dead snakes, no longer with the power to threaten me.

A few men wander lost across the scene. Dozens of pairs of men were moving in halting paths, carrying makeshift slings, as they passed among the human debris. These men stopped occasionally. The bearers turned a body or touched one with the toe of a boot. When they found a wounded victim he was rolled onto the sling then they slowly wound through the other bodies, toward the base camp where there was the first field hospital I had ever seen operating on a battlefield.

A few men were standing, just staring or staggering lost across the scene. Others sat sobbing in their own unnamed grief, with heads buried on their knees. Through my deafness a shrill scream came from someone. Its pitch was wavering in volume and agony. It was a madman's lament at the end of the world. The intensity of the prolonged vocal scale of horror would not cease or quiet and went on longer and longer. The odor was overwhelming of the excrement released in the throes of death which emptied both bowels and bladders. Soldiers who had fought with continual diarrhea added to the stench. These smells overwhelmed even the acidity of the spent gunpowder. Thousands of dead lay about with the dying horses writhing in squirming, squealing mounds. Over the entire panorama that looked like the gates of hell was a lovely blue sky, almost unreal in it serenity.

Seeing nothing near me, I fell backward from my crouch, loosed the numb clutch of my bruised hands on my gun with its bloody bayonet. I allowed the weapon to fall to the earth, soundless because it had struck the back of a dead, blue comrade. My body fell flat, backward on the ground, and blank emptiness overwhelmed me into exhausted unconsciousness.

Finally, the discomfort of the heat combined with a light drizzle which had began to fall on me, roused me. The flies and gnats on my face, and the odor drying blood from the dead bodies began to break into my conscious senses. Rolling onto one side, I saw the scavengers of boots and weapons. Survivors and corpsmen were still moving among the human debris of the Hornet's Nest. In the mugginess and drizzle of April, my right hand, on which I had lain, scratched the crumbling soil, as small pebbles and dry grasses filled my fist. I looked down on the bruised fingers of my trigger hand which were swollen. Through shreds of fabric the purple back of that hand was visible below my blue sleeve. I had a large, scabbing cut which ran from thumb to wrist and above it a burnt, gapping hole in my sleeve that a bullet had torn as it passed through the fabric.

With a slow, pained effort, I rolled over and got to my knees. Without warning, my stomach retched although nothing erupted but some sour, yellow bile which I spat out. A small trail of bile dribbled down my chin.

With the greatest effort, I came to my feet, albeit in a near crouched position because of a phenomenal pain in my back from strain, bruising and latent tension that had bound it for two days.

Standing in this wobbly, grotesque posture, I felt the buttons on my trousers and vainly tried to urinate. I considered this and realized I could not remember drinking or urinating for almost a day. Replacing my buttons, I slowly turned in a circle. About a quarter mile away some tents had been erected, a U.S. flag was flying above the area. There were men walking toward the flag marked area. Some were supporting bleeding comrades. I knew my voice would not respond from my parched throat should I try to call out for help or water. The distance to the camp, in my condition, might as well have been miles, and I doubted if I could walk to the camp.

Instead, I looked on the littered ground for a water canteen. My own was gone. I vaguely pondered its absence like a sleepwalker. As far as I could see were the huge, swarming, fly covered forms of dead horses, hundreds of them. Some had white bones protruding from legs, or gapping dark holes with entrails pouring out. The damaged were still screaming like sirens, blood and foam pouring from nostrils and mouths as they hopelessly raised their heads. Far across the hill, I saw several men setting a carcass on fire. A few men were slowly wandering the carnage with pistols. These soldiers administered a few charitable shots ending each animal's agony. Slowly, I stumbled a few steps forward toward a large area of human debris and spied a canteen near a mound of bodies.

The view recalled the scene of the first battlefield I had seen in Missouri. Our new unit had been ordered to clean up after the battle at Wilson. This was where I had first realized that this glorious war I had imagined in such heroic measure was really unbelievably brutal and monstrous. That had been the first time the enemy had a face, one far too familiar. The dead faces looked just like friends or neighbors. I saw all the young men who would never rise other than in memories; their loves, dreams and potential ended.

Now repulsed, but firm in intent because of my need, I stopped and without focusing on the nearby orgy of death, I reached for a lost canteen. I lifted the circular flask, loosed the lid, turned it toward my face, and saw a neat, small hole on the backside of the empty container. The hole was surrounded with blood and soft white flecks of flesh. Involuntarily, I looked down at the ground to see the grey clad arm that protruded from under the pile of bodies. It had a large blackened hole in the hand that was now darkened with clotted blood and flies.

Collapsing backwards to sit on the ground I landed on another body. I was broken, empty, nauseous and in pain. I lay my arms on my knees, and pillowing my forehead, began to sob, crying with a choking rasp of monotone moaning which rolled from my swollen throat.

This is my reoccurring nightmare; I had never spoken of it, for I am sure it is like a plague of memory that many of my fellows share. In guilt I feel cowardly, to discuss the haunting images would simply intensify everyone's pain. Ever since Shiloh, this memory or part of it has become me. Frequently, I relive the nightmare and each time I awake in a cold sweat with a palpitating heart. The memories of the odors once more overwhelm me with a billowing nauseousness.

We had sung as we marched toward Shiloh. How confidant and optimistic we were, unaware of the destruction that was awaiting the Fifteenth. Since so many died at Shiloh and both armies retreated in large numbers, the debate lingers about who won the battle. I do know we fought well and mightily for two days in that Hell. No blossoms or leaves remained on the trees near us, and no innocence existed on that field.

When our commander, General William Wallace, whom I greatly admired, had fallen that first day, his wife had just arrived by boat while the battle was in progress. It was not uncommon for officers' wives, and sometimes their families, to visit the warriors on the battlefields. After learning of her husband's death, she remained on the site throughout the battle nursing the wounded.

Some time after the battle ended, I slept where I had dropped. I slept as though I were dead throughout part of the day. Impervious to the drizzle of rain, my mummy-like body finally fought back to consciousness. I wiped my face on my filthy uniform sleeve, found my gun, my cap and slowly staggered through the muggy afternoon warmth toward the hospital area.

Looking only toward the ground to avoid tripping over the dead, I tried to not focus on the sights about me. The only way to survive in the midst of war is a black callousness of indifference and denial. The empty numbness is even now a part of my being. This denial is a trait that only adrenaline can overcome when I need clarity or to find the energy to survive.

When I reached the active camp area the dead and wounded soldiers of both armies lay all about; many of these had fresh bloody stumps of limbs. A long series of tents and outdoor tables stood where blood-drenched doctors were feverishly working. I stared all about me.

For three days we soldiers who survived worked on the field, moving the wounded and burying the fatalities. We rested our bodies as we could and prepared for the next troop movement.

The next morning after my restless sleep at the outpost in Vicksburg, I completed eating, shaving and drinking more coffee. Then the mail came in a dusty leather satchel, carried by a slender, freckled, red-haired Missourian. I knew as I reached for a letter that angels were red-haired Missourians. That letter was a touch of home, of a real life. These epistles were my only thread of reality in the dirty march, fight, eat, sleep, and wait existence that owned me body and soul.

In sympathy I looked at the men who never got mail, some without family, some illiterate. That is why so many of us read the less personal parts of our mail aloud in small circles after we had absorbed these saving missiles from home or loved ones.

A fat, parchment letter and a packet that had been passed to me was gripped in my hand. Turning them over and feeling their texture gave me a warm, deep pleasure. The long day of boredom and sudden, brief battles was to be broken by Father's letter. In the worn package I knew there was a book—a brief escape. The book, as soon as read by me, would be passed around and shared in the camp. Reading was a great escape.

The thunder of battle on top the hill was once more echoing down the valley's gullies. Shots and cannon were unstoppingly expended in various in conflicts. Many of the shots were by Federals shooting their compulsory hundred shots a day. General Grant had encouraged each soldier to fire their weapons thus. This was as much a show of power to the Confederates as a direct attack. The Southerner's woeful lack of armory kept them restricted to conserve firepower to active, direct action.

The daily battle sounds were mirrored in contrast to the dead silence of cease fires. These cease fires were called to retrieve the soldiers who fell on the battlefield. I was familiar by then with the bloated, maggot infested, odiferous bodies. Also retrieved were the living dead, a few short breaths away from joining the dead.

I had seen these soldiers on many other battlefields. The poignancy of knowing after the battles there would be faces I recognized among those fallen always created a twinge of fear and loss. After the dreadful cease fire silences to retrieve the wounded and dead, lumbering carts would come down the road toward the river. Blood would sometimes drip from between the boards. There were the moans and cries for aid filling the air. Walking beside the cart, holding onto the sides, were the weak, injured or blinded. As the hospital wagon passed, these walking men would be the blank-eyed staring past or through everything, in an empty self-control which might actually save their sanity.

Cupping a hot, tin cup of coffee in my hand, I stiffly paced over to the south ridge lookout with my letter stuffed into my pocket and the wrapped book tucked into my armpit. Resting the tin cup in the fork of a tree, I opened the buttons of my shirt to cool my body and loosened my belt a notch for comfort. It was now almost three in the afternoon and the humidity was rapidly increasing. Tiny bugs swarm about, when they are particularly irritating about my face, I wave a hand to spread them. In no time, dribbles of sweat begin to track down my chest and arm pits. I pick up my gun, check the shot, then gather my cleaning cloth, rod and the Enfield. In conditioned self-preservation, I sit on the ground and clean the weapon methodically. Next I sight it, take several practice shots and lay it down on my jacket, which I have finally removed.

Returning to the tree to retrieve the coffee from its risky perch, I sigh deeply. The drink was now almost cold, but it rolls down my throat, moistening it.

Now is the time—the treasured time—to read the letter. This one, like the others, will be read ten or more times. Each reading pleases me like a warm breath from a far away world. From the handwriting, I know immediately it is from my father, Henry, in Wysox Township.

I picture him sitting at the small, mahogany desk in the library. He is in a shaft of dust-flecked light facing the morning from the south window. I have viewed my father throughout my life in this place where he writes letters. A cold cigar would be resting in a dish at his side. The pen, ink and sand in the small, silver pen tray are sitting to his right at the top of the desk. This older man, with white, full hair, would be haloed by light entering through the window; so many times I have watched him from behind his back.

The window overlooks a small, rural cemetery across the road that I know will hold the new stones of Shiloh and other battles. This is the resting place of the fallen, they are friends gone forever. These graves are those of neighborhood families who have been fortunate enough to retrieve bodies months after their loved ones death. Some were returned by the black hatted, funeral insurance men who come to battlegrounds prior to each battle to sell the soldiers burial insurance. Some of the new stones are also those of broken warriors who had come home to die.

My pipe is loaded with tobacco from a small leather pouch and tamped. I light the bowl, and draw on it until the charred, ashes glow red and the fragrant smoke wreaths and circles upward. Checking the woods around me carefully, I note my fellow sharpshooters at their posts and feel safe enough to drift away for a few moments of quiet. Peacefully, I savor my privacy, which is a rarity in war. The rhythm of gun and cannon and the shrill whistle of rockets is like a distant thunderstorm. The ceaseless noise becomes only an uneven background rhythm for my reading.

First, I carefully unwrap the book to roll it in my hands. I open the back to check the number of pages, which tells me how long I can draw pleasure from it. It is "Les Miserables," a most popular novel and rather long. It tells the story of the French Revolution. This is a brave book about soldiers like myself.

With a pocketknife I slit one end of the folded paper, holding the letter and taking caution not to tear the dear epistle.

"June 16, 1863, Mt. Carroll, Illinois
My most esteemed son,

With joy we have received several letters from you in the last weeks. Although we are recipients of this good favor because of your boredom it still gladdens our hearts. With trepidation at any danger you have or will face we are first of all reassured of your safety at this time. We, secondly, are appraised of the nature of your spirits at each momentous turn in this brave conflict.

If the press is to be believed General Grant has taken a firm stand in Vicksburg which we can only believe will bring our honored troops victory. We try to keep ourselves apprised of the action you are involved in. The General is our bravest son of Illinois and I maintain complete confidence in him.

Perhaps we will soon see an end of this wrenching chasm in our nation. The President who until a year ago was speaking of Black colonization now is enlisting Black Union soldiers instead. Twice in the past the legislators proposed enlisting the Negro and Mr. Lincoln vetoed these efforts. I wrote and spoke often to encourage the forcible freeing of the slaves still in bondage and feel that to include them in the battle is right and honorable.

The scourge of slavery, as true Whigs knew, must end. The quandary of the fate of the Negro after that is still of serious consequence. What will their free state do in our communities, where will they go? How can such simple people survive? Do they crave revengeful violence? These questions are not without merit."

Pausing, I dredge the last bitter brew in my cup, fling away the grounds and spit some from my mouth. I pick the remaining grounds from my tongue using two fingernails. After knocking ash out, I lay the cold pipe on the ground.

"Concerning Carroll County now, of late, your brother Henry Clay has been pacing like a steed to become involved in the conflict. Still, his wife, Angeline, the children, the flour mill, and quarry demand his labor and attention. Yet drawn by his heart and patriotism, he would enter the fray. It would honor our family to have all of our valorous sons defending the Union. Yet the fear and dread of losing our sons' precious lives is an unremitting agony. Such fear keeps us hesitant of encouraging Clay to also enlist.

My dear friend, Isaac Spenser, he lives to the southeast. His father, Naamn, migrated to Illinois in 1839 when we arrived here as newlyweds from Indiana. He and his son occasionally work at Clay's foundry. The man has had the dreariest news. His granddaughter in Natchez was married for a brief time to a carpenter there named Scothorne and she had a tiny baby boy.

The young couple's son, Henry, Isaac's grandson, died of illness on December 15.

Her husband was fighting with the Rebels near the Red River during Banks campaign there in March. The young gentleman fell with a heart attack on the Louisiana side of the river, near Bayou Sara, south of Wilkinson, Mississippi. You will note that this is where my grandfather pioneered The epistles from the young widow that Isaac receives are morose with her loss. It has left her not only in sorrow, but also in great need.*

*The "Confederate Muster Rolls" notes Conners' Light Artillery had 160 troops. Two died of wounds and fourteen died of disease, including William Scothorne.

The supplies in Natchez are short and prices inflated almost beyond reach, shoes cost $300. The city is occupied by our troops and thousands of wandering freed Blacks. The whole city is rampant with disease. The deaths in Natchez are epidemic and with the heat of summer may only increase. The widow must rely on the Scothorne family, who are themselves wanting. Life requires the sale of many of her remaining goods to survive.

Isaac Spencer has sent what funds he can spare to see her by and has begged her to come north. Yet he fears her disdain for the North especially now they have killed her husband will prevent her from escaping to safety. The conditions this widow faces are dire. Our troops occupy the city yet we cannot yet but sorrow for the suffering of the people. This is especially true since this city did not choose to secede and ended the conflict there by quickly surrendering.

Your mother and I fare well. We have managed the crops we planted and since weather has been moderate we may expect an adequate crop in the upcoming months. The foals have been many and look promising. I made several good sales and have won every race I have entered. It appears to be a good year.

With humor I remind you of the story I tell. Do you remember, when I drove our whole crop to Chicago, being optimistic of a good price, I returned with only a few silver tablespoons to show for profit. Yet, in the long run, Illinois has been good to Mary and I and we prosper.[11]

The community cheers and rallies at each triumph of our boys in blue. Goods, clothing, or bandages flow ever plentiful from the hands of the women in Carroll County. Your mother and sisters have made you new stockings, they may arrive at any time since they were sent two weeks ago.

I have not been into town for several weeks because of the need for me to tend to the farms, and the horses. I am repairing the stables, this has occupied me continually during the summer.

As I look from the window toward the cemetery, I remember the sad day several of our brave boys who fell beside you at Shiloh were placed there. I recall the dreaded and difficult trips of parents from here to retrieve their loved ones' remains. It is a journey, God willing, I may never need to make.

Recently two of our soldiers, William Brown and Robert Burnett, mustered out and returned home. I have had no news of their condition but shall seek more information. Perhaps your fellow soldiers know the name of the officer from here who has lost a leg at Shiloh and is now in a prison in the south. The rumors about him vary.

Your most respectful, proud father and mother,
Mrsg. Henry C.W. Hunter and Mary"

As I fold and smooth the paper I close my eyes for a moment. My throat tightens with homesickness and I swallow to move the knot that threatens to choke me. Checking about me, ever wary, I prepare to move back down the gully to camp.

Chapter 5

# Victory

Now, on the near dawn of July 3, I have been in this weary and bloody battle since the twenty-second of May when I had been placed on this investment line. The black powder haze lies like a fog for miles around. The fight has been continual for around forty days. In a half doze, I roll over in my tent and kicking try to cover my feet with my blanket. I inhale the black powder odor and it tickles my nose; I gag up some phlegm.

In a half sleeping haze, my mind wanders. The war has seen some improvement. General McClernand was relieved of duty on the eighteenth of June. His inadequacies had been most costly at Vicksburg. His insubordination of Grant was a great deficit. The men had hated him. In general, most of the enlisted dislike the officers and they grumble continuously. Those leaders that are trusted and respected almost assume a Godlike aura to the soldiers.

There is endless discussion about the events and the personnel in this battle. My Union comrades are, of course, guessing in many cases or considering reports of biased information. The reports in our press are usually made much in our favor, I am sure the Confederates do the same. Once we had found a battered Vicksburg newspaper that had been printed on wallpaper; the news hopefully announced the eminent rescue of the Confederates by Johnston. All the troops on both sides hang on every message and rumor. They are hungry for hope and encouragement. Soldiers are also wary of any increased threat that a change may suggest to our armies or our persons.

Mulling the latest gossip, my own weary spirit finds little encouragement. In the darkness, coldness grasps my inner being. There is the general opinion of soldiers that in the last two weeks the Rebs are ever weaker; reinforcements and goods are still not forthcoming to relieve them. When the opposing sides call or trade across the lines the Rebels thinly disguise their need, perhaps for the sake of their pride and strategy. It is believed they have for some time only been receiving half rations and are quite hungry and ill. Some of our men hate the Confederates so deeply that the soldiers relish their enemies' suffering. Yet, for the majority of us there is some compassion for these courageous and proud warriors. They are ourselves in mirror reverse.

The songs that echo down the hills at night from the nearby rebel's camps seem ever more mournful. These ballads are slowed, sorrowful versions of songs like "Bonnie Blue Flag." Their voices send chills down my back as they roll in slowed cadence across the battlefield in the dark. The boys in butternut and grey sleep in the open and their incessant coughing sounds down the hills at night.

Most of our own men grow ever less full of bravado, more respectful of their enemies' suffering, and most of all impressed with their courage and determination. This attitude we witness in the demeanor of their men and officers is poignant, yet the irony is that we still feel relief because of the Confederate weaknesses. This gives us a strong advantage and a hope for victory.

At the top of the Confederate command is the sensitive, yet indecisive Jefferson Davis who was reared in Wilkinson County, Mississippi. He is a refined man who was called upon to be the President of the Confederacy despite a truly lackluster military school record. The "Little Creole," Confederate General Beauregard, publicly called him "that living specimen of gall and hatred." The Confederacy's own Vice President undermines him, which adds to the divisiveness of their war effort. Some of the Southern officers see him as a man who is capable of anger and retaliation, and a prideful man who is either demented or a traitor.

Most of the Rebel soldiers take pride in him and honor their president as a symbol of their sovereignty. He is a man who well represented them in Washington prior to the war. The majority of the Secessionists take great pride in their cause and the overwhelming effort the South is putting forth. When the Fifteenth Illinois attacked his Mississippi plantation they cut rugs up for blankets. Papers were found from his service in Washington, D.C., confirming his duplicity against the United States while serving there in the name of Mississippi. I was to later meet a Colored soldier who was from the Davis plantation. This man said that though firm, Jefferson Davis had been a fair master to his "people."[3]

The immense amount of land the South defends keeps their armies spread thin. The desertions they suffer weakens them. Missing on the roster may mean a soldier has died undiscovered. Many others simply walk away, full of war weariness. Southern troops are in continual search for deserters.

Negotiations for support from nations overseas have failed the South again and again. Little of the required goods and military supplies were ever manufactured in the South, so the escalation of need for these undermines their troops' efforts. The destruction of the railways from Jackson only deepened the deficiency. There is a lack of confidence in the currency the government is printing which increases their unbelievable inflation rate. The morale of our adversary is sorely tested.

My daily reality and that of the soldiers around me are the only real substance of my own day-to-day survival. Vermin and lice are constant companions. Blankets, quilts and clothing are an obsession. Much of our usable clothing is sent from home. We barter, play cards, scavenge or purchase clothing from each other continually. Shoes are always in need for we have marched thousands of miles in these three years. We simply marched ourselves right out of dozens of pairs of boots or shoes. Most of the time, footwear is the wrong size and knife-sliced for relief or stuffed with straw because they are too big. Removing a dead man's boots is not considered theft or desecration, shoes are for the living.

The most plentiful food that we have is hard tack. We soldiers say it is hard as a "ten penny nail," which would be soft in comparison. The hard tack is a three inches by three and a half inches, dry, heavy square of flour and water. We usually receive nine or ten of these a day. Often they are wormy or moldy, but we soak them in bitter coffee, sop up grease or broth when we can or crumbled them into our soup. Sometimes, we have skillygalee made by soaking the hardtack in fried in pork fat and serving it with condensed milk and sugar.

Of course, there are beans and more beans. We eat potatoes, beef and salt pork quite frequently. When supplied with ground corn we have mush. On raids we steal chickens for our pots, take hams found smoking in small sheds, or capfuls of eggs from a hen house. These disappear into our bags when we have a chance to forage in the countryside. A special favorite of the troops is securing a pig. A few times we have decided that horsemeat is better than no meat.[12]

Just as I begin to slip away into sleep once more, I hear a hoarse voice and a quick slap at my tent. Instantly, I respond, the reflex of anticipation to battle is something that we all have developed. I pull on my cold boots and grab my weapon. My tent mate and I both crawl out together, ready for action of any kind.

Our small sharpshooter outpost of twenty some men and one officer work well together. Now, what we all dreaded has occurred. We had our first casualty. Our Captain George Stearnes has been killed.

As was his practice, the Captain had been moving about the woods checking the watch posts in the dim light. Guards heard a shot, then silence. Listening warily, there was no answering weapon fire. The Sergeant took a gun, and dodging for cover, he worked his way to the spot where there had been fire.

After half an hour he came back. "Damn, outpost heard the shot but saw nothing and as I worked back from the last outpost I came across the Capn'. He's been headshot, a clean shot, and he is dead."

Motioning to me the sergeant ordered, "Report to headquarters, and let them know we have lost Stearnes. I left the capn' where he lay. We can't do nothing, no how, till we get light to bury him by."

Turning to the others he ordered, "The rest of you spread out and make sure the murderer has cleared out. Don't panic and shoot each other. Follow the procedure we implemented to patrol the area. I am going to the outposts to tell the sentries."

I armed myself, checked my weapon and filled my canteen. Going to the "sink," which is a shallow trench not far from camp, I relieve myself. Then I begin to weave my way carefully up a gully toward the first crest. Quietly, I moved past watch posts, I made the birdcall password so our men would know I was not a Reb.

It took almost an hour to get to the Illinois headquarters as I had to evade some active areas. The rebel camps were beginning to stir in preparation for morning. The raging battle has spread for miles across an uneven, scarred terrain. It is hard land and in the heat of early July it is also unbelievably muggy and hot when the sun comes on full, causing sweat to run down my body. My cap is tucked under my jacket to make me make less detectable. The lump of stiff fabric has become uncomfortable and is rubbing my side raw. As I move, sometimes on my knees, through the gullies, my face and hands are becoming scratched. The scratches burn as the sweat trickles down my face.

I finally find the Illinois command post and make a report. For some unknown military cause I received no answer, only another command. Two ranking officers, only half dressed, consulted a moment, then one returned to where I was waiting. His voice still sleep coarsened, informed me that I must go on. With sour breath that I have to resist reacting to, the command comes, "Just go right to the main command post. Find someone there to report the break in command to. They will assign a new officer."

Once more, I assiduously began the difficult path on up across the hills toward the summit. This route is more peopled and probably quite risky. It is an even more challenging task because of the foliage and vines.

Just before I arrive at the command post, I realize there was an eerie silence all around me, not only down the gully, but over the whole field. The lack of weaponry this time of day is almost more frightening than the constant thundering I have been living with. I tell myself it is perhaps a truce for burial detail and removal of the wounded.

When I arrive at Command there is an unusual number of people just milling about or doing nothing. I stop as I come near a shack where a slender young soldier and his stocky, bald comrade were sitting.

"Is something happening?" I inquired apprehensively. "Maybe, the Rebs hoisted a white flag a couple hours ago," the heavy soldier replies with an optimistic pitch to his voice. "Pemberton wanted to make a breakthrough and escape but his men are too weak and worn. Late yesterday, he contacted Grant and this morning he ran up a truce flag. They say that when the flag went up the men in the trenches stood, and the opposing lines were sometimes only twenty feet apart. They both had been digging every night. Those zigzag tunnels were getting closer and closer. We all been resting and waiting to see what is going to happen."[3]

My spirit jumped. The shaky relief that washed over me was amazing.

The man continued, "Grant sent messages back to the Rebs and said he would accept only the unconditional surrender of the city and all the garrison. General Pemberton consulted with his commanders, he then he sent Bowen to deliver the message that the Confederate leaders would meet with General Grant between the lines at three-o-clock today," he continued.

"Ya know," the bald man drawled, "Grant and Pemberton fought together in Mexico in '36. Pemberton's really a traitor now 'cause he is from Pennsylvania. His brothers fight Federal. He still chose to join the secessionist dogs. Yet might be, old buddies can settle this matter more easy."

Pausing I considered what I heard. Then I realized that no matter what is happening, our unit needed to know who our officer would be. I also realized that I still needed to make the casualty report. I went, openly walking across the field, toward the well-guarded area. A sentry passed me through, showing total disinterest. As I moved to the center of the compound, there was a surreal, relaxed attitude among the soldiers.

As I approached, I was told that I must wait. I found the coffeepot, and sat in the shade. It was about eight in the morning and every half-hour I would wander toward the command post and the sergeant would nod me away. Finally I found some food and more coffee.

When a captain came past where I was lounging at about ten, I leaped to my feet. Saluting, I explained my dilemma. He was puzzled and anxiously looked over his shoulder toward the largest tent. Then he shook his head, "I don't know. With so much happening I am not sure whom you tell about this matter Private."

He went to the tent and stepped inside but immediately stepped back out and nodded a negative to me by shrugging his shoulders. Then slowly leaning on a nearby tree, the officer nodded his head toward the tent he had just left. "Seems the rebels want the troops paroled and set free, but General Grant will only take an unconditional surrender. They may have killed more of us but we know they cannot go on with the battle without reinforcements or supplies. This battle has to end soon. Hope we can just get on with the negotiations."

I took my seat again in the shade, and realized that this day I would have some real information to share when I finally got back to the outpost. It was getting hotter and I was going nowhere so I unlaced my boots and pulled my feet out for relief.

My anticipation for an answer and sharing the news gripped me. Perhaps I should just take a nap, but instead I stared all about me. The arrival and departure of all the brass was of interest. I hoped to get a glimpse of General Grant. I, like all the Illinois troops, took pride in him, our native son.

The hope of a finalization seemed a dream to end a nightmare. Sweat ran down my neck and trickled between my shoulder blades. I raised my knees, crossed my arms over them and rested my chin on them.

From the trees at my left a slender, young, very dark, Colored man in his twenties slowly made his way in my direction. He ambled in long, slow steps. He was of medium height, around five foot six inches. He wore no shoes, and had a loose hopsack shirt over baggy trousers. A unique aspect of the man was the fact that he was wearing a military kepi cap on top of his close cut hair. With a slight curiosity, I watched what he was doing.

He stopped near me, and avoiding eye contact, began to look all about himself. He seemed interested in the lack of activity in the area. After about ten minutes, I realized he was standing in the direct sunshine beyond the shade of the tree where I was sitting. With a slight nod I caught his eye. "Would you like to come by the tree, out of the sun?"

The golden cast of his dark skin was a contrast to the white teeth he exposed in a wide smile. Nodding in agreement, he came closer and sat down in front of me. Where he seated himself was about four feet from me and being turned half in my direction I had a good view of the fellow.

"Sho 'preciate the offer, Suh. Dat sun be right hot today."

I nodded and turned my head to look away, not wanting to stare and having no idea of what conversation to make. Thus the two of us sat in silence for an awkward ten minutes more

Feeling discomfort with the quiet space between us, I began a simple conversation. "There is some hope they will make peace today. At three today they will meet in that field over there." Taking my chin off my knees and stretching my legs, I pointed to the field as I spoke. "I have been here a long time and would welcome an end to the battle "

"Yes Suh, I been here since two months befo' the fighting start."

With some surprise, I looked the man in the eye. "Do you live in Vicksburg?"

"No Suh," a wide grin reappeared lighting his countenance. "De Massa bring me up from Wilkinson. We come from de home place with lots o' other niggers. They put us to digging places for de soldiers and making hills to hide em when de battle come."

With a change of tone the young man looked down. "De shu done work us hard. Sometimes we dig all day and all night. De be lots o' us and de Massa be in a shu big hurry to get de job done. Some de soldiers be watchin' us and be real mean."

*What a curiosity this story was.* "If you were in the city with the Rebels, how is it that you are now here in this camp?" I was always wary about spies.

With this the man rose to his feet, threw his shoulders back and stood ramrod straight. "Soon as Grant get here, I jus creep across the hills at night an come ova here. First soldier I see, I come right up and den I say, 'I come to be a soldier.'"

"Well, dat man look at me a while. Den he say, 'Follow me.' He take me to a soldier with a feather in he hat. Dat man say, 'You don say, you don say.'" With the smile this time showing a warm, good humor, the unique story continued. "De man wid de feather he say 'Follow me.' De take me to two more men in a tent. Des men be real happy to see me. Dey say, 'You don good boy, you don good.' De one takes a paper and he makes the marks. Dey say, 'You wan be a soldier, you make a mark here,' and they shows me how."

"'What yo name, boy?' I ups an tell em. 'My name be Buck Murphy,' they ask where I come from an where I was born. I say South Carolina in the 1840s. De needs guess how old I be. I tell em I be married. I say Maryanne Waters and I jump the broom. When dey ask what I do I tell em clear. I be a driver."

With blooming pride the man looked me in the eye. "Now, I be a driver for the Union Army. I get this hat. When de battle over, I get a whole uniform and even a gun."

The man's pride was infectious and I smiled at him with congratulations. "What a fine thing you have done." I thought, *so this is where the Negro soldiers come from.*

Setting again the man seemed excited. "Yes suh, soon dis battle be done. I goin be a real soldier with a gun. I go to lots mo battles. Dis boy goin make sur I not bein a slave no mo. One time early on, de officer call me to de tent. De ask all kind o' things about the earthworks I don help build. I tell em where de be, how big, how many. Dos officer tell me I don good and I be a good soldier."

His eyes glittered as he went on enthusiastically, "De food be good. I get all de food I like. I think I maybe get shoes someday. Goin be free fo eva, goin eat and goin work at what I like to do, an when I like to work. No mo slave, no—now Buck be a man."*

As the sun changed position on the quiet battlefield, the two of us moved around the tree, at what I supposed to be about two thirty. I saw a number of soldiers moving northward. After small thought, we were swept up in the movement of these men.

I pulled on my boots and joined the small crowd slowly moving northward. There was no longer a line and no battle where we were headed. I wanted to be part of what was happening as we reached a small meadow.

There was no activity for a while, then a small line of grey clad men appeared on the far side. They stood at the edge of the woods. From the east, General Grant came with a corresponding group of twelve officers. He dismounted, buttoning his jacket.

I quickly moved toward the edge of the meadow where I might more clearly see what was going to happen. At three o' clock, General Pemberton and two other officers stepped forward from a copse of woods north of the meadow, and walked over a hillock toward the rendezvous.

All the leaders met in the middle and stood together. They were stiff with military bearing. The motion of heads and gestures of hands were like a dramatic pantomime from my position. After a long time, Pemberton and Grant withdrew and moved to a large, dead tree where they sat together quietly talking and eating. The others gestured passionately and interacted with great energy.

I'll tell you about that tree where the two leaders sat. Every man at Vicksburg took a piece of it home after the next day because these two brave and honorable men had finally come close to accomplishing what they needed to do. The siege was to be ended as soon as terms could be agreed upon. This peace came after this forty-seven days of battle.

The battle resumed late that afternoon. In the moonlight on July 3, I decided to carefully follow the trees on the road back to camp. Tomorrow I would be able walk that road rather than crawl on my belly through briars. Tomorrow would be soon enough to have an officer assigned to our post. Exhausted and relieved, I started along the road leading southward toward the flood plane.

The next day was July 4, 1863 and the Union had won the battle of Vicksburg. To save his men and the city, General Pemberton and his officers had finally come to a complete agreement. General Grant had gone back to his tent on the third to put the terms of the surrender on paper, and the Confederate officers moved back over the hill. This meant that on the Fourth of July the city, all the army stores and all the men were surrendered.

Individual Confederate soldiers were each to sign a document of surrender and a promise not to return to war. All did, except some seven hundred that chose Union prisons in Ohio and Illinois and so did not sign the surrender. Then the Confederate men were all paroled.

When I later heard all the terms, it seemed General Grant felt as I did about our brave enemy. Vicksburg had been a bloody place where thousands had died. The courage and deprivation suffered by the Rebels created a

**Jackson family history notes this authentic story of a Fiftieth Company H soldier.*

strong respect for the Confederacy. Their tenacity seemed to have touched him also. Not only to reduce rancor and anger, but in compassion, he and our men showed almost no braggadocio when the paper had been delivered at seven on that third of July night.

As the brazen sun finally lowered, white handkerchiefs or clothing were posted on the Confederate lines. They looked like fields of waving lilies in the wind; relief swept over all. Those flags had been exhibited in the Rebel camps as the message was passed and the final word came. Union soldiers immediately crossed the lines to provide food for the desperate troops and the citizens of the city.

Our troops felt the beginning of hope that the war would end soon. With the greatest caution, both troops on the eastern hills tested the silent peace. First by peeking over the rifle pits, then standing. Slowly, a number of soldiers numbly walked toward the other side to talk, to embrace and a few to weep as they looked behind them at fresh graves of fellows who almost survived until the end. They sat in clumps that night, meeting men whose voices they had known for over forty-seven days. While the weary soldiers now sat face to face, the conversations wound about like an unraveled rope.[9]

This battle was important, but it was also destructive. How it came to an end was different than might have been expected. One result was men respecting men who had been enemies. This was not as it had been at the bloody withdrawals of Shiloh or Corinth. Soon we would hear by wire of the battle at Gettysburg. We would learn of the toll and our final success. The wire written by General Grant that day to President Lincoln arrived the same time as the announcement of victory at Gettysburg on the third.

The Fourth of July I was told the scene in front of the courthouse was dramatic. Seventy-five thousand Union forces watched as the 29,511 Confederates marched out to lay down arms between the lines, there was silence, except from a Union division honoring the rebels as they gave three cheers for "the gallant defenders of Vicksburg."

At ten in the morning on the fourth of July, each Confederate stepped forward to deposit their military accoutrements and company flags. There were sometimes visible tears. These troops were emaciated, exhausted and tattered. Still, they stood tall; looking neither right nor left. [3]

The officers were allowed their horses and a sword. Part of the night's debate had been that these officers might retain their personal possessions, which in most cases also meant their personal servants. Grant had resisted the request because of the former slaves' welfare. Officers would retain side arms. The Calvary and officers would each have a horse. Soldiers would keep no weapons, which was good fortune for our soldiers, many of the Rebs carried excellent weapons that they had come to war with from their homes. Many of us traded our weapons for those left on the field.

A year earlier, Colonel James L. Autry, Vicksburg's military governor, declared he would not surrender. "Mississippians do not know and refuse to learn how to surrender to an enemy." He would now suffer the difficult, humiliating occupation by the Union and 3,000 Black soldiers.

Prior to the invasion, the city of Vicksburg had hosted the Confederate defenders. When they heard of the impending attack by the Union, many citizens had swarmed out of the city by wagon or carriage. Others had rushed to the crowded railway. Many of the town's people made the decision to stay; trusting and confident that they would be protected by their army.

By the end of the siege many of those who stayed in the city resided in or retreated to caves they had Negroes dig for them. By the Fourth of July, the merchants had only empty shelves and citizens were forced to eat mule meat and rats to survive. The town was battered. Through the streets, sleek and well-fed Union troops paraded on the Fourth with their bands playing. Inhabitants stayed inside to only peek out from hiding.

The soldiers planted their flags on the pillared courthouse that sat high above the city. Somewhere, I guess you could say from everywhere, I could hear thousands of Union voices raise the tune of "Rally Round the Flag." It would then be sounded by thousands more on every hill. After long singing the refrain, I could hear the "Star Spangled Banner" raised in solemnity. That evening a weary, but satisfied General Grant, with his son and orderly, Fred, rode to the river to congratulate Admiral Porter.[3]

The soldiers, blue and grey, sat quietly talking; only steps away from the blood baptized fields and the graves of their fellows. The Sanitary Commission had opened city buildings to be used as hospitals. The Sanitary Commission ladies worked at nursing, as the surgeons went on with their grisly tasks.

I had heard of these Vicksburg people as they picked up the pieces, and proceeded to face a new day. They were like harvesters who glean the leavings of a crop. The following day, a rain tried to wash the soiled world.

Chapter 6

# Officer

The elation of the surrender at Vicksburg was invigorating. Because of the wire about the Union success at Gettysburg all our troops felt energized and even had a hint of optimism. Personally, I was almost impatient to rush forward so that I could help hurry our army toward ending this War of Rebellion.

Ready and able troops move and that is what happened after the surrender at Vicksburg. The Fifteenth Illinois regiment and many others moved immediately. On July 5 our soldiers, who were still physically able, were marched through the heat and the rain once more to Jackson, Mississippi. We skirmished with the enemy a number of times as we moved forward. We marched under the command of Major General Sherman, Department of Tennessee.

We arrived before the siege of Jackson, which lasted an entire week. The assignment of the Fifteenth Illinois was to do reconnaissance on the Pearl River. On the fourteenth of July, the Confederates flew the flag and asked for permission to bury their dead and care for the wounded.

On the sixteenth of July, the city of Jackson was evacuated, and our Army fired many of the buildings that had survived our earlier attack on the approach to Vicksburg. We spared the State House and governmental mansion. The cavalry pursued the enemy forty miles to the east. The army once more tore up the railway tracks. Then we recovered our wounded soldiers and buried our own. We moved back toward Vicksburg via a route through Raymond and Mississippi Springs arriving on the twenty-third.[3]

Vicksburg was now a command post headquarters, with thousands of the Black troops on duty. This proud bastion of the South was under the bitter control of military rule that brought curfews, passes, search and seizure of goods, and verbal insults. Speculators leased nearby plantations, trying to take financial advantage of the owner's painful position.

The citizens of the city were forbidden to correspond with others in the Confederacy. The only mail contact came by the cleverness of wily mail runners whose contribution to the Southern effort was continual and daring. One mail runner, Absalom Grimes, had delivered 2,000 letters to Vicksburg last May. He arrived by river right under the nose of the Federal gunboats.[13]

There had been scattered acts of pillage by some Union soldiers on the Fourth of July right after the surrender. General Grant retaliated against such behavior as soon as he was informed. A few war weary, hardened soldiers got drunk, fought, rampaged or looted, and ended up in jail. Scattered civilians were likewise arrested for a variety of accusations.

The military officially took possession of numerous buildings and homes, and even used the Catholic convent for the duration of the occupation. Oaths of allegiance were the first requirement of occupation with passes required of all citizens and occupants of the city to move about.

Families who had fled to the countryside prior to the battle were slowly returning to the city, often to find their homes ravaged. The rancor between the townspeople and soldiers was galling. The poor condition of the town and the neediness of the populace were painful to see.

I was not assigned any task during my regiments' brief stay in the city. Several times I stood for hours at some vantage point studying the dreary scenes around me. Once I was able to walk all about the city on an errand. For most the day I mentally recorded the visible scars within this lovely city on a bluff. Up close, I looked through the broken windows into stores with empty shelves. I slowly moved down the shattered boardwalks that required me to move into the street to pass. Some homes were boarded up and empty. I wondered where the residents had gone.

During the forty-seven days of bombardment, many citizens had spent much time in the protection of caves. The damage from shell and fire left much of the city in destruction. There was a great deal of glass missing in windows and doors. Some people claimed the houses looked like "eyeballs in a skull."

One scene was amazing. Some townspeople had taken to the habit of piling "iron fragments and unexploded shells on their lawns—there was up to a ton of it sometimes at one location."[13]

Freed slaves poured into town with their possessions and families; it further added more problems and tension. Col. Samuel Thomas of the Freedman's Bureau made efforts to bring order out of chaos, but the task was almost impossible.

The Union was making an effort to provide food for people. The series of passes, bureaucracy and the provision divisions required humility of the populace. Yes, the Confederates could apply for the necessary rations but it was a bitter pill for the people to swallow. [14]

My fellows and I had arrived in Vicksburg August 15. Illinois troops were soon ordered sixty miles south to Natchez, Mississippi where the Ninety-fifth Illinois was already stationed on garrison duty. The First Corp was left behind in Vicksburg.

We accomplished the trip downriver by riverboats and barges. This was, after all, a river which the Union now completely controlled. I lolled on the deck studying the clay banks west in Louisiana and east on the Mississippi shores. The foliage was thick, with only a few people visible on the riverbanks. I saw only an occasional Black fisherman staring as we floated past.

There were a few docks; which in prosperous times would have been the sites for loading cotton bales that were just beginning to be harvested. I had a depressing view of two locations that had obviously been fine homes. They were now only naked chimneys sitting on charred ground that was littered with bricks and melted pieces of metal.

The river rolled southward, a writhing, rich brown passageway that looked like living velvet. As we approached Natchez, I was shocked to see an amazing sight on the east bank. Under immense, loess bluffs I saw a huge pen or stockade. Within this boundary were thousands of milling Black people of all ages. I could conjure no purpose or end to such a confinement of so many people.

A short distance further south on the shoreline, were hundreds and hundreds of Negroes wearing Union uniforms. Many of these soldiers were sitting idle near very long, rough buildings. Dozens more of these men were moving up and down one of the longest stairways I had ever seen. This steep passage went from the riverbank far to the top of the cliff that reached three hundred feet above the river.

Forming a unique and mysterious triad of bizarre locations, we then arrived at the third phenomenon. Only a few miles beyond these first two unique environs, I viewed the infamous docks, taverns and shops called Natchez Under the Hill. As we floated inland and finally bumped to a stop at a dock to unload, I felt almost anxious.

This site swelled with more idle Negroes and people hawking food or handmade products. I had never bee surrounded by so many dark faces. My Northern youth was a different world than the one I viewed now.

Freedom had drastically changed the racial balance of the South. To walk away with their families was a Freedman's lifelong passion. When it was finally possible to do that, thousands found freedom had little to offer their families but hunger, discomfort and new dangers. This hopeless freedom was a bewildering disappointment. The displaced people had no defense, no employment and little understanding of the world beyond the isolation where so many generations had spent their lives.

Many able Freedmen had joined the war in the service of the Union. These Union soldiers stepped forward to fight for what they had wanted—freedom. A few, still wore the grey uniforms. Those in grey had fought to protect their ancestral home and their families.

The Negroes at dockside were of no obvious threat, but I still felt vulnerable. My experience with the Underground Railroad in Illinois had never involved so many ragged people at one time. In addition to those standing in my near vicinity, were the two locations north of here I had seen. There were many thousands of people of Color at those places by the river.

After I gained the deck of the barge, I stood with my haversack in hand. My cap was pushed to the back of my head as I waited in line for my turn to walk a swaying gangplank of rotting wood onto the dock We made a ragged formation on the landing in sweltering heat.

The day was very unpleasant with rotting odors of the debris floating about between the docked ships and rowboats. Some of the source of the waste was apparent, as there were people all about the docks selling garden produce. There was more fresh food available here than I had seen in a long time. Obviously, the discards and cleanings went into the quiet water near the dock.

Here and there a carriage or horseman wound its way slowly through the throngs of people. Somewhere, I could hear screaming and swearing so I assumed a fight was in progress just out of sight. I saw glimpses of dandies, elaborately dressed gamblers and there were painted women looking from upper windows in several buildings. Many of the women were waving or making vulgar motions toward the soldiers.

It was late afternoon by the time we had all disembarked and off-loaded our gear. Our ragged, hot men were called into formation after about an hour. After that we marched up a steep curving road to the level where the city proper lay.[3]

As we emerged on the crest of the bank, Natchez became another world, one of flowers and beauty. The roads through the small city were straight and clear. Small, neat homes were set about with carriage houses, barns and gardens adjoining them. There were a few dwellings indicative of the Spanish influence of about a hundred years previous. The foliage everywhere was verdant. Trees had massive, dark trunks sheltered by almost impenetrable canopies of leaves. Hedges were lush with even more greenery and flowers.

Summer blooms on shrubs and gardens were brilliant in the intense sunlight. After the desolate views of occupied Vicksburg, this seemed to be a different world. People walked up and down roadways. Horsemen or carriages were all about; intent on pursuing their daily lives. Occasional groups of citizens stood visiting. These casual and warm vistas were unlike any war experience I had thus far witnessed. I deeply inhaled a fragrance which was free of gunpowder and rich with the very greenness of the city.

We passed a large, lovely, pillared home flying a Union flag. I later found this was a home was being used as General Ransom's headquarters. The house, Rosalie, had been conscripted from a local family. There were neatly uniformed troops about the lawn, and again more Negroes in Union uniforms. This was quickly becoming a fact of Emancipation. Black soldiers who were active in the service of the Union became a solid reality but one that I could not quickly absorb that day. In the tragedy of Vicksburg, these troops had been a part of the bizarre situation. In Natchez, they looked foreign to me. These men, like an army from some other country, were dressed in *my* uniform.

The soldiers already stationed in this city, both the Black and the White, seemed oblivious to us as we passed by. Natchez was occupied and no longer under the authority of the citizens; it belonged to the Federal government. Armed men filled every sector of the town.

The city had not voted to secede when the South went to war but were swept along with the momentum of the war anyway. They saw themselves as a merchant society. Their international trade status, the basis of their livelihood, was a predominant thread in their society and existence. A number of the planters and merchants maintained homes in other states and overseas. They vacationed in New Orleans for great lengths of time. Elegance surrounded us and beauty bloomed in an oasis in the war.

The Fifteenth Illinois camped in a small park overnight. The road going north and south paralleled the park with huge trees overlooking the swirling, muddy river. The park hid the grotesque Under the Hill from view but, in the muggy heat, the location could not mask the sounds or even the odors of that raucous, bawdy place.

The next morning, we marched one and a half miles toward Fort McPhearson on the northern edge of the town. In half an hour we were climbing to the top of the cliff I had observed from the river before we arrived at the dock.

As we crested the cliff there was a sudden view of earthwork walls with a few strategically placed guard posts. The earthworks were obviously still being constructed. Workers, mostly Black, were moving about the buttresses as far up the hill to the north as I could see. Here and there inside the walls were buildings and barracks. I glimpsed five or six large plantation homes of several stories. All around were lovely ancient trees that I had seen on the lower level of the bluffs in the city.*

In the center of the huge earthwork fort, near the parade grounds, were several rough, wooden structures true to military style. There were guardhouses, parade grounds and stables with rows of idle vehicles. I could see cannon and rifle pits. The fort itself was an earthen barrier with tons of soil moved, mainly by Black labor, to create reinforcements and gun emplacements.

At a number of strategic points were more permanent, brick fortified structures like guardhouses or watchtowers. The Marine Hospital stood north of McPhearson, outside the wall.

We were marched into the center of the stockade and commanded to set up camp. This was easy to accomplish for we had been doing this time and again for three years. My mate and I immediately staked a four foot by five foot area. Then we built plank bases for our tent. The bartering and scavenging had made each new camp a challenge. Eventually, we also created writing and eating areas from improvised, salvaged crates and barrels.[3]

Serving at the fort were a large number of other regiments and including more Illinois troops. Fifty men, living within a fort, creates a crowded, bustling effect. Barracks are full and overflowing, as is the hospital. The regiments overlap in duties and activities causing no small confusion.[15]

The Fifteenth Illinois hardly got established before we were ordered to guard a train of wagons to Kingston, twenty miles east. There we were to secure twenty thousand bales of cotton. As we accomplished this duty, there was a lot of rain and 'wet' was the word of the day.

While in Kingston, we found the tables there were rich with food. The Ninety-fifth had even secured a keg of beer to which they treated their friends in the Fifteenth. A few of us could not walk straight. The duty, as we protected the cotton, was a real luxury compared to our usual military life standards.

The fort sits on a 300 foot cliff. On the lower level of river bank, between the river and the cliff is what is left of a lovely home with beautiful gardens and a lumber company. There are several other small dwellings and sheds. This is also the location of the horrible Kraal, the pen I had viewed as I approached Natchez. It probably holds at least 20,000 poor dispossessed souls.

**There were five other homes within the boundaries. The Wigwam, The Towers, Cottage Garden, Airlie and Riverview. These homes were in the service of the army now and housed officers, provided hospitals and were put to use as need demanded.*

Nearby is the long flight of steps that I had seen these had been built originally for the workers at the sawmill. Just south of the steps are the rough barracks for the Colored troops.

The Union had accepted the surrender of Natchez earlier on July 16. The actual arrival of our army had been so quick and quiet that the citizens hardly noticed the surrender. This had been the second surrender, the first one having been ignored. Upon the arrival of the Northerners, Negroes flocked into the city by the thousands, around five hundred arrived to be fed each day. Able bodied men were put to use as labor. Anxious, Brigadier General Ransom had begged the government to explain how to handle this desperate situation.[15]

McPhearson, as I found it upon investigation, still had six homes. One, the magnificent home called Clifton, was set all about with formal gardens. Many such luxuriant gardens in the city even had full-time European designers and gardeners. This particular garden was famous and a site of tourist interest. The home was also known for its hospitality to Union officers—the owner often inviting them to social events. While I was there a petulant, young officer was offended that he was not invited to a ball. The young man, in his fury, immediately demanded that Clifton be destroyed. Without notice, it was burned to the ground and razed.

Spirits at the fort had been high when we had arrived. I was told that in late July Brigadier General Ransom had reported a conflict on Washington Road near Natchez. Here Logan's Calvary was approaching with 1,500 men. In the encounter, we suffered two wounded, they lost about fifteen men, with numerous casualties and we took many prisoners.[10] This was one of the few occasions where active war came so close to the city. Thus from the beginning, I personally felt this location would eventually become the site of a major battle.

In early August, the Fifteenth Illinois completed a five day foray into Louisiana and captured Fort Beaureguard.

We later marched eight miles south to Forks in the Road where there was an empty slave market with numerous sheds and docks. This was also the site of the Quitman plantation where four companies of our regiment resided. This plantation, called Monmouth, was rented from a Quitman relative for use as a home plantation by our army. The family had been moved to an upper level with all their possessions. *

August 30 we marched to Woodville, located about thirty miles south. In our spare time we cleaned weapons and drilled. We competed by regiment

**John A. Quitman had been a primary leader in the region and a major slave owner. His hatred of the North and his desire for secession was a fact. He had been a highly successful officer in the war with Mexico some years before–capturing Mexico City. He was now dead and his descendants were living at Monmouth.*

for the esprit de corps on our appearance and skill in the drills. Our command took great pride in our order and military bearing. [3]

Recruiters came among us seeking enlistments and reassignments to the Colored troops. At first I only listened, then as a few of our regiment considered applying more seriously, I also began to contemplate the possibilities. I would miss my fellows who had become like brothers to me. The money would be a boon, for after the war I would need to start a new life. Increased pay, if I could qualify as an officer, would set quite well, to my mind.

It was tempting, the position offered one months advance pay of thirteen dollars upon reenlistment. The first installment of bounty was sixty dollars with a two dollar premium. To be an officer and wear that elegant uniform was a much different way to become an officer than before our regiment attached. Our first officers had been selected in a voted election when we originally formed our regiment in Freeport, Illinois. The possible advance in rank appealed to my ego. I imagined the increased power and authority I would have.

That night I wrote my parents about what I was considering. I neglected to remind them that the Rebels had announced that the White officers of Black troops, when captured, were to be shot as traitors and Colored men returned to slavery.

This had already been proven at "...the battle of Milliken's Bend north of Vicksburg on the Louisiana side. In this battle the integrated troops had participated in a violent battle. Upon the defeat of our army the Rebels had executed an officer and several of his Colored troops. Eyewitnesses reported that captured soldiers were executed on the spot and that Confederate soldiers had bayoneted the wounded in the next two days. The Confederates had even entered the hospitals and executed seven wounded Black soldiers who lay in their beds." [16]

On July 30, after several other vicious acts where the Rebels had singled out Black troops for retribution, President Lincoln declared that there would be retaliation on grey prisoners for every injustice to Black soldiers. This danger was real and of concern to me, but I felt undeterred.

One sunny afternoon, as the recruiter left the Fifteenth, he tacked a small poster on the side of one of the horse stables. I was one of a number of men who carefully read it.

> "NO PERSON IS WANTED as an Officer in a Colored Regiment who "feels that he is making a sacrifice in accepting a position in a Colored Regiment, or who desires the place simply for higher rank and pay. It is the aim of those having this organization in charge to make Colored Troops equal the best of White troops, in Drill, Discipline, and Officers. It is more than possible that Colored Troops

will hereafter form no inconsiderable portion of the permanent army of the United States, and it should be the aim of every officer of Colored Troops to make himself and his men fit for such an honorable position. It can be no 'sacrifice' to any man to command in a service, which gives Liberty to Slaves, and Manhood to Chattels, as well as Soldiers to the Union."

The poster listed the high expectations for those becoming an officer of the Colored Troops. I was somewhat confident I could do well in the competition. I still wondered about the difficulty of the test. I had heard that some potential applicants went to New Orleans to a school, prior to applying to the testing board, to be better able to succeed in the test.

On the eastern seaboard there were also several schools to prepare officers prior to accomplishing both the required test and Casey's board. A few days later, I finally decided to take the risk. My father and our family had always felt that slavery must end this would be the most visible witness that I was in agreement with them.

*The Manual for Officers of United States Colored Troops* was my best resource in studying and preparedness. When I was ready it was with trepidation, for I was not entirely sure of my own ability.

Finally, I took Casey's board test. About half the men who took this test failed, as the standards were very high. There were lots of military questions, which, as a veteran, were second nature to me. The week before the testing I had read several books to fortify my knowledge of general history and mathematics. With great relief and comfort to my ego, my scores were high.

The second step of the enlistment process was to stand before the board for a personal interview, which lasted four to five hours. Each member of the board asked me many questions in turn. The questions varied from how I felt about slavery and Negroes to military matters, geography and military ethics. In the War of the Rebellion, there were eventually to be 9,000 applications to the Colored Troops with only one in four being accepted. [16]

Now, I held the document in my hand. My heart thudded with excitement. First, was the notice and congratulations on my acceptance. With elation I read it several times—I would be a Captain. There was increased pride at the rank, which was higher than my expectation. It was a real reassurance.*

The enlistment papers described me as single, 5'8' tall, light skin, black hair, blue eyes, 26-years-old and in good health. On August 25, I

**Rank at that time was Colonel, Major, Captain, First Lieutenant, Second Lieutenant, Sergeant Corporal and Private.*

was accepted as Captain William Hugh Hunter. On October 13, I would be discharged from the Fifteenth Illinois to join company K to the Sixth Regiment of African decent, heavy artillery.

My assignment for the first several months would be to direct military procedure and drilling, to observe the operation of my unit and to recruit more troops. When they issued me the authority to put on my uniform my heart almost burst. I had been led by so many fine officers in my war experience and I yearned to live up to their standards.

At the first possible moment I made a trip to the Natchez's business district. There I purchased two extra officers' shirts from Hoppe, Wolff and Company, on Main Street. Right near that shop, I went into F.H. Clark and Company to have three daguerrean taken.

One photographic image I would send to my parents, and one I planned to keep for the future possibility of a gift to someone. The clothing I now wore included a broad brimmed, dark hat with insignia on the front depicting a bugle for infantry and a brass number of the regiment and company. The blue, woolen, dress coat was a long jacket with a high, stiff collar and epaulets on the shoulder. There were light blue trousers with brass buttons, a flannel shirt, dark boots, flannel underwear and stockings. A leather strap reached from my left shoulder under my right arm to my right hip. I did, to my notion, look very fine and felt great pride in the new uniform.

As soon as I could post a letter, I sent the daguerreotype to my family. I also instructed them to purchase the farm I had been dreaming about, if it was still available. I had them draw on funds that I had mailed home to the bank. I had them put in my father's name in case I did not return. If that resource was not sufficient, I inquired if he would ally that amount and on my leave, which surely would be soon, I would bring more money. The prosperity of the new pay gave me a sense of security.

In an attempt to acquaint myself with Natchez, I secured old newspapers from the other officers and spent evenings in my tent, sitting on a barrel at a plank table, reading by lantern light. The papers posted announcements from the commander of the fort and the headquarters of the Army of Tennessee in Vicksburg. These were mainly for the information of the public.

There were also listings of merchandise arrivals and merchant's advertisements. Often the paper had snippets of humor, mostly about the war. There were sometimes tragic poems commemorating the loss of loved ones and battle reports of the Confederate troops. These were very simple, without emotion because of Union censorship.

In each issue were listings of recipients of mail that was to be picked up at the fort. These consisted of rows of names; first the women, then the men. The censorship of mail was one method the military used to keep citizens in order, although very probably, smuggled mails were still the mainstay of the community. Postal goods were to be recovered in person at Fort McPhearson.

There were important messages in the paper about provisions that those within six miles of Natchez could receive if they had signed Oaths of Allegiance. Goods and food were issued from the military by requisitioning them at the fort.

The newspapers posted evening curfews of eight for Colored and nine for White citizens.

Notices firmly reminded everyone that all persons seeking access to the fort or crossing through, must go to the provost marshal's office as soon as arriving on post. This would include those going to northern plantations or to the city cemetery.

It was encouraged that produce grown locally be marketed at the fort and individuals doing so should also have proper passes and permits, and report to the provost marshal.

Carefully worded, specific instructions on the hiring and lodging of Negroes were recorded. It was strongly encouraged that the community do so to help relieve the thousands of Contraband, Freed and homeless Blacks who flooded the near area.

This sample is typical of an attempt to supervise the homeless Colored community.

"PROVOST MARSHAL'S OFFICE, Natchez, Miss, Sept. 14, 1863
Special Order #1

All persons residing in the city of Natchez are hereby ordered to lease no buildings to contrabands, and those owning houses which are already leased will report the name of occupant, date of lease, time specified herein and situation of property to their office immediately.

John M. Marble
Capt. and Ass. Provost Marshal"

The same newspaper reported the following:

"Every day we see strange faces in the streets and on inquiry find that they are carried by persons who have come within our lines, so to escape rebel conscript officers, others to get into communication with their relatives or take comfort beneath the protection of the old flag.

On Sunday we saw a party of the former class, conscripts, who had made their escape from the camps in Arkansas, and were tired of the firm."

"A roving, young Irishman who had rambled from the west through Arizona down into Texas and been conscripted into Edge's battery, Cullsom's brigade, Walker's division, concluded he would ramble further, and get among "White folks" again. He was engaged as nurse to Cpt. Wallace of a Colored regiment who was wounded and captured in a fight at Milliken's bend last June or July. The rebels were mad and wanted to hang the poor captain, but were prevented by the entreaties of the surgeon attending him.

They say they hate the 'niggers and low down Yankees' that is the Irish because "they are so rough and hard to handle in a fight." Negroes then make good fighting soldiers, our enemies themselves being witness and so we can afford to get more of them; and trust them better than before." [17]

Southern humor or tongue in cheek was recounted concerning North Carolina.

"Our neighbors in the east are having merry time in the way of elections. The people of Chatham, Orange and Alabama held a large convention, at which the following pointed resolutions and others were passed:

RESOLVED that we will cast off our suffrages for no man to represent us in the Congress of the Confederate States, who declares himself opposed to negotiation and a general peace convention.

RESOLVED that no man shall stay AT HOME and advocate secession who uses his influence to get other men into the army, and his money to keep himself out.

RESOLVED that we are opposed to sending any more men to congress who are in favor of prosecuting the war until the last man is killed, and the last dollar is spent, except themselves and their dollar." [17]

I took to familiarizing myself about the area of my assignment in free moments during my first months in Natchez. When possible, I walked my horse through the streets, nodding and tipping my hat at the women and smiling at the children. Women of all ages and conditions quickly looked down to hurry on or even to dodge into shops. Children would sometimes give timid grins before being pulled onward.

Black servants looked down or occasionally stole quick glances, probably to see what a 'Northern Devil' looked like. The Colored population were, in general, deeply afraid of Union troops. This was possibly because of the total disruption we brought to the society or maybe because they had been told terrifying tales by the White families they lived with. Those with more direct stares were perhaps considering the possibility these blue clad men were somehow going to come and take them away from their own families.

On one of these rides a sharp sting on my thigh caught my attention and I saw a stone roll to the dusty street. Looking up I saw a twelve or thirteen-year-old boy make a dash into small alley leading from the street. I must admit I felt some anxiety and it increased my sense of isolation.

When I was first commissioned, prior to my final assignment, my days were somewhat free. At the Adams county building I went to sit at long, rough tables studying maps, taxation, bills, and slave sales; making copious notes for use when I began seeking Colored troop recruits in the area.

From my notes I hoped to learn where the plantations were with large numbers of young male slaves. Many of these had as few as ten, though several had over a hundred. About one third of the males seemed to be of the right age. The majority of our Black troops who were already enlisted had come from other states, but local recruiting was encouraged.

The ranking White officers at the fort frequently instructed new officers, explaining how the Black troops were to be instructed, ordered and we were encouraged to recruit. They also oversaw daily proceedings and schedules.

For some reason I never saw our commander, Brigadier General McDevlin. Several times we were called to parade for him, stood around, and then were dismissed. I knew from past experience that reports and orders should regularly be read to us, but this never happened either. Somehow, there seemed to be a serious break in command.

Several Sundays, I went to the Episcopal Church where I was ever conscious of the parishioner's eyes on my back; they never looked into my face. Real contact was only the handshake from the priest on my departure. When I spoke to him there was a quick smile, a nod and then he would quickly reach for the next hand.

Downtrodden with disappointment because I had hoped my new captain's uniform would impress them, I would slink back to my horse and slowly make the ride north through the town, then up the hill, to return to Fort McPhearson.

The next week after church, I sought out a couple of gentlemen engaged in visiting. I mentioned my grandfather and great grandfather, both Henry Hunters, who had lived nearby. I told them proudly that one of them was the first state representative from Wilkinson and the other a successful planter. Suspicious, the men looked at me, up and down, slowly they said they were not familiar with these names but perhaps older parishioners might know them.

When I asked about a family named Scothorne, the men remained silent.

There were a few Black parishioners at the church. These seemed particularly wary and actually scurried away when I neared them. I tried, out of courtesy, to avoid obviously viewing the women at church. There was a predominance of younger ladies sitting alone or with children; far too many were wearing black and black veils. None of these could be identified as the widow Scothorne, whom I hoped to visit with.

During the lectures, there had been some suggestions of potential soldiers: field workers, younger and strong men, to avoid enlisting those who might be weak or ill, or seemed unable to understand instructions. It was also recommended that we avoid those who seemed filled with hate or anger. They might just transfer that hate to Northern Whites, in particular their own officers. There was among the White corp an undercurrent of fear of the Negroes; it lay just under the surface of our daily routine.

The next day of duty I took a pass and selected a strong, nice looking Sixth African Descent Sergeant. I collected a clean uniform and shiny boots from the supplies, using bribery as a stimulant for the allotment. I did not look the sergeant in the eye or question him but simply spoke from my horse, "Follow me."

Under a tree I dropped the clothing to the ground and ordered him to change into it. Pacing my horse at some distance, I left him to remove his usable, but worn clothing and replace them with the new garments.

Normally the Colored Troops walked, but today I wanted to impress field workers with the majesty of Black Union soldiers. I selected a large bay horse, had it saddled and now ordered the sergeant into the saddle. I dismounted and walked around the man to inspect him. I felt he would well impress such simple people as the possible recruits I would be seeking.

With a small hammer, nails and a bundle of handbills in my saddlebag, we headed north through the fort and eventually toward the Tennessee Trail, or as the Northerners referred to it, "The Trace." The long trail leads eventually to Nashville then to the Ohio River. Riding on the rutted road we passed several horsemen. A large, Black woman approached carrying an empty basket, I pulled up to her. "I have a paper for you," folding one of the handbills I held it toward her. There was some fear and confusion in her visage. "Doan read sir," and she prepared to go on.

"Perhaps you would pass it on, I am seeking Negro men to become soldiers. We pay them, give them clothes and weapons." I held the handbill toward her, she reached toward it—almost against her will. Then she stopped, her eyes more alert and her posture straight. She glanced toward the mounted soldier following behind me, suddenly withdrew her hand

and rushed on past us toward town. Over her shoulder she fearfully stuttered, "Massa, no like me take dat paper."

Depleted, I realized this would not be easy. As an officer, I would be expected to recruit troops, but how, there was my problem. With a hand motion in the general vicinity of the sergeant I rode on.

Soon, passing a harvested field, I saw a group of Blacks hoeing at a small patch of young trees and weeds with an aim to enlarge the field. Checking the area within my vision, I saw no White overseer. I turned my mount off the road toward the workers. I was quite close when several began peeking at me as they continued to work. The group was predominantly women of various ages, the men were mostly very old or very young.

"I call your attention to a notice," I pronounced in an authoritative voice, knowing these people were used to receiving commands. They paused and looked blankly at me, making no response. "Let me tell you good news, you are now free and any Black man who is strong can become a soldier."

The group of perhaps a dozen included four boys who were probably too young but might have some soldier potential. All the workers stood staring, first at me, then at the sergeant who sat quietly behind me.

"Sir," the sergeant quietly said.

While turning to respond, I realized I had not asked the man's name. And so simply answered, "Yes," instead of responding with his name and rank.

Politely the young Black man peered; his face a rich, olive tone with large, unusual green eyes. "I think you need to say different to these people. They doan know who you is and what it is you want. They is scared."

I was a Captain, albeit a new one, and this young man was probably an illiterate, former slave. For a moment I paused. "Thank you. I can do this."

Again I faced the farm crew, holding several handbills toward them I informed the people I was trying to find men to become soldiers.

*Are they stupid?* I asked myself, becoming impatient and continued to hold the papers toward them as they stood in stone-like silence. Finally, throwing the papers on the ground, I returned to the trail, riding on with my companion following some distance behind in silence.

As I turned a curve in the road, my curiosity demanded that I look back. Each laborer was back with the hoe in hand and the papers were blowing across the field.

All day the two of us rode about the countryside in a large circle. At road intersections I nailed handbills to posts or trees, and checked my maps. When we finally returned toward McPhearson at dusk, the bills were gone. I was tired, angry and embarrassed.

The sergeant, unused to the saddle, did not complain nor had he spoken because I never spoke to him. As we passed each intersection I knew in my heart the bills had been taken down by planters or overseers, not taken by strong, likely, Black men. One posting I passed had been shredded, there were hundreds of tiny pieces of paper fluttering about in the grass and bushes with only a scrap of the handbill clinging to the nail.

At the fort we dismounted. Without a word, I handed my reigns to the sergeant and stomped off, leaving him to care for the horses and stable them. At the mess I gathered a tin plate of beans and hardtack, and a steaming tin cup of coffee.

I withdrew to sit alone, against a tree to eat and smolder with anger. The next day, I repeated my plan for recruitment but rode east of Natchez with the sergeant. The results were the same pitiful failure.

The sergeant appeared at my tent the third day. I gave him a gruff answer, "Not today," and retreated inside. I paced all morning, evaluating my failure. If I approached the other officers I was fearful they would see my inadequacy.

*These dumb darkies. Did they not want to be free? Hadn't we come down here to the heat, bugs, and war to free them? How could they not admire me and want to follow me, a handsome, fine soldier on a horse? Me, a hero!*

Anger, humiliation and pride ate at me all day. That night I could not sleep.

Exhausted, the next day I ate my breakfast slowly, watching the officers and listening to their conversations but finding no clues or answers about recruiting. I was too humiliated to ask questions. Then, after sanding my tin plate and returning it to the cook, I took a cup of coffee and slowly approached the fringe of the Sixth African enlisted area. At the edge of a group of men, I saw the sergeant who had accompanied me quietly watching as I sat there.

Standing at some distance, I listened to the chatter of the troops at rest. The wide gestures they made as they talked and laughed, coupled with their unique accents both puzzled and fascinated me. There was an obvious warmth and camaraderie between them.

The speech I heard was somewhat hard for me to understand, thick with accent and Southern imprint. The fast talk and solemn looks when things of importance were discussed impressed me with its passion and honesty, which I could understand. There were mysterious fragrances from large pots that were simmering here and there among the groups.

There were several contraband women and children nearby who had come from the camp far below on the riverbank. They lived in that horrid shantytown of desperate souls and seldom were seen at the fort except when they arrived on some chore, like laundry or sewing, that was paid for by the officers.

The whole community called their location by the river, a Kraal, after the animal pens of Africa. Some of the women and children I saw up here were obviously family, others appeared to be delivering laundry or were food sellers for the enlisted men. These people had climbed the same 300 steps near Brown's Garden arriving from the river where they, the troops of the Sixth African and the other Colored troops were assigned to barracks.

Slowly, an idea began to form. These were a different people, a unique people I could not understand. When the Union used the Black troops at Vicksburg, in my mind, they had seemed just like me, with the same reasons to fight, the same feelings, and simply had fewer abilities. To me they had been Union soldiers who wore the same uniform but were Black. With little contact, I had just viewed them at a distance as comrades in arms. Now I knew what I had to do, I must learn their ways, to live and work with them.

Wearing a uniform and having a weapon did not teach them to read or to understand military order. This important task fell to the army. A few of the officers at the fort were spending time drilling, instructing and working with weaponry from rifle to cannon. Some of the troops were teaching reading and mathematics to their troops each day. Yet, that did not instantly transform them to 'behave' White, or fit these Black men into the new society.

*Where were their families, those not in the contraband camp? Were they people with families and ambitions like the White men? Can they be soldiers, and equals? How can I lead them when I do not understand them? Who are these Negroes? What can they do?*

I made my way back to the officers' mess with a new question. *Can I, in fact, lead Black men?*

It was several days before I began to recruit again. I filled those empty days reading and writing a cheerful letter home. The marches that had filled the war had ended. It was good to be free to wander more, and to occasionally have time alone. During those days, I eavesdropped on other officers and the men in the Black camp, mulling and pondering what I observed.

One day I rode to headquarters which was a large, white house called Rosalie near the park. I had been sent there with a dispatch, which I delivered and then waited three hours for a reply. During that time, I wandered the small city, watching Negroes on the street, now with more inquisitiveness. I noticed the variety of color, size and the large number of Mulattos among the Colored community. I compared the attitudes of the Blacks who were soldiers to those on the streets. Now, I studied them carefully and objectively.

When I decided to recruit again it was because I had been blistered with embarrassment by an inquiry from a ranking officer as to why I was not about my business. I sought out the same Sixth sergeant. The soldier did not seem surprised, it was as though he had expected me.

Again we rode, this time we went south along the river and into town. "Sergeant, what is your name?" I asked with a sincere interest.

"Sergeant Anderson," was the crisp reply.

"Where are you from?"

"Alabama, Sir," came his military response, smothered in a slow accent.

"Have you seen battle?" The Sixth African Decent had a fine battle reputation.

"Yes, Sir." The answer was humble and had the quiet confidence of someone who had no need to brag.

Seeking some identification with this soldier I asked, "Why did you enlist?"

"Got a wife and two young-uns in Alabama. We don jump the broom, but the massa gone to the war and the place gettin' poor. They may sell da nigas off and break up my family. I am need the pay and send it back to save up so we can be freemen an make a life. The war be over some day. We be free, free mean we goin to go whole family together. Cap'n, Dat all I want. My family and be free."

"When you were freed by the President why didn't you leave the farm, all of you?"

After a long pause the man squared his jaw and replied, "I ran once, night riders foun' me, thought I be dead. After the massa overseer beat me I almos' dies. But they so poor de need evry Nigga. I know how hard it be to run with a family and the night riders still get ya. I be free when I can walk away, all of us. I be a soldier so I can make me an da family really be free. I be a self emancipator."

"When we rode out before, you said I should talk to the field workers in a different way. It would be appreciated, Sergeant Anderson, if you could tell me how to talk to them." I was now humble and sincere, welcoming his or anyone's good advice.

"Sir, you jus' needs to do it quiet. They know who you am. De doan read so jus tell them how and when to join. Saying they be free ain bein' free. They is still in fear o' bounty hunters, of overseer, of other slaves who tattle. It not be good talking in the open and not a mark wrote on paper. Only a few can figure marks on paper. Those darkies know what men of them might go join. Find out who they are and where to find them."

"I 'preciate this fine horse. Me ridin a horse doan impress dem they knows we Colored walk. Dey jus wan to know why I be on that horse, anyway. To them it be like, 'tricky.' Mos' important to all de man is de family. Dey doan just walk away and leave them lone. You got to get da family safe fore they will go be army niggas. We got to spread the word in town. Then come Sunday we go to a gathering where dey be far from the massa an the ovaseer. Des men not 'fraid to die, just to be caught and beat or have they family beat or sent away to Texas."

Nodding at Sergeant Anderson's suggestions, I said I would see him early tomorrow and wandered back to the camp.

The disease season was slowly closing. The small pox hospital was less full. The heat and bugs were still oppressive. Underlying our regiment was the disquiet of the breech in the chain of command. I would like to speak with someone ranking about the questions I had in recruiting. The confusion from the top down made it hard to decide with whom I might speak. General Ransom was effective, though it would be inappropriate to bring such matters to him.

Brigadier General McDevlin had been a hero at Shiloh, but here he was almost invisible. It was not uncommon that war weary men collapsed, perhaps this explained his behavior. There was virtually no control at the fort other than by the officers under him. They said when he arrived in Natchez he did not even order closed quarters and allowed both Black and White troops to wander the town and seek shelter anywhere they chose, often to the danger and inconvenience of Natchez's citizens. This resulted in numerous fires, arrests, fights and even the deaths of both citizens and troops.

Some of the things I had seen were appalling. Many leading citizens were detained or arrested. We saw them marched, forcibly taken, and locked in the stockade. The rumor was that they could only be released by ransom. The confusion among the officers was rampant. In the midst of the continued building of the fort about them, a broken chain of command allowed slackers to shirk. Supplies were not provided or distributed properly, or disappeared into thieves' pockets.

Desertion from some of the other companies was rampant and I wondered what the root cause was? What problem was turning these soldiers sour? No, I would not have an opportunity to speak of recruiting questions with the staff of Brigadier General McDevlin.

Nothing in my three year's experience at war had provided this former private with the experience, authority or insight I needed to recruit. I wandered the camp looking for the right White officer to talk to. Then at a drill area, I saw a Captain I had met briefly. I had observed him as a proper, military example.

Major Howard was about forty, a stout man who had commanded the Sixth African Mississippi Volunteers for over a year, so I knew he had as much experience as might be had at the fort. He was standing near the edge of the drill field watching a Lieutenant marching men to and fro across a well-tramped clay area. I knew the record of the Sixth had been excellent which spoke well of their command.

It would be to my advantage to have more contact with this veteran military commander. Some of the men of the Sixth African Descent would be named as a part of the Fifty-eighth Colored which was about to be formed. Many of the new officers that had been recruited would become a part of the Fifty-eighth. The army made an effort to incorporate and intersperse our new men, veteran leaders and soldiers.

Respectfully, I approached from the rear and stood at attention behind him for some moments gathering my thoughts. "Sir, may I speak with you a moment?"

Major Howard grunted and grumbled, "Just a moment." He left me standing for about ten minutes.

As the troops finished drill he turned. "Forgive me, Captain, the new men are having some trouble finding a pattern of movement with the drilling. I suggest that drilling is the first step to making the Colored feel like soldiers and part of a military unit. If they can't march together, they cannot shoot as a unit either." Then the man cocked his head to one side as though to inquire what I wanted.

"Sir, I have been pretty inactive this last week. It seems that I am to recruit about fifty soldiers. These, with some of the Sixth assigned will begin to form Company K. My attempts to recruit have not been fruitful and I seem to be at loose ends. Perhaps you could offer some advice."

Major Howard stared directly into my eyes for long moments to my great discomfort. Then he turned heel and over his shoulder requested me to follow him.

He quickly strode toward his tent with me dogging behind. He grunted to me without turning. "Green, bad case of green," then he gaffed, "green with Blacks gets you nowhere," he chuckled.

Sitting on a campstool, he squinted at the unbearable morning sun, then he stood and moved the stool into the shade on one side of the tent.

Slumping on the seat he loosened his collar and shirt buttons, and leaned back. "Get a seat, boy."

I moved a stump from the sun into the shade and sat on it facing him.

"Who are you, where you from and what unit were you with?"

"Captain William Hunter, I have been with the Fifteenth Illinois Volunteers since '61."

This he mulled. "Good regiment. You come down from Vicksburg?"

"Yes, sir." I snapped the reply, trying to be courteous.

Then Major Howard took the lead "Most of us had at least some military school before the war and we still don't know a damn thing. This war is something you learn, you sense it, then you do it. Coming as a private, who has taken commands to become an officer, giving commands and taking responsibility is a major leap. The confounded Black troops are not like anything anyone has known before, but if you get a chance to watch them fight, like my troops have, you'll know what for. They are, on the whole, good men and good soldiers."

"Sir, I had hoped to see McDevlin or his staff for advise."

With my comment the officer spat and snarled, "Be lucky if you never seen him. The man is no officer and not much of a man either. If we get the job done in this war it will be in spite of men like him. I tell you, keep yourself out of his way and most of all keep your men away from him."

Laughing warmly he added, "If you ever get any men, that is. That bastard is evil—but being a loyal officer, I never said that."

Beginning my tale of woe, I confessed, "I took one of your sergeants and for several days tried to use handbills to recruit. I believed they did that in the East. I failed dearly. The sergeant says he has an idea to recruit by going to Sunday gatherings, but says I must get the families safe or the men won't come."

"Is it a good idea to go out in the woods to where the Negroes worship? What do we do for the families? Is there more to offer the families than the Kraal? How do I find recruits if I do not try this plan?"

Major Howard replied, "Well, other officers, Blacks and assigned recruiters have done it lots of ways. Some are good plans, some bad. A couple just kidnapped them. Some recruiters locked men up until they 'decided to enlist. ' Most lie about the length of enlistment and family safety. Most just have to find them, and yes, take the families to the contraband camp or some Freedman's home. If possible they find a place for the families to work for pay or hide them in cabins in the woods. If you intend to move the whole family then steal some horses or mules, and take supplies for the families."

"If the men are willing to fight, and you carry their people away to safety, they are grateful and give you real loyalty. The only thing slavery gives these people is a deeper loyalty to and need of family—more than the two of us can ever understand."

"If you treat these Negroes badly they will desert, disobey or destroy the general morale. These are the deadly 'Ds' of a command." The man squinted and looked me in the eye with little change of expression. "Young man, you ever personally know a Black man?"

I had to reply, "No sir, I have not, only Sergeant Anderson with whom I have attempted to recruit."

"These men are a strange commodity, but really just like Whites. Some are lazy, some bright, most brave but all are hungry to end their ugly way of life. They never had to decide things for themselves and sometimes lack confidence. To be changed from a life that they have always known is a real powerful event."

Laughing the older man chided, "It is much like you suddenly being an officer." Again, he gaffed. The Major's face showed little change of expression, and revealed only the guttural sounds of ragged humor.

I looked at light grey of his eyes peering from under heavy, dark brows which were a strong contrast to his white, streaked, collar length beard. The man struck me as direct, strong and knowledgeable. The effect of his personality was comforting to me, although not calming. I still could not picture myself, dressed in my shiny buttons and blue uniform, ever having any success in this otherworldly situation.

"You have an assignment. Listen to Sergeant Anderson, I knew he was with you. He knows how to do the job in a way that no White man can. What a nigra wants and who they are, of course Anderson knows these things. Next, be firm and demanding of the troops, expecting the best. Give them what they have never had, a uniform, a gun and a little schooling. But the quality that is most important to offer your soldiers is hope and self-respect. If you can do that they will give you everything they have to give, no holds barred."

He continued, "When this war is over be able to look them and yourself in the eyes and know that you tried your best. You and I are tired of this war, but what must men who have lived for generations in the hell of slavery feel? How tired must they be? In my heart I believe we are close to the end of this war. I dream of my own home. If we were to lose this war, these soldiers of color have no home, no hope, no life. They risk all in this war and I do mean all."

"My respect for these men has grown since I took command. In the sick season they die of the fever and I walk by their stacked, dead bodies. Those dead people have come so close to real freedom, but will never to see it. I wonder who and where their parents are. I wonder where their wives and children are, and how they are faring with their men dead."

"Yet, I know I cannot really understand in my heart where they have been, who they have been and what they will become. It will be to your everlasting good conscience to care for them, lead them well and protect their welfare. Not all the officers do so, I fear. The abuses, dishonesty and mismanagement of their training and treatment in service is a disgusting travesty. I beg you not to become a part of that, thus heaping agony on their pain. Should you live through this war, live as a man of conscience."

My comfort at his advice and my amazement at his words left me dumfounded. I sat looking at a scuff on the toe of one of my new boots for some time. Raising my eyes, I found his steel gaze fixed on my own face. Words escaped me and I was still overwhelmed by the task and responsibility ahead of me.

After a moment the older man pensively, in a reminiscent tone, began, "I was a brave, young lad, glad of the opportunity of a good education and raising my status when I went to the military academy. The classes, the drills, the weapons and strategy all increased my confidence and courage. Afterwards, there were two boring assignments in Washington D.C. followed by a very unproductive station in St.Louis. There the politics unwound every knot I tried to tie. I left the service and taught at a college for a while, married and had children. Then this damned war began. I was hesitant to leave my family, but full of foolish courage. I knew I could probably end the war in months, and saw the adversary as less than able or strong. Then, on the battlefield, I saw death and the stench of violence that was like a purple fog blinding humanity. The debris of hope lay in the rotting stench and the bravado in me melted. The foe was brilliant, determined, courageous and fighting a battle with everything that they had. I wondered would anyone win?"

"Then came this command. No matter the war, I knew I needed to be a part of giving these men freedom and hope. With almost no exceptions, my men have met my expectations. Nothing but pain and destruction will ever come from this war except, I hope, a new life for this tawny people."

"How many battles have there been for you Captain Hunter? You have seen a dozen battles then Shiloh and Vicksburg. You have marched thousands of miles, so I do not presume to tell you about battle or war. But I would presume to tell you that perhaps you could find at least some meaning here by meeting the tasks and goals you have accepted. Becoming an instant officer is a small reward, even if you may have done it only for your ego. God willing, you will be up to the job. You're dismissed Captain Hunter, good luck."

I quickly stood, saluted and went back to my quarters. Taking out my small leather bound diary I wrote some of my impressions of the quest the Major had assigned to me. Then, mulling with a full pipe, I began making my plans for tomorrow.

That Friday morning I rose early, a soft mist was rising to the hilltop from the river. The world was pink in the sunrise and the usual musk smell of moldering vegetation was as fragrant as sage. I took my tin plate and cup and secured some gruel and coffee, and then lounged at a trestle with half a dozen other officers listening to war gossip and news from homes far away, but did not join the talk. I did not linger but went to where the enlisted were eating, and called for Sergeant Anderson.

While he was preparing, I went to the quartermaster with trepidation. Although it was not my first visit, I had heard from other officers of the frustration I could expect. Taking a deep breath, I strode into the dank, dark interior of a huge shed with several rooms. Here were stored goods, barrels, bags and cases stacked to the rafters. Sitting at a table toward the back were several men, including a corporal. A dozen Black service men stripped to the waist bustled about loading, unloading and storing materials.

"I am here to make a requisition."

The fat corporal, perspiring generously from reddened cheeks, looked at me with some degree of arrogance for he knew his own power. He pushed a paper and pencil toward me. I wrote for five minutes listing the goods I wished and then pushed the paper back across the table.

Glancing, he pushed it back. "I need your name, unit and purpose of request."

Intimidated, I scribbled the additional information. Then I tried to resume my composure, pretended determination and pushed the paper back toward the corporal.

Quickly he scanned the list. "Don't know captain."

I stood straighter, "Corporal, this material is needed by Sunday morning." He paused and looked me in the eye.

I assumed an impervious, although phony, air. "Sunday," I repeated firmly.

Nonplused, he stared.

"All of it," I firmly stated, then I turned and strode out.

My first major quartermaster experience was complete. Frankly, I was still uncertain that I would receive few, if any results.

I went to the prearranged area, found the Sergeant and my horse. I had ordered that the man saddle it. At a slow gait, I walked the gelding south along the road toward Natchez as he followed and we arrived on the river walk. Here and there citizens were moving about or working at early gardening so as to avoid the heat that would arrive later in the day. Passing the now empty slave market warehouse, I snuck a sideways glance inside, the reality of it chilled me.

Turning east we approached the courthouse area. There was more foot traffic in this part of town, wagons were moving goods and a few carriages were tied to posts or offloading people at the boardwalk or by churches. We slowly traveled the streets, this time with a new eye to study the Negroes who were gathered or working. I studied each male especially close, evaluating him. In a very quiet tone, I suggested our destination and pointed out possible recruits several times to the sergeant. Many, upon closer inspection, I felt were too old, young or crippled.

In a highly haughty tone Sergeant Anderson stated, "You not be too picky."

I felt the rebuff of my recent failures. After about an hour, we headed back westerly, past the mansion which had become headquarters and on toward Natchez Under the Hill. The stench, noise and bustle there were, as always, unrestrained.

As we passed an alley near a tavern, with a brave voice my companion said, "Here, turn here, an tie up de horse." The enlisted man walked well behind me. We two continued down the short space between buildings to find half a dozen Blacks lounging in tattered clothing. They stared and stood as though about to break and run.

"You wait," Sergeant Anderson demanded and he approached them alone. Moving them back behind the building the whole group disappeared. For twenty minutes I waited. Peeking around a corner, the sergeant finally waved me to join them. These men seemed suspicious but on encouragement from my companion I made my offer, remembering to promise security for their families.

Arrangements were made to meet them on Sunday where a number of families gathered at a clearing downriver. This was the regular meeting place for worship and fellowship. Not all but most of the planters, gave their people this time each week.

Finding only one more opportunity in Under the Hill to make a recruiting contact, we made our way back to the city. At a vegetable market we were able to speak with a group of five women, sending the message with them back to their families and fellows. That afternoon we rode among the contraband and were able, here and there, to pass the word. We inquired about sanctuaries where we would meet and make contact. The underground would send the message, despite their illiteracy, communication among the Colored was both fast and accurate.

Thus began my recruiting. On Saturday, with a group of twenty soldiers, we rode to a large plantation north of the fort and commandeered three horses and a mule. I selected a half dozen of the seasoned troops for the next day.

Sunday morning at dawn, I rose and went to the quartermaster. He made me wait on a pretense, as a show of power. I had my troops help move the goods outside. My men began loading the supplies onto our horses and mules. As I supervised the loading there was a skinny soldier, stripped to waist, wrestling some ground corn in a bag onto a mule. My eyes fell on his amber back. Forty or fifty grey welts the size of my finger slashed across his back in monstrous zigzags. The revulsion at whip scars swept bile into my throat. As the man turned, I also saw part of one ear was missing and a large scar lay on his face in the branded letter W.

Viewing my bounty, I took inventory then strode back into the dark shed purposefully.

The corporal was unaware of my presence at first. I asked about the canvas I had requested and he stammered, "I...." "The canvas," I demanded. After a moment, he said, "Maybe we have some." In a few minutes he returned with a fat bolt of the fabric.

That Sunday when I returned from my rendezvous, I brought with me three men, eight women and a child. Their ages ranged from three to eighty years of age. We arranged a small canvas shelter for the families at the north end of the contraband camp. Then I proudly rode into camp with my troop of three soldiers; a sixteen-year-old, skinny boy; a forty-year-old fellow with one eye who had a immense barrel chest; and a handsome, tall man of twenty-five who carried himself like a king.

As I watched, a Corporal stripped them. They threw their shreds of clothing on the ground outside, lice and all. Used to no privacy, they stood naked as a doctor looked at teeth, eyes (all five of them), examined them for cuts, studied joints, teeth and all other parts. When they turned, each one of them had whip scars of varying severity. These were located anywhere from heel to neck. The men were sent to bathe and wash their hair with lye soap. I sent Sergeant Anderson to retrieve the new uniforms, although shoes would have to come later.

In one hour I viewed them again. They were renewed, proud and more than emancipated—they now felt free. Each stood tall. I overlooked any flaws they might have because of my pride in them. I felt like a new father.

## Chapter 7
# My Men

Next Sunday, I would return to the same meeting place; sure that the message would have been passed throughout the Black community. As my success recruiting former slaves grew, I became more confident and soon was filled with special insights. Before long I could be assigned regulars, my company was in the process of being formed. I was, in fact, finally feeling like an officer.

I would begin assigning and ordering the drills. We would start classes to teach the soldiers how to read and write. In a couple weeks, I would again confront the quartermaster to find them weapons, uniforms and, hopefully, shoes.

Into early Autumn, the recruiting and training continued. I was ever more comfortable dealing with the soldiers. Their passion to show their courage and manhood, and their desire to learn made them willing troops.

Two men were drummed out of another company because of their continual drunkenness and disobedience. It was a dramatic event where all the men stood in review as the two solemnly proceeded around the parade field to the ominous tattoo of drums. Stripped of all military insignia and gear, and in humiliation, they marched off the field, no longer soldiers. I feared for my own troops.

The continuation of family problems among my men was wearing. Food, housing and illness of relatives required my continual attention and caused incessant worry among the troops. Several men reported their families, who lived nearby, were threatened and punished because their men were now a part of the Union army. One old grandmother had her home pulled down over her head.

At this time, three men in my company are critically ill. This was probably because of the living conditions in the barracks, which had been placed on the riverbank so near the Kraal. The Kraal is a source of many disasters like fires, violence and of course sickness. In a month and a half, four men of the regiment had died of illness. The knowledgeable said, in the yellow fever time it would be catastrophic. There would be unnumbered deaths of the Colored enlisted and their families.

Ironically, these problems also allowed me to better know and assess each of the family men in Company K, as they came to me with problems or questions. The single men, both the very old and the young, were less apt to draw attention to themselves. The numbers of soldiers at the fort had grown to almost 4,000, a number so large that even in my own regiment there were many soldiers that I was less than familiar with.

Sergeant Anderson was assigned to see that the enlisted men might be taught to read and write. Many of the non-commissioned White soldiers accepted this task, as did several of the Colored troops like Alexander Turner. Anderson kept me in touch with the individual progress of many of our men.

I watched the soldiers closely in drill and rifle practice. During these observations I could pick out the personalities and aptitudes of my assigned troops. Expecting to eventually go to battle with my men made me very conscious of being able to assign and put confidence in those who were showing the most leadership potential. Likewise, those soldiers who were slothful or troublemakers did not miss my attention and I recorded such names in my journal.

The increase of men under my authority made me ever more responsible for their needs. Knowing in advance that getting needed supplies would be difficult made it no easier to requisition clothing, especially boots. Only half as many rifles were issued to the troops as were needed. At least once a week, I made my quartermaster visit, usually to receive only a portion of my requests.

Never the less, despite the many problems the Fifty-eighth was slowly growing more cohesive as a unit. The former Sixth troops were already soldiers. Probably most would have preferred to remain with their old regiment, rather than be transferred to the Fifty-eighth as it began forming. These men held themselves as a group, almost apart from my men.

An inspector came to see the new fort. He was critical that our construction was not as it should be. Planning was flawed, although the overlook of the river made it a proper choice of location. The fort was too large, in his opinion, the fort proper covered too much space and required far too many men to man it.[15]

There was also much illness among the officers at the fort. A man I had for some time known, Lieutenant Daniel N. Clark, of Illinois was struck down. I had spent a brief, but close, period with him after Shiloh where we fought together. He had enlisted as a private in Company B of the Fifteenth and had been advanced to lieutenant, in the same rapid manner as my own commissioning. He was first admitted to hospital with congestive chills and I visited him twice, but on the third day when I arrived, September 23, I was told he had died. There was a hollow acceptance of his death in my heart. The mood was almost that of negative hope. *I should have known he would die.* I told myself I would also probably die as well. *Just accept it and go onward.* My optimism was dashed for some time afterward.

We were given a week's notice that we would be sending half our men and some of the Sixth African Descent to Gillespie plantation on the Louisiana side.

Skirmishes and operations in the area were to continue. In early September and mid-October, several expeditions of other units left the fort on forays. Skirmishes had occurred in outlying countryside. Many of these transpired while the troops were in the field. The agitation and risk to the civilian population was continual. Their safety and civic order was part of our responsibility in Company K.

Over the entire town, hung an evil ax, adding to the fear of Union control—it was the possibility that prominent hostages might be held for ransom under threat of execution. This was the gossip I heard about Brigadier General McDevlin's deviousness.

My own men were ordered to sleep near the Kraal in barracks down the 300 steps by Brown's garden. Work was still ongoing with the fort's construction. The troops had to be accounted for at dusk and dawn. They performed drills, gun practice and various assignments. Families would visit on Sundays which, although it was a day of duty, was more lax.

One Sunday morning, as I finished my pipe and coffee I looked across the parade ground. A large bodied, tall, coffee colored, civilian man in his twenties walked from one group of troops to another. Suddenly, with shoulders back and his head held high, he strode directly toward me across the long field. He stopped about five feet from me and looked me in the eye. His very manner had dignity. The directness of his posture was not as most of my men when I first met them.

"I be Matthew Hinter," he stood silent, his gaze unbending.

"Yes, Matthew," I looked at him with curiosity.

"I come be a soldier," his directness left me somewhat uncertain.

"Do you know about the pay and enlistment?"

The young man looked very determined. "No suh, I jus wan to be a soldier," he spoke flatly.

"Very well, welcome." As I rose, I looked at his strong broad shoulders;

he was bare to the waist, barefoot, and his trousers were worn. Assessing his health and mental condition, I congratulated myself on this powerful, new recruit. He was one of the more impressive men I had enrolled.

I led the way across the open field. Remembering my prescribed duties, I questioned, "Do you have family?"

"No suh. I be a new slave 'round here. Come from Virginia, a year ago. Left all my family behind."

"Go to the mess hall over there," waving in the direction of some benches outside a building just off the parade field. "Get some food. Later, we will go to the doctor for an examination. I will enroll you and you will get a uniform of your own. I will send someone for you in an hour."

He stood a moment, still erect. There was a defiance gleaming in his eyes. Then he turned on his heel and strode back across the parade ground toward the benches and food.

When he turned, my eyes widened. Although I had seen scars, never were they fresh wounds. Across his rich, black back slashed three, ragged tears. Two ripped from shoulder to waist and a short, but deep, cut bisected these.

Judging by the clot of blood on the rear of his trousers, the two vertical wounds appeared to extend to his buttocks. In a grotesque X, the cut that slashed across the other two was at an angle just above the waist, blood was still slowly flowing in several red rivers to his waist band. Slabs of dark skin and white tissue hung from these. A wave of nausea washed over me, and sweat broke out on my brow. Looking about to see if anyone else had seen, I found myself alone. I experienced a surge of helplessness. Walking to the west, I stopped on the river cliff. Then, I slumped to the ground looking at the dirt at my feet. I felt the revulsion turn to guilt. *What manner of man would do this. Why?*

Then I remembered my grandfather, and before him my great grandfather. They had slaves, how often had they or their overseers done this, or worse. Even a rebellious stallion would not be thus treated. *Could I, too, be a part of this cruelty?* I was certainly a part of a nation that had allowed calling fellow humans "slave." This policy had meant not only beating, but raping, tearing families apart and keeping people in hovels. In death, they would often be dumped like dead animals for their fellows find and bury.

I knew some of our officers treated these Black soldiers little better. Many White soldiers showed the Negroes disgust and belittlement in their every action. These malignant officers screamed insults at the Black soldiers and gave them filthy duty without recognition. Often the men were ridiculed in front of everyone or given rude instructions, only to publicly allow others to laugh at them or physically mistreat them in the name of discipline.

Why am I here, in this position? What can I do? Am I no better than those other callous White officers?

I had to admit, I had taken the commission mainly for better pay, my ego and more prestige. Remembering Matthew's defiant eyes, intense with the heat in them that burnt into my heart. When I had interacted with the troops they were not men to me, but my responsibility. Of course, they were not my equals. I observed these people as strange, and in a unique position to follow my orders.

I remembered the talk with Major Howard, his defense, consideration and respect of the Coloreds. *Could I say the same?*

Guilt made me nauseous again. Gathering the bitter spit that filled the back of my tongue, I spat it out. Looking down the cliff toward the contraband village and the long steps, I strove to see the people I was slowly learning to view as a community.

*How had I understood them till now?* They had the same fear, love, loyalty, joy and pain as I. *Must they, too, feel the same loss fear and disorientation that my mother, father and family felt as I entered this war? Was this how Negro relatives felt when their son, husband, lover or father served the Union?*

My family felt pride. *What of these, whose loved ones for the first time stood as independent people, with their soldiers holding out the opportunity to keep them all free? If failing in this battle, what fate would befall them all?* Pondering the weight and gravity of responsibility each Colored soldier carried, the cold sweat again beaded on my face where it itched and stung. I sat over an hour before I gained some small composure.

Upon returning to the fort, I sent a soldier to find the doctor. Another went to search for Matthew. As I had so often done while enlisting men, I entered the hospital and walked to a young clerk seated at a table. Taking a seat beside him, I said nothing.

Officers were required to see five muster rolls and two enlistment papers be prepared for each soldier.[16] This time the enrollment was not my personal success of finding a new recruit. This enlistment had become of import not only to the recruit, but this time for myself, as well. After a while the doctor came in, removed his jacket, snapped his blue suspenders and rolled up his sleeves. Coming to the table the tall, the wiry, middle-aged man nodded. He rested his behind on one end of the boards of the rough tabletop.

The doctor was humming under his breath; the slight movement of his mustache seemed hypnotic in its rhythm. Hundreds of times he had done this exam for enlistment. He had even completed my own when I entered the Fifty-eighth. *What would his reaction be to Matthew's horrible wounds?*

*Was I still a coward after so many battles?* I was loath to warn the doctor to the damage this new man would display, so I sat in silence. After quite a wait, the door darkened across the room. Matthew stood in the door, he weighed more than 200 pounds and was over six foot tall. As he stood there, an eastern light threw his long, exaggerated shadow across the floor and over the table in the small anteroom.

My breath caught, unexpelled in my chest. As I released it, he crossed the room toward us. The huge man stood quietly in front of the simple table. The air was filled with the odor of dust, sweat and blood from his body. His solemn glance moved between the three of us. I looked at the doctor who also seemed taken aback by the man's presence and carriage. The doctor rose from his perch and stood, turning full face toward the young man.

Clearing my throat I asked, "Matthew, you want to enlist as a Union soldier?"

"Yes sa," his voice was clear and strong.

"Then you must sign this paper with your mark. Do you write?"

"No sa." The clerk held out the paper with his left hand and dipping a pen with his right he extended it to the richly, browned man.

I stopped him, "Wait, I want to read this to him." The chunky, freckled clerk looked up quizzically, knowing I had never done this before.

Continuing I told the enlistee in clear, simple terms what he was committed and obligated to do. I explained what we expected of our soldiers. Somehow it seemed to me doing this would add dignity to this event by telling this wounded man exactly what he was signing.

"Three years?" he questioned.

I nodded affirmation then and added, "We will give you a uniform and a gun when we can obtain one. You will be paid thirteen dollars a month."

Regretfully, I wondered how many of these men really knew what they had signed.

With little pause, Matthew reached for the pen, and holding it awkwardly, made a scratching mark, while inadvertently moving a large drip across the page with the heel of his hand.

Reaching toward the man, I asked, "May I help you?"

He nodded slightly.

I held his dark, chapped hand in my own tanned one and led the pen across the mark in a contrary manner forming an X.

"Now the doctor will examine you." Moving toward the center of the room the doctor pointed at a spot a few feet from him. "Come here and take off all your clothing."

I turned in my seat to view the scene. The new enlisted man was facing a wall to my left and did as told. "Open your mouth," the doctor intoned his usual order.

Matthew obeyed as though this were an ordinary request. The doctor peered in, "All teeth, front on right chipped." He rattled on to the clerk.

Taking a measure he called, "Six foot, three inches, broad and heavy build." The doctor held each of Matthew's arms, checking for damage he examined the fingers and knuckles on each hand.

The clerk read off, "Age?"

"Moen twenty, name be Matthew Hinter."

"Family?" came the next routine question.

The recruit answered, "Got a granma in Ginya"

"Had yellow fever?" Was the next question.

"Nope."

"Been in jail?" Was the next query.

"Nope," answered Matthew

Without looking up the clerk asked, "Skill?"

"Don' know what you mean Massa."

"What jobs do you know how to do? What are you good at doing?" I questioned quietly.

The dark young man replied, "Farming and horses."

"When did you leave the plantation?"

"Las night, befo mornin," was Matthew's answer.

Standing to relieve my own tension, I glanced at the written record and gasped in silence. The clerk had written Matthew Hunter.

What did this mean? Why was his name Hunter? Was he from our family plantation? Somehow were we tied together in history?

The doctor continued to look into the man's large eyes, at his legs and between his toes.

Then I heard the command, "Turn around." My eyes flashed upward.

A high pitched gasp escaped the doctor, causing the round-eyed clerk to look up.

"My God," the doctor stood, stunned.

This time I studied the wound, which did in fact, extend to the man's buttocks, his nakedness somehow making the wounds even more grotesque.

Recovering his composure, the doctor straightened, "Young man, follow me to the infirmary. We will care for these wounds."

The shirt-sleeved doctor and the wounded, naked, Black man walked toward the door at the end of the room that led to the hospital. The wide-eyed clerk silently looked at me in shock.

The haunting experience held me, in quiet moments for several days as I went about my duties. Then one morning, I saw Private Hunter sitting in the shade near the hospital, his feet still bare but wearing clean, new blue trousers, with the suspenders hanging loosely at his side. Fresh white bandages locked his shoulders and wound about his chest.

I approached, "Are you feeling better?"

"Yes su." This time there was some cheer in his reply and he made a motion to stand.

Shaking my head, I motioned him to stay seated. I was looking at his feet, "You have shoes yet?"

"No su."

"I will see about that soon," I tried to estimate the size of his feet. "Did you get any more of the uniform?"

"Yes su, I get a jacket too. I come to be a soldier. When I start?"

"Not until the doctor says you are recovered and ready. Eat, rest and become strong."

Looking at me with intense directness, he firmly, slowly asked, "When I get my gun?"

Simultaneously thinking of both the deficiencies of the commissary and of his wounds, I paused. Then I answered, "It may be a while, but you will get a gun and we will teach you to use it."

"You are now Private Hunter." I started to move away but at a thought I turned. "I was Private Hunter, also, until recently," I moved off on my previously intended errand.

Many of my men were being sent to Monmouth, a plantation, east of the city. Several area farms and homes had been taken by the Union, and were being farmed for the army's welfare. They were now sources of income and food for troops and the Kraal.

Five White soldiers were assigned to the home plantation. Often the Black soldiers would be working at the same jobs they had while enslaved. They were not slaves nor yet soldiers. Their humiliation and disappointment was absolute. In an effort to ease the discomfort, I allowed a few of their families to accompany them and provide housekeeping services for the troops.

The work crews, both Black and White, began with the stolen harvest of the previous owner, proceeded to prepare ground, or arrange lodging inside the home for the officers and non coms. The enlisted men lived in tents in the old slave quarters or raised a few simple shacks of their own.

My sorrow was that the education and military training was put on hold for those assigned to work on the plantations. I rode out several times a week to receive requests and to oversee delivery of provisions, then carried them back to my superiors and wrote many reports. My own Midwest farming knowledge helped some, but the land and climate were so different. Frequently, I called on the knowledge of the very men we had freed. Now we only sought to use them again, like mules and slaves. Only the whip had been removed, military reprimand had replacing it.

There continued to be a tiny trickle of volunteers coming to the new

Fifty-eighth. A few came because the other soldiers had sought them out and persuaded them to join. One day as I left the fort, I was introduced to a new driver. He leapt from the wagon and saluted smartly.

When he looked up, I noticed the twinkle in his eye and looked more closely. As I examined the man I suddenly remembered several months ago I had met him. During the pre-surrender at Vicksburg he had only worn a Union cap, today his uniform was complete.

Observing his stripes, I nodded and smiled "Private Murphy, it will be good to have you with the Fifty-eighth."

He saluted again, "Su, I be goin' to Monmouth."

Since I would be going that direction, the private accompanied me. We visited as I rode beside the wagon loaded with supplies. The few months since we sat under that tree had been remarkable for both of us. Now I was an officer, and he was fully a soldier.

The men I oversaw had daily duties and the White sergeants or non-coms kept me informed. I would often walk about the fort in the evening to see the progress of classes teaching my men to write their names and do numbers. That was about all the educational advancement most soldiers made, but there were some that found Bibles or books, and struggled late at night to learn to read.

As the rifles became available, we practiced with them. The weapons were usually unloaded during drills but we were beginning live target practice. There were those whose diligence paid off quickly, making them good marksmen. Several of my men had been experienced hunters prior to joining service and were truly expert marksmen.

Several of the men of the Fifty-eighth had been previously hired out for pay by their owners. They were skilled in many trades like blacksmith, harness makers, carpenters and masons. All this labor we put to their trades about the fort.

As I walked among the men, I always keep an eye open for Matthew Hunter. His duty assignment was to the stables, he seemed skilled in caring for the horses and masterful in handling them. Occasionally, I would look up to see him quietly watching me.

One day, needing a horse to ride into town, I went by the stable. I found him brushing a fine mare down. "Is that horse ready?"

"Yes su," he answered respectfully.

"Would you saddle her?" I watched him at the task and decided to ask what had been on my mind for some time. "Are you from Hunter plantation here?"

"No su."

"How have you come to be named Hunter?"

"My family been here a long time. We come from Hunter in Virginia."

A new question was raised in my heart. This one would need an inquiry of my father in my next letter.

Just after harvest, my father's letters said that Spenser's granddaughter in Natchez was finally returning to her own home. Her grandfather inquired if I had met the woman.

That Sunday at the church I lingered until everyone was gone except the priest. I explained the information my father had written about his concern for Isaac Spenser and his family in Illinois. This time the clergyman did not brush me off.

His eyes showed recognition, "May I ask, young man, why you are inquiring?"

Looking him directly in the eye I honestly replied, "Out of genuine concern for my neighbor's family, sir."

He seemed to mull this then replied, "The widow Scothorne is indeed in mourning for her husband. Her loss is especially tragic, as her family is not living in the city, and her tiny baby is also gone."

"You can report she is dearly cared for by her husband's family and is well." There was an air of reticence that told me this would be all the information I would receive. His protection of the woman and her in-laws was solid.

Taking my hat, I placed it on my head, "Thank you and goodbye," and I quietly departed.

The following Sunday, when I attended services, there was only slightly more warmth in the priest's handshake. A harvest picnic was planned and I yearned to go. This congregation was as close to a normal life and home as I could find here in Mississippi. The excessive coolness of the people, with their reserved politeness seemed like a barrier that could not be breached.

My human emptiness after three bloody, tired years made me willing to face any rejection just to have some hint of normalcy. Again this week, I stayed after church until the congregation left. Running behind, I caught up to the Episcopal priest as he hurried to his house.

First, I spoke of the weather, finding it hard to breech the subject. "Reverend I would like to attend the picnic, if it is acceptable. It would be an honor to provide the coffee." Knowing how scarce supplies are in Natchez, I felt such a gift might pave my way. With a little bribery at the fort, I knew I could secure a generous supply of coffee.

The awkwardness of his reply was proof that I had put him in a difficult position, of course I knew that under military law he could not block my attendance. But I also knew I was not really welcome. "Of course you may attend," he stated in a stilted manner.

The next week, accompanied by a White corporal from Illinois, and armed with coffee in my saddlebag, I attended church. After services we moved west down the hill to a park on the bank above the river. The first Natchez settlers had planted trees in a ceremony there which were now huge and spreading.

Planks had been placed on trestles for makeshift tables, and the ladies, alighted from carriages, to begin to cover and fill them with food. After making an inquiry, I went to a fire pit where a large coffeepot was waiting for delivery of the coffee. The preparations took about an hour; that allowed the strolling parishioners time to walk about the park and visit with each other.

The few Black parishioners who always sat in the balcony were sitting at the far end of the park, playing with children and visiting. The women were busy unpacking food they had prepared, and putting plates onto their table.

The atmosphere was all I had wished. The corporal and I leaned against a tree, silent and staring in wonder at what was almost 'normal' life. The children, oblivious, ran and played. Once, a ball rolled to our feet and amazed children shyly smiled as I threw it back to them.

Because of my presence for the last three months, several of the older women actually nodded at me as they passed. There were the usual stealthy glances over shoulders from groups of men who lay about the ground or were visiting. These men stood in groups, bending like willows as they talked.

Remembering the lavish feasts in Illinois at church outings, I realized this one was different. The community was poor and in bondage. Their sharing was from want not plenty. The table was lovely, with pretty bowls and platters, garden flowers and sparkling serving silver. There were bowls of beans, lots of vegetables and some apple cakes. There were real biscuits that were soft and fragrant, which was remarkable to me after a continual hardtack diet. Someone had provided a turkey, but conscious of the scarcity, the parishioners took small bits and I would pass it by entirely.

After prayer, the men began to pass around the tables with plates and forks, and we followed behind them. Then came the women who shared their plates with the children. The food was eaten with gusto. The eyes of those sitting near where the two of us ate focused on ground. These people carefully mentioned nothing of war or any debatable subject within our hearing. With the atmosphere created by the command of Brigadier General McDevlin, and the control of military law the citizens were most wary.

As the eating slowly ended, the pastor came toward where we were squatting. "Captain, we appreciate the coffee. Thank you."

I offered, "Please keep any that is left for yourself." Then, remarkably, he gave me a smile, not a warm one, but a smile.

As the corporal and I rested on the grass, a trio of young women mounted a bandstand and sang a lively song. Next, a fiddler played a toe-tapping round. Several of the children were called up to recite a group of bible verses. With the babble of voices of varying ages, the children recited with Southern accents; it was hard for me to understand all their words. Yet, their adorable visages won the hearts of all present, ours as well.

There were several very young, flirting couples. *Would the emptiness of my own heart ever be filled?*

These youths haunted me and filled my homesick heart with pain. The corporal and I rode back to quarters late in the afternoon, very slowly and very quietly. What filled him I do not know, what filled me was pain. My real life was gone so long. My home and all the people I love so far away. Families and children who easily smiled at me or spoke to me were hundreds of miles away.

Would this war ever end?

In October, I received my permanent assignment at the fort.

Following the protocol of Order 85 we were to try to create order among the thousands of freed Blacks in the city.[17]

Our instructions were:

1. Freed Negroes under protection of the Army would be put into labor but are to stay within our lines unless in military service, or leased to plantations. Servants may use passes to proceed to any Northern point.
2. Abandoned cotton may be harvested by Negroes, one fourth going to commission, remainder to said Negro.
3. Superintendents of camps shall encourage Negroes to support themselves, remaining in camps only temporarily.
4. Pay to Colored troops will be post dated for pay purpose to time of enlistment.
5. Nominations for officers for vacant spots are encouraged.
6. Non-commissioned officers may be selected as need by commanding officers.

One morning I was kept at the fort with yet, another battle with this commissary. The damned Enfield rifles were slow coming for my men. The muzzle loaders were better than none but the frustration wore at me. I promised my men the weapons would arrive soon. Most of them were ready and practiced in their use. *When might we be called to go to battle?* An attack by Confederates while we are in such straights might be disaster;

small skirmishes continually erupted here and there all around Natchez. My troops needed to be ready.

Finally, about ten that morning, I began my ride north toward the home plantation to review the operation. It was a two-hour ride at a slow pace, one I had been making three times a week for over a month and a half. The landscape was forever of interest to me because it was so beautiful and unique. I observed the plants and trees closely. Occasional small game scurried in the woods and on the trail; birds flew and chattered about their business. In my mind, I would sometimes play at imagining my Grandfather coming here almost seventy years ago. I imagined what he might have seen as he rode this way, for there were plantations that had been here since Spanish times. As I rode on, I first passed Weymouth, a lovely home that sits at the road to the cemetery and had been there for years. Another plantation, the Gardens, was a lovely home built during the Spanish period, about the same time as when my family arrived here generations ago. I would play at a conversation with ancestors—full of questions. No matter, I come from Illinois and his roots were here in Mississippi. *Perhaps, someday I will visit Byou Sara.*

Suddenly my daydreams were interrupted, ahead of me, near the Natchez cemetery was a black, one-horse carriage. On the narrow, rutted road I needed to pass cautiously. There was an old, Colored man driving. Inside the curtained carriage I could barely see a woman with a black, veiled hat. I tipped my hat and pushed my mare to a trot as I went on my way. Just a bit farther along, I realized I did not hear the creaking carriage and glanced over my shoulder. The carriage had turned into the cemetery and was headed east down the main road between the headstones.

Today the visit to the home plantation went well. I rode across the plantation, advising and reviewing the implementation and planning. I heard reports, requests and complaints from the soldiers. A corporal from Illinois and I had a long visit about news from home. I copied some of the bookkeeping and reviewed the stores.

In late afternoon, I started to return and my horse threw a shoe. Luckily, there was a blacksmith nearby, an old Negro. He could do the shoeing but we had to send someone to find him, which took over an hour. Impatiently, I wondered if both the runner and the smithy were dallying while building the fire and shoeing. It seemed to take far too long. I was quite disgusted, for it was dark when the task was accomplished. Even with a lantern, it would be unwise to go on the road alone. I was obliged the stay overnight at the plantation. As the ranking officer, one of the non-commissioned men gave me a hammock and a blanket inside the house. A pleasant outcome of this unplanned visit was that the Corporal and I sat into the night gossiping about Illinois, and dreaming of going home to get on with our lives.

The next morning I ate a far better breakfast than those at the fort. One of the enlisted men's wives prepared eggs, which the plantation provided, sweet potatoes and biscuits. Feeling full and relaxed I dawdled over coffee. Then mounting my mare I began the ride back to McPhearson. The sun was well up and the chill long gone.

As I came along the north border of the cemetery, I saw the same carriage I had passed yesterday. It was parked on the down slope in the center row. Though it was some distance from the road and across an open field, I could view the slight form of a woman in black. The wind was pulling her skirts behind her as she moved among the stones. The old man stood by the horse, his hand on the bit. *What loss had this woman had?* I wondered, *how many widows stood in how many cemeteries?* I rode on to the bustle of the fort, and the business of the day. There would be reports and more problems.

Chapter 8

# Dear William

"Dear William,

Your mother informed me yesterday that we had just received a letter written by you after the glorious victory of the fourth of July in Vicksburg. The epistle said that you then followed the war to Jackson, Mississippi. That letter has been delayed almost a month. It is so satisfying to receive your mail. As soon as you pick up pen, do inform me about the military movements and your part. Of course, pray tell us that you are safe, your Mother Mary is so anxious."

The Courier informs us that the 15th Volunteers did reconnaissance on the Pearl River. Then the 15th had departed on a return to Vicksburg. It is with relief other letters from your fellows reported that you, personally, are removed unharmed. It is to our armies' credit that we seek to end the enslavement of a people. Here, about Wysox over a hundred and seven of our men have left to the battle. These personal letters arriving from the 15th Regiment soldiers say they also expect to regroup at occupied Vicksburg. Eventually they will move toward Natchez and a new fort there called McPhearson.

Of our ten children, yourself, and Washington, are now serving and Clay is anxious to follow, it is supposed James will enlist also. What an honor it is to have all my sons participate in this glorious crusade to once more unite our Nation. The Whig party is ever rousing the nation to that cause, and I do all I can to that end."

The letter went on full of news of Wysox Township, Carroll County and the rest of the family. This first letter must have been held up, for the next letter from home arrived within a week. The second letter came as a response to my own correspondence about my acceptance of a commission, and the assignment to a permanent duty station at Fort McPhearson. This communication from my family also responded to my request for the immediate purchase of the property that I desired to own.

"To my beloved son, William,

Your news was of particular poignancy for it ignited tender memories of my own birthplace, and later visits as a boy of 6 or 8 years to Natchez, Woodville and Byou Sara. The beginning of our family history in Mississippi was South of Woodville at Pinckneyville. The community was platted after your great-grandfather arrived and Pinckneyville eventually became a territorial county seat with about 1,500 souls. The community boasted inns, taverns and shops. It was quite near there that my grandfather Henry and your grandfather Henry Junior resided.

I beg your patience to reminisce, like an old man, lest you be unaware of the roots, which bind you and your heritage to that clime and domain close by the great Mississippi River. Far too many men fail to tell their sons of the family lineage and it soon becomes lost in the fog of the past. When this omission occurs a whole family lies in limbo with no sense of history or their place in it.

Our family heritage began in this country early. My ancestors arrived from Scotland to Suffolk, Virginia in the region that is now called the Carolinas. William Hunter served in the House of Burgess in 1650. It was there that the family first met the Narswothy family, who had migrated to the Isle of Wright. It was into this family that William's grandson eventually married Anne Narswothy in Kentucky. This great uncle was my grandfather's brother. Narswothy Hunter, William and Anne's son, was my grandfather's nephew. He also helped found Mississippi when it became a state in 1802.

My grandfather Old Henry had supplied the Revolutionary soldiers during the war. He already carried the entitlement of Colonel as a colonial militia title. As a resident of Carolina who had supported the cause of independence he was offered bounty land for his service. This first land was probably in Tennessee. He left Camden, South Carolina for Mississippi.

In a matter of years he was also offered 2,000 acres of bounty land in Spanish controlled Mississippi. In 1792, the Hunter family departed on the Holston River ferried by two flatboats on the Ohio River west to the Mississippi River and then southward to Natchez.

The harrowing journey was made by his whole family. They faced the weather, the risk of Indian attack, rapids, and lengthy portage where everything needed to be carried along the shore. Drowning and sinking were common disasters on such a trip, as was violence. Sharp curves in the river, wild animals on the shore, sand bars and snags in the river were the natural dangers they also encountered.[18]

When he arrived in Adams County the Spanish Governor Gyoso greeted him respectfully. I have saved a copy of the translated document.

'Report of Americans arriving at Natchez, April 17, 1792

I send you the enclosed account of two flatboats which arrived at this post from Holston listing the individuals and the cargo which they brought. Mr. Henry Hunter a native of the United States, the proprietor of one of them, a person of worth and special talent in all mechanical work, was Colonel in the American service in the last war, and of whom I had previous favorable information concerning his conduct, which my dealings with him have confirmed, has taken the oath of fidelity with the intention of settling in this district with his family, which is mentioned in the enclosed account.

The other individuals who came in the other boat are also settling in this district. According to the information that I have, they are persons of honorable conduct and masters of useful trades.

All of this I repeat for your information.

May the Lord keep your Lordship many years, Natchez April 17, 1792

Manuel Gayoso de Lemos, Senor Baron de Carondelet.'"

Accompanying the foregoing letter was an inventory: "Account of two flatboats which arrived from Holston to this Post with passengers and cargo.

First boat settlers: Proprietor–Mr. Henry Hunter, his wife and seven children and fifteen Negroes which belong to him.

Cargo: Farm tools and household furniture for his use.

Second boat settlers: Proprietor Robert Munson, his wife and four children, Jesse Munson his wife and one son and a slave. John Grady, his wife and two children and two Negroes."[19]

Henry had received 2,000 acres adjoining the land owned by Gerard Brandon, who's plantation came to be called "Columbia Springs."[20] Later, Henry purchased a piece of land just to the west of the village of Pinckneyville, closer to the great river. These properties would eventually be called Hunter Hall. The land there rolls rusty and vine covered with hardwood forest. It possesses clear, running water like Byou Sara.

The location of the plantation was seven miles south of Fort Adams and the adjoining town Wilkinsburgh. This was then a bustling riverboat landing and commerce area that also had a rough and ragged area of taverns. Between Fort Adams and Pinckneyville is a way station called Pond. They dug a deep pond for planters to water their stock as they moved cotton to the docks at Fort Adams. Often, those from a distance camped overnight there. Woodville was north and somewhat east, and in equal distance from the plantation was St. Francisville, Louisiana to the south. This general area was referred to as Byou Sara.

Soon after he arrived my grandfather went to Natchez to purchase more slaves as it had some of the largest markets. The majority of slaves who arrived with him were house slaves or skilled in trades. Those new slaves were chosen for strength and endurance. Several of these, my father said, were so newly arrived from Africa that they spoke no language we could understand. Many had unusual markings in patterns on their faces.

My grandfather Old Henry; his sons, William and Joseph; your grandfather Henry Jr.; Narswothy; Field Pulaski and the slaves began to create a home. As was the custom, the flatboats they arrived on were dismantled for the lumber. They built a first house that had no outside doors in the shotgun style. This had a long open hallway through the house with rooms entering from the hall on either side. The additions eventually included a gallery on the front and the porch on the back.

A locked storeroom was located on one side of the porch. By the time my father was a man and had purchased his own land, this first house had expanded with a pillared gallery, as was the custom. It also had a gallery on the second floor. Several separate buildings had been added for laundry, cook houses and sleeping space for the cook or primary house servants. They were separate from the main house because of possible fires—a dreaded disaster in the colony.

While some servants were building the barns and the houses, others were set to clearing land, tearing out cane and vines and briers. The rich soil only needed seed to be sowed over the decaying trash. The land needed no plow to produce a crop.

Only a few crops were even planted that first year. In all, clearing the land and preparation of it took many years. The virgin land was so rich that the crops planted in season were bountiful. When the land began to fully produce there was plenty for family, slave needs and for sale or export. The crops were finally planted, the majority of land was allotted to cotton, then tobacco and indigo. There was great hope for Pinckneyville, then a tiny village of only a few houses and shops, but growing.

At the house there was an original cistern that had been dug and lined with brick with a small shed over it. Other cisterns were located near the slave quarters, including the large one beside the main house. The property had a laundry shed with access to the water. The smoke house was near enough the house to stop intruders seeking to steal the smoking meats. To further protect them they were moved to the locked pantry on the porch when properly cured.

To the north, where tobacco was grown, was a large drying barn, and the slave quarters. The quarters included both long houses and some individual quarters. One small house had two rooms, as I remember, was later used for the overseer.

The stable, likewise, was near the house for security and availability to the steeds. My own love of horses was nurtured on that property while I was still a boy. In the areas where horses or cows would be placed and near the house, mock orange was planted. The thorny shrub made adequate fences and boundary markers. A fond memory of mine, is the beauty and fragrance when these neatly trimmed "fences" bloomed. At that time in Mississippi history, there were hundreds of miles of such hedges.

Because of his means, over the years our family had added much lovely interior décor to the items they had brought with them down the Holston on the flat boat. Many of these furnishings had been ordered from Europe or were custom made in the region.

It was the habit as life became more settled for the family to spend lengthy time in New Orleans at certain seasons. The whole family would go downriver to that city for a time of parties, concerts and plays. There they would shop or order clothing. Provisions would be purchased for the upcoming year.

Each time before they returned, they would find gifts for people who lived at the plantation. As the loyalty and service to the family by the slaves expanded, the gifts seemed to expand also. The excitement when they returned to Hunter Hall was like a celebration, as a young man I observed this once myself.

Old Henry's sons oversaw all efforts and jobs, and worked alongside the slaves. His daughter Elizabeth; youngest child Mary, who had been born in Mississippi; and his wife Lucy also worked beside the servants inside the house and gardens. They wore simple skirts and bonnets, working barefoot in the gardens. With the large fireplaces it was particularly wise that their skirts not be wide enough to sweep into the fires.

With such a large responsibility for caring and providing for so many people, there was always careful planning, selecting of provisions, and record keeping of the division and distribution to the whole household and servants. This was a continual and daunting task. The poultry and swine were provided by the land. Guinea hens had been brought from Africa with the slaves. Their eggs were found on the finest tables. The wild game or fish that were hunted or caught were the first meat of the plantation. There was some occasional trading in Woodville, Fort Adams or St. Francisville for extra spices, vegetables and dried fruits. Cows provided milk for the table and kitchen use, in addition to calves.

Old Henry's helpmate and wife Lucy was very strong and organized, which is good as such a large household was a dear responsibility. I remember them both well. They were trim and soft-spoken. Yet, they each had humor and wit. They were quick to defend their opinions or chastise those who needed direction.

Grandfather Henry, as a young man in Camden district of South Carolina, had been a sheriff and he eventually served that same purpose in Wilkinson County as a representative of the county. He also became the first Speaker of the House when it became part of the United States. I remember hearing a rough song that was made about him by the opposition during the election.

Party loyalty separating the Federalists and the Republicans ran high. The parties sang doggerels about a number of members of the state house. The one about your great-grandfather began, "Old Henry Hunter was a Bocher of the Gins" and rolled on in rowdy form—my father would tease us by singing it.[21]

In the 1805 census, the old man still held sixteen slaves. This categorized him as a second planter since he owned less than a hundred.* Lucy died in 1818 at eighty years of age. Old Henry was buried on his property in 1822, at the age of eighty-two. The location of their graves was along the Woodville-Pinckneyville Road.

In 1805, your own grandfather, Henry C.W. Jr., had nine slaves. He had been widowed by then and had three small children and three young women living with him in Wilkinson.

Memories of my grandfather exist, not only in personal recollections of my early childhood but also because of subsequent visits. These memories also exist because of my father Henry Junior's stories. I am grateful for his information and hope it never becomes lost.

When in 1811, my father and stepmother Isabella moved to Liberty, Indiana, there were three small children. These included myself and sisters Mary and Elizabeth. Isabella, Rebecca, Sarah and his son Frances were born later in the new marriage.[27] Some of your grandmother's kin, part of the John Heavenridge family, accompanied us from Mississippi. A family named Spenser from Mississippi also arrived in Indiana at the same time. The land in Indiana was a good investment and Father, then a young man, saw the opportunities.

It was a different life, more settled. Hired labor was used instead of slaves, who had been a burden to feed, doctor and care for. At first Isabella took her servant with her, but in that part of Indiana there were almost no slaves and abolitionists were active. The family freed the woman and then hired her. The older woman had been my mother's mammy, and was dearly loved and we looked on her as part of the family.

* *His sons Narsworthy and Thomas were living with him as was a daughter, making his household four adults, two children under 21 years of age and four females.*

Among the ancestors I loved to hear of in my fathers' stories was Narsworthy, Old Henry's nephew. Of course I have no personal memory of him but take pride in the position he rose to. Narsworthy served in Mississippi as a captain of the militia in the district that had been formed in 1793, the year he had arrived. For a year he was an inspector of forts on the East Side of the Mississippi River. This was quite an important assignment, as security for the people and goods on the river was vital. In that rough time, there were still many pirates on the river. Criminals and ruffians abounded up and down the waterway.*

Narsworthy Hunter became the first representative to United States Congress from Mississippi . The gentleman had gone to Washington in 1799 to put forth the petitions of the territory by a committee which stood in opposition to Governor Sergeant. He was successful in enlisting congressional support so that Mississippi territory was given a general assembly long in advance of the time at which it could be expected under the terms of the Ordinance of 1787. When, in 1800, Mississippi became part of the United States, he was their first congressional delegate, probably based on his performance of the other assignment.

Narsworthy, regrettably, died in office, March 1, 1802. It was the first death in the national capitol of a congressman or senator while in office. The members of the two Houses of Congress, their officers and the heads of departments marched from his residence. At that time the home was one of six buildings at Pennsylvania Avenue and Twenty-first Street.

The procession ended in Georgetown, where he was interred in the yard near Mr. Balah's Meeting House. Eventually, Narsworthy was moved to what we now call the Congressional Cemetery, in Washington, D.C..

This letter will address a matter of issue that is of great importance because of your new position. As I said I remember the celebration when the family gave gifts to the servants at Christmas or on return from New Orleans. To think of my father or grandparents being cruel seems impossible. I was so young, and did see firm direction as a necessity.

Now in this war to free the Negro, I look back at the time I spent in Bjou Sara with so many slaves about. Perhaps, I just accepted what was a way of life we had inherited and what seemed to be a necessity. I did see discipline applied to keep order and see that work was done properly. Was I blind? I do not know. I never saw violence.

I would stand by my window on a Sunday night and watch the dark

* *Narsworthy was born in Virginia to Henry's brother William and Anne Narsworthy, daughter of Thomas (Court at Isle of Wright). William and Anne were married in 1753-4 near Suffolk, Virginia. They still resided in Kentucky when our branch of the family and Narsworthy moved west from Camden, South Carolina. Narsworthy had only one sister and she was handicapped.*

figures around a central fire as they rocked and sang. From the house I heard the strange music. Now in the light of an adult conscience, I see the buying, selling and owning a human being as intolerable. Here in Illinois, I saw many escaping who rode the Underground Railroad. Many of these tragic humans had been maimed or torn from their families. There were very young girls carrying half White babies. There were men with branded faces. or ears or noses missing. How can I reconcile this with what I saw as a boy and young man? I cannot. Yet my conscience demands that I take a stand and my heart demands that it be abolition.

Enough, my son, of the ramblings of an old man. The news of the family is quite optimistic. James' wife was relieved for a few days from teaching because she had influenza, luckily she has recovered and is back at work. Henry Clay and Angelina are doing well. Since the foundry and mill is just down the road I see them often. It is because Isaac Spencer works there that I hear of him. Thus am reminded of his granddaughter who is still in Natchez and I wonder about her condition. Have you been able to talk with her?

The men from our area who did not reenlist are slowly returning, others are home on veteran's leave from the Fifteenth Regiment. These men are no longer the lighthearted boys who left Carroll county. How naive we were to expect a quick and easy resolution to this dreadful conflict. Now with the fall of Vicksburg and Gettysburg, perhaps it will not be long before we at last overcome. Yet, what a price we have paid. So many of our men will not return, others, who do come home, are very broken and damaged.

What ever will happen to our nation? I see a new flag being flown. It is made of white stars, forming a five pointed star, on a blue ground. These few stars are all that remain of our shattered nation.

Your letter was received late yesterday afternoon. I wonder what adventure the letter has been on, for it was quite muddy and one corner was torn off. Luckily, the message therein was readable. I found your words most interesting especially as the country around about you is that where I was born and that which produced my own dear father. It is thirty years since his death and I miss him still.

I'm pleased to hear you will be returning on leave soon. We shall anticipate your visit. I spoke with Roberts who owns the land you want to purchase and we began the process.

Your Mother has added a postscript,

'You look most fine in your brave uniform, dear boy. The derrogatype [sic.] made my heart dance. I congratulate you and feel honored to be the mother of such a fine officer. Your visage has changed so greatly, I yearn to see you in person. The empty space in my heart will only be filled as I see your face when you come home to visit.

Your father was able to see you in Tennessee last year, but it is a long hard three years since I have seen my Son.'"

Then William's father added yet another note.

"After your mother wrote her thoughts I considered and realized I had given you no details on the Robert's land. They are holding the seventy-five acres west and north of our home. He is prepared to make the deed and sell it to you from the funds you have been sending home. By becoming an officer you will be even more able to settle yourself after the war.

The riverboats are far more pleasant and quick this time of year as the trains stop so often. They are stuffy, overcrowded and become sooty if you open a window. I hope you will be able to secure passage on a paddlewheel instead.

Your Father,
The Honorable Henry C.W. Hunter"

The letter was satisfying and I folded it, placing it carefully into my breast pocket for future rereading.

Chapter 9

# The Mission

It was October, I had just received my permanent duty assignment. It was to command the Fifty-eighth Colored troops, Company K. We would be assigned to be in charge of security. As I read the *Natchez Courier*, I read a notice, one I was familiar with but now it had been published for the citizens of Natchez. It pretty much outlined the responsibility I would enforce, along with the men assigned to me.

"SPECIAL INSTRUCTION,

For the guidance of Guards, patrols and pickets.

1. Competent, reliable and intelligent officers must be placed in charge of pickets, guard posts or stations.
2. The men of the picket or guard will not be allowed to straggle away from their posts–nor enter houses, gardens or enclosures–nor commit any depredation. They must attend to their duties as guards or sentinels all the time.

Negroes with carts or wagons loaded with household plunder, will not be admitted inside the lines; no man and no Negroes with or without passes will be passed

> in or out during the night. They will be kept near the picket lines and not allowed to straggle...they will be sent to the contraband camp on the river." [17]

Using my knife I removed the article from newspaper so that I could post it to my family in a letter describing my permanent duty assignment.

It was now officially my job to ride north of the fort to the home plantation. I had been doing this unofficially and now the duty would include riding all the way south in a wandering path each day. Much of my company was already stationed at the southern-most home plantation. Now all on the Monmouth plantation would also report to me. I would visit at each guard post in between the two home plantations. Aside from gathering information from home plantations, I would also be required to make some minor decisions at these farms. Minor infractions at guard posts were to be administered to as well. My final daily responsibility would be to prepare reports at the fort. Each day would be spent entirely on horseback.

On most Sundays, I attended services at the Trinity Episcopal Church in the center of town. If Corporal Hobart was available he would occasionally accompany me. After services I made it a habit to drop off some food to the priest for his own use or to forward to someone needy.

Each time I came in from the bright light into the dark of the church to take my seat in the visitor's pews at the rear, I found an element of calm and comfort. The other members of the congregation sat in pews their family purchased, which provided additional income to the parish. A few people of color sat with these families to care for the elderly or small children. Any other Negroes sat in the balcony. I assumed that the numerous Negro baptisms that were announced were occurring at some outlying location. Many planters provided spiritual guidance for their people.

As I became more familiar, Father Perry and I would speak more personally, albeit briefly, after church. These were rather superficial conversations about casual things like weather, crops or a fire in the town. This relationship was not really a friendship, but still was the only civilian activity in my life. The emptiness of my world of war ate at any reality of my past that still existed within me.

Eventually two other soldiers, one Black and one White, began to attend also. The men were only allowed to leave the fort with a supervising officer. We would ride to town together, then take the assigned seats at the back of the church; the Colored soldier would go to the balcony.

The services were such as I was familiar with in Illinois, though the announcements were more signs of the times. There was always the required prayer for President Lincoln. Sometimes during the service, there were notifications from the Union Army of some regulation or change. No public prayers were allowed for the army who wore grey.

With some deviousness, I learned of a bit of pride that the congregation had in connection with the war, no one would have willingly told me. It seems that in 1862, General Beauregard had sent a public plea for all metal that could be melted for cannon. Reverend Gideon Perry and his vestry had offered the church bell to that purpose. It had been gratefully acknowledged, but with respect, the gift of the bell to the confederacy was declined.[22]

As in every congregation across the whole nation, there were the dour announcements of deaths of soldiers. One of these announcements was of a sixteen-year-old boy who had died from an illness. I had felt the loss more strongly because of the special poignancy for child soldiers that I always felt.

After I had attended services a number of times I recognized that certain wives, children or mothers had disappeared from the church. When the family returned, after a lengthy absence, they were clad in proper mourning clothing. Apparently Southern wives and immediate family must not be out in public for some time after the loss of a soldier. What length of time I could not assess. The many black dresses and black armbands on the old men emphasized the importance of social customs of Natchez. The women seemed to return to a few community events at randomly prescribed periods. The custom was hard to decipher. I assumed that this was why I had still been unable to contact the Widow Scothorne.

The baptisms of babies or announcements of marriage bans were a comforting joy in the church, because of the many tragic events around the entire city. My attendance at the church meant that I had some closer observation of Natchez citizens. The pace of the community became more real and I began to find empathy with personal struggles in this lovely town so torn and battered by loyalties and personal tragedies.

I was able to receive communion regularly, and was working to find the determination to talk to the priest or one of the officers at the post about a serious sense of guilt I felt about my own family's participation in enslaving Negroes.

Because I worked alone or was on horseback most of the day, my contacts at the fort had become more limited. I was amazed when Major Brown called me to his tent at dawn, one fall morning just before I would have begun riding my prescribed route.

He told me I was to see Brigadier General McDevlin by noon. This was an order I could not understand. With respect, I paused a second as I considered the situation and possibilities. Then I inquired for the reason of the meeting.

"I have no idea what he wants. He just sent a message requesting one of our better officers with reconnaissance experience. He wants that officer to see him before noon at the headquarters." Under his breath the lieutenant swore, "Damn fool McDevlin, it could be anything. I have only seen him twice. Then it was about some of his skullduggery. Just watch yourself, Hunter."

Looking at me, Brown shrugged his broad shoulders and shook his head with a look of helplessness. "You are released from duty until your business with McDevlin is concluded. Assign someone else to take your position temporarily. Arrange any accompanying orders and passes thus."

After completing the personnel transferal and paperwork that were necessary, I went about my preparations with some acceleration, for fear of being late. These orders seemed momentous and I was complimented that Major Brown had recommended me. Although the officer had instructed me in a few small matters in past months, we had little direct contact with each other. I had no way of knowing if my performance was meeting his approval until this assignment indicated his confidence. I took care in my dressing and shaving; trimming my beard short and shaping my mustache. I went to the stable to pick my own mount.

The mare I had been using was quite a calm and sturdy animal. As I walked into the musty darkness of the alley between stalls, I neared Matthew. He was busy, a rake in his hand, as he cleaned a stall.

"Private Hunter, good morning. I am looking for the roan mare I have been using."

"Yes su, follow me." He laid the rake aside and walked on down the row, glancing into each stall.

As we moved along the aisle I instructed, "Private, I would like to have you save that mare for me from this time on, until notified. I need her daily as a mount to go to the plantations and for my own use." It felt good to be able to have the authority to give such orders and see to my own providence.

"Yes su. Su? She 'jus come in season and might be skittish."

"I know her and feel I can control her. I do not want her bred."

With a second thought I gave the condition some consideration. Pausing to question, "How old do you think she is?"

We came upon her pen. Matthew lithely climbed into the board-walled interior which was topped with chewed lumber. He backed her into a corner and pulled her moist, velvety lips apart. "I spose she be three or four years Cap'n Hinter."

As the man stood beside the horse, I saw him gently rub her chest and shoulder. He seemed very sure and gentle with these animals.

"Are you happy in the army?" I made the inquiry with a sense of responsibility and concern.

"Yes su," the private's face opened to a wide smile.

"Are you learning to read?" Since I had been secretly observing him I knew he was studying with his fellows on a regular basis, and it gave me hope for him and his eventual success as a civilian.

"Cap'n, I be reading real good and can cipher lots too."

Looking at his face I saw pride and enthusiasm glinting in the dark eyes, this was a far cry from the pain, anger and defiance that fired him on our first encounter. There was still the determination I saw that first day he came to enlist.

"You are doing a good job, and I know you're learning." Pausing again to look into his happy gaze I stated, "Private Hunter you are a good man."

His eyes went wide and his jaw dropped. He stood, frozen. It surprised me. "Is something wrong?" I stared with confused concern?

Slowly, he mouthed the words, "Neva been call a man befo." He was tall, strong and several years older than I. Still his face looked so plaintive.

Shocked, I could think of no reply, so covering my own emotions I nodded toward the mare. "She have a name?"

"Ruby."

"Did you name her?" I quizzed.

"Yes su." he said with a sentimental look toward the horse.

"Why do you call her Ruby?" I quizzed, thinking of the bronze color as a possibility.

"My wife name Ruby." The soldier mumbled over his shoulder without turning toward me.

"You said you did not have a wife."

"My Ruby died in Virginy. She don birth my boy and the massa send her to the field next day. She don start to bleed, and he say she still got to go. Three days she get a fever, an she dies. Guess her milk be bad too, the mammy nurse the boy, but a week afta she die, den he die too. Not too long they sell me off."

"I be chained with other niggas and marched in a coffle of people clear from Virginy to de Forks here. No, I don have no family, not no more."

His voice was low in his chest. Again the pain, sympathy and the awful guilt swept me. The man looked at the ground. As his hand caressed the horse, I froze for long minutes.

"You saddle the mare for me, I will wait outside. I'd like the lightest saddle you have." Later he led the small, saddled mare out, I took the reins and mounted.

As I turned the steed to trot toward the small city he called out, "Capn' I take good care you horse, fo you, that I will."

This was the first time since I put on my captains uniform that I was being picked out for something: a battle, a special assignment, or an advance. Pride puffed my chest. It took self-control not to pull out of the trot and ride hard just to get to the commander's quarters. I wound down the trail, past the park and turned east for several blocks.

McDevlin's headquarters was a large, white mansion that was surrounded by lush, blooming magnolia trees and shrubs. The green lawn was shabby and untrimmed. There were some officers sitting on the porch, seeming to be only present to visit. On the steps there were several young, Black boys giggling and scuffling. An old Colored man, with an amazingly, bent back, was raking without much enthusiasm at the fallen twigs and blooms on the lawn. Dismounting, I arranged my jacket, then checked my buttons and bent to dust my boots. My boots really were in pretty good condition, although two sizes too wide for my narrow feet.

Straightening, I approached the porch, climbed the wide stairs, stepped between the center columns and strode across the porch. Looking to either side, I respectfully nodded at the officers of my own rank lounging there. One winked, and nodded his head right to left in an exaggerated slow negative sign. It was not intelligible to me exactly what he meant, so I smiled.

I reached for the ornate door handle and opened the door. The long hall was cool and dark except for a light's golden halo farther down the way where a door hung open, allowing light to flow out with dust mites dancing along the rays. I paused to gather my wits, then slowly proceeded. Someone had nailed a rough sign on the lovely, mahogany panel of the open door, DO NOT DISTURB. The door on the other side of the hallway was shut and a string held a card on the knob, I SHALL RETURN IN AN HOUR. A staircase rose on one side. I looked up the wide, grand ascension to a landing where a window was covered by a lace panel that cut the light, and lay patterns of shadowed design on the mahogany treads that were falling downward toward me.

At one wall on the landing, a carpet appeared to be rolled and propped vertically in a corner. Above the lower hall and stairs hung a brass chandelier. On the wall beside the stair hung two portraits; neither painting was hanging straight. As I continued down the hall, it seemed like I was in "Alice's Adventures Underground," the strange book that my parents had sent to me. I recognized everything, but nothing around me was quite right. *Was I, in fact, falling down to some underground world?*

I had a strong urge to turn and leave. *What had that nod and wink on the porch meant?* Now I could hear voices from the open door in front of me. The predominate voice was that of a man who was loudly swearing, with no coherent words interspersed between the curses. There was still another doorway in the wall, on this was pasted another sign, CLERK. I knocked on the clerk's door and a voice called me in showing my entry little interest.

A washed-out man sat inside the room. He was crowned with snow-white hair. Bushy, white brows lay over pale eyes. He stared at me from behind a cluttered desk. In this room there were unused, ornate side chairs in a stack and another rolled carpet. This time the rug lay along a wall. Straddling it were two more overstuffed side chairs. These stood in front of the desk. There was a matching sofa, its back toward me.

"Sit down, Captain," the man mumbled, motioning to the couch. With disrespect, he barely acknowledged me nor did he salute. I walked around the couch and seated myself. Turning my head to the right, I watched the enlisted man at the desk.

The clerk rocked on the back rungs of his chair for a while studying me. My eyes evaded his by looking at the book-lined wall beside him. "What you come about?"

"I am here to see Brigadier McDevlin."

"McDevlin don't see no one." The man snapped, looking back at the clutter on the desk as though he had never seen it before.

"Major Brown sent me. He received an order from Brigadier General McDevlin to send someone."

"You don't say?" One bushy, white eyebrow raised and the pale eyes focused on me more interested, "You don't say," he repeated, as he cocked his head to one side in a manner of curiosity. "Well, we just see about that. You go wait on the porch. I'll come tell you."

Standing and turning to leave I caught a glimpse of the rest of the room. Some small cane bottom chairs were stacked against the front wall, and on a side table a number of paintings were stacked in a messy pile. Remembering the rumors of government requisition of homes, it crossed my mind to wonder where the people who owned this house were.

Out on the porch, the man who had winked humorously chided, "Might as well take a seat lad, might be quite a wait, if ever."

I walked to a hedge where I would be able to look over toward the waterfront. Then I sat down on the sparse grass, with a sigh I realized that in fact it might be quite a long wait.

In an hour, I took out my pipe. In two hours, I went to the front lawn and paced off the forward lawn several times. When I returned from this exercise I sat closer to the other officers.

"May I conclude, Captain you 'spect to see McDevlin?" the officer taunted me. The other men also looked at me with the same quizzical expression the clerk had used. This mysterious hole I had fallen into was making me damn nervous.

I had been considering finding the outhouse when the door finally swung open and a short fat officer with a red face rushed out allowing the door to slam behind him. He virtually leaped off the steps and ran down the brick walk to the street.

The snowy head of the clerk then leaned out of the door. Peering both ways he caught my eye and nodded me in. At his own door he turned in and over his shoulder with no show of military rank grunted, "Next door down."

I adjusted my jacket, straightened and strode to the indicated door. I made a sharp turn and entered through the casing to stop just inside. A blond man with thinning hair and a very square jaw was sitting on the edge of the desk. His shirt was open to the waist, exposing a hairless chest. His suspenders were hanging at his side. In his hand was a crystal glass full of what was probably whiskey.

"You from Company K? Major Brown sent you?"

"Yes sir," I answered, standing ramrod straight.

"Close the damn, shitting door," he boomed.

The man before me was legendary within the fort. He did not communicate with his men, not even to relay orders from headquarters to his command. Ironically, his previous military career had been exemplary. His courage at Shiloh created an aura of magic around him. Now he was a recluse, ugly rumors of his mistreatment of both White and Black troops circulated. The whispers about the kidnapping and extortion of Natchez citizens were rampant and might well be true.

His visage and the deep-set eyes that were visible under fair brows, were so intense as to give an impression of insanity. In fact, I wondered, *could the man be crazy, a victim of a war that had rolled on for over three years.*

Squinting his eyes he studied me slowly and very carefully. *Could possibly be the same McDevlin that took control at the battle Shiloh.* He was known as a man among men there only a little over a year ago.

Sitting the glass on the delicately, carved side table, which was already marred with a white ring scarred surface. He stood and paced up and down the room in front of his desk. He wrung his hands behind his back. Occasionally, he would pause on his turn and study me as though evaluating me for something. In my heart, I wanted to please and meet his expectations but the hairs at the back of my neck were standing on end. Once more an urge to run washed over me.

After ten minutes of pacing he stopped, straddle legged in front of me, his hands still clasped behind him. Squinting, he leaned his head forward on his short neck. "Jesus, boy come here."

I took two long steps and stood there in front of him. "You blithering jackass, I said step up your blue ass."

I moved until I was ten inches from his blotchy face, the whiskey sour breath was warm on my face.

"You piece of shit, you know this God forsaken county round here?"

" I know the countryside for about ten miles in perimeter outside town. I have also actively recruited to the south and east for some distance." I tried not to sound shaky.

"How far south?" he boomed with a sneer.

"Twenty miles, Sir." I tried to keep the appropriate military composure. *Had I been sent here for some kind of reprimand? What could I have done? How could McDevlin know anything about me?*

Abruptly, he straightened, turned and moved behind his desk. Reaching into the knee space he pulled out a folded map. He spread it on the desk, in the process knocking a stack of papers to the floor and upsetting the partially empty drink. The glass lay on the desk with the liquor running in a puddle and off the edge of the desk to dribble onto a lovely, but soiled carpet.

In a low voice he said, "Close the door and come round here. Keep your damn voice down."

Doing as commanded I followed his orders. I was sick at my stomach and felt full-blown panic. When I stood at his side, he reached an arm around my shoulders and pulled me to him until we were pressed side-to-side above the map.

"This is Natchez," he grunted as he pointed to the map. "Here is the Wilkinson county line and down here is the town of Woodville. It is a bit more than twenty miles. You see?" he whispered gruffly.

"Yes Sir," I whispered in a barely audible, scratchy voice.

"This trail is the one that is used the most," pointing at the main road; one I had been part way down numerous times.

"There is a footpath closer to the river." He traced it with a long dirty fingernail. "Might be some grey boys hiding there, but usually not. You listen boy, damn it. I want you to reconnoiter. I don't want—not one damn word about this, not you or your men. You take maybe six of the niggers. Get horses and three days provisions. Go down this small trail, real quiet and real careful. Avoid any notice."

Looking up, proud of himself he said, "Maybe even go at night and hide in the day. Yes, that's good. Go at night. Go as far as Fort Adams. Check the fort out for one day and night; see who comes and goes. Count any cotton bales. Then go to Woodville, check that cotton warehouse one day and night. Then the most important part! Count every bale of cotton you find anywhere from below fort to above Wilkinson. Take this map and you mark everything you see."

Turning from me and taking a step back, he spun and grabbed two handfuls of my jacket, giving me a rough shove. "You let anyone know what you are doing and I will have you court marshaled and hung. You hear me you asshole? You pick your men careful and leave tomorrow afternoon. Get your hind side out of here now," he growled.

As I turned to leave he yelled, "Stop, what's your name?"

"Captain William Hunter, Sir," I snapped a crisp reply since I was sincere in my desire to not further raise this man's wrath.

"Hunter, you stop at the clerk and send him down. I will issue you commissary requisitions. You and the men need passes in case you meet any of our troops. Take this map," he threw the rolled paper at me. The document fell at my feet and I picked it up. As I stood to salute, the man had his back to me and was moving to a decanter sitting on a table in the corner.

It took the clerk only a few minutes and some loud curses from his superior to receive orders about the creation of the documents. He returned to the desk and began the paperwork.

Angry and offended as I was at the whole experience something in me wanted to find some redeeming qualities to the assignment. I wondered if this duty was of such importance that it had caused McDevlin to act in such a manner. Perhaps being an officer had personal challenges I had not imagined. Then remembering the swearing from the office earlier, I had second thoughts of any excuse for his behavior.

Whatever else had happened, I found that the commissary documents I was issued were the most effective tool I had found in my ongoing battle with the corporal there. The provisions and goods were promptly provided and stacked in a corner to be picked up.

"On second thought, there are a few other things also," I told the man, using the opportunity to the fullest, I finagled some other supplies I had been short of for my men, previously. The insolent sergeant only eyed me, said nothing and immediately ordered these last goods placed in a second pile that I would have picked up and distributed today.

*Power feels good.* I smugly thought to myself as I strode out.

When I returned to the stable with my mount, I sought Matthew out. "Private, I have an assignment and would like to take you away for three days. Are you a good shot? Do you know your weapon?"

"Su I do da best," he responded, his shoulders thrown back.

"I will tell your company officer to free you at noon tomorrow. Come to the parade ground near my tent and just sit down, like you are waiting. We will be sleeping on the ground and riding for this assignment. Have my mare and five other horses ready and tied at the end of the barn. The other men will come one at a time to get their horses. I trust you. This is something you must not speak of with anyone or do anything to attract the attention of anyone at the fort."

I next sought out Sergeant Anderson, who had helped me recruit, gave him instructions to select a man who was single and totally trusted. "Take two horses and pick up the goods at the commissary. Meet me at two tomorrow, at the river bank south of town, two miles past Under the Hill."

Suddenly, I remembered the private who was assisting in reading classes. I struggled to remember his name. *Yes, Private Turner.* That was the right name. I sought out the noncom who supervised the classes; from him I was able to locate Turner. I inquired about his use of a gun and satisfied, I also swore him to secrecy. His confident and clever mind would be an asset on this mission. When I found he was from Wilkinson County and familiar with all the surrounding area, his value was further increased.

While watching target practice I had noticed a soldier of around eighteen who was an excellent marksman. I sought him out then ordered him to meet me on the main road out of town in the late afternoon.

Searching my memory, I remembered a Sixth African who was assigned me when I first arrived at the fort. This soldier was one that had proven himself in battle. It took until evening for him to finally came to my lodging. He seemed glad of an assignment away from the boredom of the fort.

"I respect the Sixth, and am sure that you know men of your company who are very clever, good shots and can be trusted to observe secrecy. Select one man to accompany you. Midmorning there will be a horse for each of you behind the stable. Ride south out of town and on the road along the river wait for me in the early afternoon. Here are passes."

Finally, in the early evening I sought out the respective commands and reported the men I had selected for temporary duty. I stated that they would be "on picket" which would seem an ordinary duty for me to need a few extra men.

With my first mission as an officer underway, I was anxious when I retired to my quarters for the evening. Turning up the lamp, I spread the map on the packing box that I used as a table and sat on an upturned bucket. I studied the map for several hours. Night duty in a place I did not know might be a challenge and preparation needed to be very careful. At least two of the men I had selected had been from plantations near here and claimed to know the whole country. I hoped they were not bragging.

The next morning, after breakfast, I was nervous and walked about checking the troops, then stopped by Major Brown's tent to say I would be gone for three days. "What," he started to inquire, then with a strange look said only, "Very well." and looked down as though I had said something of no matter at all.

Just before noon I went to my room, washed, shaved and put on clean socks, that were worn but more comfortable. I found an almost worn-out pair of boots which fit better than the newer ones. I rolled my oilcloth with what goods I would be taking. Then I cleaned my weapon and lay back on my bunk, with my hands under my head and tried to be calm and rest.

I heard a slight sound, "Matthew?" I questioned softly.

"Yes su," his reply was whispered from outside.

I rose and joined him.

Private Hunter and I approached the hitching post where only our two mounts were tethered; the selection and primary instructions to my men had gone as planned. I watched as the private secured my oilcloth. Setting the pace, I rode in front very slowly as though I were going about on a casual ride. My heart was thumping in my chest like a finger snapping. We rode south on the dusty road.

Just outside of town, at a crossroads near an old slave market, Private Turner was lounging. He rose, mounted and fell in line behind Private Hunter. Next we cut back toward the river; at a grove of trees I saw the Sergeant's horse and another.

When we rode toward the men, they moved from the grove, mounted and fell into line. Following the riverbank southward, I felt we probably had gone three miles. With the cotton fields stripped, vision was open but I saw nothing. We rode on another half mile.

Just as I pulled up and felt my chest for the brittleness of the map, I saw a head pop up from a ditch leading to the river. Another man rose to his feet and the two final contingents of the troops stood. Turning, they each pulled at the reins of their horses which struggled up the loose soil of the gully to fall in behind the line of horsemen following me.

With a sigh, I waited for these last men to close ranks. It was now close to four in the afternoon, I pulled my watch out of my inside pocket and studied it. Using my minds eye and memory, I tried to recall the trail on the map and headed toward where I expected this small path to begin.

Feeling lucky, I found the almost hidden roadway. We all moved silently, except for horse and saddle sounds or pebbles unloosened from soil that marked our progress. The seven of us moved along what could better be described as an animal path than a clear trail.

I led the small, silent band onward until hills and trees provided cover. Then I pulled up; dismounting we moved into a copse of woods, breaking a path to get off the trail. There was no clearing or space in the location I had selected.

For the first time I spoke, my voice almost shocking as it broke the silence. "Do any of you know of any open area near here?"

Private Turner handed his reigns to another soldier and joined me. On his suggestion, we moved back to the trail, and leading our horses, proceeded a short distance to where he had indicated we would find a small patch of grass off to the east of the path. There was an old fire site there, and I was comforted that he did, in fact, know the land. We dismounted, made a fire, cooked and ate. Then we all lay resting quietly until about nine in the evening. The full moon was our only light.

The men visited in low voices, with accents I still found hard to follow. Sergeant Anderson came to sit beside me, but we were carefully quiet as we spoke. Once after hearing a round of soft, muffled laughter I inquired about it and he said Rube was telling a story about treeing a possum, and he doubted that the story was all that true, he softly chuckled. The soldiers homey talk reminded me that they were men who learned early to be quiet. At nine thirty we moved out riding at a slow, careful trot.

Private Hunter rode up beside me. "Sir."

"Yes private."

"There be dogs live up ahead. I hate dem dogs and they do make a racket."

I pulled up and motioned the sergeant. He and the private named Nate whispered and then the private rode on ahead at a quicker pace; the moonlight allowed him to see more clearly. I heard some barking, then soft yipping.

"Sir."

"Yes Sergeant?" I questioned.

"We got to go now, and fast the next half mile. The private took care of the dogs."

Increasing the pace we moved along. As we passed the location where the dogs were I heard some growling and yipping, but not a bark. In the muggy dark with sweat rolling down my back, I led as we kept up the pace for another hour. Finally, I pulled up, and called softly, "Dismount." We relieved ourselves, stretched, drank from our canteens and checked our mounts.

"Private," I called under my breath and soon Rube was beside me. "Private what did you do with those dogs?"

"I run onct and an old niga tol me, jus take the toughest pig rind you can get. Throw it to dem dogs, keeps um busy if they not bein' run by no midnighter."

Pausing to take in the import of his story, I asked, "Did you get away?"

"No su, but warnt no dog got me," he laughed triumphantly.

"Thank you, go back and rest a bit. I figure we are near Wilkinson and as we pass the town we need to be quiet."

After a short break, I gave Matthew some cloth and he divided it. We each wrapped the horses' hooves, as I had seen some spies do. I rubbed dirt on my face and turned my jacket inside out so the buttons wouldn't catch the light. My men, I suddenly realized, did not need to darken their faces. Again, I instructed Matthew and he inspected all weapons and canteens to make sure no metal would clank as we moved.

Then I called the private forward. "Do you know the cotton dock at Wilkinson?"

"Yes su, I take lots of cotton there both 'for and afta the Union burn the mill."

"I want you to lead us past there and on down to Fort Adams. I want to be there before dawn. Will we be able to make it?"

The young man shook his head slowly and his posture seemed to slump somewhat. "Don' think we be that far," he spoke softly with remorse.

"Do you know the fort?"

"Not so good, but I been there."

"Go and see if any of the others know the fort."

In a few moments he returned. "Su, Private Hunter know dos parts."

"Very well, you lead the way and I will be right behind you."

The next few hours were tense as we proceeded. We heard voices once and pulled into the trees just off the road. Two young Black men came wandering slowly down the road. One seemed to weave as though drunk, and stopped to urinate in the road near us. We held our breath. Finally, the man who had paused, rushed to catch up with his companion. Then the private led us onward.

Occasional wildlife or owls moved; birds rustled as we passed. At the northeast edge of Wilkinson, the full moon illuminated the town enough to see the shapes of buildings and homes in the distance. Passing, I vainly tried to study the trees to see where we might have a vantage point to study the mill dock. It was far too vague in the shadows to make out anything distinctly. A couple miles further we turned west through rolling hills toward the Mississippi. Near a widened area in the road we pulled off, taking break once more. I studied the sky but saw no indication of light. My watch was useless in the dark but with the tension I felt it seemed we had been on the road for days.

Following the break I mounted and heard the creak that indicated the men regaining their saddles.

"Private Hunter do you know this country very well?"

A cold knife of a voice replied, "Yes su, I know this part too good. I be made a slave about one mile from here."

"Do you know Fort Adams?"

"Yes su."

"What we want to do is to get near enough to watch the dock without being seen and hide out all day. Do you think you can lead us there?"

"Yes su."

"Then we will follow behind you."

The soldier's horses took off at a trot, slowing only when the ever-narrowing path was less than visible. At one point, he pulled the horse up, dismounted and studied something. I moved closer to him, left my saddle and walked to his side. A large tree had fallen across the trail. "Wait," he murmured softly, then tied his horse to the branch of the downed tree and moved off into the woods. It was a several moments before he came back. Untying the horse he said, "We got to go roun'." We backtracked a short distance and took a winding path had probably been used by others to bypass the deadfall.

About four in the morning he halted again. Most of the time, we could now hear the gurgle of the muddy river as it rolled southward. An occasional break in the trees showed reflections of the moon on the swiftly moving water. When we halted this time, I could not hear the river. The disorientation was giving me a feeling of being lost.

"Private, why are we stopping?"

"We here, su."

Looking around, I felt I should take charge, *but how*? I did not even know where we were. Dismounting, we fumbled for places to tie the horses, unsaddled and removed the hoof wrappings. Trying to become comfortable, I sat against a tree, removing my boots and loosening my clothing. Carefully, I checked where my weapon lay and tried vainly to doze. The dampness of the earth and the humidity of the earlier evening was replaced by a cool, crisp fall dawn. One of the men snored with a low whistle, thus rest is not how I would describe my repose.

It was less than an hour before light began to change the sky. Peeking though the canopy of trees, I could see the peachy pink of the sky growing ever more rich through the foliage to the east. We appeared to be about fifteen feet into a grove of thick trees. There were fence hedges of Cherokee rose, which in April would be pink with blooms. These shoulder high borders protected us on two sides. About a quarter mile toward the river was a more open flood plain and I began to make out shadowy forms of small buildings and other shapes. Above, on a high cliff, was a more massively built structure.

With the increased light I was able to check my watch and began to mark in a tiny ledger with a pencil each quarter hour. "You can rest in shifts. I do not want a fire. We need to water the horses, Private Hunter."

"Yes su, I take um down a ways to a creek," motioning the two youngest men to join him, he took my mare and they all started off.

"Wait, take your guns and all our canteens." They did as ordered.

The fort was not as I had expected, only a small building high on a yellow clay cliff with a wharf some 400 yards in front on the sandy edge of the river. The name of fort had made me expect a rough outpost. Yet, nearby was a small village. No crafts were moored at the docks and there was no activity to indicate early rising people. At the fort there was a small pen holding four horses and a chicken house was nearby. There was not even an outhouse.

Morning was well into light when two men finally came out, and went to feed and water the horses from pails they filled at a large barrel. Very faintly in the stillness I could hear a rooster. The one rewarding sight I found was a large pile of cotton on the wharf. I pulled out a spyglass.

Unfamiliar with the bales I spent an hour counting, recounting and multiplying. From this angle I could not make a sure count. Disgusted, I finally threw the glass down and looked up the see my soldiers watching me in silence. Embarrassed, I sat there sullenly. Finally, I explained, "I am trying to count the bales."

A big grin broke across Private Hunter's face. His broad forehead wrinkled and his large eyes twinkled. He studied the mound of bales without the aid of my spyglass. After a surprisingly short time, he confidently looked me in the eye and announced, "Two hundred three." Suspicious of a man just learning to read, I squinted at him. Handing him the glass, he peered into it, then looked up briefly with pleasure. He again studied the white mound, carefully, "Two hunda fifty. Capn', how you count em?" I struggled to sound authoritative, "Yes, our count is close."

"Private how did you learn to count bales?"

"I learn to count de wagons when they load em. They stack be three high, dat pile be ten wagons wide, I just count the wagon load. That be two wide, then I count fingers. I don count every bale. I wonder, spose some dem be massa Sullivan cotton bale?"

I turned to Sergeant Anderson for conformation. He nodded solemnly. I queried him, "Sergeant, what kind of fort is this?" "It used to be Spain's long time ago. They build it long time ago; got no soldier, just people to guard and load de cott'n."

"Sargent I want you to take command while I nap, if anyone comes near us, or goes on land or water to the fort wake me."

Comfortable now on my oil cloth, I lay on my back, chewing hardtack and water. Then I rolled to my side and dozed. When the sergeant eventually touched my shoulder, I roused, feeling rested, and raised on one elbow, suddenly attentive. "Su, de wagon come."

I saw a wagon with cotton lumbering toward the wharf. I watched it wind west through deep gullies in the clay hills and as it unloaded and returned south down the road. This tally was added to my notes. "Is Private Hunter awake?" I asked.

The young marksman I had inquired of moved to a form curled in a ball under a tree at some distance. Rousing the private he returned to sit near me. In a bit Matthew came and sat down. "We need to go farther down river to see if there is any more cotton. Do you know the way south of here?"

"Yes su they only four more plantations for Louisiana. They big uns." He volunteered brief descriptions of each and the approximate locations. My curiosity was piqued.

Leaving sergeant in charge and sworn to keep track of any changes at the fort, Private Hunter and I mounted and began to slowly wind southward up deep gullies through the trees. The two of us rode several twisting miles of groves. As the undergrowth increased, we followed the forest at the edge of the plain. After about ten miles the private pulled up. "Dat be de plantation of Sullivan; dat be my plantation."

In the distance I saw through the trees, a hillock with outbuilding; no house was visible. "You don' need look fo' no cott'n. By this time he don' take it to Wilkinson."

No matter how much I had grown to respect this man, I still did not have complete confidence. "Let's get closer." He moved us stealthy just beyond the house and then in closer. I studied it through the glass and, in fact, found no evidence of cotton wagons or piles.

Nodding to the soldier, we moved west and south once more. We had only begun to ride when he held out a hand to halt our movement. There was the sound of talking and rustling. A young, chocolate colored girl of less than fifteen and an old lady were struggling along a path trying to tow a dead, bloated pig toward some unseen destination. His front hooves were secured by rope, but the size and the stench were making it a slow, difficult task. They were complaining and stopping often, as they struggled down the path.

We halted, stopped in dead silence, and stood hidden in the woods. The couple passed near us. As the girl glanced back at their load, she caught a glimpse of us and squealed. In fear, both women looked at the Union uniforms. Like most slaves, they were terrified of the soldiers.

Then looking at Matthew they broke into squeals of joy. "Matthew you be live! How you be a soldier? We think the nightriders get you when you run away afta Massa Sullivan's ovasea beat you." They ran to his side and reached for his hand, clingling like long lost family members.

Once more I wondered at the closeness of those from the same plantation. I had observed this at McPhearson. I could see Matthew sit straighter in the saddle and it reminded me of my own pride in my new uniform when I went to church the first time.

The women excitedly jabbered and laughed. Finally, head held high, he moved the rifle to his other hand so that they could notice it.

He said using a deep solemn voice, "I soon be ciphern' too. I read some and I be paid cash money." His face took on an intensity and his voice lowered in threatening tone, "I not be no one's niga no mo, I neva be beat again. Now you don be tellin' no one you see us fo this week. Then you tell the men folk to bring da people to the fort at Natchez and they be soldier too, and de family be safe. I be doin' soldier work now and we got to go."

I had been viewing this strange reunion in silence. The women suddenly looked at me. They cast down their eyes, dipped their heads and began to drag the carcass on down the path.

Hunter and I continued on for about an hour, and then took a break to stretch and eat. We lit a small fire and boiled some coffee. It tasted good.

Pulling the map out and looking at it I figured how far east and south we had come from the fort. A sudden realization stuck me. This final plantation had to be that which had originally been the home of my own great grandfather, Henry Hunter. I could see the location as we were so near the Louisiana border and also the river.

I stated to tell the private of my excitement, but it was short lived as a wave of guilt and shame struck me. I could visualize the bleeding flesh on this man's back the day I first saw him. *How could I admit my own complacency and my family lineage?*

Sipping coffee and gaining my composure. I guilefully said, "We need to go to the next place." With this selfish, foolhardy act I was not sure I wasn't going too far south—it was seven miles from Fort Adams—to please McDevlin. My motive was to see this piece of my own history.

Silently, the private moved and swung into the saddle. I followed him. "Not far now cap'n, they doan use the west road much, mostly de take the road da otha way to the main road past the Pond."

He led us inland through thick cover on an overgrown path. "Be quiet now. Der be a warehouse, don think they have no cotton, but you can look."

When he pointed ahead I could make out the weather beaten peak of roof. "You stay here and hold my horse," I commanded. Taking my rifle, I stealthily moved along the tree line until I could see the entire cotton shed. Checking carefully, I jumped across the path so that I had a view into the yawning open door of the outbuilding. Inside there was no reflection of the white or grey bales as a few shafts of light fell to the floor and I could see the other sides of the shed, "Nope, no cotton."

My eyes shifted beyond the barn to where the path widened, and there on a knoll, 1,000 feet beyond was the house. Not the lovely, columned house of the headquarters but a two-story, wooden building with numerous additions, including a washhouse and a smoke house. A dog was on the porch; the hound stood and stretched, then slowly lay down again. My heart resumed beating. Stunned and alarmed, I dodged back across the path.

I hurried back, mounted and we quickly began our return in silence. There was a strange, new sense within me. Seeing Hunter Hall, and reconciling it to the memories my father had shared in his letter, my mind wandered backward in time, imagining people and activity about the property.

*What would it have been like with the gardens and hedges neatly trimmed? Could I have seen the place where three generations of my family had made a home, that would have been remarkable. To have walked to the porch and have been welcomed in, instead of this furtive stolen vision, peopled only by a hound dog?*

Some miles down the road I heard a voice behind me, "Su, dat be a Hunter house too, yes su, three generations." My heavy silence returned. With relief I realized that at least he was not from the Hunter plantation.

That evening my small band again sat near the fort, watching the nightglow. We were able to build a small, protected fire and cook gruel that we ate with hard tack, and coffee. Taking turns, we sat all night watching. There was a total lack of activity in the small settlement in the distance.

Starting several hours prior to predawn, we were able to ride consistently but slowly. We were at a new camp at sunrise. The sergeant reported to me in an efficient manner on the days' activities at Fort Adams, this being a much busier port and tiny community during the preceding day. There had been the delivery of a number of wagons of various goods and some cotton. Private Turner gave me a tally. The bales were now filling a large portion of the dock.

During the day, I recorded his report. As the day started to dim we rode in a wide, winding arch through thick foliage, and followed a gully for several miles that wound west and north toward Woodville. Here we repeated the count and night watch.

That following evening finally took us back to the path we had followed when we had arrived. We camped with a sentry at each end of our bivouac, and waited for dark to make our return to Natchez.

The acting sentry on the south, the stealthy young man who was such a fine shot, returned. Whispering, he reported a small band of rebel soldiers bisecting our path from the river. There was no reason to think they would suspect our presence. Our horse tracks, if found, could not be identified. Still, we cautiously cushioned all our metal goods, and buried the fragrant coffee grounds. We lay on our bellies for two hours in dead silence, praying the rebels would just pass on eastward.

In fact, we had been quite lucky that we had not had more than a few human contacts during our time in the woods. All about the countryside were deserters of both armies. There where criminals and bandits seeking any gain they might find. Many former slaves who, fearing interment in the Kraal or capture by the dreaded night riders, were simply hiding in the woods; others too old to work had been turned out and were existing on the land.

When we felt safe, we all rose. I sent the sergeant to the north sentry as a replacement and Private Hunter to the other post. The muggy, afternoon heat made this forced idleness less than comfortable. We were only able to endure it as necessity demanded until dark.

Finally, as evening came, a soft mist began to fall, and then the splash of rain. This slow rain continued in a quiet evenness the whole way back to the Natchez. We were soaked. The odor of the horses and leather was pungent. The horses' hooves were no longer wrapped so that they would more sure footed on the slick clay of the path. The noise our movement made was of less consequence tonight because of the rain. It also provided us protection as we passed the home where the hounds lived.

When we were within several miles of town I pulled the mounted men together. With great emphasis, I demanded their absolute secrecy, remembering the threat from McDevlin of a treasonous trial and a hanging. I threatened them with punishment in jail and being kicked out of the army. I sent the sergeant and his man on ahead to wind down through town. Waiting a half-hour, the next two were sent off toward the fort. Again it was Private Hunter, the young soldier and I left to take our turn to leave.

By now there was a pink glow to the sky and the rain finally stopped. Hunter, myself and the young soldier rode onto the west road along the river. As we passed McDevlin's headquarters the others proceeded to the fort and I turned off. Wet and dirty, I dismounted and tied my horse to the hitching post in front of the dark house. The mare stood bleakly, water soaked and surrounded by muddy puddles. Her head, usually held high, simply hung.

As I approached the house a young, White, enlisted soldier with a gun stepped forward from a shadow. I pulled out the pass I had been issued, he studied it and went to a corner to stand, allowing me to climb onto the dry porch. It was good to reach the dark porch and have some shelter. I plopped down onto a straight chair, folding my arms and resting my chin on my chest to doze and wait for some sign of life within the lovely dwelling.

After resting for some time, I checked my pocket watch—it was six—I stood and began to pace. An officer I recognized but did not know well, joined me after tying his large roan at the post beside my mare. He gave me a silent glance and sat straight on another chair. Finally, I heard a door slam inside and the front door being unlocked and opened. As I might have expected, I heard muffled swearing inside. Immediately, I stepped in. The clerk was just entering his office and stopped to look at me. "Captain, wait on the porch."

Surprisingly, this time the wait was only five minutes. The clerk opened the door and signaled me. He nodded toward McDevlin's office and I went down the hall to the open door. Stopping on the threshold, I saluted. In a gruff whisper, McDevlin, wearing a stained dressing gown, demanded I come in and close the "damn door."

"You do what I told you boy?" he growled with burning intensity.

"Yes sir," I reached into my jacket to retrieve the map and ledger which were dry but clammy with body heat and humidity.

Brigadier General McDevlin rose and opened the drapes behind his desk. He made an effort to furtively scan the lawn both ways. As he moved, almost in a panic, to make sure no one could spy on us, I studied him. Although unkept, I could see he had been quite handsome. His hair was closely cut, in its mussed condition, some tendrils fell across his brow. His beard and mustache were full. In the dressing gown, which clung closely to his body, I could see he was trim, lithe and about five foot eight.

When he turned and those strange, burning eyes drove their heat toward me, I sensed in him almost a madness. The dark circles around his eyes were a strong indication of some driving passion. These were the kind of eyes I had often seen on the battlefield. They were the eyes of war weary, angry, beaten men who had lost their very souls.

"Come here, behind the desk." He grabbed the map and spread it. Then, dipping a pen into ink, he heard my report, making marks on the spots I designated. He was totally absorbed in getting all my information about the condition and locations of the wharves, landscape and any visible, posted guards.

The number of bales was of such importance that we hovered for an hour listing them carefully, again and again. This was not surprising to me as both armies counted the power and wealth of cotton in many ways for its possible use to their armies.

McDevlin straightened, and with a craggy hand, clamped on my shoulder in a firm grasp. "Anyone finds out—ever, I hand your sorry ass over the hangman! Hear me boy? You go now, fast. Leave by the back door and go around the house. Hear me! Go!" Repelled by his lack of military bearing, I felt offended and disgusted.

I saluted in a vain gesture and answered, "Yes sir." I left quickly, feeling relief to be freed once more. I was more than glad to be gone from this insanity.

As the back door swung shut behind me, I heard some commotion in front of the house. It seemed to be coming from the road. Rounding the corner, to my dismay, I saw the cause. The roan, with a long erection, was being pulled and whipped by the other officer and an enlisted man. My mare was prancing, foam on her neck and a small cut on her shoulder. I approached her from the side and carefully guided the nervous animal by the halter some distance before I took to my saddle. Talking in a soothing manner while I fought for control of the skittish animal, I rode her north in the direction of the fort.

When I returned the nervous mare to the stable, Matthew was waiting, obviously for me. With disapproval, he eyed the mare and I felt accountable.

"She got caught." I explained defensively, and strode away. After surrendering the reigns and retrieving my goods from the saddlebags, I went to the bath shed, returned to my tent and slept until mid-afternoon. After my nap, I went to see if there were any beans or meat left in the cookhouse, but they only came up with some mush and dry, cold corn bread.

I sat at a table with two officers who were idle. They tried to engage me in conversation, but I felt groggy and disoriented, so only answered in short sentences. The soldiers went on with their own line of talk.

As I completed the meal, I looked across the parade ground. Near the brig, a civilian, White woman stood with a basket on her arm. She appeared to be crying and begging the two armed guards to allow her inside the stockade or to answer some question. This caught my attention. After dealing with the Brigadier General, I suddenly found this scene most curious. *Was he, in fact, taking civilians as hostages?* I watched until the woman was turned away, holding the basket in front of her, head bowed and shaking in tears, she returned to her waiting carriage.

The next morning was Tuesday. I took an early ride to Monmouth home plantation and back. I made a late afternoon report and called on the enlisted noncoms for reports. One of the men casually asked where I had been Saturday. "Just out of the fort," I answered.

I did not have to wonder long what our sortie was about. The news came back that our troops had attacked Woodville and once more had burned the cotton. This seemed a reasonable purpose for the assignment my men and I had accomplished it. *Why were other units from the fort not used for reconnaissance and why the total secrecy within military ranks?*

The real bomb dropped a week later. A flatboat of cotton was taken from the river. The men manning the boat were some of our troops, and they had passes signed by Brigadier General McDevlin. These soldiers claimed he had ordered them to pick up cotton from Fort Adams, south of Natchez, the night the Woodville cotton was burned. The soldiers said they had been told moving the cotton was by direct order of General Grant. After a wired reply to the negative, the men who had been held in the brig were suddenly missing, no one witnessed their departure.

McDevlin was missing from the fort, and the enlisted men's story could not be collaborated. Not more than a couple days later, Brigadier General McDevlin was found moving numerous wagons of cotton northward using government wagons and horses.

Quietly the brigadier general was relieved of command and sent back to his home state. As I mentally evaluated the information, a sour taste and hot anger arose in me. I had been used. As Shakespeare had said, "something was rotten in Denmark," and this time it was named McDevlin. My mare and I had suffered the same treatment.*

**Such rumors or crimes did occur during the war but many were never prosecuted.*

Chapter 10

# Fort Life

More comfortable with the atmosphere of worship in the church, I finally made the decision to speak privately with Reverend Perry. It was my reasoning that with his welcome to the Black parishioners there might also be sympathy with my own personal dilemma. Sending away the two soldiers I had attended church with, I again lingered behind, waiting until the priest was free.

"May I speak privately with you about a spiritual matter?" I waited not at all sure that this quest for comfort was wise. It was a strong possibility that the man would not be willing to speak with me.

With only mild surprise, he responded, "Do come with me to the parsonage." Leading the way, he moved down the street with me following. The pastor stopped at a stone house not far from the church. Climbing four stone steps, we entered the classically styled doorway. Despite the warmth of the early afternoon outside, the entry hall was cool.

"May I take your hat?" he held out his hand and I surrendered my hat as I stood just inside. He took it to a hall tree to join some canes, an umbrella and a formal top hat and we moved to a study on the right.

As he crossed the threshold he nodded for me to follow. The sunlight sliced through the many paned glass in the two street-facing windows. Between the two windows was a small, beautiful mahogany writing desk. Moving behind the desk, he sat on a carved, dark chair with tapestry upholstery on the arms and a tall back.

"Captain, won't you sit down?" he motioned to a maroon, upholstered

Chesterfield armchair.

Settling into this seat I looked at either side of the room that was lined with bookshelves. The room had wide-board, polished floors covered with a colorful, woven carpet. There was another small side table and several other comfortable chairs.

Realizing that I was being rude by starring, I stammered an apology. Other than the headquarters, I had only been in private homes three times in four years. "Sir, I did not presume to stare, but I have not been in a house, such as this, for almost four years."

With sympathy, he slightly nodded his head and looked with empathy into my eyes. The gesture reminded me that with this nation split by conflict, none of us were completely comfortable being in contact with other sympathizers in any situation. The tribulations of the men on both sides were the same; that empathy created some type of bond, though loose. The differences were in the goals, not in our individual determination of achieving the ends for either the Union or the Confederacy.

"May I make you some tea or offer you a drink?" Realizing his lack of means, and my own impatience to get on with this awkward discussion, I demurred. "Sir, I thank you, but I do not mean to selfishly take up more of your valuable time than necessary."

Planting my feet solidly in front of myself and sitting straight with my hands clasped in my lap, I prepared myself to speak. By this time I was not at all certain this was a good decision. My personal quandary might necessarily even prove to be offensive to the clear-minded clergyman.

I knew that unlike the local Catholic priest this Episcopal pastor had signed the Oath of Allegiance when it was demanded by the Union. I was also sure that, with his example, almost every man in the congregation had also signed the pledges. He routinely recited the prescribed prayer for President Lincoln at each service. This was a church that also included Black, baptized members. Since the clergyman had a New England background, he surely must be sophisticated enough to understand the slavery issue from several perspectives, no matter where his own sympathy might lie.

"Young man, you desire to speak of some spiritual matter?" The slender, greying man leaned his sharp featured head forward in anticipation and professional openess. To my own discomfort, he seemed to also be covering some impatience. His eyes narrowed and his brows knit in intense concentration awaiting my narrative.

"When I first arrived in the congregation I had asked about Henry Hunter, my great grandfather who was a citizen, planter and political figure in early Mississippi. My grandfather, his son, left the state for Indiana many years ago. Through a strange turn of events I have been able to see the plantation the family founded near Pinckneyville on Byou Sara. It was nostalgic, yet poignant because of my current assignment in Natchez. The unique circumstances leave me with great personal conflicts of concern and guilt."

I found it hard to put my discomfort into words although I had rehearsed the speech many times in my head. Taking an awkward pause, my mind went blank for long moments while the priest waited patiently and compassionately.

"Both my grandfather and great grandfather were slave owners in the area. Now the personal guilt I feel toward the Black men in my command is overwhelming. I knew few Negroes until this war, although I was abolitionist by choice.

"When I took command of Colored soldiers I was advanced from private to captain in a matter of days. Frankly, my first observation of the men was to find the Coloreds very strange and simple. In fact, I felt no respect for them at all in the beginning.

"As I have continued with my command, I find the enlisted, Black troops to be as talented or lacking in talent as my own fellows from Illinois. When I examined each physically, upon their joining the army, I have been especially troubled by the scars of whipping, mutilation or branding that almost half of them carry as witness of owners' cruelty. The dire situation of their families, some perhaps because of my own family is most troubling."

Then my mouth went dry again and I looked at my hands in my lap.

Gathering composure I continued. "Upon the realization that I too have had a hand in this cruelty; I feel hypocrisy and compliance in the institution of slavery. In the underground railroad in Illinois the issue was clear and uncomplicated. It now overwhelms me with a sense of dishonesty to those in my command. Frankly, it may only be my need to confess the guilt I feel, yet the need to speak with someone I respect has been growing for a number of months.

"I am still firm in conviction of the rightness of our abolition of slavery. Now that I have seen the innocence and unprotected situation the Negroes will suffer after the war, I feel almost as much guilt as I feel for my own family's participation in slavery. My spiritual problem overwhelms me and it is guilt. The guilt is cold, heavy and weighs on my heart."

There was a very long silence, Father Perry leaned forward on his desk and studied its glossy top for some time, weighing his response.

I realized I had perhaps placed him in an awkward position, in consideration of the prevailing, military situation. There were so many restrictions for the citizens, especially the leaders, in Natchez. The man might even see this conversation as an attempt to entrap him for some infraction of military order.

I started to rise, "Sir, I am most sorry, perhaps I have put you in an untenable place." I moved quickly toward the door.

"No, young man. Please sit down. I offer you total confidentiality and would respectfully request the same courtesy for myself. I am most glad to speak with you, although I will of course not be specific to any one person in particular, other than the two of us.

"I came here as a boy from Connecticut. My father was a merchant. We owned three slaves for labor, a household girl to help my mothers and sisters with a large house and busy family. My father owned one nigger who helped with the shop and one who cared for the garden, horses and the grounds of our small home here in Natchez. When grown, I went away to seminary in New England. I was married here in Natchez for some years, until widowed by smallpox ten years ago. I owned two slaves and feel no shame in it. I was fair and kind, though firm.

"Both my father and I punished servants for unruliness, sullenness, drunkenness, dishonesty or disobedience. Neither of us ever broke the skin of one of those poor souls. Like children, they needed guiding, chastisement and without such they would take advantage, steal or become lazy."

"Slavery is an institution we all inherited, but we cannot survive without it. From the beginning of this church, the planters have brought slaves here for baptism. We have served them, always, as a part of our congregation. Among these at Old Trinity are also a number of skilled freedmen. The freedmen in Natchez are almost two hundred in number and serve their employers and themselves."

"The town of Natchez has always been a source of malamutation for slaves by owners. Many of the Colored community have found freedom. Often, freedom comes by their owner's wills upon death. Others eventually earn enough to buy their freedom, while also assigned to earning income for their owners by working for pay.

"The true cost of maintaining great properties, large populations of family and slaves has been overpowering to the planters. The skills and labor of this people has allowed the city to build what abundance we have had in Natchez. Even now as they become free, that freedom is like a death warrant to their fellows who remain on the plantations or businesses which they leave.

"There is a delicate economic balance in the community. The men are an important source of income for the owners and their own families. A young male worker is worth about $1,800. There is a great investment in such service. Their departure leaves the planters much in need. Nigger lives are tied, even unto the fifth generation to a single family. Although it is not a Black family, the owner's family has often become their own history and family, in a matter of speaking.

"Cast out without support and protection, how many of these Colored will survive? Yet it could well be asked, what of their fellows left on failing plantations or businesses?

"Guilt, my boy, is a fact of maturity. Only a man of no conscience can exist without the knowledge of responsibility or of some guilt. God is our judge, but we can be our own witness to our personal guilt. A man who sees himself totally innocent is a fool.

"Your ancestor, like all the settlers here and even the Cherokee, learned that it is not possible to prosper with paid labor or with only their own power. This country is hard. The power of the slave labor is not free or without responsibility, but this manpower has made the our life possible.

"Eventually the economy would have demanded some changes. The end of slavery would have been one of these. But with the necessity of the huge amounts of labor that are currently needed, the demand cannot be changed quickly.

"Perhaps some overseers or owners do take liberties with the females and in the punishment of the chattel. Despite your sensibilities, some of these simple, Black people deserve or need severe punishment. They are first a necessity, second valuable, and because of this they are generally well treated, fed and provided with doctors when necessary. In my congregation no White plantation owner has ever confessed to me violence. Neither has any Black member so complained of cruel treatment. I do know this violence happens, but in secret and despite protective laws put in place many years ago. Such reprehensible behavior is seldom exposed to public view. Owners and overseers who abuse break the law.

"Especially distressing, have been the nightriders harassing and murdering slaves and former slaves. They are cowards hiding in the night. The justification they give for their actions is that there is some chance these thousands of dark people may rise up against the White people. If Negroes had run free, encouraging others to run away, we would have had bedlam, violence to our own families and anarchy.

"It is most alarming now that emancipation has made a sudden, knife-like incision of change to our whole society. The whole community is restless, lost and disorientated. The Negroes, the city, the owners and the planters are all in dire straights."

Reverend Perry sat back and looked at the ceiling as though pondering his next statement. In this moment I absorbed what I had heard. It was especially of worth to ponder responsibility as a mirror reflection of guilt. He had said it was a price of maturity.

Clearing his throat, the clergyman slowly began to speak again, this time with less certainty. "In the north I found a lack of understanding that the whole community here in the South is sympathetic to Black's welfare. Our people especially respect those loyal servants who support them in these dire days. These individuals are treated like family members, sometimes they are even buried in family plots at the city cemetery."

"There was, until recently, a Negro freeman who was a barber in this town. He was a respected person, landowner and even was a slave owner. He was literate and successful. He is but one of several. This community appreciates good businessmen and commerce, so there's a place for niggers here."

"Among many of my associates in the north, are those with no sympathy for slavery. In our continued correspondence we may differ. Yet, having lived in this region for my adult life, I know there is an unavoidable historic and necessary quality to the institution. The caring concern of all our citizens for the welfare of the Blacks far outweighs the many deficits. These are a simple people who would, in the most, find it impossible to make their own way in the world as the few exceptional freedmen do.

"I tell you these things about myself because I too have a personal investment in slavery or the end of it. Only I feel the responsibility and concern, not the guilt you feel. I can accept the inevitable and do my duty to see after the Colored congregations' welfare while still serving my White congregation."

Again the pastor made a pause and his stern visage softened, as he looked me in the eye. "What guilt you have is not personal if you have not whipped a man, dishonored a woman nor caused hardship to their families. That is, unless this new military position of responsibility causes you to put them into such a dangerous situation that it will bring more pain to them.

"Perhaps you need to concentrate on bringing what good you may to your soldiers. Better that your energy be invested in what will become of them, however the war may end.

"I would suggest what you feel is not guilt but sympathy for the few individuals who have been mistreated. You also feel the weight of a responsibility to care for and guide them in your own capacity as their officer. Are you making an attempt to prepare them for the future? In whatever way you choose—education, protecting their families or supervising their pay; you need to put into action what you stand for if you truly are an abolitionist."

My eyes did not leave his face as he spoke. For a long moment, we looked into each other's souls. Perhaps there was some solace in this visit. Slowly I continued with what I had thought of sharing. "The guilt I feel for the past makes it difficult to look into my men's eyes, especially one private. Yet, I do know the sin is not mine, I did no violence or purposeful evil to any of my men."

With a professional tone the Reverend seemed to finalize our conversation, "It is my recommendation that you take time in scripture; much is said there about the slave. Then ask forgiveness for any duplicity you might carry and pray. Bless you," making a sign of the cross, he rose to signify the end of our talk.

At the door, he shook my hand firmly and returned my hat. As I exited, we stood a moment and he nodded to me from his place on the threshold.

"Good luck young man, your task is like Don Quiotix, the windmills exist but it is not always very effective to attack them."

As I rode through the town in the late morning sun, I watched the few people move about. Women were holding shawls around their shoulders. Despite the flowers and green grass there was a soft, moist coolness to the air. My uncertain mind shuffled through our talk for the insights I had received from priest.

Last week a letter had appeared reminding me that Christmas was nearing and pangs of loneliness filled me. Then a vivid memory appeared in my mind, the torn back of Private Hunter on the day he had enlisted. Next, I saw images of the widows and grieving families in the congregation. My mind's eye glimpsed Brigadier General McDevlin. Finally I seemed to be looking into a mirror, feeling lost and fearful. *Who and what was I? How did I fit into this diverse collage? The world has gone mad, dragging me along with it unable to help myself or others.*

The following Sunday I had stayed at fort. It was as though I felt I needed to find some kind of peace before I returned there to worship. A soft mist began to fall and those of us left idle at the fort gathered just inside the stable. I visited with other officers, then played several card games.

After that, taking my pipe, I went to lean against the open stable door. I was not intending to eavesdrop, yet I could still hear the gossip of the Black enlisted men sitting under a lean-to that was covering on some hay.

They discussed at some length the promised pay for their three-year enlistment. Several bitterly renounced the difference of what they were really being paid compared to the White enlisted pay.

Their opinions varied about whether they would ever recover the money which some of the Union officers took and claimed they were holding for the Negroes. When they had inquired or requested their collected salaries, the officers had given them no direct answers. Then to my alarm, the men discussed a specific fellow officer from Tennessee who was holding their pay or promising to send money to families who lived far from Natchez. I had known the practice of extortion existed in the Colored corp yet had no idea that such duplicity was being practiced here at McPhearson.

One young man then shared with excitement the birth of his first, freed son. He had named the child Moses, of course. Another soldier complained of the hunger suffered by people in the Kraal. He mourned the old people who lived in the squalor. Haltingly, he described the sickness of one of his own young children.

I heard the well spoken voice of Private Alexander Turner, and took a furtive peek to make sure that it was in fact him.

"I wonder if the Fifty-eighth is going to battle soon?"

From this question the small group went around expressing their confidence and courageous intent to become warriors.

Private Turner went on once more about his personal concern. "I am from the Hedges in Wilkinson County. My massa was my father. It was him taught me readin'. Bout the time we all be freed my pappy was goin' to war. I come up to him and say that I goin' be a Union soldier. He was upset. He begged and even tried to bribe me not to join the army. He offered me cash money, even. He wanted me to go fight with him. He say nothin' bout me being free, jus like it wasn't true. One thing I sure of, that man love me. I jus stay quiet cause I know what I goin to do."

His attractive tan colored face calmed, and he continued, "Know what my Pappy say? 'My son, if we meet on the field of battle I will fire over your head. I would hope that you would do me the same honor.' I just want to fight. But I sho do hope I do not need to decide if I kill my own Pappy."[23]

The group of soldiers was silent, each person lost in personal evaluation and awe at the man's story. The situation as they compared it to their own emotions was strange to consider.

After a bit more family gossip, the conversation turned. I was probably becoming accustomed to the Southern Black accent for I could now understand much of what was being said. One Colored enlisted said he had been raised in Mississippi and would not be happy away from his home here. Once, he had been taken to work in New Orleans and it was far too busy and big. In Mississippi, he would be among people and land he knew. His dream was to find a small farm, right here, and work that land to feed his family. He wanted to sell enough produce for shoes, to send his children to school and to buy a beautiful dress for his wife.

Although he was in the shadows, my senses sharpened when I next recognized the voice of Private Hunter. "I will learn more, be smart, and find a business, perhaps my own stable up north or in Virginia." The voice was the same but it was different. His companions noticed the accent immediately with some resentment they chided him.

"What you be doin' bein' White? Massa Hunta?" they laughed.

"I have been thinking, did any of you know that freed barber that got killed here in Natchez a few years ago by a white man?" Several murmured their acknowledgment. "He spoke very well and all the town people treat him like he be white. One company in this town has a freedman owner, by two generations they already be rich." Private Hunter continued, "If I read books like I been doing and I practice I can talk just like them, too. I be just like a gentleman."

With some sullenness one of his fellows warned, "They still treat you like a nigga. That barber is still dead. We still only get part o' our pay. Any officer or doctor here can whip us if they wants. How you goan change how you look?"

With embarrassment I drew back around the corner of the door, hoping I had not been observed eavesdropping. In my heart I knew that no matter my own compassion and the growing respect I felt, there would always be distance and a lack of complete understanding of my men.

I withdrew, walking the length of the stable, and made a dash through the rain over to the mess hall to see if I could find something hot to eat. Luckily, there was the evening meal and I secured some porridge and fresh bread. I ate a large helping, topping it off with bitter, hot coffee. Then, with long paces, I moved across the parade ground and north to officer quarters. A few weeks ago I had been moved to a mansion, used for that purpose, within the fort.

When I removed my boots, sweat and moisture had dampened my feet, as soon as my knitted stockings were removed, I wiped my feet dry and wrapped them in a blanket. I lit the lamp and wrote a letter to my parents. Then later, I made a few notes in my small leather bound diary. Undressing, I lay on the cot, wearing only my union suit.

The sun had just dropped away when I stared through my west-facing window. I saw figures on the parade ground huddled against the mist as they moved about. Several Black families were grouped together and talking on the crest of the steps. Their shapes were outlined with the last faint pink glow. In the distance, a few horses whinnied.

It should have been a peaceful time, but I was truly disquieted. My roommates had not yet arrived in our room and I had unusual privacy in the cramped quarters. I lay there lonely, pondering many issues, both personal and spiritual, and those of war.

I began to silently pray for the end of the war and a peace. I prayed to lose the emptiness within me. Remembering the overheard conversation, I prayed passionately for my men and the future they faced. Tears dribbled from the corners of my eyes and rolled warmly down my cheeks.

As always I was surprised when I woke at dawn in relative comfort. There was mist rising from the ground. Pulling my trousers up, I wandered to the outhouse and returned. I wiped my feet with a bit of rag and replaced my boots and socks. Dropping my suspenders, I pulled my shaving gear out and shaved my face, then trimmed my mustache. Turning the mirror to a good light, I used a tiny pair of scissors to shape it carefully. I combed my hair and tilting my head, plucked a white hair out of the crown. I was too young to become grey. I had not even begun my life, six years of it would be gone before I returned home.

The daring man that I had been was gone. I was no longer the man that made the manly trek to Pikes Peak in 1860 and returned in the Spring of the War. That man's idealism was gone. The war had worn my spirit as my view of death and violence had hardened some internal part of me.

People like Brigadier General McDevlin tore to shreds all my trust and faith in people.

There was a God, at least I hoped so. It was some comfort to talk to the Reverend last week, but I am not a schoolboy. It was myself, not some wisdom from somewhere else, that would absolve my guilt. My only job for today was to do what was needed, to be honest, dependable and respectful.

God willing, I would be in no more battles or see no more blood. If war came to the Fifty-eighth, somehow my men would need to be ready for battle. That was the first of my responsibilities.

I breakfasted, went to the command post and spent several hours filling out papers and forms. Then, just before the early lunch, I went to the stable to order my horse prepared for me and went to eat again. The time spent going to the northernmost plantation today, would be longer as I knew the rutted trail would be an almost impassible muddy and slick byway.

My premonition about the road was correct. *What a mess!* The Loess clay was slippery where it was semi-dry. Along the whole course there were uneven pools and puddles. The grasses were tall and irritating if I rode to the edge of the path, so in the main, I walked my horse.

I saw a now familiar carriage ahead of me, but this time it was not moving. The old Black coachman was in front trying to guide the horse to the roadside and out of a mud puddle. As I approached, I could see one wheel mired hopelessly and the other riding high.

As I pulled beside the carriage I asked, "Might I help you?" With relief the driver saw me. He first looked at me timidly as I stood beside my horse. Then the man climbed into the seat, speaking quietly into the back of the vehicle and then looking back at me.

"Thank you, Su," he responded with obvious relief and gratitude.

I mounted and rode to the other side to check the situation. "Have you had any luck backing out?"

"No su."

"I think we will need some branches or something." I looked toward a section of scrub bush and small saplings. Dismounting, I cut an armful and lay them in front of the mired wheel. Remounting, I rode to the front and pulled the trace up with no success. Then, taking a rope from my gear, I tied it to my saddle horn and through a metal loop at the front of the carriage. I nodded to the old man and instructed. "Now, when I say drive, pull the horses forward and to the left."

When the command was given we both strained and encouraged the horse onward. The animal strained and the carriage wobbled precariously; it rolled a bit but came to a dead halt. I went to cut more foliage and threw the branches behind the wheel while the older man unharnessed the horse and brought him to the rear of the vehicle.

We repeated the process pulling backward this time. The carriage suddenly lurched out of the hole at a wild angle. I retrieved my rope and left the servant to reharness the horse. Riding to the front of the vehicle I drew up. "Madam, are you safe?"

A voice, younger and sweeter than I expected, answered from the shadowy interior, "I am just fine. Thank you for your help."

I could see little except prim, gloved hands folded into the black fabric of her skirt. The lady wore a small hat with a long, heavy black veil that hid her face. I could see the shape of her face and a mass of brown curls under the hat.

"If I might be so rude as to make a suggestion?" I spoke with careful courtesy for fear of somehow offending this widow.

"Of course, I am in your debt," her light, sweet voice spoke warmly.

Gently I began, "I have seen you many times on this road and know it is your practice to visit the cemetery. Perhaps today you might delay the visit, you may have further troubles in the mud of the road or cemetery. It would be unwise to be disabled with so many ruffians about and this near the Trace."

"Oh," she whispered with a shaky voice that seemed on the verge of tears. "You may be right, it is kind of you to offer such service and to be considerate of my welfare."

I listened to her appealing, female voice, heavy with a smooth, slow, Southern accent. Not wanting to be invasive, I tipped my hat. "I am about a task and regret I cannot see you home, good day,"

"And also to you, sir," came her earthy reply.

For a few moments I wondered at the woman, who was obviously a widow. Now, I realized the lady was quite young, if her voice was true measure.

Then my errand at the plantation filled my mind and the vigilance of keeping my own steed on sure footing took all my concentration. I passed the Devil's Punchbowl every time I went to the plantation. This was a strange sunken area, which seemed to be caving into a dark underworld. Because of the shifting earth, no one had ever farmed or built on the location. On the undisturbed ground were treeless, grassy meadows. At the river's bluff edge were a few ancient trees.

Since I had been in Natchez, I had heard the legends of river pirates hiding bounty here. It had a haunted reputation of thieves and murderers. Many felt it was the site where a meteor fell. Ironically, it was a favorite prewar picnic location for citizens from the town. Perhaps the mystery attracted them as well as the beauty.

As I passed, I smelled smoke and there was an eerier silence. I pretended not to look in that direction for I knew at least several hundred dispossessed Negroes where hiding there in deep gullies. These contraband were deathly afraid of the Union soldiers, nightriders, or of being found and forced to go the Kraal. The poor people were in no danger from me. Even this eerie place was preferable to the Kraal.

"Edwin," I called when I saw Hobart. He was the Illinois corporal who was temporarily placed on duty here and was assigned to a different company in the Fiftieth. Hobart was sitting on a stump near the road when I approached the plantation.

"What are you doing out here?" It was easy to be warm with this friend.

"Captain, I am just wondering and wallowing. Wondering what I am doing in this forsaken war, planting and plowing, and wallowing in the mud."

Standing, he came to walk beside my horse as I approached the long lane to the house. "The roof leaked all night, every pot and pan was called to Union duty. The bedding of those sleeping in outlying buildings was wet. In the middle of the night, everyone crowded into the house. The sleeping was wet, smelly and uncomfortable. All the White enlisted crowded into my room, sleeping on the floor wherever there was not already a drip pot."

"The land is too wet to work, the men can only feed the stock, and do simple tasks about the house and barn. I just had to escape the house and so walked away a bit," his complaints continued.

We tied my horse to a post, and walked to the porch where we sat among a number of people. I turned to a private and requested some cold water. He soon returned with a pitcher and a glass. The first two glasses I downed greedily, then sipped on the third.

"Is there news from town? I shall be glad to come to town next week for a few days," Hobart said with bitter emphasis.

"Will you accompany me to church next week?" I inquired.

"You know I am a Catholic but I always like to go to your church," was his answer.

I continued in the easy banter we had always adopted, "That is fine though, the Catholic priest in Natchez was so reluctant to take the loyalty oath that his church is still being punished for his defiance, at least the Episcopals were not so stubborn."

Pausing, I murmured, adding a pall to the mood. "I wonder when I am in church if our churches at home are so full of widows and orphans?"

Edwin looked at his muddy boots and sighed, "Our whole nation is in mourning," he murmured sadly.

We sat silently. Finally, looking excited Edwin brightened, "One of the soldiers' wives had a baby—big, strong and beautiful. Makes me wish I was not a bachelor and was going home to such a child. The father let me hold the babe and it was so soft and warm and sweet. Babies have always frightened me, but this time it was hard to return the child to its father."

Pausing to recall a new memory, he then continued, "The men

stationed at this plantation are so disappointed and humiliated to be here instead of at the fort behaving like 'real soldiers.' On each Saturday we practice with rifles, although each man does not have his own. At least six of them were already excellent shots and the others now shoot quite well. Each night we use the blackboard and study words. The entire group of children and women crowd in to watch. Though I have not asked, I think they are also learning to read."

"Lets walk," I suggested and we took to our feet and walked through dripping weeds in the meadow between the house and the road.

Edwin quietly reported, "Several men are so discouraged I am afraid they may desert. Two of these are men came here with a bitter hate of the other because of some past problem. Twice, they have appeared with wounds from fighting, which they of course deny. I have not seen the fight, and no one would report it. I have taken no action. I am afraid that this disorder can eventually cause a real problem."

"The women with husbands here add much to our comfort and earn some money by cooking and doing laundry. But there are four girls around fourteen years of age, with twenty lonely bachelors, that could also be explosive."

"Edwin, I think you may have a good feeling for possible solutions to future problems. Do the men follow orders, respect and obey you?"

"Yes, and you know Captain, I am beginning to understand these Black men. Several are real strong, good men; men I would gladly fight beside."

"I know what you mean, Edwin, my tendency is the same. Even President Lincoln does not know where they will go after the war. My father writes that the North, though hateful of slavery, fears the freedmen will undermine employment. This summer there were riots and lynching of Negroes again. When this war began there were two million slaves, not counting freedmen, they are an eighth of our population."

"So many souls with no homes. Where and what will they do?"

We began to wander back toward the porch; an idea struck me. I straightened and stood before the corporal. "Corporal Hobart, your men are available today, since they are idle I will do a pass in review on the grass in this meadow in the late afternoon. Have your men prepare and tell me when they are ready."

The men nearby, who had eavesdropped, straightened; several even stood, saluted and then rushed off.

In the following hours I reviewed the journals, bookkeeping and records. The corporal and three other White noncoms encouraged and instructed the men. Edwin came back into the house to give me his official reports and requisitions.

It was around three in the afternoon when I was informed that the unit had formed in the meadow. I had, as a ranking officer, participated but never before had I called a review. For the first time in my new position I felt in command.

I groomed myself carefully and slowly walked to the porch. To one side of the wide yard were all of the families. The children were round-eyed and excited. Most of the men had been sent to this plantation as soon as they enlisted and they had no experience with such things as a pass in review.

"Are you ready Corporal Hobart?"

"Yes Sir". He replied loudly, smartly saluting me. Then he called his men to attention. Slowly, I walked the line making only a few, small corrections on posture or buttons. My heart sank as I saw at least a dozen men were shoeless and most were armed. Several soldiers had no jackets. An unusually, large man had a jacket with the sleeves halfway to his elbows and a large gap in front that bared his naked chest.

"Corporal, which of the enlisted men has the most responsibility for this operation?"

"William Brown, Sir," was the quick, unhesitating reply.

Turning to the troops I commanded, "Private William Brown, step forward." A tall, skinny man with close-cropped hair; light, tan skin; and a pointed nose stepped up. "Private Brown would you make a report on this Union home plantation?" He stared wide-eyed at me in panic and silence.

"Private Brown, you may just tell me, in the easiest way, what is happening here now and how the farming is proceeding."

Looking tentative and using a soft voice that exposed his shyness he carefully planned and presented each of his phrases.

I interrupted a few times with questions. "If you continue to care for and help guide the operations here, when the time comes I will recommend your raise in rank. Thank you, return to the line."

Looking back at the men I tried to look official and pleased. "As you know our army is large. It is hard to provide goods as needed. I will continue to attempt to speed up the effort to provide you all the goods, uniforms and weapons you need as soldiers."

"Those of you without arms stand forward."

Nodding to a White private, I commanded. "You will take the names of these soldiers and make a list for me." The man rushed to the house for paper and pen.

Nodding at a sergeant, "Will you please make a list of clothing, especially shoes and jackets and an estimate of size for each of these men."

I stood with my hands behind my back in parade posture for the half-hour these tasks took. Then, I commanded the Sergeants back into line.

I climbed to the porch and looked at this strange army standing on the grassy meadow. I glanced at each face groping for something else I could do to transfer my approval of them. My eyes rested on the oversized man in the undersized uniform and I saw something, something special. His face was full of pride to be able to stand free, to stand before this small community of soldiers and family. He was proud to be a man. *I wanted to give him more, but what?*

I paced up and down the porch several times while my mind raced; they all stood silent and expectant. I wanted to give them more.

I stopped and cleared my throat. "Since it is difficult to find the goods and rifles you need and deserve, I cannot tell you when the order will be filled. I am asking all of you, though tired from your work, to find time to begin to do more practice drills.

"This is your first pass in review. When your drill is complete and I have obtained the goods; I will schedule a full pass in review for you with ranking officers at Fort McPhearson." Looking at the huge man, I addressed him, "Private, perhaps your uniform will better fit someone else, you are a Union soldier. We will find you a jacket that expresses your profession."

Corporal Hobart ordered the sergeant find a man it would fit. "I promise you a new one which is suited to you."

"Corporal Hobart is quite pleased with your work and effort. It is good that so many of you are doing well at reading and writing. Please continue to prepare for your new lives after the war. We will win this war and like all the Colored troops, what you are doing is important. Your duty is to feed and pay for the war effort by the Union. This duty is helping to defeat the Rebels, as much as on a battle field."

"With your shooting and drilling, you are going to be prepared to be called for battle when the need arises."

At the end this presentation, I had another thought. "I hope all of you will encourage your families to learn to read and write. You are dismissed."

Into the evening and as the meal was prepared, I smoked and rocked on the porch. It was so personal and comfortable, I felt almost like I was home. There was fresh pork, greens, small brown beans with a black spot on each and a spicy red soup. A fine meal and a front porch were soothing.

The other problem situations that Hobart had described played on my mind. After supper the White enlisted men and I visited for a while, then I sent them into the house.

"Edwin, who is the oldest and wisest of the women here?"

"Melanie, I guess."

I requested, "Would you see if you can find her?" He left for fifteen minutes and returned with a woman, taller than I. Her head was wrapped in a peach colored bandana, her white apron was marked by work and covered a buxom, rounded form. Her eyes were deep and dark, yet, her brows were a startling white. Only the whiteness of those brows and a slight stoop belied her age, which appeared to be at least sixty or more.

"Melanie."

"Yes su."

"Are you a married woman?" I questioned.

"No su, I be widow," came the quizzical answer.

"If I pay you two dollars a month, will you provide a service for the Union?"

A smile covered her face. "Yes su, I like do a job and get pay. Can I still be pay for the cookin' I do?"

"Yes this will be two dollars more. I am going to ask Corporal Hobart to find a room in this house where you will sleep."

She brightened and straightened. "Yes su," she was amazed.

"Do you know what a chaperone is?"

"No su."

"Well…," I groped. "You will be a chaperone for the Union Army. Many times young women are very foolish and cause themselves trouble. They also make lots of trouble for young men by flirting and tempting them. I do not want my soldiers troubled. I want you to be the chaperone for the unmarried women on this plantation. You will be their boss…their Mistress. Keep them busy all day and they will also sleep with you in your room. Do you accept this job for Union?"

"Chaperone…Mista Cap'n," she said with a twinkle in her eye. "I do agree with you and I most like ta be a chapron."

"Very well, you are hired Melanie. If they do not obey you, tell the corporal and he will see that they do. Thank you, you can go now."

Holding onto the porch column the woman stiffly helped herself down from the porch.

"Yes sir, yes sir, that was some good thinking. Nothing gets past Melanie and extra help in the kitchen and the rest of the house would ease her job a lot."

"Ed, do you know what else I have thought of? I need your advice, and go slow in putting it into action. See if this works. Those two fighters put them to different tasks. Divide the work crews very equally and keep them stationed apart. Perhaps we can turn their animosity into enthusiasm to compete with better work."

With some thought Hobart replied, "I have done that sometimes, but it has never been official. I think the one thing we have to watch for is having too much competition. It tends to become team against team. Please be conscious to reprimand and applaud them equally."

With a wink, Edwin added, "I may talk alone to Private Brown about this. He would never report them, but he might know what men to put on which team."

I dozed half the night in the rocker, until chill woke me and I went to a bed. Being an officer had an advantage. Most of the White soldiers were on pads on the floor.

The next morning the ride back to the fort was easier after almost forty-eight hours without rain. I thought of all the tricks, ploys and bribery schemes I might use on the quartermaster to get the needed goods. My men at the fort, and those on the home plantation, needed so many supplies.

A half mile before I reached the cemetery on the return trip I saw the same small carriage. It was wending its way along the paths into the Natchez City cemetery. I halted the horse and led it off the road into a small grove where I allowed it to graze. Running my hand on the horse's fine coat and increasing belly I stealthily watched the distant forms. The carriage stopped near a small tree in the northern section of the burial grounds. The driver tied it halfway from the entrance. He then helped the woman out.

I studied where she went with some curiosity. Mentally, I marked some landmark locations. She stood before a cluster of tombstones, and then knelt for a long time. Finally she rose, was helped back into the carriage and it moved slowly back out of the cemetery and into the road southward toward town.

With no reason for the lady in the carriage to look back, my stealth was unnecessary. This day I turned into the cemetery, checking to make sure that the carriage was out of view, I followed the same route that they had used.

I tethered my mare and studying the sizes and shape of a few landmarks, tried to approximate the location where I had seen the woman kneel.

There it was, a plot with several similar family names. A small bouquet of garden flowers lay on the neatly tended plot. Seeing the stone where the flowers lay, I read with shocked surprise, the stone was inscribed: WILLIAM SCOTHORNE, LOVING HUSBAND AND FATHER AND PRAISE HIS VIRTUE. I had found the Widow Scothorne.

When Corporal Edwin Hobart came in to the fort that week, his news was optimistic. The work crew idea was accomplished and was easing the tension and friction. With Private Brown's help, he felt the home plantation was seeing more success due to the soldier's skill.

I, unfortunately, had to report my futile attempts for finding the needed goods with the quartermaster. After mulling on this, Edwin asked for a copy of my request to the quartermaster. He studied it, folded the paper neatly and put it into his breast pocket. Looking at his watch, and seeing that it was nearly four. He asked the quartermaster's name and said, "I will see what I can do," giving me a broad wink before he departed.

The next morning I looked around and did not see Edwin. I went about breakfast, and the usual paperwork. "An army runs on paper," I muttered to myself.

About one in the afternoon I saw a bleary man at my elbow. It was Edwin a bit worse for the wear.

"Did you go drinking, man."

In a husky reply, the disheveled corporal laughed, "Well, guess you could say I went fishing. You will need a wagon when you come to the plantation next week or the week after. I got everything on your list if the quartermaster is good for his word." Holding a twenty-five dollar silver piece high, he continued, "and also enough to take care of a fine Christmas for my family."

"I am flabbergasted. How did you do it?"

"Guess you did not know that in Illinois I am known as a 'gambling man,'" he laughed, "That is when I get a chance and have a dollar. Took me till dawn to do it. Do you want to join me on a shopping trip?"

The idea of a day with a friend away from the fort was the bait and I was hooked. I would have never finished the paper work anyway. Sounding official, I reported I had business. Then I transferred duty to another officer. I retrieved my horse from Private Hunter and another for Hobart. I heard Matthew's none too veiled disapproval of the growing belly on the mare. Politely, I listened to his advice on how to ride her. Then Edwin and I departed, I was in the lead, but my friend was not too far behind, so we could share news.

The man accompanying me had a barrel chest, was about five eight and light-skinned with freckles and bushy brows. The brows matched the mad mass of chestnut hair which seemed only controlled by the cap perched on it. Each time I looked back he gave a comradely wink, a gesture common to his good nature and a sign of his happy easy ways.

Another habit of his was the frequent reply, "that's one for the old diary."

Today, for the third time when he said it I quizzed him, "Do you in fact keep a diary?"

"That I do, and Captain you are in it, so best be careful what you say or do."

We chatted about what we were seeking as gifts. We listed for whom we would purchase these and other such frivolous matters during the slow thirty-minute ride.

As we rode, we both remembered the Midwestern snows and cold. It would be good to be there, to see the snow. But, today the comfort here, the flowers and green trees made snow only a lonely memory.

The townspeople were well dressed, unless you stood close and realized how many garments were patched, taken in or let out. As a whole their countenance was pleasant, yet behind it there was a veil that lacked true cheer. The price of war paid by this lovely city lay just below the surface of each citizen. A few merchants simpered to gain favor with the Union officers out of greed or poverty. The majority were more courteous but still restrained. After all, the Union held this city in military rule. The whim of an ill tempered officer could deeply affect their welfare, or even their lives.

Along with the Under the Hill bedlam and crime, there were other lewd and corrupt people in the city. These were ever seeking to take advantage of the pitiful conditions of all. *What but caution could guide these Southern people?*

Many of the shops had only a few things on the shelves, some seemingly removed from elsewhere, or placed there from personal homes. In the war, merchants had no goods and the towns people had no money. The goods that were available and advertised were exorbitant in cost. The weathered opulence of this prosperous port city was peeling like the paint and whitewash on many of the houses. Yet, like the granite and composite shell stones on the houses, the city clutched with pride and dignity to what it could, until the war should end and they could begin to rebuild, again.

With the downward turn of the war against the Confederacy, a sense of desperation became ever more bewildering to the citizens. Slavery had been expedient, a force of necessity and economy; it was an inherited decision not a personal act of cruelty. If the Union succeeded, as it seemed it might now, in late 1863, how would the society reshape the vestiges of what remained.

Cotton, like white gold, fed the whole economy, and without labor what would the South produce? That slowed trickle of white gold had kept this internationally important trade and port city barely alive. Cotton still provided four hundred dollars a bale up North.

The boardwalks and covered walkways of the business district kept the sun off our heads as we strolled. We left the horses tied at a water trough down the hill. Pausing, we bought some apples from a Negress. Wiping them on our sleeves we then bit into the sweet warm skin; the juicy meat cleared our dry mouths.

Near where we stood was a small, ladies hat shop and we only glanced at it. Then my eye fell on a glint of red, and I stepped toward the window. Between two large feathered hats lay a garnet necklace. The delicacy and color drew me. Finishing the apple, I threw the core into the street and grabbed Edward's sleeve. Pulling and tugging the embarrassed young man behind me, I pushed through the door of the shop.

"What? You need a ladies hat?" my comrade mumbled from a moist, apple stuffed mouth.

The interior of the shop was cool. There were shelves lining the walls with a few hats; empty spaces were covered with crisp, crocheted doilies. Here and there were tidy piles of lace, edged handkerchiefs arranged to show various colors and styles. Behind the counter was a lovely, young, blond woman with her hair piled high, a lace collar beginning at her neck and falling down to her bosom. I smiled and nodded to her, intent on my task.

Behind me I heard Edward choking on the last of his apple.

I wondered if there were more necklaces and studied the shelves and the counter in front of the woman. When I did look at her I saw her blush and look down. Looking behind me I saw Edwin, his face bright red; *from blush or choking*? The man's head was erect, his mouth open and eyes staring.

"Are you well?" I inquired of the young man, with some concern.

Lowering his head and taking a breath my friend mumbled, "I am fine," with an embarrassed gurgle.

I paused for a second and turned to the blushing proprietress, "Is the necklace in the window for sale?" She nodded demurely.

"May I see it?" She moved away from the counter and to the window display. Like magnets as she passed, we both turned with her motion. There was a soft swish of skirts; a lavender fragrance wafted as she moved.

Then my eyes again rested on the necklace the woman was retrieving, but Edwin's eyes never moved from the soft, lavender dress and the blond hair. The woman gracefully moved back behind the counter and carefully lay the necklace on the black, marble surface.

There was a chair and a mirror in front of the counter and a small oil lamp with crystals was glittering close to the mirror so women would see a complimentary view when they tried on hats. Today, the lamplight, mirror and crystal illuminated the necklace. There were clusters of garnets cut in teardrop shapes, hanging on a delicate, black wire of some type. The center stone was larger and reflected light. It was of the same shape but smaller. What made it so appealing to me were the jewel's color and the delicacy.

"Are these garnets?"

"Yes sir, Czechoslovakian garnets, but the setting is quite unusual. The center stone," she said touching it, "is a fine ruby, small but perfect."

I touched the stones delicately. Real jewels were an unknown quantity to me. "May I touch them?" I asked as an afterthought.

The sweet reply was, "Of course." Picking the necklace up delicately by the chain, I watched the transparent, red stones shimmer. I could not imagine anything I had seen before that was more beautiful and luxurious. I held them to the light of the lamp. Then I turned and looked through them toward the light outdoors.

"Madam, would it be proper to ask you to put them on so I can see how they look?"

Blushing even more, she reached and took the jewelry. Nervously working the clasp, she raised the fastener behind her neck and took some time fumbling until it was fixed. The chain was long, the stones lay between her white throat and her small round breasts whose shape was much enhanced by the white lace.

With some embarrassment I stared at her chest, then lowered my eyes, "Thank you."

Hurriedly, in an awkward act, she began to unfasten the clasp. Raising her arms thus before two lonely, young, Union soldiers became ever more embarrassing. I turned to pretend to examine some handkerchiefs. Ed simply stared; his mouth ajar again.

After long, painful moments, the clasp released. Holding one end she pulled it away, only to have the other end of the chain catch in the lace at her neck.

A long soft "Ohhh" escaped the girl with a defeated note, as she stared at the free end of the chain laying in her hand. Then gathering what dignity she could, she straightened her posture and plucked at the end of the necklace with her right hand, while her left held the necklace. It required more attention, so she bowed her head and as she did, Edwin looked at me, nodded his head slightly from side to side, and winked.

At last the disentanglement was done and the necklace lay on a tatted doily on the counter. I returned to the counter and picked it up. "How much is this?" "Forty dollars." "I would like to purchase it." I reached for my moneybag, which I always secured inside the waist of my trousers from the belt loop. The pretty girl found some tissue and carefully wrapped the red necklace, placed it in a tiny box and handed it to me.

"Thank you," she said shyly. I saw her glance at Ed from under her eyelashes.

A moment of pique struck me. Surely, a good customer and better-looking man, she should have looked at me that way. But, the possession of this wonderful thing warmed my hand. *Why had I purchased it? For whom?* I simply wanted to own it. Something was so special about this lovely necklace. Pushing the box into my trouser pocket I moved to the doorway and out. In a second, Ed followed.

We moved up the street and he was breathless, "that is the most beautiful woman in the world." He stopped, and after a couple steps I turned. "Wait, I need some handkerchiefs for my mother. Removing his cap, he smoothed at his hair, replaced the it, tugged at his coat, and checked his buttons, before rushing back into the shop. I waited ten minutes and finally he returned flushed and smiling.

Glancing, I noticed he carried no package. "Did you find your mother's handkerchiefs?" I schemed to tease him.

"No, I have to go back later, she could not cash my silver piece with the money you gave her and she has no other change," then he winked.

We shopped for an hour. I found father a fine book and my mother a pillow adorned with handiwork. For the brothers and sisters there were knives or small china figurines. It was the first time I had shopped since I was an officer. It was a good feeling to have cash, since during the past years I had been mailing almost my entire pay home. I could not remember moving in and out of shops like this ever before.

Just before five in the evening, Ed took some of the small change he had after another purchase. He bought a single, lovely flower from a young vendor. Then, prideful, the young man returned to the hatter, and in fifteen minutes left the shop without the flower, carrying a small, white package wrapped in paper. I wondered if he might choose to start a handkerchief collection.

The fort was dedicated on November twelfth. There were drills, so I brought the men in from the Northern Home Plantation. Fort McPhearson had been established in July and many of these Colored soldiers had been there the whole time. I wanted them to see the operation and layout of the fort to its best advantage. This dedication was a real highpoint for everyone.

Rebels roamed the whole region around Natchez. Two to four miles from the city the countryside became a no man's land. These rebels burned cotton and crops. They threatened the lives of field hands if they were caught growing cotton instead of corn. The Southern farmers were ordered to grow only corn, so cotton monies should not be available to the Union.

Because of this real danger, our plantation had been protected today by a few of our most skilled marksmen and most of the women.

All the troops were at their best; wives and families climbed from the Kraal up the many steps to the top of the cliff to stand watching. Bunting and every American flag that could be found hung on all the buildings. Flags of every sort, American, regimental and company, were carried.

As the Sixth marched by in review, I envied their officers. These brave men had seen many battles and marched with true pride. Even today, a detachment was in battle near here.[23]

A few dignitaries or suppliers from the town attended. Yet, most of Natchez must have been unaware of the festivities. When we released a round of ceremonial canon and rifle shot, many townspeople were alarmed and thought there had been an attack. Good food was in abundance. I was especially aware of the Kraal residents' joy at the quantity and quality of provisions.[3]

Each morning the troops are allotted one tin cup of whiskey and in the evening one more. The ration was more than generous today and by afternoon a few men appeared inebriated.

All in all, the day was encouraging and the morale of all seemed lifted. At that moment, we stood at McPhearson with 1,200 White soldiers and 1,500 Colored. Six heavy guns were in place high above the great, old river. The earth works were complete.

The next morning Colonel Edwin Hobart and I groomed carefully and rode down to the Episcopal Church.

I was especially antsy and distracted during the service, and found myself staring and analyzing the backs of those sitting in the Scothorne pew. I waited to leave until after they had departed. None of the women were young, except one who was too young, although dressed in black. I watched as they spoke with several people and left walking north along the street.

After Ed and I had shaken the pastor's hand we mounted. I guided the horse's path north. As we passed the corner where the Scothornes had turned, I looked at the house they were approaching. There was no sign of the carriage, but as we passed the alley I saw a large carriage house behind their home. The carriage would be my final proof of Sarah's presence there.

## Chapter II
# Leave

Since my enlistment at Mt. Carroll in May 1861, letters from home remained my greatest comfort. I had one visit around a year ago, when my father and two brothers rode down to find me. We were in Memphis, Tennessee when they came. It had been several weeks since I had written them. By the time they arrived they had to follow me to a different camp some ten miles out from the main location of the Fifteenth regiment.

The trip had been harrowing for them. They had feared they might meet confederate troops, or thieves that lurked on all roads and followed the army like scavenging buzzards. The trip was arduous and long.

Many other families had visited their soldiers at our camps or even arrived at battle sites. Some friends and family came to deliver bad news. Most came bearing abundant food, aware of our appreciation of such gifts. Such bounty was usually shared with all. Fewer women or wives made the trip to see their men. The women usually were present only in their gifts of clothing, fruitcakes and cookies, which they continually sent to their soldiers. All visits were brief and poignant.

My family's considerate effort to seek me out was greatly appreciated. On this visit we sat apart from the camp talking and drinking coffee and some wine they had brought. They carried derrogatypes, for in my long absence, children had grown and my family had greatly changed. There were moments during our sojourn that I forgot this constant war. The next day, after they left, I found myself quite homesick.

Now, in December, I was finally looking forward to my veterans' leave. This was due to me, having completed my first enlistment commitment to the Fifteenth Illinois with no furlough. I had submitted a request to headquarters in Vicksburg. I had seen no leave or furlough for two and a half years. Then arrived the notice from headquarters at Brookhaven, Mississippi that my leave of twenty days had been approved. It would begin on December 10. I was to leave my command of forty-nine men in charge of First Lieutenant A.L. Sellingham, and Third Lieutenant James McCann.

In preparation, I had my clothing and uniforms cared for so as to be clean and crisp in appearance for the trip and visit to Illinois. Many of the women of the contraband living in the kraal did laundry for the soldiers. I rode to Vicksburg, signed my papers and went to the railhead to wait for a train. I had considered my father's advise to take the steamer but was attracted to the train because it cost less and the train was speedier—every day of my leave was precious.

As I waited for the train in the throng at Vicksburg, I almost felt giddy. Every aspect of my grooming was attended to and I felt such a glow of pride and accomplishment to be going home as a success. The time was compounded by my excitement into what seemed interminable. Finally, I was able to join those entering the train.

There were many Union soldiers on the train. When I climbed up to board, I did find an empty aisle seat alongside an older woman. Tipping my hat, I nodded toward her.

"Is this seat taken?" I inquired. With disgust, she simply looked toward the window. I was abashed and stood a moment assuming she was Southern and hated all of "us."

The train began to slowly pull out. Finally, I took the seat, relaxing into an easy posture, for despite the lady's disgust, I was not willing to stand. I folded onto the vertical seat with hard cushions, and pulled my rucksack behind my feet on the floor. It was early morning as we noisily lurched up the track; smoke seeping in the windows of the passenger car.

For long hours I looked out at passing landscape. Once I dozed off to sleep briefly, until a local stop wakened me. There were stops at many small towns, but we moved onward after these brief loading and unloading halts.

In mid-afternoon we stopped for half an hour in Southern Tennessee for water. Most of the passengers off-boarded to stretch and for convenience. I lit a pipe and found some shade. From this vantage I looked about.

Near one end of the depot other Union soldiers were standing in a small group. I saw several small boys come behind them to call out insults. Then, as the soldiers turned, the ten to twelve year olds pelted them with rocks. The children ran quickly away, laughing. It was a portent of what my trip home would be. There seemed to be animosity toward the uniform. The soldiers had been informed that they were not allowed to ride in first-class coach.[24]

As the trip proceeded I was not physically comfortable in the train for it was stuffy and smoky. Realizing I had chosen a railcar too close to the engine I was disappointed. Any window left open, even a small bit, allowed smoke and ash to enter. My fellow traveler remained silent throughout, never acknowledging me at all.

For an entire night of total discomfort I tried to sleep. The journey was jerky, and each stop interrupted any peace I found. I pondered the antagonistic atmosphere at the Tennessee stop. The angst against the Union soldiers I observed had probably been Southern hostility.

Yet the next day in the North the treatment of all of us soldiers was equally distressing. Newly boarding passengers, and people at the stations, continued to be rude and insulting to the Union uniform. We either waited until last to be served food or were not served food at all at the stops. I found buying fruit from venders was wise. We were called, "horse eaters, murderers, nigger lovers."

Everyone seemed rude and impatient. Several men took gleeful pleasure in asking us if we "had nigger wives yet." One White enlisted soldier standing near me informed me that in Illinois he had not been allowed to vote because as he was told he was "a damn black soldier."[24]

My shock at the response of my own nation's betrayal made me wonder what I would find in Illinois. I had dreamed that we would be viewed with the same respect father gave the Elk Grove veterans. After three days on the train I was dirty and exhausted. The most telling emotion was how completely drained I felt.

What joy I did find when I arrived at Savannah, Illinois was my brother, Henry Clay, in a carriage. He was still drowsy from waiting four hours for the train to arrive. He tethered his fine, chestnut mare and leaped down quickly to walk the length of the short passenger train, watching each person disembark. As I stood in the aisle I bent to peer out the sooty window. I realized how these years away had changed him. He was now thirty years old and married. His lean body was somewhat taller than my own and he was fuller in the chest than myself. As an assistant to the local surveyor, he had hopes of obtaining that position for himself eventually. He was also still operating the Hunter Mill and Foundry on Rock Creek where he lived, not far from my father's farm.

As I stepped down the steps from the train, he yelled out an exuberant greeting, "William, William, here!" A great grin was smeared on his face.

We rushed together, embracing. I had hoped to cut a grand figure in my captain's uniform but wrinkles, sweat and ash impugned that. "Oh, it is grand to be home," I whispered in his ear.

He grabbed my haversack and led me through the people on the platform toward his carriage. Being used to the condition of the war weary horses and carriages of the South this sleek, shiny vehicle looked fit for a king.

At a fast trot, the hour drive to Mt. Carroll and then north out of town to Elk Grove, which was another five miles, gave us time to talk. He was full of information about other veterans who were home wounded or those who had previously passed their veteran leaves visiting in the county. The fresh, cold, crisp evening was a relief. The heavy blanket on our laps was needed. I was also grateful for the woolen hat and gloves Mother had sent with Henry Clay for my use.

Then they hadn't departed Natchez until November. The Fifteenth had seen more duty guarding Vicksburg after I left them to join the Fifty-eighth. These men who had returned on leave were changed men in Clay's view. I thought *if only you could understand how changed, for even we cannot know who we are now.*

Next there was family news, my father was fifty-nine and mother was sixty-two, and they were doing well. Henry's wife Angelina was happy with the new baby, which they were quite proud of. I felt a twinge of envy that my brother had a home life and I did not.

I felt some reticence as he asked about the trip I had just completed from Mississippi. I had been left with a sense of shame because of the treatment of the soldiers, especially in the North. I perhaps expected some gratitude and respect that did not exist among the civilians. I could only compare it to the loyalty and support all the soldiers in the field give each other. I was out of an emotionally unified world that I had become familiar with due to the bonding of comrades.

My brother solemnly asked about the battle of Shiloh. Once more I was also not entirely truthful because of loyalty. I recited only the glory of the charge that General Grant had led. I could not bear to be brutally blunt about the horror of the battle. I could not list men that left our county with me, but fell or were fatally wounded at Shilo.[8]

After all, I was wise enough to know that the civilians really wanted to hear only of glory and patriotism. Next, I told him about Vicksburg and what I saw of the preparation for surrender. It was not until that evening in the family parlor that I also talked of my assignment, and the black soldiers. My Republican father, I knew, would be supportive.

Again, it seemed I was too weary and disorientated to give any details about the kraal, the dysentery and small pox. I just told the family about recruiting. Of course, I was mute about the disastrous foray for Brigadier General McDevlin. Finally, promising to later tell father of the city and Byou Sara, I begged to be excused and climbed the narrow stairway to the second floor.

Exhausted and disorientated, I lay in my childhood room in my own bed that night. My mother's bright quilt covered me and a down pillow was supporting my head. I stared at the star lit ceiling of the room. *Why was I not be able to just step back into my old life?* I was like a different person, perhaps I had become someone even I did not know.

One at a time I thought of fellows I had fought with. I counted each one who was dead or maimed. I thought of those whose families who would not see them on veterans' leave. The thought made me sense my own unworthiness and guilt at surviving. *Yes, we were different now, we would never be the same.* I viewed this warless environment in Illinois as though I was an observer, seeing through glass, I felt removed and vacant. This was a world that I was no longer a part of. It was a strange world to me and somehow unfamiliar like a blurry memory.

The morning light woke me. I had dreamed of sleeping around the clock and although rested and relaxed, I could not lay there in my bed for long. My mother and sisters had prepared some of my civilian clothing. They lay on a chair beside the bed. I fingered through them selecting a familiar shirt and trousers.

When I put the pants on the belt could barely be pulled tight enough to keep them up and the shoulders of the shirt were too tight. It was though my body was not the one I had when I left Illinois. Previously in the field, I had given little thought to my physical condition and changing dimensions. Not only did I feel alienated, I must even look like a different person.

A hearty, farm breakfast was served by my mother who alternately wept and laughed, then repeatedly reached to touch me. Excusing myself, I bundled myself in warm outerwear and walked alone about the farm; for hours observing the sameness and also the changes. I looked at the horses, stables, the other livestock and land. Then, I walked a bit over a mile to my brother's home for a brief visit.

Later that afternoon, I wandered through the cemetery across the road from my father's house There, I noted the new stones that had been placed as the consequence of the war. It haunted me; *why was I spared and not buried here.*

A few days later the whole family gathered to celebrate my return and an early Christmas. My oldest brother, John H., his wife Alice and their children Henry Frederick, John W., Emma and Nellie arrived. Henry Clay and Angeline with their three children were gathered at the house. My sisters, Laura, Martha, and Avline were also in attendance. Mary and James George Washington arrived later in the day.

I gave each family member the gifts I had selected for Christmas. The day was festive, especially because John was home on leave as well. The nephews and nieces were charming but it was alarming because they had grown so much these three years I had been away. Several new children had been born and these I became acquainted with.

During the next two weeks, I renewed acquaintances in the town of Mt. Carroll. As I would walk down the streets it was common to see someone I knew and stop to visit at length. One Sunday my parents and I went into Mount Carroll and attended church. I made stops at the school, the doctor's home and various stores to see special friends. The visits were usually brief, but it was rewarding to see those I respected or had a relationship with.

One afternoon, when it was late enough that I hoped to find Isaac Spencer at home after work, I rode a horse to his farm. I sat by him a short while as we huddled near a fire in a cast iron stove. Withholding information had become quite natural on this trip home. I did not tell the gentleman that I had in fact identified his granddaughter and even had a furtive glance and brief conversation with her one muddy day. Instead, I passed on the generous encouragement of people within the church who had told me she was doing well. Explaining that my assignment kept me very busy, I vowed that I would still see her in person soon and so notify him.

Isaac shared his anxiety for her welfare. From the monthly letters that the two of them exchanged he had learned that she would be moving into her own home, leaving her in-laws. With a sinking feeling, I realized that after all my spying to finally find her domicile, she would soon disappear again and be further protected in anonymity by the community that sought to protect her privacy. My only hope would be that the widow would become more regular in her church attendance.

I spent much time nearby visiting my siblings, with the exception of John who was living in Iowa. After arriving, bundled against the cold crisp air, I spent evenings sitting in their homes just resting. The cold was like a resurrected memory after my years in the South.

One day Clay and I rode to a barn on the hill at 8500 South Grand View Road. This was only a short distance northwest from Clay's stone quarry.[8]

The barn we sought had been a horse thieves' hideout. Later this same barn was one of two used as stations on the Underground Railway in the pre-Civil War days. In view of my new position this location was quite haunting now. I looked into the dark, somewhat decaying interior; it seemed haunted by the frightened, huddling humans I had glimpsed as a young man. This time, when I looked into the barn, I could truly understand the horror they were fleeing from in an attempt to reach Canada.

Many of those who came to the two Carroll County depots had moved furtively by river, on foot or hidden in vehicles moving northward beside the Missouri River's west bank. The escaping slaves came up through eastern Kansas and Nebraska. They were hidden in a riverside cave near Nebraska City, Nebraska. The cave was disguised as a vegtable storage area. Then north of the city they crossed the river into Iowa.

There were still bounty hunters and hateful people seeking the large, advertised rewards. These people would betray these refugees and see them returned to slavery. There were also supportive people. Dozens of waystations, depots and individuals hid, fed, healed and protected them. For instance, many communities like Lewis, Iowa had hiding places on the river. This town sheltered runaways behind a basement wall in the rural stone home of Pastor George Hitchcock, who having been raised in Massachusetts and for spiritual reasons, was opposed slavery.

The 'freedom passage' that went through Carroll County came westward across Iowa. Then the route cut northeast across Illinois. This is how our travelers had arrived and where we helped them on their way toward Canada.

In that barn I felt the ghosts of runaway self-liberators and my memory isolated several of the more memorable Negroes I had helped escape. This experience relieved some of the guilt I continuously struggled with.

During the visit, several important things transpired. My savings from soldiering and bonuses had been placed in the bank. Using my savings, I completed the final legal acts to purchase the seventy-five acres I now owned.

One situation at home, both a matter of pride and yet of some apprehension, was the safety of my brother, Henry Clay. My leave had further influenced his decision to enlist. Now he had signed up to leave almost immediately in late December. The departure from his young family and the jeopardy of leaving the business in his partner's hands was of great concern.

After the unpleasant train ride North, I went to Savannah for the return trip and took passage on a paddle wheeler on the Mississippi. To save money I did not take a cabin, preferring to sleep on my haversack and carry on my person the books, writing materials and the gifts my family had sent with me.

Having lived most of the recent past unprotected had toughened me. I turned up my collar, and wrapped myself in a quilt my mother and sisters had pieced for me from woolen scraps. For the trip I snuggled between packing crates and bags. Watching the familiar landscape float by, I wool gathered in empty thought. My leaving home had been trancelike. To say goodbye for what might be another several years seemed like leaving for another world—and it really was.

On the second day of my return trip I was smoking at the rear of the boat while a light mist from the wheel washed over me. A portly man, dressed in a heavy, expensive overcoat and a fine beaver hat, joined me. At first he stood silently at the rail as we watched the paddles' wake of muddy bubbles.

There was little ice on the river this year, having been somewhat warm for December, most of it was only clinging in light patches to the banks. The ship's captain maneuvered skillfully around sandbars. The boat brought us to a dock now and then for passengers or goods to be received or discharged. The shrill whistle announced each landing and departure. The smoke from the stacks was pungent but pleasant with a woody smell that pleased me.

Turning to lean his back against the rail, the gentleman pushed his mittened hands deeper into his pockets. "Are you going back to duty?"

I nodded, somewhat braced for what might be another unpleasant experience with civilians, as those on the train had been. There was an awkward pause and then seeing a wide grin on his full cheeks I responded.

Feeling more secure with his attitude I relaxed and answered, "Yes, I am stationed at Fort McPhearson in Natchez."

His face lightened, "Ah yes, Natchez. I lived there for many years as a clothier. I have even spent time there in the last years. Have you been there long?"

"Yes, I have been there for five months, it is a lovely city."

"One of the most lovely on earth, isn't it," he murmured. "My favorite vista is the road through Woodville to St. Francisville, Louisiana. There are, in season, great walls of blooming Cherokee rose hedges five to fifteen feet high. They are so dense in many places as to shut out completely the view into the adjoining fields. At frequent intervals the orange flowers of the cross vine are mixed with the white blooms and glossy, green leaves of the rose. These are used as division fences between plantations in the near area. At least a thousand miles of this type of hedge exist in the state." [21]

"Natchez," he reminisced in soft tones, "is like a lovely, secretive woman. It is the living dream of prosperity, safety, power and elegance. There are six or seven generations of dynasties based on wealth that would not be possible without the river or the cheap labor of slaves. The planters are mostly educated in the East or Europe. Many still hold ties and even land in Europe. As the cotton land plays out many rotate back and forth to their other Carolina properties."

"The quality of life is unparalleled in that small city. The women hold unusual legal rights to property and inheritance. They are a people rich in dignity and pride, yet resentful of the lack of respect shown them by the rest of the nation. They hold more wealth per capita than any other city in the nation—even New York City."

With a pause the fellow traveler turned his back and overlooked the wake, "This makes the present Union occupation there even more painful." The man rambled on like a lovesick swain about the region. He recounted Natchez history such as the tornado of 1840, which killed over three hundred people and destroyed most property of' Under the Hill. The loss included three steamers and sixty flatboats that were sunk. I then realized that in just the last twenty years the community had survived numerous other tragedies and rebounded. I hoped they could recover from this tragedy as well.

Knowing he had my rapt attention the fellow continued the impromptu history lesson.

He smiled in a smug but inoffensive manner and began his tutelage, "Some prehistoric people built mounds all along the banks of this great old river. These mound settlements extended all the way to the Gulf. These people have left few traces. The Natchez are the only tribe that existed here when France settled the area in 1716. The population of the region grew after that occupation to over 700 people. In 1729, the Natchez Indians attacked and destroyed the settlement, slaughtering, burning and taking captives. The retaliation by the settlers was swift. The army found the Indians and slaughtered the entire tribe. At the end of the French and Indian war in 1763, the English were granted ownership of the land. Between 1768–1780 the village consisted of a handful of cabins, a couple houses and four stores. There were only about seventy-eight families living there at that time."[21]

"When the American Revolution came, Spain declared war upon England and took over the region again. Spain did not abandon their claim until 1795, although it took three more years to deliver the territory to the United States. Agriculture and imports there depend on free labor. By 1809, planters frequently owned as many as one to three hundred slaves. Three years ago, less than nine hundred of the 35,390 citizens of the region were whites who owned more than seventy slaves."

"Slaves were costly and maintenance was dear. It took the planter fourteen and a half bushels of meal a week, 250 pounds of beef and fifty pigs to feed sixty-two slaves. Slaves often raised their own chickens or kept small garden plots. The plantations usually had Christmas feasts and a Saturday distribution of crops that were raised at the plantation such as peas, pumpkins, milk, butter and potatoes. There was at least one distribution annually of head handkerchiefs, shoes and flannel for the old and infirm. Each Christmas, sugar and coffee was freely distributed or the slaves could purchase these."

"Thus, in fact, free labor had a price and food was only one responsibility of the institution. Small pox, scarlet fever, influenza and diphtheria attacked the Coloreds in the hundreds. Doctors were usually sent for immediately by owners because of the value the owners placed in them. Personally and economically this was a great expense."[25]

"By 1812, while the population of White people was small, the community was booming and varied. [21] There was a financial panic in 1837 that was unsettling and quite a setback for the whole populace. That unique city is dependent on commerce, trade and river traffic. Most of the growth of town has been on top of the bluff, and already a sharp distinction was evident between the character of that part of the town and the character of Natchez Under the Hill. The upper town was closely allied with the surrounding plantations and the lower town allied with the river traffic. There were, necessarily, business dealings between the two, though socially they were far apart."

"When I returned on brief business in 1861, I had found that a number of planters had driven their slaves into Texas. The trips were difficult, danger filled and carried high fatalities. These were owners seeking to save and retain this valuable, living property in 1862. One family moved to Texas with their slaves. Their own baby died and the mother's breasts were so engorged with milk that she nursed a puppy to relieve them. Since Mississippi came to the aid of Texas in force during the Mexican War there is a deep bond between the regions. Many families are related across the borders. The South hopes that Texas may become a safe refuge should the war turn. With the war of rebellion Texas is actively involved, but distance has caused it to suffer less action of a military nature."

"Last year, I found inflation was strangling the city. Salt, needed to preserve food, had risen to fifty cents a pound. Pork was forty-five dollars a barrel." His voice slowed with meditation, "Yes, it is quite a city, but today it is in definite distress."

The day was passed thereafter with more light conversation that bypassed the war. This educated fellow talked on with no pause but I considered it a blessing to pass time with such an informed individual.

One of the charming tales he told was of the raucous history of the dance halls and gambling houses of Natchez Under the Hill. With ominous drama he described the crime and violence. Much of this evil was attributed to the gamblers that inhabited the area or moved in and out along the river. Eventually the Under the Hill authorities, and likewise those in Vicksburg, threw out all the gamblers with a brief notice of a couple days. With tongue in cheek he recounted many paddlewheel stories like the boat that took a day to pass because it was so long.[13]

I shared with him my grandfather's history and he said he knew Pinckneyville well. He was well informed about the location of that original land grant. The man was a walking history lesson. While chatting, he spoke of merchants, buildings and churches of the town. He knew names of several powerful people like the Brandons, who had been my ancestor's neighbors, and the Quitmans, who owned Monmouth, where the Union had the home plantation I took responsibility for. Feeling I might have need of knowing such names and their history, I requested he repeat such information. He carefully listed information about a few citizens for my benefit. The next day I left him as he continued down river toward New Orleans, but I accepted his calling card. With my own familiarity with Adams County and the new information, I felt much better prepared to understand the area where I was stationed.

Upon returning, I found that the battle of Natchez had transpired ten miles to the south. This was one of the few serious military actions that reached so near the city, although, there were often small skirmishes, forays or movements hereabout.[15]

With my first thought I inquired, but found my own company was not involved in the battle. It excited me to be returning to the responsibilities I had left. Illinois was far behind me as I returned to my post more fresh and enthused.

## Chapter 12
# Sarah

Sarah Scothorne impatiently tapped her toe against the floor causing the small walnut rocker where she sat to move backward with a jerk. Her neck was stiff with bending over her embroidery, and she felt somewhat nervous. Now looking around the small, cozy room where she sat, the young widow felt a widening warmth of comfort surrounding her. She had endured a long absence from her own home while she was living with William's parents after her son had died and later when her husband had also died. In her life, the satisfaction with being in her own home was quietly pleasing.

Her eyes slowly moved about the room enjoying her possessions. She looked longingly at the small things her dead husband had so lovingly made and placed about, and at those which she herself had made. A pile of glowing coals smoldered in the small fireplace. Her gaze drifted slowly toward the entry doors then moved toward the windows overlooking the front porch; a sharp pain struck her chest.

The stark realization overpowered her that the door would not open tonight or ever again to allow her husband to cross that threshold. She would never warm to his open smile, see him dusty white and covered with sawdust. He had always trailed the wood odor of his labors at carpentry. To her his blue eyes and golden hair had made him seem like a hero from a history book. *How could it be he was dead? Why was he gone forever? God must know she needed him, why?*

The loss and tragedy seemed unreal, leaving her empty in soul and body. This vacant quality was hard to bypass. The last two nights she had lain awake all-night, tossing and peering through the curtains into the moonlight. The other side of the bed was cold and empty; there was total silence.

Once when she drifted off to sleep, she dreamed of herself sitting perched on the edge of the bed ready to go to the baby cradle where her tiny son lay. In her dream she heard his cry. Her mothers' heart had instantly responded. When she suddenly woke there was only death's emptiness and the draped, empty cradle that was dimly visible at the foot of the bed where she lay.

*Perhaps she should return to her in-laws?* she now asked herself. Although the Scothornes' small home was full of hospitality, it was crowded. At their house she had not been so overwhelmed by the dead silence as she was here. The burden she had caused, at the Scothorne's home, although never spoken of, had made her feel more the victim and quite guilty for imposing on them. Her mother and father-in law had shared all they had to comfort her through the death of their grandson and then their son.

Her own parents lived in the country an hour away. Travel was risky now with the Yankees in possession of the area. She knew that she could go home and stay if she wanted to, even though she resisted visiting them very often. Even her grandfather offered her a distant home with him up North. Yet, the security of this home and her garden were the small resources she possessed that really belonged to her.

Large, quiet tears rolled down her cheeks and fell on her bosom. In dead quiet she rocked slowly, her hands lying limp in her lap on top the stitchery. Reaching to the table beside her, she turned the lamp lower; she felt shame for her fear and weakness.

*How could she betray everyone by being weak?* Her dear Will, dead in the Cause, had been brave, wise and protective of all he loved. Other war widows were holding their heads high and provided not only for themselves, but their children and homes using whatever means they must. Somehow, she must also find the courage to honor all her loved ones. Self-pity was a commodity no Southern woman could afford.

The young woman, her chestnut hair piled on top her head, was wearing a dark grey silk dress accented only by lace at the collar and cuffs. She had olive skin and large brown eyes. Her shapely breasts moved slowly with each breath. She now smoothed the cool silk and continued slowly rocking in the dim light of the Natchez moon. One window, opened just a bit, allowed a musty, river flavored fragrance into the room. With a weary sigh she rose and moved to this open window at the front of the house.

The cottage sat on a low knoll at the edge of town; to the west she could view other houses. Over their roofs she saw a small patch of watery reflection that was some distance away. This same river had brought Will and she a good way of life in a formerly prosperous, secure community. As a carpenter, her husband was always busy, repairing someone's home or building slave quarters on one of the plantations.

Though they had been married less than two years, he had accomplished so much in their own home. He had built cabinets, wardrobes and shelves before he left for the war with Conner's Light Artillery.

That same Mississippi River that provided for them had also made Natchez a Union target. The position the city held on the Mississippi and the resources in trade and income it provided for the defense of the Rebels had marked it valuable to both armies in the war effort. With no means of defense, wisdom had demanded the city surrender or be defeated by the advancing army and navy. The merchants and townspeople, most in sympathy with the Southern cause, recognized that their economic possibilities as an international trade center demanded that they capitulate to be destroyed. In fact, many also opposed secession. A brief, earlier attack by cannon from the Union forces on the river had caused the death of a small girl and a confusing situation where the city's first surrender was ignored. Natchez finally, successfully surrendered to the Union last year, in the summer of 1863.

When Mississippi seceded in January of 1861, Natchez reluctantly joined the secession. The city then formed fourteen companies. Many of the men of the small city had enlisted and left to fight. In 1862, one of these companies, Conner's Light. Artillery, formed with 1,600 men. Isaac William Scothorne was one of those serving that regiment with company H.

After his departure, her handsome, blond husband was hardly able to visit her or their baby son, Henry Isaac. Twice they had planned a rendezvous. One time, she traveled to her parent's home in the countryside taking Henry to meet her husband for a few days.

For two weeks during a wave of respiratory disease, she had fought death for her son's life in a losing battle. Her eight-month-old son, Henry, had died. That death had been about a year ago. When their son died, Sarah had smuggled a letter out of the city and informed his father of the tragedy. She had been required to bury her child without the support of his father, this was matter of great heartbreak for both parents.

The cemetery had been empty when the small group gathered to inter the tiny casket. In the cool, winter breeze she stood and looked southward where she knew her husband's regiment was serving. Silently, the veil on her hat hiding her swollen face, the grieving mother imagined her husband somehow mystically pulled to look up from some task he was involved in. He would turn for a moment and stare toward the distance in the north as the Natchez cemetery accepted his beautiful son. In her grief, the woman dreamed of the imaginary uniting of their eyes across the miles.

Feeling a soft tug at her hand Sarah had then reached to grasp her sister-in-law's gloved hand. The firm warmth made her feel safe. Then she felt the kind hand of her father-in-law on her shoulder. With a shudder the woman had begun to weep again.

In 1863, William was only able to sneak into the city to visit her one night. That had been just a short while after the child's funeral. The time the couple spent together was one of weeping in each others arms then an exchange of their bodies that was more comfort to each of them than passion.

In March of 1863, the young woman was called for at her home by a servant from Scothornes. Sarah sometimes spent brief times at her own house to maintain it and protect it from vandalism. When called she went immediately to Will's parents house. There was a sick dread in her being. Such requests in this war scared city usually foretold bad news.

A dirty, young man, out of uniform but from Conner's light artillery, was at the house. Before he could speak she looked at her mother-in-law. The agony was visible on the older woman's face and she knew what the message would be. The soldier told her of the battle on Black River where her husband had been struck with a heart attack. William had been taken down river from Simsport on the Louisiana side.

After a day of weeping, she had returned to her own home once more. This time she went to secure it, and retrieve clothing and valuables. After baby Henry's death she had frequently slept at the other house. Now, with the help of her houseboy and her father-in-law, Sarah had moved to the Scothorne house near the business area of the city.

Her husband's family went to retrieve the body. Within days Will had been buried in Natchez with honors provided by a service at the Presbyterian Church. The only comfort she found for the two tragedies were her daily visits to the cemetery which was located north of town through the fort.

With her funds she purchased and erected a stone and in honor of Will and had it inscribed.

SACRED TO THE MEMORY OF WILLIAM B. SCOTHORNE. BORN NATCHEZ, JULY 2, 1835, DIED SIMSPORT, LOUISIANA MARCH 23, 1863 AGED 27 YEARS, 3 MO AND 8 DS.

A KIND FATHER AND AFFECTIONATE HUSBAND AND A DUTIFUL SON. NONE KNEW HIM BUT TO LOVE HIM. NONE KNEW HIM BUT TO PRAISE. MARK THE PERFECT MAN AND BEHOLD THE UPRIGHT AND THAT MAN IS PEACE. ERECTED BY HIS WIFE.

She had been at her own home in this sitting room since late afternoon after she had completed a light supper. Now it was quite dark and, because of the Union occupation and curfew, the streets were entirely still. Suddenly, she heard a carriage approaching with a muffled creak. She rose and went to the window, stepping back where she was not visible. Sarah dropped the sheer panel of curtain and watched through it, uncertain of who might be breaking curfew.

With some fear she saw the vehicle pull onto the apron of her lawn, under a large magnolia tree. A male figure jumped down and tethered the horse, smoothing its muzzle to quiet the animal. After whispering into the carriage he turned toward her house.

Quickly she moved to the door and checked to see that it was locked. Pressing her back against the door, she self-consciously grasped a handful of the silk skirt of her dress. She tried to quiet her breathing.

A light knock sounded on the other side of the door but she remained still and soundless. Then, in a rough whisper, she heard a familiar voice. "Sarah? It is Joseph. Are you there, Dear Sister?"*

With a deep sigh she filled her lungs, then straightened and hurried to open the lock for her brother Joseph, wanting to protect him within the house. The tall, slender man pushed the door open and quickly stepped inside, pulling it shut behind him. His sharp features, dark skin and straight dark hair reinterpreted the distant Cherokee heritage they both shared. Although, he was built quite differently than she, the family resemblance still marked them as kin. He held his arms open and she fell into them; secure, comforted and relieved.

With the close embrace he lay his chin firmly down on the top of her head. He whispered hoarsely, "May I turn the lamp down?" Feeling her nod of acquiescence, he moved to the table and almost extinguished the lamp.

Taking her hand and accustoming his vision to the moon's reflected light, he led her across the floor. They stepped onto a hooked rug that lay in front of her settee. He sat, then reached for her hand to guide her to a place beside him.

"Is mother well?" Sarah pleaded in panic.

He answered solemnly, "They have been raided again, and more servants have run away. But, she is well and continues to persevere."

Sternly he ordered, "Mother need not know of my visit tonight, for her own protection."

A chill filled the young woman. *What sort of portent did this visit carry?*

Her brother leaned so close to her that she could feel his breath against her ear. "I come on behalf of someone who is in sore need of your help. What she requires has risk and will require courage of you." Then Joseph paused.

**It has been difficult to trace the Spencer family. There are indications of a Native American heritage. The family of most interest is found in "Cherokee by Blood," Heritage Books, case 417, George Washington Plummer, Elisha B. Spencer, Gracsy Creek, N.C. The line may run through a family named Sizemore.*

In her heart she knew she was a coward who could only hope to survive herself. *What kind of task would she be capable of? Who might seek her, of all people, for aid?*

Taking a breath she found herself unable to speak for a long moment. Her voice betrayed her, it was shaking and husky, "What can I do, how can I help?"

With the naive enthusiasm that her older brother had always shown, he took this as affirmation. He leapt up, "I told Abigail you would help." He headed toward the door and went outside.

Her temples throbbing, Sarah felt breathless and vacant. *What did this all mean? What on earth was happening to her? It could not be true.* She, herself, was helpless and weak. *What could Abigail need of her?*

In a few moments the door smoothly slide open and beside the lank form of her brother was a shadow of a short, stout, older woman wearing a shawl and bonnet. Carefully, Joseph led the woman across the dark room and guided her to a chair sitting to one side of the settee.

Sarah saw the woman was Abigail Talon, a neighbor of her parents, since their move to the country from Natchez. Yet, she had known the Talon family her whole life. Indeed, Sarah had been special friends with Mary, their daughter, who was now married and living in Boston.

"Oh, Abigail, what is your distress?" Sarah leaned toward her and softened her voice with sympathy.

The plump, greying woman reached into her sleeve, removing a hanky and dabbed at her eyes. Sliding from the settee, Sarah fell to her knees in front of the woman, concerned and confused. She took the older woman's soft hands in her own.

"When my two boys went to fight my John wanted to stay at home to take care of our place and me. For a while he hid out in the woods. Then, when a man down the road refused to go to fight and was executed, John had second thoughts. He joined the war and left."

"First, I heard my boy, Theodore, was killed and his body could not be brought home. Then last spring, my husband John returned with one shoulder shattered and his other arm blown off. Just now, he is able once more to be up and about. The farm is only being worked by two old darkies and me."

With a gasping sob and the woman went on hesitantly, "I think I will die. All is gone, I need your help, there is no one else to turn to. I cannot do this for myself; there is no one I trust like the Spencers. Your brother suggested that because you are on your own once again and you can move about the city more freely. I need someone young and pretty, but a lady. Oh please, please," she gasped, clutching the young woman's hands to her heart.

Sitting back on her heels and releasing the woman's hands Sarah's heart ached with compassion. Much of the family's tragic story she had been familiar with, but she still had no idea what on earth she could do to assist or support this dear lady. Softly and gently she whispered. "What, what can I do for you?"

Sighing deeply, Abigail continued the story. "Now, after over two years, my boy James came home. He just walked away from war, I need him to help me but I am afraid they will kill him for leaving the war. The Union devils will kill him or the Rebels will shoot him for desertion."

Still, Sarah could make no sense of the pained and rambling story Abigail told.

"James is sick, real sick and he is hurt. I have hidden him and am nursing him. I can't let the niggers know and so I must go to great lengths to keep his presence a secret. If I don't obtain quinine and sulfa for his wounds I fear he will die." Taking a deep breath, Abigail continued her story, "There is a way to get medicine, I cannot tell you who told me. This same person has prepared a way for me to get what I need."

"A number of young women and wives in this city have contacts at Fort McPhearson who will provide them with many things. It requires knowledge, a pass and money."

Reaching under her shawl Abigail withdrew a small leather purse. "Inside here is the money and a pass. Will you take it to the fort and secure medicine? This may be my only hope to save my dear James?"

What Abigail proposed was terrifying and repellent. Sarah's breath sucked in and she held it for fear her compassion would overwhelm her and she would say yes. Then a sound though soft seemed to echo in the room. *Had it really been her voice?* She had said, "Yes." She had whispered the word out loud. It was shocking.

Grasping the younger woman's hands and pushing the small purse into them Abigail sobbed, "Oh, thank God."

After a pause to gain her own composure, the old lady began to speak in a conspiratorial voice. She tried to be clear in her instructions. "Girl, have you seen the garment the women use to smuggle?"

"Yes, Mam," was the young woman's reply, "the bags they have are like aprons that are a pocket they wear under their skirts inside their garments."

Abigail went on, "Well, prepare one with the opening behind a slit in a full skirt hidden under some trim or bows. You may slip the medicine in there when the soldier at the fort gives it to you. Next secure some vegetables, greens or fruit. Wrap them in paper and put the purse in inside one of the wrappings. Then put the purse and produce into a basket. To protect the money and yourself you must carry these goods without help—by yourself."

"Oh, I hate to put you at risk, but I must stay with James. A pretty young woman finds it far easier to go about the fort," Abigail paused then resolutely went on.

Opening the purse, the distraught woman removed a folded piece of paper. Smoothing it, she lay it on the settee. In the moonlight it was impossible to read and Sarah only turned her head toward it.

"This is a pass for the day after tomorrow. Fill in your name. Go to the fort between nine and eleven in the morning. Any earlier will arouse suspicion, and later you will not be able to contact our agent. Go first to the provost marshal for access to the grounds."

"In the fort inquire about the commissary. When you arrive there ask for Sergeant Riley. He will look at the produce, pay a small amount of money. Then, as a signal you say, 'this is worth twice what you offer.' At that password he will take you to his desk to wait. He will leave briefly to get the medicine which eventually he will hand to you very carefully."

"When he goes to put away the produce he can check for the money. Then he will return the basket. While he is gone very carefully slip the medicine through the slit in your skirt and into the hidden bag. Put the coins he gives you into your purse. Take the empty basket and leave the fort. I will send my house servant to pick the medicine up after dark, he will come to the back door and knock."

"This is alarming, I don't know," Abigail whispered with panic in her voice. She once again carefully went over the information. She pleaded and wept while Sarah sat listening silently. On Abigail and Joseph's, departure the neighbor woman kissed the Sarah's hands. When the wind from the open door touched her Sarah Drucilla felt the woman's hot tears on her face.

If sleep had been fugitive previously, tonight it was impossible. She simply paced in the small bedroom all night. Just before dawn she lay fully dressed on the bed and dozed fretfully. It was midmorning when the fragrance of food wafted up the narrow stairs to the single dormer bedroom and intruded into her awareness. The Black woman she had hired to help her was humming to herself and making quiet sounds in an effort to not disturb her employer. It took some time to groom, change into a lightweight cotton dress of dark blue and go downstairs.

"Nell, good morning." The slender, older woman with a blue bandana on her head turned, "Got ya some water for tea and some corn grit." Sitting at the table Sarah allowed herself to be served. For the first time in ages, she was truly hungry. Perhaps her terror was promoting hunger.

This day she carefully went thorough the several dresses she owned. She found a gown with a very full skirt but she needed to manufacture a flounce from another dress. The peplum would be hiding the slit in the back of the skirt over the smuggler's bag. The particular dress she had selected to wear was of a light yellow color and was usually worn in the summer more casually. Thus the gown was quite simple in design.

Finding another garment, with a complimentary tan color, she cut this up for the flounce. Next, she formed a rectangle twelve by sixteen inches, folding the longer part inside her summer gown and stitching it snugly. Tearing long strips she sewed these two long tails at either end of the bag. Then stripping to her petticoat she tied the bag at her back under the skirt. When she reached back she found that by tying the bag snuggly the top of it was too tight to allow anything to be slipped into the opening. If only she had a pattern or some advice, but that would be dangerous and was not possible.

When the woman practiced tying it loosely it sagged and did not feel secure. Finally, she found that taking a small tuck in the fabric next to her body allowed the front part to gap slightly.

Next Sarah opened the a five inch slit in the center back seam of the dress, and tacked the fabric with tiny stitches so it would not tear more or allow frayed edges to be visible. Stitching the flounce and stuffing it with light crinoline she adjusted it to proper length and fullness. Now she put on the bag and the dress with the peplum trim.

Next, she practiced slipping a bottle of perfume into the receptacle while both standing and sitting. Repeatedly, she dropped the bottle and in frustration realized that this would be very difficult.

"Sarah Drucilla Scothorne," she scolded herself out loud as she walked toward the mirror. Then with a phony smile she simpered, "You lil' ol' Southern Belle, you can sure fool those silly soldiers." The woman then watched her own reflected expression to make sure it did not change as she practiced the deceitful act again and again.

In her reflection she realized with some vanity that her garment looked very nice except that the bustle was a tan color and of a bolder mixed floral pattern. Somehow the dress seemed unfinished. Laying extra strips of the second fabric about her neck on the bodice she decided to use more of the fabric as trim at her throat so that dress looked more planned in color and design.

Stripping down to her petticoat she ruffled and hemmed a collar of the coordinating fabric. Sarah replaced the dress and looked into the mirror. Suddenly, she realized while wearing this light colored dress, that it was the first time in almost a year she had been out of dark widows' weeds.

Her reflection revealed a young woman full of color from her afternoon's efforts, her hair was still lying loosely on her shoulders in soft ringlets. The russet browns reflected in the window's light. Her high, rounded cheeks were rich in an olive-rose color. She had almost forgotten she was a person, and a woman. It seemed less than noble to see herself as other than a grieving widow. Steeling herself, Sarah realized that after all she was perhaps capable of fighting, of defending her own, of being a southern woman with dignity and...strength.

It was late afternoon when once more in her narrow skirted blue house dress, with her hair pinned back on her head she returned to the first floor.

Nell appeared quizzical in her view of this new employer. She was new at being a paid employee and not a house slave. Perhaps town people in Natchez kept this strange schedule.

"Miz, you want me make yo bed, or make yo suppa?"

With a pause, and cautious to hide her secrets, Sarah tried to be calm and decisive. "Nell you do not need to tend to the bedroom today." With a firm instructive tone she ordered, "You may prepare my supper. I will come into the pantry and see what we have. We probably have only vegetables left."

"By the way, I need an early breakfast tomorrow, by six in the morning, I have errands to do." This, Sarah realized, was also a departure from her reclusive life. She would be busy; she would be going out. Her day would not just be occupied with the household chores or visiting the Scothornes. Tomorrow, she would be entering a mysterious new life that was all her own.

Again she slept fitfully and at dawn rose and began dressing in the gown she had prepared the day before. She washed her face, and dampening a comb pulled it through her wavy, brown hair until there was an order to it. Then with quick fingers she braided and pulled each plait across the crown of her head where she securely pinned them. Finding a light bonnet she tied it about her neck, and sitting in a chair pulled on her stockings and carried her shoes.

With a clumsy gait she descended the stairs and moved to the kitchen. She sat in a chair and requested that the servant lace her shoes. The woman knelt and put a foot into her lap and began to fix each of her shoes. Finishing one, she reached for the other foot and repeated the service.

"Nell, I am going to the garden and would like to eat when I return. Do we have tea?"

"Jus' a dab," was her maid's immediate reply.

"Please make me a cup of tea for my breakfast and some mush." Sarah replied without sitting.

With a distracted but steadfast determination she reached for an apron to cover her dress and took a large, woven basket from a peg beside the door. She lifted the bonnet onto her head, retied it and immediately strode out into the gated garden. She stood assaying what remained of the produce.

Carefully, she pulled some sweet potatoes and then went past a low greenhouse in the ground moving toward a small shed at the back of the house. Unlocking the door with a key from her pocket, she swung it open on creaking hinges. Fumbling past tools that were hanging on the wall or propped about, she moved to the rear of the shed. Here she reached into a basket of hay; digging through the hay she plucked out five apples. Begrudgingly, she put one back, stood, then reached down and picked up the fruit again and also another for good measure. She found a small hard squash.

Returning from the dark interior into the bright sunlight she squinted at the basket. With some dismay she realized that the basket was not full enough. She secured the door and returned to the garden where she pulled up more sweet potatoes. Food was scarce and she was wary of not having enough for herself to last until spring. Yet, with too little produce to hide her contraband her life might be at risk. The women's prison in Natchez was full. Entering the kitchen she sat the basket on the floor, and moved to the basin where she washed her hands, then dried them. Loosening the apron, she slipped out of it and hung it on a peg.

She turned to the table; it was good to see a breakfast nicely set. "Thank you Nell," she removed her bonnet, hung it on a peg, then sat to eat the mush and drink her tea.

"Nell, would you wash the things I have brought in and dry them while I am eating? Then go to the Scothornes and ask if they will send their carriage so that I may go out. Tell them I have a morning errand. You may wait at their house and ride back with the driver."

Trying to stay calm Sarah forced herself to eat slowly. When the slender, bronze woman dried her hands and hurried out the back door, she sighed and sagged in her chair. *How ever was she to accomplish this subterfuge?* Looking at the vegetables and apples she tried to rehearse the scenario that Abigail had laid before her. *I think the purse was to be wrapped with an apple?*

Staring at the pile of produce she suddenly remembered something and ran into the parlor. Dumping her embroidery and spools on the floor she squinted at the basket, which had held them. The basket was smaller, but deeper and would be more secure from snooping eyes. Rushing to the kitchen she rearranged the goods into this smaller basket and removed one squash. Now she was pleased with the appearance and hefting it she felt the weight—quite comfortable to carry.

Returning to her own bedroom, she straightened her hair and pinched her cheeks and lips with a practiced look of arrogant confidence. Sarah found the small bag Abigail had given her in a drawer, dumping the purse onto the bed, she removed the folded paper and returned several silver dollars to the small leather purse.

Taking the paper to her writing desk, she sat and carefully signed *Sarah Drucilla Scothorne* on the blank line of the pass.

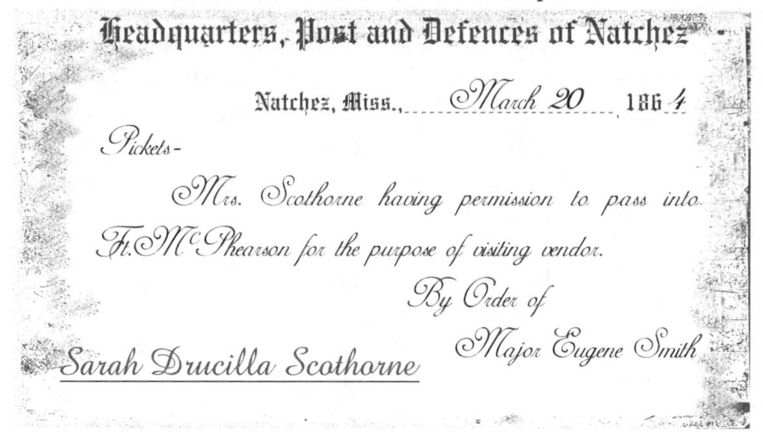
Headquarters, Post and Defences of Natchez

Natchez, Miss., March 20 1864

Pickets-

Mrs. Scothorne having permission to pass into Ft. McPhearson for the purpose of visiting vendor.

By Order of

Major Eugene Smith

Sarah Drucilla Scothorne

She sprinkled sand and waited for the ink to dry. She blew the sand away and folded it, using her nails, she pressed a crisp fold. She put the paper into her own bag that hung on her left wrist.

For good measure she walked to the mirror and looking into her own stiffly smiling face, she smoothly picked up the perfume bottle, smoothly slid it through the slit of the skirt and into the pouch hidden in her clothing. Throwing her skirts into the air she plucked the perfume out and replaced it on the dresser.

Grabbing the leather money pouch from the bed she rushed down stairs and into the kitchen. Then with sinking heart, she remembered that she must wrap the goods. Paper was scarce; she dug through several drawers, then remembering something, rushed upstairs to open a trunk beside her bed. Pulling at a bundle of crisp white paper she threw it on the bed and tore the paper away from a creamy, golden colored garment that it had been protecting.

In horror, she looked down at the lovely lace and silk dress that lay half off the bed. It was her wedding dress. A wave of nausea swept her and sweat beaded on her forehead. Breathless, she stared at the dress as waves of grief, shock and bewilderment swept her.

Sarah slumped onto the bed, feeling weak and out of breath. At her feet she saw a scrap of paper that had been torn from a notebook. She bent and smoothing it, read the familiar and tender list, dated 1860:

ALTER DRESSES, 1.00
2 UNDERDRESSES, 1.50
4 DRESSES, 6.00
5 CHEMISES, 5.00
7 APRONS, 3.50
12 DRAWERS, 9.00[26]

When she found this list after William's death, she had placed it with her wedding gown. It was the record of the first clothing her new husband had bought her. The man was so meticulous in all his business records and diaries that even this old personal record was left after he died.

Then with a deep breath she stood straight and knew that what she was doing would make her Will proud. She reached to the gown, which lay on the unmade bed, smoothed and carefully folded it, and then replaced it in the trunk.

Folding the paper, she returned to the kitchen. She carefully cut each paper no larger than necessary and wrapped the fruits and vegetables. Folding the left over paper she laid it in a drawer, and surveyed her work. Then with a start, she removed an apple, placed Abigail's purse under it, wrapped it twice and placed it on the bottom layer of the basket.

Tying the bonnet on her head, she walked to the table, swallowed the last of her cold tea, primly picked up the basket, placing it on her right arm, and went to the front porch to wait for the carriage. After a few moments, she wisely decided to sit the basket down close to her skirt. A few people she knew walked past tipping hats or waving. She realized their warmth was encouraged by the lightness of her dress. They seemed to recognize that her mourning time was over; little did they know why, so she slyly smiled back.

When the carriage arrived, Nell and Thaddeus came to the porch. Thad reached for the basket, but halted when Sarah said she would carry it herself. "Nell, you may see to your morning chores now." "Yes mam," the woman replied and moved toward the back of the house. "Nell, should anyone ask I am doing an errand and visiting the cemetery. I should be home before noontime."

Thaddeus helped the woman into her carriage, assuming they would be going north of Natchez to the cemetery. The driver turned the carriage in that direction. As they moved across the small city, the even clopping of the old horse and their scurry at intersections to take turns passing, filled the driver's attention. Before the carriage began the incline upward toward the top of the bluff, Sarah told him that today he should deliver her to the main gate of the fort.

"Thaddeus, do you know what time it is? I did not bring my watch." "No mam, but Ms. Scothorne say it after seven when I leaves the house. Do think bout afta eight now." Her breath was coming short and her temples were throbbing. *How on earth did this happen, a widow yesterday, a smuggler today?*

It took some time to reach the main gate of Fort McPhearson. There was the usual hubbub there, even this early. People were lounging near the gate. Black women were selling food and goods. Small colored children were running about nearby as they played. Numerous soldiers were standing about, Black faces above blue uniforms with brass buttons. The sight was still repellant to Sarah; it was like a charade. The presence of their guns gave her somber thoughts. She told Thaddeus to pull up and find a place to wait. He tied the horse to a shrub on the east side of the dusty road, and came beside the carriage where he stood quietly.

Head tipped slightly so she could peek from under the brim of her bonnet but not be observed, the young woman stared at the fort and tried to form some mental order and see where she must go. Assessing the situation she moved to get up, and allowed Thaddeus to help her down. He reached to be handed her basket, which she almost grabbed from his hands. She alighted, "Wait here," she knew that approaching with a servant would make her more conspicuous in this fort full of former slaves.

She pretended to settle her skirts as she gathered her courage. Then, slowly, she walked toward the gatehouse on the south wall.

Just as she approached the entrance, two soldiers stepped in her way. "Where you goin?" "I have a pass and have business inside the fort." It was the first time in her life that any Black had ever confronted her. It was far more offensive that frightening. "Wait," the older soldier demanded. One of the men went inside and she stood quietly looking the other soldier in the eye. He stubbornly refused to look away and returned her stare with no change of expression that she could read. Thus they stood for perhaps ten minutes until a stocky, white Union soldier with a red beard came up.

He beamed, looking at her appreciatively. "You have business here?" he inquired. "Yes, I am here to sell produce at the commissary." He held his hand out. Awkwardly, without sitting the basket down, she loosened her bag and pulled the pass out. Holding it toward him in her left hand, she plastered on her brittle, rehearsed smile. The ruddy man winked and read the paper, "Sarah Scothorne, don't believe I have seen you here, before."

"No, this is my first visit to the commissary, I will need directions where to go." Giving her a big smile he turned, nodded at the gate guards and said rudely with half-hidden salaciousness, "Follow me."

As they entered the huge area inside the earth walls she looked about. Visible were buildings, troops, tents, horses, cannons and a few distant houses. Most of the troops were lounging; a few were occupied with various tasks and a few groups were marching.

"What kind of food you bringing?" the man tentatively tried to start a casual conversation. With her phony smile applied again but now with more breath since she was suddenly being washed with the excitement of the adventure. "Oh, just some late garden produce," and more demurely she looked toward the ground and tried to keep pace with her companion.

After stopping at the Adjutant General's office, they moved across the courtyard and stopped just short of a long, one-story, wooden building that had three doors opening toward the parade field. He paused, "That's the commissary. Just go in the center door," he directed with a nod of the head. "Do hope you come again, my name is Corporal James, just ask for me if you need help."

I was just returning from checking the outer plantation in the north and writing a report of a rumor of smuggling. I entered into the fort by the Marine hospital, which sat on the northern border of the fort. I reigned in just beyond the gate and saw numerous horses tied at the post to one side of a mansion, which we had commandeered for our army's use. There was probably some sort of meeting inside the house. Many of attaché and several sergeants lounged on the porch and lawn awaiting need by the ranking officers they accompanied.

As I shifted in my saddle and leaned my cheek on the neck of my roan mare to relieve my sore body. There was the cadence of hoof beats approaching from the east. The horseman neared. Then I heard a creak and loud chuck of someone reigning their horse to a stop. "Well Captain Hunter, you seem to have retired early the in day," it could only be my friend Hobart. Tartly I replied, "You truly lack sympathy and loyalty." Raising myself back into position, I shook my head and flashed a sarcastic look. Reseated, I turned my steed to face Edwin.

"Haven't seen you at church. I made the excuse that you are busy investing in handkerchiefs. They have inquired of your soul and I told them you are condemned to hell. I also told them your soul was black and lost." My comrade shifted and spat Union tobacco, at the ground in front of me.

"I need to be off toward the Quitman place, so must leave now. If you're free, do ride along." We headed across the rolling grasses on the path toward the main fort and east gate, exchanging personal news, gossip and other fort events. In about twenty minutes, Edwin rode off on some task of his own.

Moving into the area near the center of the fort, by the parade grounds, I approached the stable. Seeing Private Hunter, I raised a hand to catch his attention and asked him to check my mare's front, left hoof for a pebble. She had been favoring one leg all morning. Smiling at the young man, I handed the horse reins to this man who had earned my respect. With an afterthought I thanked him. This was received by the enlisted man with a modest glow. Then I started across the grounds toward the commissary to get some pipe tobacco.

I stretched my legs and slowed, walking in long strides. I was glad to be out of the saddle where I spent so many hours every day. I met several of the troops at the back door of the commissary, when I entered they saluted. Then I quickly moved into the storage area, as I crossed the rough plank floor I stepped over a cat sunning herself in a shaft of light. I passed into the main area where personnel usually worked. It was almost empty now.

Across the room a woman wearing a light colored dress and sunbonnet stood stiffly with her back to one wall. She was standing behind a table, with stacks of woolen garments and bolts of fabric folded and piled to either side. The pretty woman was standing awkwardly in a strange posture facing me with one shoulder against the wall. Quickly her eyes fell to the floor as I nodded and crossed the room.

Just before I passed her I heard the light clink of glass and as I looked down I saw a vial on the floor, I bent to retrieve it as it rolled toward me. The corked vial was filled with a bright yellow powder, which appeared to be sulfur. Rolling the object on my palm I narrowed my eyes in consideration. *Where did this come from?* I looked about there were no similar goods in the merchandise stored nearby. No one other then the lady and I were in the room at that moment. The only object, other than the cloth goods, on the table was an empty woven basket on the counter between piles of clothing. My eyes went to the civilian female leaning on the wall and staring at the floor.

*Smuggling?* That, after all, was my forte and it was not uncommon for townspeople to try to steal, trade or smuggle. Of even more import, was that this might also imply that someone in the commissary was involved in this deception. My hand closed tightly on the vial.

Holding the unmarked vessel, I crossed to stand in front of the short, shapely woman, "Mam?" The bonnet raised and the face looking into mine was somehow familiar. She had held large brown eyes, and full lips. There was the pinkness of her cheeks, which appeared to be soft—were I able to reach out and touch them. My throat tightened as I looked fully at the olive skinned beauty with a heart shaped face. There was a wisp of a curl peeking from under the bonnet at her temples and her heavy lashed eyes were set deep above sharp cheekbones.

I caught my breath and only stared in silence. It was the lady from the cemetery; I had helped remove from the mud. She straightened and brought her hands in front of her waist clutching a small purse. Defiantly, her chin struck forward, she stared back at me. Then her eyes widened and her mouth opened and I realized, she too, had recognized me. The stilted sound of our breathing seemed to echo in the barn-like room. Both embarrassed, surprised, and somewhat attracted we looked into each other's eyes and a slight pink of blush crept across her cheeks to her whole face. My own pulse was racing, and my breath became short.

Nodding and smiling I finally retrieved my composure. "Madam, what brings you to McPhearson?" With a sweet smile she replied coyly, "I sold some small produce and fruit." Then she brushed past me toward the counter where she reached for the basket.

Stepping into her way I said, "I'm Captain Hunter, no insult is intended but it is my duty to inspect your pass." Loosening the strings of the small-embroidered bag she carried Sarah once more plucked out the folded paper. She passed it to William.

With an even sharper shock of recognition I read the name, Sarah Drucilla Scothorne. I looked at it long, understanding the import. *Could I possibly interrogate this widow whom I had been seeking for four months?* I turned and paced a bit trying to gather my composure, then I stopped to look at her and paced some more. *So this was Sarah Scothorne, she probably was smuggling* but I felt unwilling to confront her. I felt a loyalty to my family and her grandfather but I had to be honest about my other motive—she was also far too appealing and feminine.

I took a long step toward her and smiled. With obvious relief she returned a tiny, nervous grin, "Very well, allow me to walk you to the gate." Nodding and looking at the floor once more she stammered instructions as to which gate she had entered by and where her carriage waited.

Reaching for her elbow I held it as she stepped down the deep step from the building to the ground. Then with some embarrassment I released it, for the very touch of her arm was thrilling.

Sarah also seemed confused and nervous. Her fear of arrest and her guilt were almost choking her. Somehow, she was sure this officer knew the truth. With a plunging heart she realized she had only secured one of the two medicines. *Yet, why was she released without an accusation? Hunter? Hunter?* The name seemed to ring a bell; somehow there was an association with the Episcopal pastor or her grandfather. There was some connection; but she was too flustered to sort it out at this moment.

As the couple walked in silence keeping a respectful distance, each one's mind was racing.

When I exited through the gate to escort her to the small carriage, I recognized the driver. Assisting her into the carriage created a tingling at the warmth of her body and the fragrance of her hair as it washed over me. The closeness and sweetness left a sensation of heat across my chest and loins as I helped her into the vehicle's seat. "It was so good to meet you Mrs. Scothorne. Perhaps we shall meet again." What a strange statement to make in this awkward situation? I felt embarrassed and stiff.

Her breath was rapid and stars bloomed in her vision. For moments after the officer's departure she felt faint. Then she ordered the driver to take her home instead of to the cemetery today.

# Chapter 13
# Circumstances of the People

From July of 1863 to the beginning of 1864, the entire society of Natchez, Mississippi went mad. Like a python swelling to gobble everyone, the inflation enveloped and choked everyone. Clothing and necessities cost hundreds of dollars. War widows or the elderly were often destitute, dependent on the provisions of the Federal army. Businesses closed; tradesmen and labor had little call for their services. If unable to grow food, or without something to trade, many middle class families lived in dire straights—some going so far as to glean corn that had fallen between slats in crib floors. The military were the only dependable market for any goods.

Within the city, the former slaves could only be used when employed with salaries. Familiar with obedient servants, the people chaffed under the attitudes of the newly independent people, who were much less than dependable now. To be surrounded by thousands of Negroes in uniform, and to be under their authority was a shock to the whole community.

The humiliation of subjugation especially rankled the previously wealthy and elite culture. In many households there was restlessness and growing fear with the progress of the Confederate army. Although Jefferson Davis was almost a native, coming from Woodville and having a nearby plantation, many Southerners secretly lacked confidence in him. His military leadership was not sure and confident. Frequently, he was too long in taking action, and many of his strategies and decisions were confusing or malleable.

In this atmosphere, cotton was worth $400 a bale, so the only sure coinage was cotton, it was like gold. With no means or opportunity to move cotton or to resell it, cotton was frequently stolen. Angry planters even burnt their own crops, floating the burning bales down the river, they preferred it to be destroyed rather than be so used against the Confederacy.

The bales sometimes sat on docks, like those at Fort Adams had, until they were stolen. The stolen bales were put on boats and sent down the river or they were moved North using wagons and draft horses. These horses and wagons were frequently stolen from the Union army for this purpose.

Soldiers, both Black and White, were abusive of the population having a sense of power over a people whom they resented or hated. Officers saw the same violence, two Union Colored soldiers were executed for killing their White officers.[28] On forays into the country, families and properties were arbitrarily abused by some troops and officers. The fear and anger bred retaliation. There were numerous lynchings, beatings or burnings of Negroes. Deserters from both sides, and free-wandering former slaves, plundered and harassed the countryside. The region was a no mans' land. The citizens who had opposed the secession were at first comfortable with the surrender, but as their own welfare was interfered even they now became resentful.

The conditions in Kraal overshadowed the whole community. Disease killed so many there and they were thrown into the river or buried in shallow graves on the riverbank, just to the north of the awful camp. Vagrant Coloreds were taken to the Kraal against their will, adding fuel to the fire. The federal government gave the people in the Kraal blankets and food, but little else. The Catholic priest who visited what was intended to be an infirmary found only a few dying people, in rags and uncared for. Many of those impounded had been servants; their previous owners would visit them bringing provisions. When there were fresh peaches and cherries they would take these to former servants; in future years the discarded pits generated many young fruit trees.

In this oppressive atmosphere, Edwin and I were crossing town from the fort toward Monmouth. The late winter morning was pleasant but the general attitude of the populace was not. In the eight months that we had been here the whole demeanor of the people had hardened. We had hardly been welcome before, but now the glowering looks and occasional sneers made us uncomfortable. We attempted to overlook and ignore the behavior but it was hard to be so hated.

The corporal was now in command and we visited as we cantered, after some discussion of the situation of the troops at Monmouth, where Edwin was now posted. We finally moved into more personal discussion. "Dear man, how is your handkerchief collection coming?" I inquired with some tongue-in-cheek sarcasm.

Gaining a straighter posture my companion answered, "The pretense of purchase at the shop has gone by the wayside. Only a week ago I was allowed to stop by the shop after it closed and walk Mary Ellen around the park and then deposited her at her home."

Uncharacteristically, I made no comment and we rode a bit farther into the center of town in silence. Edwin noticed my distraction, with sincerity he inquired, "My friend, what is on your mind? Do you have some problem?"

In fact, I was manipulating our path to pass streets with which I was becoming familiar. I had begun riding on this street each day as I passed east on my rounds to Monmouth. With inquiry, I had been able to ascertain where my lovely smuggler lived.

Now, seeing this particular small, brick house on the next block, I reigned in my mare and dismounted. I leaned against a tree to write a short note. This, I then folded carefully. I led my horse the next half block, and upon reaching the house I put the note into the slot in the door for calling cards.

As I accomplished this task Edwin had just sat on his horse. Now, he rode to my side where I was remounting. "What house is this? What are you about?"

I only smiled at my friend and remained silent. *How Edwin would tease if he knew that I was maneuvering to meet a certain widow of Natchez.*

Dear Mrs. Scothorne,

I regret I was not candid when we met at the Fort some time ago. I actually have had business to conduct with you for some time. Since my arrival in Natchez, a missive has bound me to you. This request comes from your grandfather, Isaac Spencer.

I would desire that you allow me to visit briefly on the Monday next, at your home, in the late morning. For that purpose I will call on you at such a time.

Dutifully,
Captain Wm.Hunter

That evening Sarah carried the note to the supper table. She read it, then slowly reread it. *Could this Union officer be coming to blackmail her about the smuggling?* Her first emotion was fear. There was terror that her foolish act would bring drastic repercussions upon her. Mentally, she enumerated the terrible consequences that might follow her crime.

She now knew who he was, most certainly she did. Friends and family had been keeping her informed of his inquiries about her at church. The family had chosen, out of respect and also to protect her, to not mention it at first. Then, just before she ended her mourning, Mother Scothorne had told her of the several inquiries about her by a young officer but they did not know his true purpose.

When Captain Hunter had confronted her during the smuggling, she had recognized the same soldier she frequently passed on the cemetery road. Indeed, it was this same person who had rescued the mired carriage last fall.

Sarah played the many scenarios in her mind. *What would this visit mean?* She was in no position to be rude or antagonize a Union Officer. She, of course, would accept the call. With dread she hoped it would be quick. *What would he ask her? Or worse accuse her of.* Again and again she tried to see her situation from many angles to try to devise a means to turn the visit to her own good ends.

For the next four days she felt restless and again found sleep elusive. One night she even dreamed of the man. This dream was most troubling for he seemed to be coming to court her. When she woke sweating it seemed she could still see his face.

For the four days after I rode with Edwin and delivered the note to Mr. Scothorne, I could hardly keep from thinking of the possibilities. Neither could I keep from thinking of the beautiful woman I would be spending a short time with. The approaching morning appointment filled my every free thought of which there were many, since I sat in the saddle all day. I could not sleep last night, so I got up quite early. I groomed very carefully and rode into the city with at least an hour to spare.

I was very anxious and spent time slowly watering my horse on Main Street then walking at an even pace in the direction of the Widow Scothornes' house. I still needed to waste half-an-hour within vision but some distance from the house. As I leaned on a fence, I received many furtive and suspicious glances from passers by.

Finally, I checked my appearance, mounted and rode toward the house. Her home was a small brick house with a low front entry; the roof had a pair of chimneys. The rise of the roof indicated a single upstairs room. The home was set close to the street and houses were near enough to each other to indicate a working class part of town. There was one hitching post where I tied my horse under the shade of a large magnolia tree.

I tried to walk to the door in a casual manner so that I would not appear too anxious or excited. I rapped using a heavy, brass knocker that was placed in the middle of the door, and moved back a long step to await a response. The few moments I waited seemed long, but were probably less than a minute.

When the door opened it was by an older woman of color.

"I am Captain Hunter, and have requested to see Mrs. Scothorne this morning."

The servant opened the door wide and stepped back so I could enter. She then reached toward me to take my hat. I removed my hat but nodded a negative, preferring to carry it myself, as I usually did. I was ushered into a small sitting room opposite an open staircase.

Selecting a soft, side chair at the side of a love seat, I crossed the room; motioning with her hand, the lady indicated that I might be seated. Then the hired woman went toward the rear of the house.

In a moment, the lady of the house appeared. She moved across the room smoothly, seeming to float on the wide skirts of a rust-colored, day dress. I could hear the swish of her skirts and there was a soft, floral fragrance about her. I rose to take her hand and gave it a gentle squeeze, "Thank you for seeing me."

She gave me a nod of greeting, then moved past me. After she was seated on the love seat, I returned to the chair I had chosen and sat once more.

Nervously, I quickly started to explain myself, "I have come, as I said, on behalf or your grandfather Spenser."

With a courteous but cool glance she interrupted, "May I ask Nell to prepare tea?"

Realizing that this meant she would not be shooing me out of the house on a moment's notice, I felt giddy with relief. Then to my embarrassment, I responded much to quickly, almost gasping out my response, "Thank you that would be very nice."

"Do you take sugar or cream?"

Remembering the needs of the community, I simply nodded my head in refusal.

In response, the courteous lady rang a tiny, china bell which lay on the table and when the servant appeared she instructed her to prepare tea.

With disconcerting coolness the woman leaned against the back of the divan and sat silently looking me directly in the eye. Her own expectations foreboded nothing but danger, while mine were of romance.

Disgusted with myself, I realized that my mind was once again blank. The prepared speech had disappeared, and for long moments I sat staring at her while she remained patiently, quietly waiting.

"Your grandfather, Mr. Spencer, that is, is he well?" I paused again knowing that my statement made no sense.

Taking a deep breath I slowly started, "Let me begin again. He has been a family friend of many years and a near neighbor. He has worked at my brother's foundry in Illinois. When I came to Mississippi in August, my father wrote of your difficult personal situation which is of great concern to your grandfather. Then when I came to Natchez the request arrived that I seek you out and see, for the gentleman's comfort, that you are safe and provided for."

"This is a deed which you have now accomplished," her tone was formal but kind. "My grandfather and I correspond with some regularity and I try to keep him informed of my condition of life."

"I was unable to find you, I am sorry that I have been tardy in my response to my father's request on your grandfather's behalf. When I saw your pass at the fort I realized who you were." With embarrassment I realized that I had in fact made the mental connection of her identity when I had read her husband's head stone. This information would most certainly have raised her ire, had she known I had spied on such a private act of grief.

Dead silence ensued as her eyes became cold and suspicious. Her lovely, dark eyes looked at me directly and silently.

In panic Sarah felt that this must surely be the opening of her accusation. He had most certainly called to mind their meeting at the fort. There was no reply for this statement, although there was an impulse to make some excuse or lie. Yet to do so might further incriminate her or prove her guilt.

*The tea must have been started as soon as I arrived,* he thought. For at the long, tense silence the servant entered the room with the tea service on a tray. The willowy woman sat the tea on a table by the lady of the house. She then moved a side table near to my chair, and went into the kitchen from which she returned with a crystal tray with small molasses cookies. I was given a cup and a saucer with two cookies placed beside the cup. Then Sarah was served in a like manner. The steaming pot of tea was poured by the lady of the house.

I sipped lightly at the steaming cup and pondered what I had said to raise this woman's ire. Then I realized and quickly stammered, "This madam, my visit that is, has no bearing on the fact that I met you at the fort."

She relaxed somewhat, but the ice was still not thawing. As the widow averted her eyes to her cup, I sneaked a quick look. Courteous though she was, I panicked to think how I might prolong the visit or to engage her in some more light conversation.

"Might I inquire, for your grandfather's sake, if your basic needs and necessities of life are fulfilled?"

"Yes sir, there are no needs that I am bereft of."

Then there was more silence. "Your home is quite comfortable," was my next feeble attempt.

"Thank you," more silence.

"I see that you have staff here."

Her brown eyes flashed defensively, and she snapped, "I have one servant, she is not a slave. Although, the Union allows us the holding of slaves within the city."[29]

Seeing little optimism in this train of conversation, I tried to move to what I thought might be common ground. "Both of our families came from this part of Mississippi. Where did the Spensers live prior to migrating to Mississippi?"

Brief answers seemed to be her forte. "North Carolina many years ago and Alabama. I was born here."

Sarah was tense and still feeling panic. She imagined words that had not even been spoken. *Was Captain Hunter now going to make issue of the service of her maid, or the past ownership of slaves? What ever was his direction? Was this some devious trap?*

This time the ensuing quiet after her statement allowed me to hide in a teacup and a molasses cookie. This was not a comfortable feeling. "Your own parents, do they live here?"

In a flash I realized that I had fallen into another trap with this visit. I fumbled to loosen the buttons of my jacket while trying to hide my discomfort. This angry woman was looking for a fight. She saw me as the proof of her smuggling deceit, seeing me as the enemy, maybe seeing me as one who had killed her husband. There was only fury in her. How else could such a simple question spark her anger, I had no idea, but the idea of a friendship or flirtation was seemingly a dead ember.

I looked toward her with slight relief as she began to add some detail to her last statement, "Actually, I was raised here, although, born in Alabama. Until last year, I had a family here in the city. Of my parents and siblings, a sister and two brothers; only one brother, Joseph, now lives in the area. My mother is desperate and this war has killed my father. My father, Elijah Ever Spenser, was broken. He was crushed by this disaster. He was a merchant living in town, his business was destroyed and the family moved to the country."

The flushed woman clamped her lips together and sat stiffly.

This was one of the more difficult situations I had ever been placed in. There seemed to be no topic that did not raise her anger. I had dreamed of seeing her; of a possible relationship. In my mind, the connection with her grandfather would at least open doors to friendship. I was numb.

With an empty voice she inquired if I wanted more cookies or tea. I only shook my head no and took a small sip of what remained of my tea as I fell into the hopelessness of the whole visit.

Sarah felt intense defensiveness. How dare this Yankee question who and what she and her family were! *I refuse to be cowed or threatened, I am not afraid. In fact I am proud of who I am.*

Suddenly, she sat straight, and took a deep breath. Now her eyes flashed, and color rose in her face. She tipped her chin upward, then she began a rambling nervous recitation about family slaves. It seemed that she felt that I expected some kind of explanation.

"Our family had two servants. An older fellow named Peter. He was short and fat with a totally bald head. He was like a family member. Father always planned to bury Peter in our cemetery plot, someday. Peter, I guess I don't know where he came from. My father had bought him when they were both young men. He always teased that the man was the best buy he ever made. Peter's ankle had been broken, so the price had been low. Pa didn't want a strong field hand. The reason he needed him was to care for the horses, cut wood and help occasionally at the store doing errands, stocking shelves, sweeping or moving merchandise. The clear-eyed, golden man had dignity, which he never lost. As children, we never disobeyed or tormented the man for he demanded our respect."

"I am pretty sure he never had a family. On his day off he would dress nicely and go to town. After I was an adult, I would be riding in a carriage passing the Black quarter and see him sitting under a tree with other Black men. He would be visiting or playing cards, nary a single woman in sight. I never knew him to mention church services. As the war progressed and emancipation came, he stayed on with us but told us when he would work and how much work he would do. He announced, 'I like stay here Suh, but I over sixty summers and can't lift and do the hard work no more.' As though my father was not also failing in strength and of the same age. My father would move heavy crates by himself. That change of attitude in Peter hurt my father. It made him feel that his kind treatment and consideration of the darkie was not appreciated. The balance of their relationship was changed forever."

With some relief I thought the widow's tirade about slaves had ended as abruptly as it had begun. Aghast, I realized she was only catching her breath, and she went on with another tale of a Spencer servant.

"When I was about to be born my mother needed help. She found a small boy, slender, light-chocolate skinned, with freckles. When he was older, he had still not grown past the size of a half-grown man. He was quiet and quick, but not trustworthy. Father had to whip him for drinking, stealing and lying. The minute he heard of Lincoln's emancipation act he ran and joined the Coloreds. Little man in a blue coat—just looked silly. He looked like a child in dress up in adult clothes. I've glimpsed him several times and just turn my head to save myself seeing the man."

Sarah sat the empty cup aside and turned her head to stare at the objects on the fireplace mantle. She felt empty and defeated. There was also a sense of embarrassment for she had told this man more than was any of his business.

As she stared moist eyed at a spot across the room I studied her profile. I was sure I had never seen a more lovely woman, nor a more tragic one. Was her personality always so angry and defensive?

"Sir," she began more softly, "what can you tell my grandfather? I would only hope to cheer him, but the realties are not of good cheer. My William, my husband, was a fine carpenter. He apprenticed to the same carpenter that his brother, Henry Quitman Scothorne, had learned from in 1858. At first Will and Henry worked together. When Will felt prepared, he began to work alone and built quite a successful reputation. He purchased this location and built our home, bartering for the brick exterior and finishing all the rest himself. When we were married, a couple years ago, he took very good care of me. As I was with child he had a woman come to help several days a week. I had all I needed."

Sarah reminisced, thinking of this small house on a long lot, "I also had a fenced garden and a small carriage house for the wagon and carriage. Our servant Jim slept in the carriage house and cared for the horses. During the day, he helped Will at the building trade. I had hoped to find a servant, a maid or cook, by the time the baby was two." At this her voice slowed with a slight quiver and her eyes lowered. She paused and looked across the room through a window with misty eyes and knitted brows.

While the grieving woman regained her composure my heart felt a twinge and I stared at her now fragile features. How I yearned to hold her soft hand or, almost too daring to consider, I would wrap my arms around her to comfort and protect Sarah.

"Dear woman, I am not asking for an account of your former slaves. Each day slavery moves into the past and energy needs to be directed to help rebuild the South for both the Black and White community."

"I had a sense that slaves other than house slaves lived separate lives and women often did not know all that happened. Although, I have heard of homes where the woman of the house also owned a well-used whip."

"You said Jim left." I asked, "When?"

"Not many months ago. He was becoming less and less dependable and was very rude. I seldom saw the lamplight at night by his pad and knew when he was gone. Knowing he would leave, no matter what I did, there would be no stopping him. Since my husband died I have been most helpless in many ways. One day, I saw Jim whispering by the road with Negroes I did not know. Then finally, I rang the morning bell one day when I arose to find no fire or coffee. There was no response, so I dressed and walked to his husk bed in the shed. It was empty. The blanket was gone. His possessions were usually kept in salt and fruit boxes, these were all but empty.

"Looking about, I only saw our sway backed, old horse and a poor wagon. The carriage and our pony were gone. These things would be of small use to me, since I have never cared for a horse. It would have to be sold. The comeuppance was that even the older horse was stolen before I could sell it. I wondered if it was carrying someone about or was dinner for the hungry. I finally moved the wagon outside to show a buyer. Before he arrived, ten soldiers passed by, nine were Black and one was White. The White one was riding a horse and laughing coarsely. They fixed the wagon and pulled the vehicle down the road."

Jerky and flushed the woman took a breath. Her temples were reflecting in a tiny glaze of moisture. I put a hand on her arm, "Why do you need to tell me this? To explain?"

Brushing my hand away she jumped stiffly to her feet, "Sir," she firmly stated, like a person in a trance. "We always took good care of our slaves. We provided for their homes, families and food, do the Federals." Gasping for breath the angry, young woman vented, firing flames toward me from her dark eyes. Her lightly clad breasts rose and fell under the rust-colored gown.

Then a sudden silence fell like a blanket—hot, angry and suffocating, "I'm, I'm sorry I was not asking about your slaves. I was asking about you, you the … lady," I stuttered, "I pray you can forgive me for implying a judgment on you personally." I desperately wanted to quiet the tirade. Shaking inside I was now overwhelmed with my own anger. "This war is not only about slaves, it is because the South, with deceit and antagonism left the nation to become separate. This war is about secession also, it is not about your personal consideration of the slaves you owned."

Coolly, she pointed to the door, "Do leave, now!"

I picked up my sword and buttoned my jacket with one hand. I kept my eyes fixed on the buttons as I moved toward the door. Turning the handle, I crossed the threshold then turned. She stood silhouetted with the light of a window at her back. Light sparkled on her hair at the crown and wreathed it warm, red-brown, like a copper halo. This image only heightened my pain.

"You may inform my grandfather as you choose, but perhaps he would not like the truth of the condition of our family. We did not want war or to secede or to die or to be occupied or to be surrounded by Blacks carrying guns and full of resentment. Our way of life was ending as our region matured. This city has been drug into the wine press where it is our blood that is flowing."

"My father was too old to go to battle but he smuggled and spied. Several times I think he had done so, but I do not know to where or how. Once, early on, he was gone a month and came home hitching a ride on a wagon. He was dirty, his was horse gone, and his clothing was shredded on his body. The second time he left for a week and returned with a cut on his upper arm. That wound became infected. A slave's poultice finally healed the runny open sore after months."

"The final time he left was last year. It was before Vicksburg was occupied. When he arrived back at home, he seemed to be a man I had never met. He sat vacant and staring. When he ate he only pushed the food about. Father would walk to the road and stand limply staring at our house, come in again to his chair in the front room and sit unmoving until dawn."

"Crushed, he was crushed and he finally just lay down. The silence and the pain between us and him was like a sleet storm. In a week he was dead with his face turned to the wall. His eyes and mouth were open, staring and empty."

"My mother, Elizabeth, is alone in the country with Joseph and his wife, Catherine Jane. Isaac, my brother, has left for the war; his family lives elsewhere. The roads are so dangerous that Mother has only been able to come to Natchez once in January to attend church. The next two trips she made were for the funeral service of my dear Henry Craig and Wills' burials in March. I fear and pray each day for her but seldom have an opportunity to even see her."

My sympathy was for the widow. Yet, there was also pain in my own offended dignity and the personal insult stretching the wire between us. Frankly, I was sorry for me also. By stuffing her grief and pain the dam had finally burst and it had drowned me in its path.

"Sarah," I gathered my thoughts, "Sarah, your father, your husband, the city and you did not chose this path; but because they were a part of the warp and weave they were not beyond the responsibility of the South either."

"I am also a part of this war but," and my anger once more rose, "I am not personally responsible for the tragedy and loss you have suffered. It is neither my choice nor my fault. My compassion for you is sincere, but my determination to fulfill my own duty is my bond." Speaking of all the sacrifices and difficulty I faced only added to my own indignity.

"Dear Sarah, you must choose your own destiny." With a tilt of my head, I replaced my hat, and straightened it. "Good evening." I closed the door behind me. The pain, anger, rejection and confusion followed me into the warm, muggy daylight. The sweet fragrances of a funeral, instead of a romance, filled my being.

This beautiful but furious woman wanted to lay the war at my feet and to justify the institution of slavery, which she did not create but lived within. Our relationship was hopeless.

With my full command in October, I rode each day to the northern and southern home plantations. My discomfort was raging from rheumatism and the saddle sores, both incessant and unrelieved. The command I accepted demanded that each day I was to sit horseback, for ten hours or more.

Midday, I rode back past the cemetery and fort to the military plantation, at Monmouth. I rode south past smaller homes and large plantations, several of these empty or in states of disorder. Monmouth was on high ground about a mile east of the river. The lands rolled slightly to the north. The army had soldiers, women and family there to care for the crops being grown for the troops and some cotton. The nearby former slave market was now a barracks and hospital.[29] Then I repeated the route, to end at the fort for the night. If it was too much to accomplish, I sent someone else on the long ride. Regardless, I would be in the saddle tomorrow to collect more reports of smuggling, bushwhacking and complaints of citizen suffering theft or vandalism. I inspected passes not properly prepared and other infractions.

This particular night I stayed at Monmouth. It was late so I took a basin and bathed in cool water, sprinkled talc on my swollen tissues and lay in a lower room, exposing these to the soft wind. I rocked all night in a kneeling position on my knees.

The anger and pain, after Shiloh, Hatachie, Corinth and Vicksburg in the past three years, I had strongly endured. Now my backside was to be my nemesis. Edwin Hobart, my friend and companion, forever tried to cheer me by rude humor about the seat of my pants.

I realized how often I had been less than sincere with my sympathy for skin rashes, foot rot or the poor digestion of my fellows and my men. So many of us were disabled and crushed by these maladies instead of battle wounds. We were the walking wounded who were expected to go on walking. We endured the pain each hour of each day, despite the mundane nature of ailments crippling us.

Tonight at Monmouth after finding myself unable to sleep or even rest, I loosely pulled on my trousers, not buttoning them but pulling the suspenders up across my bare shoulders. Barefoot, I felt my way out to the landing, onto the gallery of a colonnaded porch. I paced slowly, turning to cross the porch again and again.

After several slow turns, I saw a small glowing light near the shrubs on one side of the house. I tensely studied the dark shadows there. I could make out a sitting form on the fallen stump of a tree.

The stump was part of the army's destruction to Monmouth. The men had sawn down the lovely, old trees near the house. The smaller branches were cut for corral fences for the horses. Other wood was cut for the fireplaces. This wood was burned for the downstairs, which the Union Army occupied.

"Who stands?" I firmly demanded reaching to the button at my waist in case I was facing some situation demanding action. I did not choose to be hampered by falling trousers. It was enough I had come unarmed, which was really poorly considered for an officer, but being half-disrobed was ridiculous.

"Jus' ol' Phant hav'n a pipe." Somewhat relieved, I paced toward the quadrant of the lawn from which the voice emanated. I found a Black recruit, he was also wearing only a hat and trousers, and was resting as he drew deeply on a corn-cob pipe.

"What unit are you with private?" I questioned.

"Company K, I was at the Fort 'til las' week. Then I come here." His smile at night and his twinkling eyes revealed a familiar, albeit dim recognition of the man.

I looked toward the moon to estimate the time. It would be dawn in an hour or two. "Couldn't sleep either Cpn?" he asked.

"No, Private, I could not sleep either."

With warmth he asked, "You have something on yo mind?"

I am uncomfortable and need medical attention I wanted to say, but instead murmured "I should be fine. Why are you up so early?"

"My Massa always gets us up real early, my whole life I be up early. Now, I got no peace, no su, got no peace in me. Been here at Quitman place doin' nothin'. I enlist, an wan to go to real war. If this war beat us, I goan be a slave again. If I get caught in the woods, they cut off me ears and my manhood. I be scared but want to fight so I can get rid of the it. Cause you see, fear and scared different. I have no fear. I want to fight. Here, my job is jus' ride round and boss the women, children and old men raising the crops."

Quietly, he looked toward the south and viewed the hill where it sloped down to the silhouetted shapes of hundreds of tents; belonging to four companies of Union soldiers. I knew one of these tents was Corporal Edwin Hobart's, for he had finally received a permanent assignment here.

The soldier began to speak again, "I look at the big house and know now I can walk in and out as I please, but I got no house of no kind for me and mine. My mammy, sister and grandfather all penned in the Kraal. I see they get food but they is in a bad way."

"Last week, all but my sister get typhoid. My grandfather goin' and my mammy going. I be free, but what goin' to happen to me and my sister. Even if I have my family; I have no house. How I goin live? What I goin' to do? I die befor' I be a slave again but where is this war goin take me?"

"You need to do the job here first, private. That is the first thing you need to do, to be a good soldier. Private, we are fighting a different battle. Just like me and my saddle sores, there are no bullets in this battle the two of us are in, but what we have to give now is still going to be an important part of the war. We are all trying to do right thing to win the war."

"I was at Shiloh and that was a big battle. Death was strong and evil there. No one won that battle, we all lost. Trust me the gun doesn't always have the right answer, but food in the soldiers' mouth and feeding those in the Kraal may. Those boys and men in grey are also fearful and hungry. It may be food that wins this war, and medicine and tents. Yet, I am confident the Fifty-eighth is ready to fight at any moment."

There was quiet smoke rising from glowing embers of the man's pipe as I turned toward the large, beautiful house. A new light was reflected in the broken panes of a lovely shaped high window on the south. Dawn had hinted its arrival.

The soldier stopped me. I slowed, then moved back toward him, "Capn, where you from?" "Illinois," was my reply. He asked, "They want me and my sister up there when this is over?"

I turned so he couldn't see my face. Then lied, "Maybe in Chicago."

"Nope, they don want us," the private stated flatly. Sheepishly, I nodded in silence, the growing light was making us more visible to the other. Turning, I saw the fellow to be around thirty, a bit older than me. His skin was rough on his cheeks with some kind of scarring reflecting like tree bark. He had a high, shiny forehead with large eyes that were slightly bloodshot in the whites. His skin was a color between cinnamon and wine.

"Su, I am here to prove dat I mean to be free." He walked to the porch and raising a foot high, balanced one large hand on a column, as he bounded up and onto the porch. This location became his perch on the new world.

"Capn', my sister be real special. Her pa be de overseer. His chile. Dat girl be light gold. She be right pretty. De white men always chose her first. Then when they find the chance they just take her. De high yellow boys and girls dey all be special. They be so special they be the first to be taken and taken and taken. We have a good massa, but he not be able to protect her. The other Colored folks on the plantation they can't protect her either. When we be on our own she can get a job cause of her skin, but that same thing be a curse to her. The Africans spose stop coming this country over fifty years ago. Most Blacks I know been born here or Virginia. More and more have White pappies. I even hear a few white women have yellow children. These chiles have de worse time. Some the pappies keep them in New Orleans in high style. Some give em all freedom when the pappy dies. Some jes keep bein' slaves. They be treated good in society but behind the doors they be a different kind of slave."

Inside I ached because I was becoming even more aware of the Black dilemma, miserable and condemned, but safe or free they were still lost and in danger. In my heart, there was empathy but knowledge of the probabilities that faced this orphaned soldier staggered me.

"Look to the South," and he pointed some distance where I saw, on a small crest, large warehouses with loading docks silhouetted with several smaller clusters of sheds around them. These all were now in use by the army. The area had fences and pens scattered about. "See dem sheds?" I studied them as they sat silently between several roads.

"They be de 'forks'. All the slave roads come here and meet right there, high on that hill it be Hell. These roads sure be Hell." And he pointed west where the Natchez trace came from Tennessee. "That de trace," then moving his viewpoint toward the Mississippi River, "and that road where they unload boats and come down the road to the Forks." Next he pointed south-east toward New Orleans and finally pointing east he simply stated, "Virginy."

"That Hell be call 'forks of de road.' They be lots of slave markets in this city, some be almost one hundred years old, but this one de biggest slave markets in the world, I think. So much money come from it to make the plantations bigger and the people more rich. Each road bring the Black here an take 'em away. Des Nigras be sold there. Be my people some new or old. Even be free people trapped and sold again. Man and woman, family, single, old and young they be my family not just be niggers. Not just be slaves but people and my family."

"Moma and granfather come here to da forks. They say my father be kept back in Virginia. Him and two brothers stay cause they big enough to work in the fields. They be walked hundreds o' miles down the Trail chained with up to fifty others. Some folks some try to escape and be beat or killed. When they get here they all tired, sore an scared. They make em sing so they can 'pear to be strong and happy when they come in town. Da traders keep em here one week, feed, wash, fix up sores and cuts. They hid tem sores."

"De put em naked and cold in tubs of water and start feeding them lost of yams and pork fat to make em look good. When time to sell they rub oil all over the Black folks to make em look good. Lots be striped naked and poked. The sellers yank mouths open, make you show inside yo behind. Then there be screams and begging and whipping when they take de families apart."

"My massa take me here lots of times to the forks cause I drive a wagon good. We bring slaves to sell for cash money and bring slaves home for cotton fields. I stand there an' I look in the eye of de people on the dock. I see the whip scar, the broke bones that ain't set. I see the screaming mamas torn apart from de chilin. Once, behind a barn, I see a slaver knock down an old man and drive the butt his gun into the grey fuzz o' de ole man's brain."

There was a poignant pause before the man continued, "Here at de forks, when sores of the people be healed, they oil them down, put on better shirts and pants then they put the folks on the dock. The buyers come, just like looking at pigs in a barn. They be lucky if de owners buy both de couple. So for a while they be good. Just now I come from a plantation near Woodville. Hard work der, get good food and a doctor when you need one."

"We trap and fish at night for extra meal, and den we dress up an take Sunday off. The massa and missy try to be good and care for us, but couple years have bad overseers. De ovaseer get women in the family way, those overseers do. Beat the men and charge the workers cash money for food and keep de money. There some law to stop 'em, but who can complain. Final' massa see a bad beating, almost kill his good man, and fire dat overseer with no pay. Not all them niggers at the Forks got scars, but deepest scars be in the eyes. Fear, anger, empty eyes with no hope and smoldering eyes like a wild cat. They be men, women, children. Yet, somehow God seem to have forgot that."

"One day the massa buy a woman. Her was round and have butterscotch hair long, and pull back in a knot. That night I loose that hair and she be my woman. When I have permission, cause you even need that to go to yo woman, I go see her always. [29] That woman make my heart happy, and I get permission to jump the broom with her. She get yellow fever and die."

"I hear de story of de nigga called Prince, here in this city in the old days, he come right from Africa. He keep trying to tell some story. In a long time, finally a man can understand him. Seems he be a real king in Africa and he get to go home from Natchez."[3]

"I no king but I be a man. I have kin. I want a family. I want to decide where I walk. My massa and missy not be bad, but they don let me be a man. They know those sheds be on the hill, they want them be there. They take money there and they bring money home sellin' men like sows or shoats. Cpn, I want to fight. No one goin call me a slave no more."

Sighing, I collapsed slowly and carefully onto the porch and quietly said, "I don't want to fight anymore. My problem is that I will not give up." Silently, together we watched the dawn, I was slumped and tired, he clenched a cold corncob pipe in his mouth. We looked into the other's eyes.

The next morning when I left, I walked through the house until I found a satin pillow embroidered with magnolias. This I took to soften my saddle. The pillow, from a bride's wedding trousseau, had been made with love by a grandmother who was now dead. This became my satin saddle cushion.

Private Hunter and Phant were among the few of my troops that I had spoken to at any length. I had a sense they believed I might be trusted and respectful. Both were from nearby. Many of my men were from Pennsylvania and a few came from Maryland. Several had been Freedmen. I had, in talking with other officers, found that Colored men from Canada who had fled to find freedom now had come back to the Colored Troops. Negroes from as far as Africa had returned to join the battle. The men of color were standing together and fighting this—their battle.

The fragments and pain around this city mad Natchez an angry, fearful place. The three people within—citizen, Negro, soldier—were only helpless game pieces on the ragged map of a broken nation.

## Chapter 14

# The Quilt Society

Sarah pulled her wavy auburn hair back and began pinning it into a compact bun, then she wrapped it into a net bag that lay down her back. She finally turned to either side checking her image in the mirror above her dresser. Stepping back and turning, she smiled with approval; her hair was neat but had a youthful air. Then she checked the appearance of her dress which looked very nice as it shaped softly to her abundant body. The tiny challis flowers of the gown were quite cheerful and reminiscent of spring flowers; it was the same she had worn during her smuggling adventure.

Going down the stairs from her single, upper floor bedroom she crossed the small, formal sitting room and entered into the kitchen, which was now empty. She went to the kitchen door and stepped through. There was Nell in the garden which lay between the house and the carriage house. Nell was cutting some lettuce and shaking the dirt from the leaves. The early spring day was lovely with a soft breeze which blew from the river. Luckily, today it smelled clean and had a natural, earthy odor that was somehow comforting.

The young woman crossed from the doorstep and walked to the garden. She stepped carefully along the young plants, then bent to pick a sprig of parsley. Delicately she bit at the stiff, green plant allowing the bright flavor to cleanse her mouth.

Without stopping her task the dark woman spoke, "Miz, I think we bout goin' to start the eatin' season."

"Mm." Sarah mumbled agreement because she was still chewing the pungent weed. Swallowing, she instructed, "Go ahead and finish what you are doing. We can find a few chitlins and wilt the lettuce for supper. It is Tuesday and I am going to the quilt society meeting today."

"You 'bout don' with you quilt?" Nell asked with snoopy curiosity.

Sarah brushed her hands together to remove imaginary dirt and turned her back. Smiling to herself vaguely, she swallowed again and replied, "It will be a while yet. I want to be very careful with my stitching, and I am afraid we ladies all visit far more than we should."

Slowly the widow moved back into the house. She stood, carefully looking out the window at her servant who was still busy in the garden, now pulling a few weeds that had appeared between the rows of strong seedlings.

Going to the sitting room the Sarah reached for a large, woven, willow basket and put it onto a side table. She pulled a cane-seated chair designed to accommodate women's hoop skirts close to the table and sat down. Sarah placed the basket on her lap. Checking in the basket she moved needles and thread about until she found a velvet pin cushion that had been hers since girlhood. She had begun making her first samplers when she was about seven years old.

She stood, placed the basket on the chair, went to the window seat and raised the lid. There was the muslin and calico quilt, folded and bulky. She took it to the side table near the chair where the basket was waiting. Then, looking quickly over her shoulder, she furtively unfolded one edge of the unfinished quilt and peeked inside at the grey, woolen fabric and some folded blue, woolen cloth. Pulling out a small, brown, paper package tied with string from the folds of quilt, she fingered the rough, fragrant paper and felt the hard, rounded shapes within. Checking toward the kitchen again to assure herself that Nell had not returned, she refolded the fabric and put it into the basket.

Inside the keep locker in the kitchen were some cold biscuits, these she sliced using a silver knife that had been a wedding gift. She spread some tart, cherry jelly onto the biscuits. Moving to stand above the sink by the pump basin, she ate carefully so that the crumbs fell into the dry sink. The woman outside was still working and was now near the apple tree. Nell continued patiently at her job, stopping occasionally to straighten and stretch.

Brushing crumbs from her breast Sarah pumped some water over her hand. Next, she blotted her mouth and dried her hands on the hopsack, hand towel hanging by the sink. Going to the keep she removed a partial gallon of sweet cider, poured a small glass and drank it quickly.

Opening the screen door she called out. "Nell, I have made a small breakfast and you need not attend to my food. Since it is such a lovely day, I will be leaving early. I see in the *Courier* that there is some brown sugar in new arrivals of groceries. I will leave twenty pennies on the table and if that is not enough for some of the sugar, see what sweetener can be had, molasses will do. I will be home late in the afternoon. Attend to your regular chores and if it is late, leave my supper on the table. We can eat our wilted lettuce tomorrow. Whey and fruit would be plenty tonight, as I will be having a lunch with the quilt society."

Humming "Bonny Blue Flag" softly under her breath, she secured her next to the best bonnet from the peg in the kitchen. As Sarah moved through the house, she put the basket on her arm as she neared the door.

Standing on the porch she looked at her neighborhood, surveying people or servants who were caring for yards, sweeping walks and porches or standing to visit. Looking at the sun, she was pretty sure that she could still go by Isaac Scothorne's to meet her sister-in-law on the way to the quilt society; to walk together would be nice. With a sprightly pace she descended the four steps off the side of the porch and started eastward.

The city comprised only about 6,600 people and many of those lived in the north of the city in the smaller homes just beyond the businesses. Other citizens lived on the fringes to the south in larger homes. The house Will had built for them was in a neighborhood near the center of town and was mostly surrounded by the homes of tradesmen among other comfortable but smaller homes; placed four or five to a block.

Walking across the city was not an unpleasant task and on a lovely spring day it was quite satisfying. It was also expedient not to involve servants in too much with the quilt society, far too many citizens had been betrayed by their own servants to the officers at the fort.

As she started down the street, a Union officer on a horse bisected a street a city block away. Her pulse jumped and she stared, trying to identify if it might be Captain Hunter. Feeling a flush, she realized the man she had glimpsed had a long white beard.

In her excitement of the impulse to identify the gentleman, her emotions swirled from anger, of her embarrassment at the bungled smuggling, to a rush of passion that made her breasts tingle. Then she was suddenly quelled by embarrassment at her foolish and girlish reactions.

She had not seen nor spoken to this man since his visit. Coyly, she knew he passed her house often, and standing back from her curtained window, she had watched him several times. Try as she might to ignore the knowledge of his whereabouts, Sarah had become quite aware of the possible schedule of his passing. It was a compulsion she fought to be near the sitting room in the early afternoon or early evening. This emotional response made her angry with herself and she made an effort to create and maintain a defensive attitude toward him.

About six blocks from her house she stopped at the older Scothorne's house. Going to the steps of the small home she called through the open door, "Oh, Minerva, Minerva Price, are you home?"

There was a laughing answer from inside and a pretty, small blond woman a couple years older than she came to the door. Minerva was about thirty, a year older than her brother Will would have been, had Sarah's husband lived. She was married to Daniel Price, and had two children with another just announced as being on the way.

The Scothorne family had no servant except the older man who drove her to the cemetery and Minerva lived close by her parents. She often spent much of each day here to help them. This allowed the grandparents to assist with her children while she helped her mother with household tasks.

"Do come in," she opened the screen, pecking a light kiss on Sarah's cheek as she stepped into the interior dimness. There was a fragrance of ginger, hinting at baking that had been done. The neatness of the room was cozy. "I am glad you came by, I will enjoy the company, wait a minute." The petite blond scurried about, opening drawers and taking paper wrapped packages from shelves. These she placed in a fabric bag.

Did you have luck this week?" Minerva whispered.

"Yes, I found some suitable brass buttons and some blue wool. Did you have any success?"

"No," her sister-in-law replied, "I have been busy with the garden and some sewing so have had no chance to scout. I saw Mary on the street and she said she had knitted several pair of socks and found some flannel for undergarments. Well, it looks as though the bundle will be large this week." Minerva and Sarah went to the back of the house where Mrs. Scothorne was paring the last of the fall apples.

Each woman greeted their elder with great respect. Minerva thanked her for watching the two children who were playing in the back between the house and the carriage house. Then, dutifully, the younger women brushed soft wisps of kisses on Emily Scothornes' warm cheek and took their leave.

As they walked across town they visited about their mother-in law, and the state of the goods shortages. Each woman had recently been forced to make the humiliating six mile trip to the Fort for the supplies the Union provided the townspeople. Each had also gone to the Provost Marshal to retrieve a letter addressed to them.

Sarah announced, "My grandfather in Wysox Township was generous to me with a note that will see me through Christmas, if I am careful." Just thinking of the fort reminded Sarah of the terror she felt when she had been discovered smuggling. It also revived the emotions of dealing with that confounded Captain.

Sarah had never and would never, tell of her adventure and the near exposure of her own smuggling at the fort. The whole incident was still a burning shame to the young woman. The secrecy covered more than just herself—her act would also implicate her brother and their neighbors. She hadn't even succeeded in acquiring all the much needed medicine. No Southern lady would even admit to a private conversation with a Union soldier, so that medicine adventure and the ensuing episode of the visit to her home was a secret also. It could be supposed that every family and every civilian held some secret in this town of secrets.

When the two young women arrived at the large clapboard house which was their destination, they were passed by a carriage leaving the yard. The carriage carried a golden skinned, young woman of mixed birth and a dark, grizzled, old man who was driving. Mrs. Elton, the hostess, only had these two servants. They had once more been sent away, so the "quilters" would be alone for the whole day. Sarah smiled to herself.

The servants of Natchez were not expected to be loyal as they had been as slaves and might report any infraction to the Union. Such an action would probably cause the Elton family to be punished. Sarah knew this to be true, some of her acquaintances had been charged of various offences, and a few had even been briefly imprisoned at the fort. The court house now also had jails. One area, called the women's prison, was full of women of all stations of life who had been held for all manner of things, both real and invented.

It was rumored that one woman in the community would not say where she had hidden her Confederate, deserter husband. She had been executed, and although it might be the Rebels who did the deed it was supposed the Federals had been the murderers. It was common knowledge that her servants had presented the evidence.

Another carriage arrived before they could enter the house. Their friend Caroline debarked and had her attendant lift a wooden trunk onto the porch. Then she pointed at a distant clump of trees where she instructed her servant, a boy in his teens, to sit and wait for her until late afternoon when she would call him. She did give him permission to go to a nearby stream for his entertainment. "Do not come to the house for any reason, my friends and I do not want to be interrupted with our visiting and quilting."

The three women entered together after a light knock on the door; a plump, older woman greeted them. Entering, they joined six other women, this brought their number to ten of the invited eleven in their group.

Without invitation they went immediately about the great room, clearing space on tables and moving furniture. For over three years, the quilting society had been meeting to make clothing for the Confederate soldiers. These contraband supplies would be smuggled weekly into the lines by one of the loyal Black servants who had accompanied a Southern White officer of the region into war.

These men of color brought small attention to themselves, and were able to sneak out of town with burlap bags of produce which also included the bags of garments. The servants would use the name of his owner's family, which would be known to be living in the area. They would be accepted as being part of that household.

Going to their own bundles, each woman proudly produced the scarce supplies they had been able to procure over the last seven days. There was thread that had been stained with walnut husks to darken it. Packages of pins and needles appeared. Scraps of wallpaper, newspaper or tissue for patterns were smoothed and lay in a pile. The fabric, which Sarah had brought, was added to a small mound of woolens, the blue sent to a pile on the floor which Caroline would take home to dye.

As the ladies worked, they were joined by the final quilter whose grandfather had delivered her to the house. This meant that today the entire group was present, which was a rarity. Caroline went to the porch, looked about and opening the trunk took one of three bundles of quilts out. Her friends held the lid open, while others lifted and carried the other two large, quilt bundles.

They entered, moved down the hall and placed the colorful piles on a settee. Several women went out over and turned the edges of the quilts back to remove lengths of wool which Caroling had dyed grey. Few of the yardage and disassembled garments had originally been grey. The freshly colored hues of various grey ranged from chestnut to dark umber.

Caroline lived outside of town on a small plantation, so she had more liberty to dye the goods after her servants had retired to their outside quarters. She dried the fabric in a lower room, under the kitchen, that was kept safely locked. The smell of wet wool was a problem and it would occasionally waft upward. She kept fragrant herbs all about the lower part of her house. There was also always a pot of water with pungent roots that could be set to boil at a moment's notice. She told her servants that she dyed quilt pieces and left a few of the same in view to convince them of the veracity of her task.

The latecomer also opened her basket and began opening prepared paper patterns of clothing in different sizes on the two tables. Mary and Sarah moved to the workspace with scissors and pincushions. After pinning the patterns, they began to cut fabric which they had withdrawn from inside the quilts that lay on the settee. Others settled eventually to sew, working as a unit on a single garment's parts, so as to keep the sizes and colors together as much as possible. With the quilters they worked on woolen garments since knit socks and flannel underwear could be made openly at home.

There were long moments of silence and then the talk began. "Have you heard of the arrest and detainment of the jeweler from Main Street?" Mary murmured a reply and added some details that she had heard. Like women from the beginning of time, the information grew and changed in the telling. This group of old friends talked; savoring and mulling each event that was discussed.

As though taking a group breath, there was a long pause. A few women exchanged the goods they were sewing. For various reasons they chose to stitch at a different garment. An older, respected woman thought for a while and shared her opinion, "At least that terrible McDevlin is gone. I heard he was caught late last year smuggling cotton and thrown out of the service. His previous meritorious service was probably considered or it would have been more severe. His service was no boon in Natchez."

"The ransom my family paid will keep him well off for some time," another woman spat the accusation out without lifting her eyes from her neat stitches.

"The nine o'clock curfew is becoming more effective within the community. The niggers and deserters still lurk about at night, but robbing and destruction is not as frequent and they are more easily captured with booty."

Mrs. Elton seldom became involved in the gossip the younger women were so absorbed with. Now she added her own views, "The wandering Negras are still a great fear to me. Perhaps the danger is greater than it has ever been. They surely will someday rise up and try to murder us all. Ever since I was a child, I have had sleepless nights," the lady lay down her needle; the expression in her eyes was painful to see. "As a child, I overheard my parents speak of the twelve years of battle in Santa Domingo in the late 1700s. The slaves revolted and 60,000 people were killed. They burned everything, strangled the owners and the wives were abused. There were half a million violent slaves and only 36,000 White people.[30] My whole life here in Natchez, I have had a sense of the greater number of slaves in comparison to the White men. We might have more millionaires here than anywhere else in the country, but that would be little comfort if we were overthrown violently."

Paling even further, Mrs. Elton lowered her voice and glanced around the room before she went on, "We have a close family friend who was one of the judges at the Second Creek incident"

Some of the women narrowed their eyes knowingly but the others inquired what that incident was.

The lady of the house lowered her voice, to what purpose it was not known since we were entirely alone, "A group of Negroes made a plot to revolt around a year ago. It was their intent to murder the owners, take their wives and eventually to join with General Grant."

There was a collective low groan from the women to whom this was new information, those who had heard rumors of the incident nodded. "Yes, these men were from the Second Creek area to the northeast of here. They hoped to gather a large group, but were thwarted by an informant before they could accomplish the horrible conspiracy. The judge told us that it was quite lengthy and difficult to investigate, and coerce the truth from the men. Carriage drivers were instrumental in the plan and I have never seen my own servants in the same light since."

"The inquisition went on for months and a number of executions took place. Because it caused terror regionally and potentially encouraged more slaves to revolt, the matter was of the greatest confidentiality.[31] I first heard of it only recently." Clearing her throat and taking a moment the lady went on, "The danger I have always felt was magnified. This condition we are living in now, with all the armed colored soldiers is, and should be, of great concern." With a solemn air, Mrs. Elton went back to work on the clothing.

Laying her work down for a moment, Caroline groaned and tears gathered in her eyes. "It was at the old grove at Bowling Green Plantation, in Wilkinson county. Judge Edward McGhee's home was invaded. At the time, the old man, his wife and two daughters, a small child and an expectant mother about to deliver were at home. The entire family was rudely herded outdoors under the old trees while being insulted with oaths and threats. The home was destroyed and burnt; a single piano was the only possession rescued. They also burned the gin along with 350-400 bales of cotton. The respected, 78-year-old gentleman was struck on the head with a pistol. When his wife tried to intervene she was struck with a saber." [32]

Hearing this grim information, each woman paused in various postures of sympathy and pain to commiserate and murmur.

Mary's response to this information was to name the many plantations also destroyed or vandalized in Wilkinson County. "At the Brandon's Greenwood Plantation, a maiden aunt was by the fire in the sitting room one evening last spring. The Black troops and their officers were bedded on the lawns about the property. As she sat alone in the room, a window near her had been opened to allow fresh air in. She saw a black hand reach in at the window and grasp the molding as though to lift himself through. Like a true woman of the South, she made no move or action to acknowledge she saw anything. Instead, she reached into the hearth and stirred the coals with a poker. Suddenly, she turned and brought the poker down on the hand. This produced a terrible howl and no more occurred of the incident." [33] Several of the women smiled smugly.

"All about Greenwood, especially south toward the Louisiana border, there have been raids on the plantations and the army takes all the animals. The cause, the Union says, is the 'disloyalty of the owners.' Many of the homes have been vandalized, and inhabitants threatened and treated coarsely. They are simply overrun by the Black troops who are out of control and the Union officers allow it. What slaves remain are rounded up just as they do the cattle, and called 'recruits.' It is with some wisdom that the Governor of Louisiana is pleading that our army also enlist all the Black men possible, to fight for the freedom of the South."

Caroline added that she thought this was wise and good use of such men. A fifteen minute debate ensued with no one having a change of mind concerning their own opinion.

During a pause for working and planning, several women grouped together searching through all the wool to obtain enough of a close match of color to provide one more sleeve on a large sized uniform. Two of the younger women wandered to the kitchen to find cool dippers of water and also to allow them a few moments of quiet private gossip

"When the Federals burnt the mills and looms at Woodville last July, they destroyed forty looms, many of our food supplies and military clothing. They also raided the railway facilities which had been the first rail line in the state. My own family was there when it happened. The city fathers came to plead for mercy, but were ignored," a very tiny, dark eyed woman added this to the list of atrocities these loyal women were enumerating at their gathering in lieu of social gossip.

A red-haired woman of forty almost snapped in her anger, "It reminded me of when they burnt all the cotton within five miles of Natchez upon our surrender." Then when a few troops entered the town, the army enlarged the destruction to ten miles surrounding the city. They removed all vehicles of private use and commercial purpose, and the horses and mules."[15] They even went to the churches while parishioners were inside, and took their horses and carriages.[33]

"Such acts must be as much for spite and revenge against the civilians as in the cause of war." Her pale skin, with a light dusting of freckles, became red with her emotional outburst, "Perhaps the union expects us all to learn to live by eating grass as do the cattle."

The talk quieted for a while as the eleven women worked carefully but in a haste born of their sense of the need of the soldiers.

Then began the more personal litany of the loss of soldiers, both sons and husbands, or of fellow citizens and neighbors. In the small group, four were widows. Three of the ladies had lost one or more sons. Especially painful to all, even if not personally related, was the defeat that wiped out a whole Confederate company with the exception of thirty men. This company was made up almost entirely of the brave, young merchants and businessmen of Natchez, so the immediate grief and loss had struck the whole city when they fell last October at Chickamuga.[3]

As early afternoon came on, they lay down the vital chore each was investing in. The ladies all rested and had a light lunch. Mrs. Elton had obviously taken much care and long planning to provide a fine luncheon. The hostess had served it with dramatic style on beautiful table service. The food was simple and the quantity was adequate, yet a reminder of present need.

For a moment they were caught up in a memory of the elegance of their former lives. Though all were of very limited resources there was a comfort in having these small moments of ease and quality.

Full and rested the eleven worked in silence for some time. Then several mothers and grandmothers told some charming stories about their respective children and Sarah smiled with each. Yet with each story about the children a stab of pain touched her heart.

There was, near the end of the afternoon, a long discussion on what the women could do about easing the tension between the army and the Natchez society. This occupation was a true disruption of the lives of the community, yet any civility that was possible would benefit all. Good will on either side was scarce.

Several fires that occurred in the city often were fought by soldiers. Some companies of the soldiers were maintaining the cleanliness of streets and walkways. The provisions that the fort provided were humiliating to request, like charity, but were necessary, especially for those whose men were away fighting or those who were widows. At a recent parade, the military band provided excellent music. Granted, these gestures were appreciated, but the tension still smothered normal life.

It fell to the women of the city to plan and provide polite social events where the ranking military were entertained. These events, like balls, parades and picnics were balm on a wound. They were not totally sincere and joyful on the whole. Yet, they did provide an excuse to gather socially and also to make an improved political atmosphere in the occupation. To be honest there was some comfort and pleasure in such events for the women also. A number of the quilt society women were involved in the planning of these events, and all participated.

By the end of the day the "quilters" were stiff with the diligence of their task, but all were satisfied with the social intercourse and the products produced. This week the stockings, jackets and undergarments made quite a pile. The hope of their delivery of comfort to the Southern troops was very satisfying to all.

They gathered their treasures, helped Caroline fill her trunk with "quilts" to be taken home to dye and each started to return to their own homes. Minerva and Sarah were among the first to leave; the young mother felt a responsibility to return to her children as soon as possible. Sarah questioned Minerva, "Minerva, is that a family name? For it is not common as are Mary, Nancy or Ellen; your sisters' names." Her sister-in-law giggled, "The two boys and my sisters always teased me that perhaps my mother had found the name in a novel."

After a pause Minerva began solemnly, "The conversations today made me uncomfortable. Much of the pain and problems that we discussed only make us more restless and fearful. I am proud of the work we do but the atmosphere of recounting such fears as those of Mrs. Elton's are quite dreary."

*Perhaps, she is right,* Sarah thought, *I have also been left quite melancholic by our situation and the repetition by telling of the pain we are all experiencing.* The widow realized there were unshed tears behind her lids and a deep feeling of loneliness.

The ladies walked the last few blocks in silence. After a light embrace, they parted and Sarah moved westward toward her own home. She was deep in thoughts about many things when something that Captain Hunter had said reoccurred to her. It is true the individuals in this whole thing are not personally responsible. Rather they are each part of the warp and weave of a huge drama.

Chapter 15

# The Hopes of 1864

It had been long months when I finally saw Sarah again. There was a ball given by citizens of Natchez for the military several times a year.[17] The ball was a bit stilted because of animosity blowing like a strong, pulsing undercurrent below the surface. But it offered an awkward effort to curry good will among the community leaders and by the Union occupiers. The officers and noncommissioned were always encouraged to attend. The city provided the event and the Union shared by providing the music and the food.

Since a New Year's party at the headquarters of Rosalie, I had not had polite society for many months. Although it might be shallow, I was as romantic as any lad, homesick and void of female company. I had been to one of these balls in October of '63. But I had only stayed awhile, feeling awkward.

Now, I felt anticipation and some degree of freedom to be spending an evening just for pleasure. I dressed with strict attention to my appearance, and groomed the full beard I had nurtured during my leave. My hair, dark with a wave, fell just above my shoulders, but was more walnut colored than my beard which had some russet when in the full light.

I asked Edwin Hobart to accompany me and we met in the evening about nine, mounted our horses and slowly rode to the ballroom. It was held at large theater near the courthouse. When we arrived it was in a thickening dusk. We found a hitching rail to secure the horses.

Slowly we strolled across a lawn; under a spreading tree we stopped a moment to smoke cigars. We chatted about events at the fort and reminisced about the adventure we had shared last year when we had been assigned to retrieve prisoner soldiers. This incident was the beginning of our friendship.

He had joined the Colored corps after I had. At that time we had served in different companies and had only some acquaintance with each other prior to this foolhardy assignment.[34]

Edwin drawled the often repeated story; I always felt his version was only a bit more dramatic than what I recalled. Having memorized his telling, I nodded in time to the tale. When we left the fort with a military van we were to pick up several soldiers who were prisoners and transport them back to the fort. Hobart had been wary from the beginning. After an hours drive we arrived, and entered the tavern. The hair on my neck rose. I knew immediately we were not among friends. This was to be confirmed.

I wanted to turn and run.

"Remember," Ed told the story, "we just stood a long time studying the room. At the far back was a man in an apron who apparently was providing food and drink for the establishment. Then we swaggered into the interior with bravado; a patron winked at me as we sauntered toward that very unfriendly fellow in the apron."

"We were trying to give the impression we were not apprehensive. What were you thinking William?" Edwin leaned his head toward me in a cocky manner.

"I was mentally marking where every exit was, and as it turned out this was well and good. The smoke and alcohol smell was thick. Some food had been burnt, I can remember the pungent smell."

This was the place in the story where Edwin always took the narrative back. "As I became accustomed to the darkened surroundings, I realized there were about twenty-five men in the room. Many were probably drunk. As we reached the back area of the tavern, you asked the barman about the captives. He answered, and then led us to a small room where kegs and goods were stored. There we found, tied to chairs, the two bedraggled young men."

"Just then some fellow yelled an insult from inside the bar about 'Union nigger lovers.' When we turned almost all the people in the bar were on their feet and moving in our direction."

Laughing, I remembered the panic I felt.

"That's when I remembered a small hallway with a door at the end and we ran for it. Luckily that door led to an alley."

"It was a stroke of good fortune that most of the tavern patrons followed us down the narrow hall, which slowed them, instead of going for the front door."

"We sure high tailed it, racing around the building. We grabbed the reigns and jumped on the seats of that ambulance and took off. Guess the men in that bar continue retelling the story of running off the Union army." Edwin continued the story, ending with a chuckle, "Never did find out who the prisoners were or what happened to them."[34]

Like old comrades, tonight we were relaxed and cheerful. Several officers moved to us and offered a swallow of some whiskey, which warmed my throat and my belly. Then the several of our group of friends visited for half an hour.

We vigilantly watched the front entrance appraising the people entering the ballroom I am sure the other young men were also assessing any attractive woman who entered, I know I was. Suddenly, my heart stopped. An older, white haired man with great dignity to his bearing was leading an older lady and two young women toward the steps.

As the lights from inside poured on the women, I realized the gentleman was Mr. Scothorne, and one woman was Sarah. The immense skirt she wore was of some soft blue material that was gently blowing. Her hair was piled on her head in chestnut swirls with sprigs of some tiny white flowers set off against the dark tresses.

The rush of excitement and attraction warmed me more than the whiskey I had swallowed. I wanted to rush to her, then realized that her disgust and anger would close me away like a wall. Lingering as the others filtered slowly into the music filled hall, I felt nervous. There was an awkward response in my heart as I wondered if I would ever have an opportunity to speak with her again.

When I garnered the courage to join the party, I slipped into the hall and moved to a corner where I quietly stood seeking her out in the crowd. There were over two hundred people in the room, the majority were Federal soldiers. When dancers completed a round they cleared the floor. It was then I saw her, she was seated on the opposite side of the room.

Watching Sarah's slightest movements for almost an hour, I was oblivious of all the other women. A few friends spoke to me as they passed but with a fluttering heart I barely heard them. I tried to evaluate my next move. This beautiful woman was unconscious of my stares, and was laughing and talking with everyone near her. Several times she was escorted to the floor to dance. When I saw other men's hands on her waist I yearned to hold her thus.

It was almost midnight, which would be the time to dine, and I realized there would be only a few more dances until the food was laid out, served and then removed. This finally gave me the impetus to take action.

With heart thumping, I crossed the floor and stood in front of her. The musicians had just declared a waltz. I approached from one side, then moving in front of her, I politely deferred, "Mrs. Scothorne, may I have this dance?"

She stiffened and looked up, her cheeks becoming quiet pink. Her full lips parted in a small smile showing her white teeth, but she spoke no word. She just looked up at me in surprise. The waiting moments were interminable to me. Then with a polite nodding response, she offered her hand. I took it as she stood and holding her elbow moved to the floor with her.

It seemed as though we were alone in a silent room as we moved in a shared rhythm, my hand felt the warmth of her body at her waist. Her lace glove was a rough texture on my palm. I seemed wreathed in her sweet fragrance. Her hair, with the moistness of it twining at her hairline, released the sweetness of flowers or roses. This fragrance was especially rich where moisture touched her face.

I made no attempt to speak nor did she. As the dance progressed I felt her slightly relax under my hand. She would move her head to either side quietly viewing the other dancers as she turned. I felt her warm, sweet breath pass across my face as she turned her face aside.

When the music ended we stepped back and looked at each other solemnly. Then I walked her to her seat, thanked her, bowed and left. I did not want to be rude, pushy or impolite but more honestly, I had also lost both my voice and my courage.

For the next hour I found some wine and ate a bit of beef and some sweets, then moved about the room trying to look casual. Now and again I cast a sly glance toward Sarah. I was insane in my need to see where this sweet woman was, and who was with her. After the music resumed and I felt there had been a respectful lapse of time, I again crossed to her. Inquiring if she would dance, she again favored me. This time she was more relaxed and the look on her face, was not a smile yet it had some promise of warmth.

"Of course, I would like to dance again Captain Hunter," she answered sweetly and my blood began to boil.

This time I had the courage to speak, "It is a real pleasure to see you, I hope you have been well."

"Thank you, I have been quite well," was her sweet reply, yet she looked toward the dancers instead of looking at me when she answered.

Once more we were covered by a smothering silence that was like a blanket on a summer night. In a feeble attempt at communication I asked, "Have you heard from your grandfather in Elkhorn?"

"Yes, I received a letter last month. It was held for me at the post and I retrieved it." My mind raced, *was this a subtle insult about the interference of mail addressed to the citizens.* The reply had left me in a quandary; I desperately wanted to avoid any suggestion of dissention.

To my surprise, she continued, "Have you been well?" "Yes, I was in the hospital at Airlie briefly, but am recovered." "I am sorry you have been ill." The stilted, polite conversation was frustrating. I would rather have told her how lovely she was or that the fragrance of her hair made me want to hold her and kiss her. This would not have been very polite conversation at all.

It could not be avoided if I were honest with myself that she was often on my mind. Yet, until this contact, I had not realized how drawn to her I was or how love sick I was. *Whatever must she be thinking or feeling about me?* Then with a start we both realized the music had ended and we were still dancing.

The embarrassment made her giggle and I released a lung full of air in a soft whistle. Slowly I walked her back to her chair, and she moved toward the pretty blonde woman she had arrived with. The other woman carefully watched me as I retreated.

Thus the evening ended at about two in the morning. By the time I arrived back at my quarters sleep would not come, and an embarrassing ache in my body left me quite uncomfortable.

There was a nasty turn in the weather in the Spring. It made the rides I was assigned to more uncomfortable. I had heartfelt compassion for my men in the barracks by the river, and also for the White soldiers still living in their makeshift shelters instead of the enlisted barracks.

It was my habit ever since my visit at her house to ride either past Sarah's home or within a block of it, at a distance where I could still glimpse the house. Prior to the ball, I had kept my head straight ahead when I passed. I had only strained my eyes toward the residence. It was my childish assumption that at a distance she would not see me staring at her house.

To relieve my conscience and shelter my denial I rationalized this zigzag pattern across the town was the most convenient route between Monmouth and the fort.. I refused to openly admit that I had a strong attraction for her, even after a number of improbable but wonderful night dreams.

Now out of mourning, Sarah had returned to Trinity Episcopal Church. Yet with the difficult year I had experienced, including illness, military duties and leave, my own attendance had been irregular. When I arrived I would always sit with visitors in the back pew. I would try to pray and mediate, but find myself staring first at the Scothorne pew, then if I did not find her, I would continue scanning the congregation. Either way, it is fair to estimate, I probably did not hear ten percent of the sermons in 1864.

About three weeks after the ball as I crossed in front of her home my breath was forced out of me. I saw her on the porch making a small, feminine wave. In panic, like a lovesick boy, I looked over both shoulders to see if she was, perhaps, motioning to someone else near me. When I turned back I saw she was laughing at me. Embarrassment washed over me.

Almost choking in my nervous excitement, I rode to the front of the house and tied my horse. Her face was flushed by the cool wind, a heavy blue cloak was protecting her. Her hair was wrapped about in a knit, peach colored scarf. I tried to look calm and official as I climbed the side steps to the porch.

"Good day Mrs. Scothorne," was the unimaginative salutation I used. My racing mind could find no more clever greeting. I simply touched my hat and smiled. I fell into her lovely face, like falling into a warm pool of water.

"It is good to see you Captain Hunter. I do hope your health continues to be stable," and she smiled, this was my undoing, for I was struck dumb and simply stared at her. "I happened to see you passing," there was a slight increase of color on her cheeks, "and, and, well, I wanted to tell you that I have just heard from my grandfather."

"Earlier, I had told him that you had called to inquire of my welfare. Grandfather Isaac asked that I thank you. He also told me of a visit with your parents. He reports that they are well, although buried under the snow."

In my dumb condition I nodded, smiled and gasped out a weak, "Thank you," then heartfelt, I added, "I am most pleased to see you again."

The silence fell like a boulder in a roadway and just lay there.

"I must not keep you, as you appear to be on some business."

She smiled, nodded and turned to go back through the door. As she turned to close the door behind her, I mumbled a short, "Goodbye."

As I rode on toward Monmouth the bluster of the wind seemed much less vexing. I hardly felt it all. My pulse and my mind raced, and I gave up denying that I was truly smitten. The pall that overshadowed my love was insurmountable, as were the political and philosophical differences between us. A woman of her high standards would never consider me as a suitor.

During the next several weeks, I attended every social event in the city with the hope that I would see her again. This was in vain, yet twice each week she would stand at her open window and smile. Other days, if my imagination was not wild, it seemed as though I could sometimes see her shadow behind the curtains at her window.

Corporal Hobart had now been assigned to my own company K. He was under my command and permanently stationed at Monmouth, so I saw him frequently while on duty. At this home plantation the troops were especially resentful of the Quitman's who were living on the second floor of the mansion and were well known to be secessionists. The Quitmans, like most Southern people of their rank who lived out of town, had kept a fine garden of many acres. It had contained all sorts of things from onions and potatoes to pineapples, pomegranates, figs and large pecan trees. The soldiers liked to walk in that garden and steal the produce. Its close proximity to our camp enabled the troops now and then to get a taste of something delicious. [35]

The lady of the house, Louisa Quitman, had reported to her husband

Joseph, who was on the war front, that she was left with only the servants Harry, his wife and Fred's family. They were now partially dependent on these the servants, as they had been given small monthly wages. This caused Louisa to write "Oh deliver me from the citizens of African descent." The lifelong closeness of the servant, Harry, and the deceased John Quitman had been set aside now during the angst of war. Harry had even served at his side during the Mexican War.[35]

Black and White troops were living all about the property and on the lawn. For them this was a great improvement over the barracks at the river's edge. This arrangement was also a fortification and a protection against raids on the home plantation by the rebels or ruffians.

Through the last of winter and into spring, my duties and the decision to always pass the widow's house both going and coming from Monmouth, kept me preoccupied. There was almost a pattern to the times that Sarah would appear gardening or standing on her porch. Now, she not only waved to me from the window twice a week, but was outside once a week.

This increased acknowledgment gave me hope, yet no sign from her seemed to indicate that I would have the freedom to call on her. Our first visit had made me most apprehensive of offending her or incurring her wrath, again.

There was a thrill the several times when I saw her at church. Before it had been my habit to linger behind after church. Now, I rushed to be outside first so that I was on the lawn before this dear woman should depart. Several times she nodded and smiled and once said, "Good day, Captain."

These small contacts gave me hope, still I could not be optimistic. I was obsessed with her, and finally had confided in Edwin that I was, in the whole in love, but hopeless. We did commiserate then, for the parents of the "handkerchief girl," Mary Ellen, had finally decided to demand that she no longer see this "Union devil." The uneasy truce in the town did little to create any true harmony of fellowship. We were two lonely, lovesick, war weary soldiers.

One night when I was held long at the Eastern Home Plantation, I began the return ride back to the fort after dark. When I was still several city blocks away from Sarah's house I could hear screams. I sped my horse forward, and as I neared her house I was most alarmed. There were lighted lamps in both front windows of the house. The cast light showed a number of shadowy forms on her porch, yelling through the windows and pounding on her door.

Some neighbor men were standing in the street and on porches yelling warnings and threats. None of these neighbors had yet taken action, so I felt this invasion of her home had just occurred.

I drew my rifle, unsheathed my saber and leapt from my horse running to the porch. Seeing this, two or three of the neighbors also came forward to join me. "Stop, stop immediately in the name of the Union army." I bellowed. Then I bounded up on the west side of the porch and began forcing the men to move east.

Aiming my rifle at them I demanded, "Into the street, all of you!"

The intruders were six or seven Black civilian men I aimed my gun and looked at the neighbors approaching on the street. The culprits moved in confusion and then tried to bolt off the small porch and to the back of the house.

Racing behind them I could hear the other defenders at my rear. Adrenaline pumped into my whole body; I had the sensation that I always had in the heat of battle. I was always able to move decisively and take action with no fear at the moment. I was simply driven, full of energy, to catch them. As they passed lamplight from the rear windows of the house I recognized one of the Black men as a deserter from our army. Several of the men were staggering and veering as though drunk.

"Halt," I screamed at the top of my lungs. "I am going to shoot." In response, I kneeled, aimed and shot hitting the deserter in his leg. As he fell his body he tripped two other attackers. The enraged neighbor men raced to the scrambling bodies and began hitting them with sticks and canes.

I came to my feet and raced down the alley after the other escaping men. It took about five minutes, but I found one hiding in a shrub, put my saber to his chest and he came crawling out. Unfortunately the others escaped.

I marched my captive to the yard, asked the men to guard them while I checked to see that Mrs. Scothorne was safe. When I looked at the four men aiding me, I realized one had a small, illegal pistol. It took only a moment to decide to overlook this. I requested that they cause no further damage, find a cart and horse for the prisoners, and tie them so that I could deliver the three culprits to the stockade and the wounded deserter to the infirmary.

In panic I raced up the stairs, to the door and pounded once, screaming, "Sarah!" At my call, the door flew open, I dropped the saber to the floor and grabbed her into my arms. My face was buried in her soft hair, "My darling, oh my darling, are you hurt?"

She pressed her body against me, her soft breasts crushing into my chest. Tears were streaming down her face, with our close pressed bodies I could feel her heart race.

Sobbing she gasped, "I am so frightened, it is so terrible, thank God you came." Her voice was strangled, "I know they intended to rob and molest me, that is what they were screaming, I think they were drunk. One of these men had insulted me today in town and I gave him a tongue lashing."

The trembling woman pulled back and clutched handfuls of my jacket, "I was so alone, so afraid," she began to sob again.

I considered with horror how I could live if something happened to her. Without any thought but of my love for her and gratitude that she was safe, I lowered my head and kissed her softly. Then with passion I kissed her again more firmly and for a long moment. This beautiful, terrified woman did not resist, but clung all the tighter to me.

When I released her from the kiss, an "Oh," escaped through her soft lips. It was more a sigh than an expression of surprise. Laying her head against me, with her face turned over my shoulder, I felt her stiffen.

Looking, I realized that her four neighbors were in the street staring at us as we stood embracing in the open doorway. I moved back, and looking across and down the street, realized that other families were also standing on their porches watching.

My, "Oh," was not soft or tender, but gruff and embarrassed. I stepped back, reached for her hand and shook it, firmly but politely. I nodded, "Will you be safe now? I need to deliver the prisoners to the fort."

With a brilliant, red blush she mumbled something I could not hear. I departed with what dignity I could display. In all, it was not exactly a dignified exit. I could not imagine what scandal or problems we might have created for ourselves.

I tied my horse to the cart full of criminals, and drove seven miles to Fort McPhearson. I went to the stockade where I deposited three of the men with Private Licking. Then went to the dispensary and called for the Carroll County surgeon, Noyce Coates, to care for the deserter I had shot in the leg. Knowing that the paperwork would keep me up much of the night, I used a desk at the dispensary. My late night tasks were irritating to my roommates who grumbled each time I tried to do paperwork at the end of my working day. It was quite late when I finally sat on my cot and removed my swollen feet from my boots.

Each day I passed her house, Sarah now came out of her house to wave; it was as though she had been waiting. I was quite aware of nieghbors on her street watching, so would reign my horse, tip my hat and wave back, then move on.

One week later, I tied my horse and joined her on the porch. "Were there any ill effects from the break-in?" "No," she answered, "I am in you debt, thank you. A lady and her husband stayed in the house all night with me for fear the other men might come back."

As though it was a report, I told her about the men in the stockade, and what I thought would happen to them. The deserter, of course, would eventually be shot. Then fumbling in my pocket, I produced a small bundle wrapped in brown paper and tied with white, grocery twine. With surprise on her face, she accepted the package.

After she had unwrapped it, she smiled up at me. "This is a nice gift, how did you know I smoked a pipe?" I had smelled pipe smoke and saw an ashtray the first day I visited. Then I had found this small white, clay pipe. It's tiny size and soft shape had appealed to me. I felt that a gift of some more personal nature might not be appropriate. I just smiled back at her, and departed toward the plantation once again.

In a week she called to me, and when I pulled up she told me that perhaps some evening when I passed I might like to stop for something cold to drink. Of course I would. I wanted to scream with joy.

Then she added, "We could sit on the porch." I realized this would define my unchaparoned visits. The neighbors would be able to provide the chaperone service.

For several months I stopped every night. When duty pressed me for time, I was anxious, apprehensive and unable to share this stolen hour. I felt no conscience at neglect of duty, although I knew I could be disciplined. It simply was worth the risk.

We visited for an hour or two from rocking chairs facing each other. Often we only rocked, drank cold water and quietly smiled. We smiled quite a lot. The moonlight of Natchez became magic for the two of us.

There was pure joy in just being together in these hours. It was an unspoken rule what our discussions might encompass. Both of us dreaded the pain we had known before in the angry, bitter, retaliatory first visit I had made to her home. The boundaries did not need to be spoken.

While she shared her childhood and life, Sarah did not touch on any mention or inference about slavery. Of her deceased husband, there was only the briefest mention of her life with him, although of her tiny son there was an occasional sharing which seemed to somehow comfort her grief, at least a tiny bit. Never did the dear lady complain of the military control, the shortages or the insurmountable inflation in the city. Of these situations there was no complaint, nor of her loneliness and the danger of living alone.

I had also made a cautious and inflexible list of the things I would not discuss with her. I referred to my assignments only in brief reference to time spent or the relative success of some duty. Although I would have loved to share my successes and fears with her, I was discreet about my army life. Now, in her delicate hands she held my self-esteem, dreams, joys and hopes.

I spoke not at all of the fort. This was because all army personnel was under the threat of treason should any improper information be given to anyone. Also, I was still uncertain what might raise the terrible wrath she had previously shown me.

I told her of my friends, only in a social sense. We talked of the church, the beauty of the village in the natural, garden atmosphere that surrounded us for those hours. This place of dreams made us feel we were on a private island in the middle of the war. It was easy to pretend and each dreamed of sharing our love in a home of our own, or to be sitting on our own porch in a place of comfort, peace and elegance.

Of course, in my cowardliness, I never spoke of the depth of my feelings for her. If I should offend her and be sent away, I was no longer certain I could survive without her.

When I arrived, I frequently brought a small gift such as tea, or a small package of sugar. These were of such an amount as to not infer her need, or any implication of providing them in return for her company. One time, I found three lemons and brought them to her. She immediately rose and rushed into the kitchen. Upon returning she had prepared fresh lemonade.

One evening as I left, she followed me down the steps and reached to a bush planted there. She plucked a small wand of pink, flower spray, and as I left she held it to me. With my heart racing, I received the flower, brought it to my nose to inhale the scent, then unbuttoning my tunic, placed it symbolically over my heart and replaced the button to protect against it's loss. That night I secreted the fragile bloom, and when I rolled onto my side to sleep I lay it on my pillow where I breathed the fragrance; in the magic moonlight I studied the fragile shape of the petals.

The next morning I retrieved my mount from Private Hunter, then went to receive my daily orders. I rode to the west and upon leaving the walls of the fort, and I rode to the cliff above the river. Without looking down at the human tragedy below, I stood in my stirrups viewing the lovely scene of river and trees across the water near Vidalia. Glancing around to reassure myself I was alone, I let loose a whoop of the purist joy. Removing my hat, I swatted my mare's rump and galloped northward whistling with the sheer exuberance of being alive.

What transpired during the year of 1864 was a wild hurricane ride. There was the progress of the life at the fort, and major national changes. It was a year of personal struggles, and interwoven with it all was the love of my life, growing and blooming.

In my military career my office was progressing well. With satisfaction, I realized that I seemed to be competent, and to contribute my share to the welfare of the army. On a number of occasions, I had uncovered attempted embezzlement, abuse of personnel at the home plantations and very suspicious travelers who did not have proper identification.

When McDevlin had finally resigned there was great relief and the new order of command improved.[15] It was with gladness and angst that I heard of this man's downfall. This more than raised my personal spirits. For several days I felt self-righteous joy in his exposure. This because of what I felt, but could not prove, of involving myself and my troops in those devious activities last year.

Sometimes I was relieved to be armed, as situations escalated because of intoxication or defiance by those I confronted. The sentries in most cases were vigilant and competent. When they were not, they accepted my rebukes with appropriate demeanor. The Colored troops were in the majority anxious to behave well as true soldiers. A number of times I found it necessary to escort prisoners back to the stockade at the fort. This would rearrange my schedule or, most painfully, my opportunity to steal time with Sarah.

I now felt more peace and hope in the success of my own regiment and company as we prepared for possible battles to come. Then one night, as I began once more to gloat, I remembered the heroic leadership he had provided at Shiloh. With shame, I realized that such a seemingly drastic turn of his nature was a truly tragic event. A quiet compassion and shame for him began to grow within me. I grew in an understanding of the loyalty that every soldier in this army deserved.

In July, Brigadier General Mason Brayman took command. He complained that fatigue parties, that is menial labor details, were being imposed on the regular troops. "Even the streets and gutters of the city have been habitually cleaned by U.S. soldiers, whereas this work should have been done by civil or military prisoners or by hired labor paid for by the city. Soldiers have also been supplied as clerks to the treasury and post office departments. Some are even now so employed within the city. Soldiers needed for our preparedness are being used in the depots, and the hospital. These troops are to be sent back to their companies," he commanded. The morale of my men was immediately raised. Their self-esteem and pride was recovered, and my own pride swelled within me.

With a growing awareness and kinship with the citizens, I felt rewarded that the Fifty-eighth was seldom used in raids. In September, the Fourth Illinois cavalry, and the Twenty-ninth Illinois gathered 185 head of cattle and 700 bushels of corn from "disloyal" men and women. The men of the Seventieth and Seventy-first Colored also rummaged houses, and stole goods on this expedition. Many of the soldiers entered private homes and fired guns, annoying and terrifying the families. This was against their strict orders to resist such activities.

On July 15th the force at the fort was 5,000, 1,850 were White. Upon inspection, the Fifty-eighth was reported as well prepared, armed with Springfield muskets and well supplied. This was, I hope, an example of the quality of officers. The inspection found that the Fifty-eighth Colored were in sanitary condition good, discipline good, instruction was fair, and officers were good. To quote the inspector, "it promises to make a fine regiment."[15]

My pride was unbounded. I immediately wrote home feeling that in part the Fifty-eighth's success was to my credit. How I yearned to share my encouragement with the woman I loved. Instead, when I was tempted to tell her about my men I held my tongue.

My men were to be used in event of danger within Natchez. Thus assigned in February, they had been called upon on the Fourteenth of May to fight terrifying fires in the city. Among the many others, my troops of Company K fought the battle to save the property and lives of the citizens.

In another fire on May 18, we lost the government stables and many animals. I had been on duty and was riding my mare.

In the first week of August, while I had been assigned to Brookfield, the Fifty-eighth was called to march on Gillespie plantation in Louisiana. This army landed five miles below Vidalia. They went in search of a rebel brigade that was 800 strong. After departure, they made a night march, accomplished single file by torchlight for three miles. They first met the enemy's pickets at that time. The Rebel pickets fell back. By seven AM they had arrived at Stacy plantation and found the enemy had evacuated the night before. They rested then moved, led by the calvary, to Gillespie plantation. It was there they encountered 350 rebels. We suffered only the loss of one man in the ensuing battle.[15]

Of my own person, the wearing on my constitution during the war was taking its toll. In May, I had spent some time sick in my quarters with rheumatism. My joints were swollen and stiff.

During November I was kept at the hospital in Airelie, one of the requisitioned homes at the fort, with rheumatic fever. In fevered pain, I was only capable of wishing to die. I felt it impossible to breathe. Even letters from home lay bedside, unread.

Again, over Christmas, I was bedfast at Marine Hospital. On each occasion when I was ill, I had managed to have my duty replacement inform Sarah of my absence lest she think I chose to not see her. With little ado, I told her of my condition and of the disappointment that I would not be able to call on her. Upon the return of the officer I had sent with the message, came tender notes with pressed flowers folded within the paper. These, when able, I read and reread.

Weak and fevered, I was still washed in amazement when on Christmas Day she appeared at my bedside. She carried a fruitcake rich with pecans and candied fruit. This bold show of her loyalty in public and at the fort was brazen. Her action was encouraging to my spirits and hopes.

What she felt I do not know as she walked among the injured, ill and dying Black soldiers who filled the other rooms. As she approached me, her step slowed and with no shame she stared at the other Federal soldiers all about her. By my side, she laid the gift on a chair by me and took my hand. As I looked up, I could see tears brimming in her large, brown eyes.

The heavy, dark eyelashes blinked and large tears rolled unstopped down her cheeks. We said little, but the acknowledged my condition, and my appreciation for her visit. Still holding my hot hand in her own, she looked compassionately into my eyes for long minutes. I was too weak for conversation and could only observe her overwhelming emotions. They were, I knew, for my safety and recovery. Internally, I knew I had also observed her compassion for the soldiers she had seen. I hoped her loving heart could see these boys in all they were suffering.

With my romance growing it was of great disappointment that during the time from June to August I had been called to special duty in Brookfield, which was now the command post to the Fifty-eighth regiment. It was an honor to be thus under command of General Farrar, whom I greatly respected. My services were similar to my accomplishments in police work. There was some guard duty supervision, and some crowd control. A number of times I accompanied the general in the field.

At the beginning of the war the were over four and a half million Negroes in the United States. Since the ending of importation of slaves from Africa and Haiti, two thirds of these Black citizens were born within the state where they resided. All but a small number of the remaining third were born in other states. Just a few of the Negroes were born in other countries or Africa.

The enlistment by the army of Black soldiers occurred in isolated incidences around the nation since 1861. Many were used as labor, but some were also used as soldiers. General recruitment, authorized in 1863, brought many men from out of state to Mississippi. My own troops included a number of men from other states. These men were generally from 16–50 years of age. Only a few were freedmen from the North and East. Some men were literate. The further recruiting within the state, and reorganization from other Black units had completed my company.[16]

The combination of the Colored troops makeup, literate, illiterate, former slave and freedmen was a strange mix. The advice I sought from the officer while I was trying to recruit had proven true. They were special and unique. The bond I now felt was one of respect for them. Mixed into my feelings were the deep concern for their welfare, not only now in my command, but in their future also.

Of most concern to me, were those soldiers who had family in the area, or even in the Kraal. As I became more sensitive to my troops, I recognized the unbelievable loyalty and bonds in the Black community, and its total commitment to family. For effective soldiers to be concerned with their community and family was often debilitating to them. I frequently assigned lieutenants or noncoms to see to specific family needs when appropriate. Although it was always personally repellant and painful, I more often visited my men where they were quartered by the river near Browns Lumber Yard. I sometimes even accompanied them into the kraal to hear and see the plight of their families.

It was there I first met Bishop Elder as he was inspecting the ugly building which was supposedly the hospital there. He spoke to me of the agony, the filth and the lack of care of the dying; some patients were bound as they died, uncared for; lying on rags on the floor. The anger and pain of the Bishop was moving. This was a man who caused so much disruption to our occupation, but one whose integrity and compassion I could not help but respect.[36]

Each time I visited the horrible stockade, I also saw a few townspeople seeking inmates or speaking with former slaves and servants now confined in this pen of humanity. Some of them were carrying food or goods to give to the Colored people within.

Equal to the pain of the soldiers, was the especially poignant report by Colored noncommissioned officers announcing the illness or death of a soldier. Since almost half of the troops at the fort eventually died of disease, this tragic visit was far too frequent. The deaths usually left those grieving in the kraal even more hopeless and destitute. The little remaining comfort of these homeless victims was especially devastated by separation or death, as their close bonds developed during slavery were their only comfort.

There were a number of new regiments moving into the fort. Many new Colored units were also being reformed from other military regiments, just as my own began from the Sixth.

This circumstance brought about an excellent change in my life. As the Fifty-second U.S.C.T. arrived at the fort, a companion in my sleeping quarters became ill and left the service. With an empty cot in my room, a lieutenant who had newly enlisted at Vicksburg joined the remaining four of us.

The Fifty-second had originally been the Second Mississippi of African Decent. The newcomer, Second Lieutenant John W. Cadwallader from Illinois, was assigned to company F of the Fifty-second. John came into my life and we bonded immediately. He was a clever and stalwart man; yet his wit and humor was most pleasing to me. Many a dawn we sat on the gallery visiting and laughing.

Such was one of the conditions of this occupation of uneasy and conflicting ideals. No clear right and wrong existed beyond that of power. The past power of the enslavement of a people, the power of an invading army attempting to control a small city and the greatest immediate power—that of life and death battles by two armies, each convicted of the rightness of their cause.

These experiences, opinions and personal opportunities filled my daily life for an insane year. Yet I could and would not express them to the woman I loved. My insights told me that she too yearned to open her own heart and life to me. The wall of war and society still held us apart. In pain, I realized and admitted that perhaps the possibility of fulfilling our lives together was, indeed, probably hopeless.

## Chapter 16
# Private Hunter

I was slowly becoming much more comfortable at the fort with my commission and permanent assignment as a police officer. I was now housed in one of the five private homes at the fort which had been commandeered by the army for our use. The second floor room where I am assigned is full because it holds five cots, a small closet cabinet, and one desk. The curtains were left at the windows, from which the view is exceptional as they face the river. The fort which perches across the top of the high loess bluff which offers a spectacular panoramic view. I often watch the Louisiana shore; the foliage and flowers changing color with each season. The traffic on the river was always of great interest to me. Before I had only seen a vista like this when I was visiting in Savannah, Illinois as our home was nearly twenty miles inland. Thus the river continues to fascinate to me.

Paintings had been left on the wall as well, and gave some elegance to the crowded room, as did the lovely carpet on the floor. Sometimes before I go to sleep I would lay and stare at the portrait of an unknown lady and make up stories in my mind about whom she was. On the other wall is an engraving of a landscape that had been colored in by the artist. This artwork has trees and meadows with cattle. In the foreground was a small boy and girl walking hand in hand down a path. It is probably a scene from Europe and provides a lovely escape from the reality of the tenuous situation here in Natchez. There was also some egotistic pleasure in now feeling more dignified and respected.

The other White soldiers, enlisted and non-commissioned, are at the barracks or living at Monmouth in tents. My freedom from the worry of weather is of great relief. The comfort we officers have is unknown in war. The only displeasure that exists for me is the lack of privacy. The night noises of four sleeping men is not always comforting. The room has only a tiny closet and no bureau; so our possessions are piled in corners. Only our dress uniforms can be accommodated in the closet. Perhaps the best advantage is that we are fed in our lodging with food prepared by a soldier who previously was a cook at one of the plantations. Thus, we have excellent food in both quantity and preparation.

One afternoon, as I rode toward Monmouth beside Edwin, we gloried in a long visit. He told me of his birth in Illinois and his childhood, which was barely in the past because of his youth. He told me of an earlier event in his life; it had touched him and motivated him to enlist in the Colored troops. He had only summarized his battle experiences ending with his arrival at Fort McPhearson. Then began a pivotal story that allowed me to see into this man who was the best, personal friend I had made during the war.

In August the "marts of trade" were opened in Natchez; they functioned as open-air markets. The various planters and citizens, both Colored and White, brought produce to town.

Some of the soldiers of his old regiment had just appropriated an old Colored "uncle's" watermelons. The older man reported the incident to a Lieutenant. Edwin knew the men well, and was not entirely innocent himself since he was present. It was demanded that Edwin list the names of the perpetrators or go to jail. To his relief the others stepped forward and it was unnecessary for him to provide their names.

This was the cause of his leaving his regiment and joining the Colored corp. It was at this time that my young friend had became more seriously committed to improve his deportment. In deep sincerity, he expressed the desire to be a more serious and effective soldier. He had never shared with me this tale of his own enlistment.[34]

Edwards's usual jovial spirit was wistful today. He looked neither to the left or the right as we rode, he just spoke with the greatest of honesty, baring his own heart and humanity. His next experience was quite painful to hear. Thank goodness I was on duty and did not also witness the execution of Privates Geer and McBride. Edwin had witnessed it.

He reported that these were men of his old regiment; men he had lived with, fought with and felt great respect for their fellowship. The two left Natchez on a raid to the plantation of a Mr. Sergeant, while robbing the hen roost they were surprised by the planter, a shot rang out, the gentleman was dead and the men were jailed. Since Ed knew them, although no longer in the same regiment, he made it a habit to visit them in jail.

One day, through camp gossip, he was informed that they were to be executed. By order, the whole of the military were present and were marched to the field and formed a large square inside the gates. The two condemned men arrived in an open wagon, accompanied by a priest. In an open side of the man-ringed square the wagon stopped, the soldiers climbed down and the condemned stood by their coffins. The firing squad made the fatal volley, and the men died in silence."[34]

The strict, sudden authority and action by the military is always shocking. I knew it must have been a horrifying loss and lesson to Edwin. In fact, there were a number of executions at the fort while I was stationed there. Several of these, I had, likewise, witnessed, but none were my men or friends.

Our talks were of great relief to both of us as we were able to be open and trusting with each other. It was the first time I had ever had a peer of this intimacy, and felt unashamed to be honest. I told him of my Pikes Peak trip in late 1860 through early 1861, not only of the adventure but also the fear, loneliness and depression I had experienced. I shared the sense of shame at returning home feeling foolish and a failure, I admitted that this had also played into my decision to enlist and try to redeem myself by saving face.

One of the stories my friend shared this day was of how he helped oversee the disinterment of soldiers who had been hastily buried at a fort in Louisiana and its surrounding area. These were then moved to the cemetery for reburial. Like all veterans he had seen death and dismemberment. Edwin oversaw the jobs accomplished by Black 'fatigue troops' which included the infirm; those of ages not considered prime to be soldiers; prisoners; disabled soldiers or contrabands. These were the 'dirty job' workers of both sides in the war and consistently had been used for such unsavory duty.

The men wore scarves at their faces and were only able to accomplish this ugly task with the most repellance. Ed said his dreams were now filled by distorted, decaying, grotesque bodies. He described empty skulls that came flying at him through the nightmares, to him they were the bones symbolizing this war. [34]

Several recent events had improved the lives of those responsible for workers on the home plantations. It was of concern to the citizens, but to our advantage, that 'disloyal' planters were stripped of the animals they owned and their stock relocated to the army's home plantations. The prior owners were accused of secessionist views or disobedience.

This circumstance much improved the effectiveness of the home plantation operations with the improved stock. The horses made the work easier since the first animals there had often been rejects, quite sad animals indeed.

The outfitting of most of the troops with Springfield rifles was a tremendous improvement. Not only were the rifles much-improved weaponry but their arrival also freed the other guns so that my men now all had weapons. The many steps of loading and firing the older weapons was eliminated. Finally, after long battles at the commissary, this meant we were only lacking in certain clothing and a few odd things like haversacks.

There were the beginnings of a response to cease using soldiers as labor within the city and on the home plantations, and instead using fatigue troops. We now hired older or younger boys of color. Since this was a dear wish of mine to raise the morale of my soldiers, I was hopeful.

In March, Order #9 came from headquarters at Vicksburg. Strong and healthy labor over 14 years of age were to be paid ten dollars a month, those less able were to be paid seven dollars a month. With this order also came instruction to teach all Colored children less than twelve years of age. They also strengthened the command that no soldier without sufficient orders was to go to any plantation. This action much relieved my responsibilities as the soldiers going to the plantations had frequently caused a nuisance.

I came this afternoon to leave reports at the Fort. As I entered the new stable built after the fire, I dismounted, called to a soldier to take my horse unsaddle it and care for the needs of the animal. I left the barn, with my saddlebags over my shoulder and caught a glimpse of the mare I was so fond of and had so often ridden last year.

I turned toward where she was tied inside a small pen and as I approached I saw that Private Hunter was also in the pen and had her foal. He balanced the tiny animal in his arms. Having removed his shirt his scarred back was exposed. The soldier was on his knees running a hand up and down the colt's legs while the nervous mare pushed at him with her nose.

"Private," I said in recognition. Quickly he rose, "Yes Sir." During the last disconcerting year I had seen much less of this soldier. "Is the foal in good condition?" With a wide grin he laughed softly, "Yes Sir, this is one excellent horse. I like its legs, they are strong and quite long. Perhaps it was a good accident that this mare got caught."

With wry humor I remembered the scene and the incident that day at Brigadier General McDevlin's headquarters. "Then perhaps you have forgiven me, my carelessness," I attempted to make amends.

The ivory of his eyes contrasted his dark irises as he looked me directly in the eye having returned to his kneeling position. "Most certainly, it was quite a good accident at that."

I smiled warmly, admiring the tiny wobbly animal. With the knowledge garnered from caring for my father's horses I concurred with the private's opinion that this was really a fine foal. The coat was a dark chestnut, much darker than the mother's. For some time I leaned on the outside of the pen as I studied the tiny beautiful animal until she began to nurse.

It occurred to me how carefully and concisely Private Hunter was now speaking. I remembered the discussion I had overheard when he had announced his decision to speak more correctly to advance his own opportunities. I was impressed, it was little more than a year since this man had enlisted.

Trying not to disclose my privy information gathered from eavesdropping, I quizzed, "Are you still studying?"

With little of the first defensiveness I had seen in him when we met, he answered with quiet confidence, "Yes, that I am. I read and can write quite a bit. Corporal Tanner says I am his best student."

"I am happy and proud of you, you are a good man, Private." I continued to lean on the fence enjoying the maternal scene, and then decided that I needed to be about my business. So I stood straight and departed.

I walked directly to the officer of the day and took my turn to pass him the documents and reports. We exchanged a few words about some specific situations. Then he promised to take immediate action and send armed soldiers to one of the outposts; a precaution I had recommended. I took my leave in preparation for closing a long day. I would be happy to be back at my cot and out of my boots.

Because of obligations to report the incident today I had only waved to Sarah as I passed her house. She did not expect me to pass by so early and I could tell she was somewhat disconcerted. My beloved was wearing a straw hat and a dusty, long apron tied tightly about her waist. This homely garment clung to her, accentuating her waist and breasts. I found her equally as enchanting as in her ball gown the first night we danced. Without dismounting, I looked down on her as she held a large basket of garden produce. I resisted the urge to teasingly ask if she intended to take them to the fort. I was only free to speak with her for a moment before I took my leave.

Now, departing the office to head to my bivouac, I saw a fellow officer under a tree in earnest conversation with John Cadwallader with whom I share the room. I was looking forward to sharing some petty humor with the man and decided to walk toward them and talk a minute if they were not discussing something of a private nature.

With this in mind, I slowly sauntered that direction. As I crossed the drill field I glanced to my left and casually observed a tinker's wagon. It's boxlike structure was painted a bright yellow and hung all about on the outside with harness, pots, pans and shovels. Its wheels were red and orange. Painted on the side in ornate, green letters was O'MALLEY EMPORIUM. Nearby was a strong dappled grey dray horse that was trying to graze on the sparse grasses of the parade ground. Even at some distance, I could hear the voice of the vendor who was speaking with several rapt soldiers.

I squinted, shook my head and continued moving toward the group of officers. When I reached them we greeted each other and I eavesdropped on a story that was so grand it was most certainly a fable or a joke. Distracted, I kept glancing at the tinker's wagon and pondered some vague memory. Suddenly a flash of memory lighted my mind. Then with a brief apology said I was going to look at some of the tinker's merchandise.

Forcing myself to approach slowly, I moved toward the bright wagon. As I moved, my mind raced with questions and plans. The tinker looked up when I neared and we nodded; I moved about the outside of the wagon as I half listened to his sales pitch to the soldiers. I touched and examined a number of the things on the outside. Then when I reached the rear, I peered carefully into the interior where I saw a saddle on the floor.

Going back to the tinker I inquired if I could enter the wagon to see the saddle, and he nodded an affirmative but went on talking. I climbed up three high, portable steps and moved into the dim interior. With a glance over my shoulder, I began a careful examination of the roof and the wagon's sides that were hidden under piles of goods.

It was some time before I consciously realized that the conversation outside had ceased. Then I moved to the saddle, squatted and began to examine it. When I heard a noise behind me I stood, "May I take this outside?" Squeezing past the peddler, who was standing in the tight space, I left the vehicle. In a moment he appeared carrying the saddle, which he lay on the ground.

Immediately, he lurched into a description of the virtues of the saddle, beneath his voice I could detect beneath a heavy Irish accent a trace of Southern, also. As we bartered I asked some casual questions of how far he traveled and the pace of his business. I inquired lightly where he came from originally. His replies were only satisfactory.

We then spent ten more minutes haggling over the value of the saddle, he said he would be at the fort for two more days. I told him I would be back tomorrow; adding that I had some duty to perform at one of the offices at this moment. I took leave of the man as though I were quite busy and occupied with some errand.

After I left the peddler I went to the office of the provost marshal. Since this was the primary contact for the local citizens, the large room was full of people. Several clerks were busy checking passes, returning mail and answering questions. I passed through to the tiny office where I knew the Provost Marshall sat. After a knock, I peered around the half open door and smiled, "May I have a moment?" Looking up from two huge mounds of paperwork, the bespectacled man smiled back, "Of course, I will obviously never be free, so we'll simply steal some freedom."

I placed myself on a straight-backed chair, reached backwards and closed the door. In a low serious tone I requested he lock the door. From behind me I heard the slide of the bolt. The man opened a drawer of a tall desk and found two small glasses and half a bottle of whiskey. This was brought to the desk and with question blanketing his face he looked at me.

I responded quickly, "Only half a shot, and thank you."

The Captain sat, took a small swallow from his glass and leaned back with a serious expression on his face. As legal officers, the two of us had continual working contact and consulted frequently. It would also be fair to say we had developed a mutual respect. In my opinion, he was bright, effective and cooperative.

"I have some reason to be suspicious that the tinker hawking at this base is a spy. He says he expects to stay two more days, but I would like to be prepared to take action immediately should he move his departure forward. This suspicion has just occurred to me. The strategy I plan is to send four men to follow him when he leaves, seek evidence and if guilty arrest him. I believe he is here to ascertain the complete force, armament, any weaknesses and the layout of the interior of the fort and report it to the rebels."

Leaning back the Captain pondered this, if true it might indicate a possible eminent attack. Thus it was of most serious import, "You may perhaps speak with General Brayman. Simply inform him that I recommend a hearing, as soon as possible." With a serious look he leaned toward me, "Just what has aroused your suspicions? I remember the man, he was here last year, also."

"As my regiment marched unprepared toward Shiloh this very tinker passed us going the other way down the road. Then as we waited on the Louisiana side of the river to invade Vicksburg I also saw this same tinker. Both events were of no consequence at the time and I only glanced at the vehicle. Soon the battles obviously drew my attention to more dramatic events. I gave it no real consideration until I recognized that wagon today at the fort."

"Since his wagon is distinctive, when I saw it it occurred to me that in both the previous cases this O'Malley might have been doing reconnaissance of troop strength. If so, his trip here may be similar and the portents of attack may be imminent. It is possible that so close in proximity to battles, this man is not selling goods, other than coffins." In my passion I rose, placing both palms on the desk between us.

"What I will need from you is four passes for soldiers that look very innocent. My men will also need official documents to identify them should there be an arrest and papers to pass themselves, the prisoner and his wagon back through the lines. I will give you their names. I will select three enlisted men and a Colored sergeant in civilian dress for they will provide less suspicion."

The Provost Marshal stood, his face solemn, matching my own urgency and concern. "Of course, you may come to me at my quarters at any time if I am not on duty. You may receive them at your convenience. I will prepare them myself and carry these documents on my person should there be need."

Before I left I had a thought, "Please, also prepare passes for Sergeant Anderson today, I want him to watch the man tonight when he leaves the fort. I will have Anderson find you as soon as possible. It may also be helpful to review O'Malley's passes and papers as though it is a casual inquiry. We do not want to alarm or warn him that he is suspect."

I went to the stable to get a horse to take me to General Brayman's headquarters at Rosalie. As I approached, I walked past several of the soldiers assigned there and sought out Private Hunter. I found him with a pitchfork moving soiled straw.

"Private, may I have a word with you?" The man followed me as I moved apart from the stable and stood in an open area where no one could approach without being seen. Turning toward him I studied his serious, intelligent face. "Do you remember the adventure you participated in to count cotton?" He nodded in silence, yet I saw his expression change and knew he was well aware of the true nature of that event. "Should I order you to take another such dangerous secret task, but this one of honest importance, would you be ready?"

His face bright, he smiled and he nodded in agreement.

"I want you to leave immediately and find civilian clothing for four men that would be appropriate for someone who is a freedman walking outdoors for several days. Prepare by this evening, if possible. Secure a knife for your defense, a small pistol and some ammunition; take food and non-military blankets. There will be four of you similarly prepared. Seek out the men you feel the most confidence in to accompany you; like those on the assignment south. Say nothing specific, but each man must recognize the need for secrecy and the danger. The men should he be willing to volunteer to enter into this project. One man and you should gather these goods and must come to my quarters tonight so that I know all is ready. Keep close to the fort on the upper level, so that you can move the moment I send for you. Upon departure, I will instruct you in the duty required of you."

It felt good as I requisitioned a horse and rode about until I found Sergeant Anderson whom I instructed to get a pass from the Provost Marshall and carefully follow far behind the tinker when he left this evening. I instructed him to observe the man and all he did and with whom he spoke until he returned to the fort tomorrow; then report to me. As I turned toward headquarters at the far end of the fort, I felt smug. I guess I felt good because I knew these were men I could trust.

The plan I was using, of employing Negroes for spying duty, was not that unusual. As Grant made vain attempts for months to approach Vicksburg, Southern Black spies were sent out to misdirect his efforts. The seeming innocence and familiarity made them excellent for undercover work in the South. With the numbers of homeless Black people roaming everywhere a Colored spy was almost invisible. The Union used them all across the war front, just as the South did. These men and women smuggled, watched troop movements and were couriers.

Private Hunter left the stable and sought out Private Mullen. Then the two of them discussed what little information Private Hunter had been given. Private Mullen inquired, "This be a assignment like de other crooked one?"

"No, the Captain says this is honest and important, but dangerous." After a moment of consideration Mullen nodded and confirmed, "I trust de man, guess I be willin'." Then the two squatted by a barn and made plans to get the equipment and supplies. Mullen departed to find food and weapons.

Matthew headed quickly toward the long steps down to the river. At the top he paused and looked down the steep, long stairway. He viewed the end of the Kraal with anger. Since his barracks were down there, he had regularly climbed up and down these stairs each day. Perhaps they were 500 or 700 steps, he was sure they were a thousand. Still, he hated them, and most of all he hated what he knew lay at the river's edge. This was truly a staircase to Hell and a sign of the true position of the Negro in this war and in this city.

With some speed he descended the stairs and passed Brown's gardens, moving north to the Kraal. The stench reached his nostrils and announced his approach. The nearby huddled figures were sitting with their backs against a rough and ragged board fence that was a boundary instead of an enclosure. Milling about inside this horrid pen were Black people of all descriptions. Most were children, women and old people. There were only a few healthy men here and there. There were some scattered buildings that appeared to have been sheds, perhaps previously used for storage by the mill. There were also hundreds of shanties made from canvas scraps, blankets or salvaged materials.

Matthew stopped at the fence and tapped an older man on the shoulder. "I want to talk to someone who sews or does laundry that might have some clothing for sale."

The toothless man looked up and grinned, "Yes su, dey be some dat kin' here. Let me think," and he studied the milling people for a long time. Finally he looked up, again with a large grin, "Way down dat way," pointing, "where de smoke be comin' from dat chimney. Dat be the place Belle stay, she be tall and be wearin' a red blanket. You ain't find her, jus ask."

The soldier thanked him and hesitantly walked into the compound and slowly wound his way through the swarms of people, trying not to smell the odor or listen to the sorrowful voices. It took about twenty minutes to get close to the shed with the smoke because he had to detour around so many shacks and people. The knowledge of the circumstances in this place was common knowledge, but since he did not know any residents Matthew had always made a wide circuit of the pen trying to never come too close. When he approached the small shanty he reached to hold an older woman's arm; all the while wishing he were not here. He felt great anxiety and wanted to be away as soon as possible. As the woman he had approached looked at him he questioned her, " I am looking for Belle. Do you know her?"

The old woman looked at him with question in her reddened and matted eyes that were peering through her dirt-covered face and simply pointed at a shed where smoke was floating upward. The young man moved to the shack. Only a holey, blanket covered the doorway, but he noted, with relief, that the blanket was clean. From the outside he could smell the odor of wash water; the lye soap was pungent to his nose.

He called into the blankness of the woven door covering, "Belle? I am seeking Belle." There were some faint sounds, a rustle and then the blanket was pulled sideways. A woman pushed past him and stood outside as though to keep him from coming inside her pitiful home. She stood straight, with fists placed on her hips and a slightly stubborn look on her face.

Her presence left him breathless, somehow he had not expected this woman to be found in the middle of all this bedlam. She was tall and narrowly built; her height was such that they were eye to eye. The golden tones of her skin, and large, soft brown eyes were set into a clean, long face. A bright blue-checkered bandanna was wound tightly about her head. She had, wrapped about her shoulders, a solid red blanket that made her almost glow with color. The blanket covered a clean but faded and neatly mended dress of blue calico. Her jaw was held high and proud and she looked him directly in the eye.

The silence became awkward. As he stared at her finally she demanded, "You want Belle? I be Belle."

"I come on military business, can I talk to you in private?" This made her suspicious and it took her a long few minutes before she opened the blanket door to allow him into her hovel. Pointing at a soapbox she demanded, "Sit."

So Matthew did as commanded and it *was* a command. Belle remained standing and looking down on him.

An hour later he exited the home of the washerwoman. He carried an armload of old, clean garments and four worn blankets. Private Hunter exited minus his heart.

It was nearly eight in the evening when I finally stepped onto the porch of my quarters and into the house. The three men dressed in ragged clothes had just reported for duty. Anderson would soon be part of the group, with Matthew, Mullen and Alexander Turner completing the troop. I had carefully shared their instructions, then ordered them to stay outside so that I would not need to seek them should I find that the tinker was making a quick get away. I was tense because of the planning and preparing for this foray. Thus far the whole of the preparations were in place. Hopefully, my commands were being followed very carefully. Tomorrow I would need to make these soldiers available to leave with appropriate papers.

Earlier at the headquarters, it had been only a short wait before I was allowed to speak with the General because of the Provost Marshall's recommendation. I found the packet of passes had already been left for me and I filled in the blanks with the names of the soldiers on this assignment, using their real military names and rank on the second set which would allow them to return to the fort. Optimistically, I had also included documents for the transportation of prisoners.

In the morning, as I was shaving, Corporal Anderson appeared on the porch and asked for me. I went down to meet him. The Corporal looked wrinkled and exhausted, I supposed he might have been up all night; his dark skin had a pallor that was almost grey.

"Corporal, were you able to follow the tinker?" I quizzed anxiously.

"Yes su. He left here 'n went 'under the hill.' He get a boy to watch his wagon, den he go in de gambling hall. I can see him in de window an he eat. An den he play cards mos the night. He get in de wagon and drive up by da park an stay all night. Jus now he come back. Park de same place and put his pots n pans out. He did'n seem to talk to no one special or pass any paper to nobody."

"You did a good job. Go and sleep for a while. Then hang around the stable all day. Take the opportunity to speak with Private Hunter in a most secretive manner. He has clothing for you. Private Hunter will give you the location and names of the other men. When the tinker goes again follow him. He will most certainly depart in a day or so. This time three other men will go with you, I am concerned that he may leave Natchez and I am assigning you to follow him with the other soldiers."

Taking him to the back of the house, I once more outlined the whole plan. Finding Anderson later, after I went to the Provost Marshal. I gave him all the passes, handed him a chit to take to the Provost Marshall for money for this venture. Then I put him in charge of the foray, making sure he was aware that spies are shot upon capture.

"Capn' Hunter they shoot us jus fo' bein' black anyway."

Shaking his hand firmly I said, "Good luck, I appreciate your diligence." His statement was most poignant for I might be sending four good soldiers to their death.

The next evening when I returned the horse to the stable, Matthew was there with the other men lounging around. I looked at him and he nodded a 'no.' The following morning when I went by the stable Private Hunter and the other men were gone. My pulse raced and I began to be even more anxious.

It was three days later when I returned from my daily duty that I saw the horseless Emporium wagon sitting beside the brig. My heart began to race. I rode directly to the brig, tied my horse and entered. Looking about I identified the jailer.

"Private Licking, I see the tinkers' wagon is outside, does this have some meaning?"

Slowly smiling and winking Private Licking, the large, gentle jailer replied, "Sure does. He is a visitor here and will have a trial next week for he is accused of being a spy."

With a sigh of relief I quizzed, "Who brought him in?" The custodian smiled, "Corporal Anderson and some other men, one was wounded. He didn't check in alone, came with two others, a civilian and a rebel in uniform."

Wasting no time I retrieved my horse and galloped across the fort to the stable. There I found Private Hunter, obviously it was he who was wounded. There was a bandage on his upper arm and one on his leg.

Standing in the open stable door I saw him halfway down the alley; the light at his back reflecting off the white of the bandages. I spoke loudly, "Private, congratulations. You must have been successful as I see the tinker is in jail."

With obvious pride he answered promptly, "Yes Sir, we took him yesterday morning and delivered him today." I was concerned with his wounds. Motioning to a couple of piles of hay we went to sit and listen to his report. "You were wounded? Were any of the others injured also?"

"Well Captain, it went like this. We followed him that first day; just out of town, at the Devil's Punch Bowl, he pulled over. We hid ourselves and watched. In a couple hours a man on a horse pulled up, got beside him on the driver's seat and tied his horse behind. They drove off toward the Natchez Trace. It was easy to follow them there cause the path is full of trees and not many people on the road this time of year. Sir, that is one spooky place in the day but at night the deep ruts and puddles make it hard to travel. There be so many trees the moon is cut out."

"That night they went to an inn. We stayed outside, and about midnight a lone Confederate comes up in the dark and taps on a window at the back. The man inside opens the window. Then that soldier climbs in the window. Corporal Anderson and I crawl up close to the building. We be real quiet and get under the window. We hear the tinker talking all about the fort here. Then we peek in the little room and see the three of them are looking at papers on a table."

"We crawl back and talk with the other two soldiers. We figure we would be like ducks in a row if we try to climb in the window. The inn had at least eight people inside by the count of horses and wagons. They might not like four freedmen comin' in the middle of the night, so we decide to let them spies come out before we try to catch them."

"Just before dawn the soldier climbs back out the window and starts for his horse that he had tied to a tree quite a bit away from the inn, to keep it out of sight. Like we planned, I take off after him. In the middle of the night we had knotted the reins real good to slow him down on his get away."

"I tried to be quiet but he heard me come up behind him. He pulled his saber and took a good swipe at me but I ducked, and he only sliced my arm and leg a bit. I spose he thought I was a bandit. He starts swearing and calling me names. I just up and tell him I am no nigger, I am Private Hunter of the Union Army and he is under arrest. Well, all Hell broke loose. I didn't suppose he would surrender and he sure didn't want to either."

"We commenced a big fight, me trying to keep him from getting his rifle and him beating on me good. Meantime, the other two come out the front. We had loosened the a nut on the hub of the wagon wheel and when the tinker starts to move the wheel fell off. As the man gets off to look at the wheel, Corporal Anderson points his gun at the man's head and introduces his self."

"There wasn't much of a fight for some reason O'Malley just gives up. The man who had ridden with him was mounted and seeing this scene he tries to race off. The other two soldiers seem to have tied he horses back leg to a tree. The horse stumbles and the damn man falls off and knocks all the sense from him. He just lay there."

"Finally, I got my knife out and hold it at that rebel's throat I been fightin' with. He wasn't no big man so I sit on his chest till the others finally come and tie him up. We use rope the tinker has in the wagon to tie 'em all up good. We put the wheel back on, gathered the horses and tie them to the back of the wagon. Then we put them rascals all in back with Turner and his pistols for the ride home. I rode in back too cause I was pretty sore all over. I got to wrap my arm and the cut on my leg on the way to the fort. One private rode a horse behind the wagon and Corporal Anderson drove it."

"Yes Sir, you were right. That sure was a spy and we got two more in the bargain."

"Good job, Private. This is one execution I will be glad to attend. If I am right that man helped cause the death of many of my friends and hundreds of others." I squeezed his uninjured shoulder. After inquiring about the others I sought them out for congratulations. Then I started for my quarters. As I strode down the road toward the house I heard my name called. It was Private Hunter.

He was running with an awkward cantor, favoring his bad leg.

"Sir," he said breathlessly, "the laundry lady gave us all the clothes and blankets. I would like to pay her and take the things back to her." Reaching into my pocket I pulled out two silver dollars and placed them in his hand.

With a big smile, he asked permission, "May I go to the Kraal right now to give her this?" I nodded, and he took off with his stilted gate seeming no problem to his current occupation.

That evening as I smoked a pipe on the porch and pondered the successful conclusion and the probable outcome of the trial, I felt quite satisfied. Then I had a thought. Immediately I went to the desk in my room and began a letter of recommendation for all four men. It was too bad I could not also include their service during McDevlin's damn 'cotton count.' I felt especially satisfied with the thought of someday calling one of my men 'Corporal Matthew Hunter.'

After Matthew left the Captain he cut a wobbly path toward the steps, then turned and quickly returned to the stable. He found a pail of water and using his handkerchief washed his face and neck. Reaching to a crossbeam he found a small can of fragrant pomade he had hidden there. This he worked into his short hair. The soldiers kept a small tin mirror on the wall, using this he examined his face and plucked a stray hair from his jaw. He dusted and shaped his cap. Not satisfied he then borrowed one from a fellow who was quizzically watching him. With sudden knowledge the man passed him the cap and with a slow drawl inquired, "Ya got a important meetin'?" Matthew only cast a quick look over his shoulder and smiled as he once more departed from the barn. He grabbed the bundle of clothing and the blanket he had used.

The private moved down the steps more slowly than usual, he was more sore than he had realized and the throbbing leg made him awkward. As he descended his pulse raced, as did his mind. He was trying to decide how to approach this proud woman. She was so beautiful that he knew there were probably other soldiers who had tried to meet her. Then he came to a dead stop, *she might be married.* His heart fell and he began the trip downward on the wooden staircase even more slowly.

By the time he reached the bottom a second moment of panic washed over him. *What if Belle was not at her home?* How could you find anyone in that mass of people? Finally he just stopped and stood, uncertain if he should go on. Then a plan came to mind and he started to rehearse the conversation he would have with her.

Now he had hope and the courage to risk taking this opportunity. Once more he approached the desperate quarters. As he entered the pen he looked for a friendly face who was not watching his uniform or trying to identify him as a family member. He saw a vigorous older lady and approached her. "Mama, I am seeking Belle, the laundry woman."

"Ys sah," pointing toward the area where he already knew she abided. The woman added some description to his goal as he patiently waited. "Mam, do you know if she sews too?"

Nodding, the woman placed her hands on her hips and nodded. "Ys sah, she do bout everything. Sew, mend and wash."

With wide-eyed, devious intent Matthew continued falling back into accent. "She be young or ol?"

"She be young an real tall," the woman tried to be helpful. With a confirming nod the soldier inquired, "This woman be hard work'n, that fo shur."

"She be married to a soldier?" With excitement he waited as the lady squinted, thinking.

"No, she not be married to no one."

Smiling, he touched his cap and departed with his heart once more in its proper place in his chest.

Now he cheerfully wound his way through this horror, toward the shanty. As he approached the shack he saw that the blanket at the door was knotted and pulled across a nail to hold it back. Before he could approach the building, Belle came through the door with a sloshing wooden bucket of dirty water. He took long steps toward her, lay his bundle near the doorway and reached for the pail. "Let me help you, mam."

With surprise, then recognition she halted and stared at him. After a moment, she gave a demure nod and allowed him to take the pail.

Hopefully Matthew smiled, "Is there another?

With a bit more warmth and obvious relief she said, "Yes, there is rinse pail just inside the door." He reached for the pail and lifted this in his other hand.

"Now, if you will show me where to empty them."

Raising her chin she moved off briskly toward the riverside. It took almost half an hour to work their way across the crowded camp to empty the pails into the river. "Thank you, sir," she reached for the empty pails.

"That's all right Miss Belle, I want to do some business with you and will return them to the cabin for you." Matthew looked deeply into her eyes and realized his smile must be almost foolish, for he was so excited.

Once more she paced off in front of him, winding through the crowd.

When they reached her home she entered and he followed. Hanging in a moist zigzag of spider web design was wet laundry lying over ropes. This washing was mostly uniforms and shirts, hung all about and dripping onto the dirt of the floor. Matthew saw a vacant spot and placed the empty buckets on the floor.

Although it was already warm, a small stove in the corner for heating water steadily added to the swelter. With the moist clothing all about, the humidity was thick. It was good just to be near her. For half an hour he had studied her back, posture and stride. Suddenly, the soldier realized he must return to his plan.

First he stood very straight with military posture, and then he politely removed his borrowed cap and tucked it into his belt. He reached for a pail, turned it over and with exaggerated discomfort and favoring his leg, he eased to sit on the pail with a pretentious low moan.

With a look of concern the young woman inquired, "Are you in pain?"

"Yes mam," Matthew replied with perfect pronunciation. "I am just back from a mission," seemingly hesitant to continue with his tale of wounded heroism.

"Were you wounded?" she questioned with compassionate respect.

"Mam, it was minor. Really not much at all, but I could use a drink of water." From a pot that had been boiling on the stove she poured a small cup for him. As he drank he realized it was boiled river water, but forced himself to swallow at least a mouthful. Then he smiled up at her, "Thank you, mam."

With learned anxiety from generations of slavery, Matthew felt driven to pursue this woman. It was an instinct of courtship that, by necessity, must be quick and desperate. For generation's lovers were separated, they met at risk of whippings or death. Even after marriage, if they did not live with the same planter they could only meet with the permission of both owners. It was Negro heritage to find passion in direct and bold action. When the couple finally became family, the dread of separation by being 'sold away' was an ever-present threat. Probably this was the greatest control of the planters over their human chattel.

The lady swiped at her face with an arm to wipe away perspiration. The tiny space, completely shrouded in wet cloth forced her to stand quite close to him. Reaching behind her head she tugged at the knot of her bandanna. With her arms stretched behind her head, Matthew viewed her shape that had been hidden by the blanket on his last visit. This tall angel was slender, with small breasts, long through the body, with a shapely hip rounding from a small waist.

*Oh, what wonderful legs she must have.* The thought sent him tingling all over. He purposely looked at the floor so as to not stare at or offend her.

From the corner of his eye he saw the scarf dangling from her hand and looked up. Once more he raised his head and gazed puppylike at her. Her sweaty hair clung to her head. It was cut close and had a slight red color. The effect was that of a cap, circling her small ears, and emphasizing her long neck. Her eyes were large, rich brown and set deeply. Her nose was long and wide but very straight and dramatic. It ended above rich, full, purple lips. The even gold highlights of her skin seemed like sunlight to the smitten man.

He knew she was aware of his appraisal, and he felt uncertain of how she was responding as she only openly looked back at him with no change of expression, perhaps because she was also studying his features. Her confidence was complete; the silence between them and the close quarters seemingly had no effect of embarrassment. No effect on her, that is. Matthew was nervous and on fire. Now he was struggling to remember the script he had written for himself.

With great effort he gathered his wits and unbuttoned his tunic to reach into the jacket for the silver dollars. With a slight frown the woman watched him warily. "Miss Belle, the recent mission would not have been possible without your help. My men were able to move freely and we apprehended the rebel spies we sought."

Now the beautiful lady slightly tipped her head and seemed more warmed by his appreciation of her aid.

Matthew stood, forgetting to be frightfully wounded. The dollars were in his fist. "I would like to show my appreciation." Holding his arm close to his body he opened his fist, to show the coins. He saw her appreciation of the generosity and her need for the money.

"Please take these as you have much aided our cause." After a cautious pause, she slowly reached out and began to lift the money from his palm. With a careful motion, Matthew reached his other hand out and lay it lightly on top of hers.

"Dear lady, may I say something of importance to me?"

Without removing her hand she looked him in the eye and nodded slightly.

Now, with his confidence returning, he smiled and looked deeply into her eyes. "When I arrived to seek the clothing the other day I was overwhelmed to find you here, in this desperate situation. You are as beautiful as anyone I have ever seen. My official task today is to thank you. Yet this visit has also given me an opportunity of speak of my regards for you. Please, oh please, consent to allow me to see you again with no other obligation or pretense than to get to know you."

Again the silence enveloped the two. Belle searched his face and found it without guile or threat. A small smile grew slowly and her expression softened, "I will see you one more time." Looking down, both studied her golden flesh against the ebony of his hands and a long moment passed.

"Private, I like to see you in some more private place than here."

In panic, knowing how constrained her freedom and his were, Matthew could think of no place to go alone. Everywhere were military restrictions on mobility and thousands of people surrounded them. Matthew tried to think where they might meet. He was blank, "I do not know where we might see each other."

"I regularly deliver laundry to the officers at the fort and am known, so have passes. On Monday of next week I am making a delivery. While I am on the post could we see each other?"

Thus it was on Monday morning Belle arrived at the stable with a bundle of folded garments. Armed with a gift of biscuits and a jar of jelly, Matthew met her and they sneaked off for a walk to the delivery point for the clean clothing. Then the lovers slowly returned. They sat behind the stable between the straw piles and visited.

Twice a week for the next month this was their tryst. Knowing soldiers smiled as they passed the two but they never interrupted the young people holding hands and visiting. The expression on their faces spoke of the sacred time together and it's power protected them.

While I was at Monmouth near the end of the month Edwin shared some gossip. "William, that Private Hunter who is assigned at the stable came by one day when I was on post. He pulled me aside and asked to speak of a private matter. He was most nervous and the request was unique. He wanted me to read a letter of proposal of marriage he had written to a woman."

"The man takes great pride in his ability to read and write. His wish was that I would review it since the lady can read and write and he feared his skill is less than hers. He wanted me to read and copy the letter in a better hand. The missile spoke of his love and admiration of her and asked her to marry him and share his salary. He is doing well with his studies but the letter did need some help so I rewrote it, in my own messy hand."

This information was a surprise. Now, aware of the romance, I kept a keen eye out. One night as I looked out my window at sunset, I saw a couple walking near Brown's Garden. The narcissuses were blooming in white sparkles at their feet. The shapes of the lovers, though distant, were proud and tall as they walked hand in hand in the backdrop of sunset.

The letter that Edwin had copied had been in Matthew's pocket for over a week when the lovers had once more found the opportunity to be together. This time, after the soldiers had gone down the steps to their barracks, Belle and Matthew had met at the steps. It was early dusk when they climbed up a long way then sat together. She sat below him, leaning back against him. His cheek was resting on her crisp hair as he leaned over her. In the distance they could see campfires near the barracks and hear the evening songs of the men that rose to where the couple sat.

He reached into his open tunic and took the letter out. "Belle, I have written a letter to you." Withdrawing it, he unfolded the paper then read it to her in the dim light. The task was not that hard as he had read and reread it many times and all but knew the words by heart. Then he carefully folded it and handed it to her.

"I love you so and need you to be my wife. I do not know when or where we will go after the war. I just know I want us to go together. Take this and read it and consider what I have written." Then he rose and helped her up. In the new moonlight they embraced, then kissed long and passionately.

After he had returned her to her house he went to his bunk in the barracks. Laying on his back in the dark he knit his fingers together behind his head. *Yes, it was good to be a man and to be free.*

On the next Monday when Belle came to the fort, her suitor was especially nervous. After the delivery of the laundry, they returned to their private straw hideaway. In the dusty fragrance of their crisp bower, his beautiful woman lay on her back then rolled to face him where he sat.

"Matthew I have read your letter many times. I have considered it well. Although we have known each other only a while, we done talked a lot. I had decided to not tell you about myself. Now that you have proposed, I feel I need to tell you who I am."

"I was born and raised on a plantation in Alabama. The master came to my mother for my mother's whole life and also several other women at the quarters. He was my father. When I was little I cared for the master's children. I served in the house later and was able to teach myself to read and write. The sewing and laundry skills I have, my mother taught me."

"Because of my work and because the master thought I was pretty, he was proud of me and showed me off to company and neighbors. Sometime times White men took me. One time I be pregnant. My son was born when I was sixteen. He was killed in an accident when he was three. A carriage ran over him."

"Five years ago, when my mother died, my father freed me. When I be free I go to Natchez. Until last year I lived in a tiny cabin behind a White man's house in Natchez. I did all the laundry and sewing in return for the use of the house. As times got worse many de Whites quit hiring me for their work. Then when the owner of my cabin got scared by the war, he moved to a house he got in England. I was left without a home. The order came from the Union last year that I was to be removed from the city and sent to the Kraal, cause I had no job, no place. During that time I been desperate and scared, I do lots o' bad stuff—steal, lie and all."

"All I know dat I have been a slave and I been a free woman. I know I am afraid and lonely all the time. I know, if I have more children, I want to have a family for them. I want a real family with a father. I love you. You be a good man and I do not want to be alone no more. Now, that you know where I come from, you know who I am. What I want to be is your wife. I do not want to jump the broom. I want to be married by the real preacher."

Chapter 17

# Triumph

It was early spring of 1865 when some excellent and uplifting things occurred. "Congratulations Edwin," I clapped my comrade on the back after his swearing in ceremony. "I will now have to address you as Second Lieutenant Hobart."[34]

"Yes, Captain Hunter, and I also will expect a lot more respect," Edwin leaned forward and whispered.

We shook hands heartily as he glowed with pride. Then others stepped forward to also congratulate him and we all stood, enjoying the moment. Pleased as I was, this would mean that he would now be reassigned to Hazelhurst just north of Brookhaven, Mississippi some seventy two miles to the east, which would soon become the headquarters of the Fifty-eighth.

I was standing on the fringe of the group as various non-commissioned officers and enlisted filed by to shake his hand. I saw Sergeant Anderson and Privates Netter, Turner, Sanders and Mosby, all natives of the region, pass. I could not help but smile for I considered them *my fine men.*

Not much later, I saw a face from the past and pulled the man over after he had passed through the congratulatory line. By the time I reached him a small timid woman was at his side. It was the wagoneer I had waited with under the tree at Vicksburg as peace was formed.

From the darkness of his face came recognition, "Well, I be!" with a grin, Buck Murphy laughed. "Private Murphy are you still attached here?"

"Yup, I be a cook with Company H of the Fifty-eighth so I be at the kitchen and not much on the parade groun'. I thought I see you once, but from far. This be my new wife, Louisa, we been married proper."[37]

I nodded to the couple and shook their hands, then made some small inquiries of their welfare before I moved on to the end of the next line.

From my viewpoint I saw Corporal Hunter step forward for a brief congratulations and it was quite heart warming. My best friend and this new Corporal that I had such high hopes for stood together for a moment. Each of the men had been recognized for service and their personal qualities. Probably because of his injuries Matthew had been selected to fulfill my recommendation instead of all the men.

The stalwart Confederates battled on, unyielding but ever more desperate until April 29 when the final surrender was ratified and announced by the new president. Confederate President Jefferson Davis was being held in prison in an unprecedented arrest of the president of a defeated country and had no offer of parole. [34]

Ironically, at the final Confederate Congress, the proposal of Black soldiers had been a serious possibility, although thousands had already served and would receive pensions. [38] The proper enlistment of the Colored troops would have added strength to their cause and had been considered for some time. What manpower that might have contributed, no one will ever know.

When I heard of Confederates grasping to recruit Black troops for the South I recalled the story of one soldier who fought with a weapon at his owner's side for two years. With an abiding sense of loyalty when his owner was wounded at Gettysburg, the servant pulled him to safety, then walked boldly across the field to the Union to lines to join. *Could that loyalty have been harnessed?*

This Spring had also brought several tragedies. In this nation where one eighth of the population were former slaves and many others were freemen and women, they had been a presence in the capital. In Washington, a city where almost everywhere the wounded and dying lay, four companies of Colored troops had marched in the inaugural parade.

The President had included these words in his memorable speech concerning the former slaves and the war. "Woe unto the world because of the offences! Now, God wills to remove (slavery) and he gives to both North and South this terrible war, as the woe due to those who by whom the offence came, shall we discern therein any departure from those divine attributes with the believers in a living God always ascribe to him?... All the wealth piled by the bondman; two hundred and fifty years of unrequited toil shall be sunk and until every drop of blood drawn with the lash shall be paid by another's drawn with the sword."

On March 4, Abraham Lincoln had been sworn in at his inaugural. Following his speech the president had sought out abolitionist Frederick Douglass. "I saw you in the crowd today, listening to my inaugural address, " Lincoln said. "How did you like it?'

Douglass demurred, "I must not detain you with my poor opinion," he said. But Lincoln pressed on.

"There is no man in the country whose opinion I value more than yours," he said. "I want to know what you think of it."

"Mr. Lincoln," Douglass replied "that was a sacred effort." [39]

The president was killed on April 15, 1865. Having seen the end of slavery, but not the violent, destructive war replaced by a peaceful and unified nation.

On April 18th at Natchez we relieved the following order.

> "BY ORDER OF BRIGADIER GENERAL J.W. DAVIDSON GENERAL ORDER # 16.
>
> The national calamity, the assassination of Abraham Lincoln, President of the United States and it's Secretary of State, William H. Seward, demands a public expression of mourning and respect.
>
> Ordered: that minute guns be fired from Fort McPhearson from sunrise to sunset tomorrow; all flags to be displayed at half-mast; all public offices and buildings be closed throughout the day. The churches of the various denominations in the city will be opened at sunrise and continue so for payer through the day."

The second tragedy was ironic. Some days earlier Edwin had been standing on the bluff and watched the ship *Sultana* pass Southward on the river on the way to receive released Union prisoners. Her flag was half-masted and her bells tolling at intervals of half minutes. Soldiers asked the cause from the shore. Calling out, the reply had come, "President Lincoln has been assassinated." Thus at Fort McPhearson in Natchez, we had received the sad news, not by telegraph—that was not always dependable—but by the word of a doomed ship. The ship had most probably heard of the affair in Memphis or Vicksburg. [34]

This same ship was destroyed on April 27. There were on the ship 1,886 paroled prisoners of war. Only 800 paroled Union prisoners that had been held in the South were to have been on the ship *Sultana* for the return. Twelve commissioned officers and 757 enlisted men were saved when the overloaded ship exploded and 1,117 were drowned, cut apart by debris or scalded.

My parents kept me well informed of news in Carroll County and of my brothers in the army. Their letters also described the movements of the Fifteenth Illinois, my old regiment.[40]

One of the more dramatic Civil War stories had evolved there. At the battle of Shiloh, I had last seen Captain Adam Nanse. Born and raised in the East, he had migrated to Carroll County and was the sheriff of that county, residing in Savannah, Illinois at the time of the call. He had enlisted early and was with the Fifteenth Illinois when we formed at Freeport, thus he was elected a Captain of our regiment. In the battle of Shiloh, he was wounded and taken prisoner. That battle had cost our regiment dearly, of those from Carroll County he was but one.

Captain Nanse was taken to Memphis to a rebel prison where his leg was amputated. Later he was moved to Jackson, Mississippi. The whole of his time in this deprivation he had only been able to send two letters, so his welfare was of great question in Savannah. His wife, Rebecca and children, son Frank who was six, and his daughter Hattie, knew the greatest distress. Then he was moved to Vicksburg where he was paroled in October of 1862 by way of an exchange for a rebel Brigadier General.

In the same year he procured an artificial leg and returned to the fray in December. He was promoted to Major and fought with his fellows until the fall of Vicksburg, The Major found such difficulty in mounting and dismounting his horse, that he admitted his military career was at an end. He resigned about the same time I became a Captain in Natchez. He then served as a recruiter for the army in Carroll County. Much of this I had heard of and was quite satisfied that he was now safely home.[8]

Of real distress was the information that a company of my old regiment had been surrendered by their officer, with no single shot fired and were sent to a Southern prison. Those who survived would be released now.

My daily duties continued, including my regular reports of smuggling, and the arrest of either soldiers or citizens. Our prison, and that at Vicksburg, were full. The city jail at the courthouse had a full women's prison. The dynamics of war, the varied people and the region's problems were continual and a volatile caldron, despite the end of the war.

I never neglected to stop by Sarah's for 'porch sitting' unless it was too late and I had stayed over at Monmouth, or if some information I carried needed to be moved immediately to the Provost Marshall.

It had been early spring when my beloved had first informed me of her painful situation. The dear Scothorne family was most concerned with the well-known circumstance that I was courting her. That public knowledge had been immediate and scandalous as soon as the foiled attack had occurred. The contact between us had not been planned or decided by either of us and we had been both vulnerable and thrown together.

She timidly admitted on one night that a number of neighbors, community merchants, and friends, even at church, were shunning her. I had empathy because of my own treatment in Natchez.

I remember my question, "Sarah, you will not rebuke or reject me? I could not exist without the hope of your companionship."

With quiet tears in her eyes she straightened, and looked into my eyes. In the utmost pain, I rocked forward and reached for her hand. She placed the soft warmth of it into my hand. With her chin raised defiantly, and her voice only mildly filled with her pain, came her answer, "I have struggled again and again with the quandary, yet know that it would be most painful to never see you again. Your company and person are my only comfort in this time of travail. I cannot tell you how lonely I have been since I lost my husband and son."

"Last week came the most painful blow of all," she confessed. "For many years I have been quilting with a group of friends. I received a note informing me that I would no longer be needed." At this information her voice broke and I had a full sense of her isolation, pain and loss. The agony I was causing this woman I loved was beyond my ken. The enormous reality of our rejection and the impossibility of a lasting bond was like an insurmountable wall between us and we sat quietly that night for almost half an hour. I do know my mind was racing. I could not face the horrible thought of giving her up. I scrambled for an idea of how to rescue her in some way from her rejection. Then in a deep gloom, I thanked her for the cool drink, kissed her forehead gently and rode away. I knew nothing to say to encourage and comfort her.

Only on four festive occasions had Sarah and I left the porch. Once we were in public at a picnic and then at a parade near her home; one other time we attended another ball. She had indicated that she would attend the ball with the Scothornes so I was not allowed to escort her and we acted with strict decorum. Yet, though I had held her at a respectful distance as we danced, my passion was overwhelming and from her expression I could tell that she also welcomed my touch with matching yearning.

On the occasion some months ago, of Edwin's advancement to Sergeant we had made a celebration. We invited Sarah and her sister-in-law, Minerva Price; Alice 'the handkerchief girl,' with her mother; and a fellow who had been with Edwin since he enlisted. We had hoped the party would be large enough and the chaperones adequate so that the young ladies would be able to attend. There was to our favor, the unspoken obligation of the community to be accommodating to the Union officers. To our relief and excitement they all responded to the written invitations we had tendered.

That night we rented a carriage, and by arrangement arrived for the four ladies. Edwin and his friend rode along side on horses as we went to the most elegant hotel in Natchez.

In our plot Edwin and I had planned the event for early evening, and of course made every effort to linger as late as possible. This night was the highlight of our whole time in Natchez and I would not allow any shadow of fear to pierce it. The younger women were light hearted, the hotel and food were lovely and the price was quite high. To the two of us, that evening of celebration was well worth the several month's pay.

It was near midnight when I deposited Alice, her mother and Edwin at their home. He took some time to say goodnight, then intended to ride back to the fort. The other man had left straightway from the hotel. I delivered Sarah and Minerva at the Price home. First I helped Mrs. Price from the carriage, and she went toward the house as though intending to leave the two of us alone for a moment.

Sarah remained in the carriage looking down at me sweetly. She was effused with appreciation for the evening, and was thanking me. This was the first private event she had occasioned since her widowhood almost two years ago. Unspoken were her feelings for me. I could not concentrate on her words with the pulse in my head pounding and my whole body throbbing. The joy of my life was to stare at her face in the dimness of the Natchez moonlight as I studied her every movement and attribute.

With a breathless gesture I finally reached to help her from the carriage to the step.

As she alighted, I grasped her waist and pulled her to me where we stood for many minutes embracing. Our breaths inhaled into each other's mouths. Her taste had the small reminder of her dinner wine, which only sweetened its wonder by adding more intimacy. Finally, we withdrew to shiver with passion in each other's arms. I simply needed to touch her, to see her more closely. Then aware of the propriety and in her defense against more scandal and public rejection, I turned from her and took her arm.

It was sure that I was holding her arm too tightly, but her hand on my arm matched my own pressure as I crossed my left arm over and lay that hand on top of her hand. We arrived on the dim porch where only a small light was sneaking out the open door. We stood for long moments staring closely into each other's eyes. We were vacant of all thought except love.

In total agony I felt her hand release my arm and I allowed her to free herself. As she stepped back, she dropped a small beaded evening bag that she had carried. It fell with a soft plop and the rattle of the beads. I immediately retrieved it and straightening looked into her eyes. There was a mischievous twinkle in her eyes and a warm smile. I made a small movement to come closer, paused and in total joy realized the smile had only widened.

Now I held her warm and close for long moments and felt no resistance. Moving to place a kiss on her cheek, I felt her rise on her tiptoes to meet me. I kissed her forehead, her two closed eyes and then I allowed my kiss to trail down to her lips.

I clutched her once more, feeling the wonderful softness of her breasts. With frustration, I yearned to be able to pull her whole body to me, but her many skirts and hoops withheld that reward. The length of this last kiss and it's passion made time inconsequential as we occasionally moved our heads or bodies into a new and more exciting position as to be able to reach the other's person in more wonderful ways. When I knew we must part it took all my strength do so.

Finally, with a choked and quiet voice she whispered, "Thank you, William. I cannot tell you just what this evening has meant to me." She smiled, looking deeply into my eyes and I knew without any doubt that her love was deep and complete. She had put herself into my hands without a word. Then my beloved moved into the quiet house.

Through the whole ensuing courtship we had never behaved with impropriety, other than the breaking of the barrier of Union and Confederate. The stifling of emotions had been wearing and difficult for both of us.

No matter my own need, I had determined to do no more damage to this poor woman than she had suffered already. Sarah remained quiet in the doorway trying to regain her breath and her composure. Bewitched, I stared at the red-golden halo the light behind her cast onto the piles of curls on her head as she passed into the Price's house.

It was perhaps a week later after her confession of her ostracization, on a momentous Wednesday. As late summer neared, the bugs and heat were stifling, that I had finally been forced by duty to visit the terrifying smallpox hospital. Although there was some recovery, the smallpox took far more souls away than were spared. This hospital was within the grounds of the fort so all of us stationed there were ever aware of its ominous presence. Now, I had been required to seek out a Colored soldier who was confined there. He had been witness to a drunken brawl where there had been a death. As I entered the doors, a most disgusting odor took my breath away. The smell of the pox was overwhelming. Those stationed there always wore masks. I stepped outside and removed a hanky to hold over my nose before I returned inside. As I wandered among the cots I witnessed soldiers in various stages of this scourge.

There were those just showing the first evidence of the grey pustules and individuals writhing in the throes of fever. Nurses sat here and there attempting to feed patients who immediately vomited the total contents of their stomachs, adding more awfulness to the odor of the pox and diarrhea. Among the many were those who in delirium screamed or recited insane empty conversations. Since the blisters usually gathered in one place, that location when visible was horrible. A face or some other part would be covered with grey pus oozing from sores and mixed with bits of blood. Also among the beds were those patients who were far too quiet, those were the dead and dying.

I did not find the soldier on the first floor and moved to the next. I had paused a number of times to gag and try to keep from retching. Most of the patients on the second floor were Black and soldiers. People from the Kraal did not receive any treatment here.

Finally, I found the poor young lad, and with relief I saw that he was conscious, although obviously in a great fever, he made no complaint. With pained eyes he stared at me vacantly as I questioned him, and only nodded yes or no. When I was required to ask for specific names, times or locations, he forced the words across a dry, swollen tongue. I wanted to give him a drink, but my horror of the disease prevented me. I knew true shame and do to this day. I only took notes and before leaving sought an attendant to seek him out and offer the man a drink.

Now in August, it being several days since my duty had allowed me to steal these moments, Sarah was not on the porch. Fresh from the horror of the Pox Hospital, and having completed my appointed round, I was anxious but resolute in the decision I had made. I needed to see her tonight although it was well after eight in the evening. I knocked on her door. In a moment I heard her question who was there. Hearing my reply, she threw the door wide. With breathless abandon she stepped on the porch. Although still dressed, she had loosened her hair and it lay in soft waves about her shoulders and down her back, this was a glorious wreath I had never seen before. Each quality I had found in her during my courting only heightened my love and desire for her.

"Oh, William, I was afraid you would not come tonight." Her expression was one of complete joy. With so much practice, we moved immediately to the two rocking chairs, which had become our most dear locations on Earth.

In our conversations she had told me at length of her life while still a girl. She told me about her sister Louisa, her beloved brother Joseph and of his marriage to his wife Catherine Jane who was a Pitmore and their baby Rosa. Having heard of her father's death made the stories painful as she told me of his love of her. Elijah Eyers Spencer's attentions for his daughter's welfare had been his first priority. She shared just a few stories of her marriage.

With some trepidation she spoke of her long ago Cherokee heritage though a grandmother who married a man named Sizemore in Alabama many generations ago. I wished I could know her family and thought of the bonds they held for Sarah here in Mississippi.

My beloved seemed more vivacious and talkative than usual, then slowly she quieted. We slowly rocked staring at each other, yearning for touch and closeness. Then taking a deep breath, I stood and placed my back against the porch pillar for reinforcement as I began my rehearsed speech.

"My dear Sarah, I come tonight on the most important mission of my life. I love you with my whole heart. Soon I know I will be returning to the North when this unending war finally releases me. Even before that I know I might be called away at a moment's notice and leave without even a chance to say goodbye, I cannot live without your sweet presence. Please consider marrying me and accompanying me back to Illinois when I leave."

In panic, I shook as I waited for her response. The immediate indication of her response was a blush and a wide smile, and then with a lowering of her face. Her faint voice began while my heart fell and I was washed with trepidation.

"Dear Will, I do love you so. You are my only happiness. All I know of you I admire and wish to be with you. Yet, I must tell you of what I have considered. For I too have longed to marry, to be your wife and to be together forever."

"So many people have turned their backs on me, partly I am sure, because they fear my shift in my loyalty would lead me to implicate them to you or the army for treason or betrayal of the occupation. My condemnation here in Natchez makes me well aware that even if we should not marry. I will still never again be a part of the life I have enjoyed in the past. We, of course, should we marry, must retreat North. This would mean leaving my sister Louisa and my brother Joseph and my mother whom are the only family I now have. That though, is an agony that causes me great pain."

"My life with my husband was quite happy until the war, and his family has been loyal, loving and supportive of me. They are now disapproving; yet have had the courage and integrity to not abandon me during our courtship. Many is the times they have defended me despite their own reservations. The very fact of marrying any man would cause them pain because of the memory of their son. To wed a Union officer of Colored troops who is part of the occupation of their home would be a true insult to their son's memory. That treasured image is of one who died defending the South and all they believe in and love. The tragedy of hurting those dear people is almost unbearable. I have confided in Minerva, but even she cannot support this marriage."

"I am embarrassed to say that I went behind your back, not long after Edwin's dinner party. I wrote my Grandfather Isaac in total honesty, describing my complete quandary. His reply took some time, for he gave it long consideration. Because his own Southern heritage, he understands much of the influences we face. A part of him chooses to be in my company in Illinois, to protect me and to know me better. He had to fight to keep this self-interest from his epistle. His letter gave complete recommendation to you and your family. His one caution was that I not choose to marry you simply to escape future pain here in Mississippi after the war."

My whole being was quaking with fear and pain.

"Beloved, I have thought on this for months. I have pondered many of the same reasons as you have. Please, please say you will become my wife. In my heart there is no other answer. My fervent love for you is the core of all my being." I hoped this came to her without the panic or weakness I was feeling.

She sat silent, looking at her hands, which were folded in her lap. With a breath of hope, I too looked at her hands and noticed her wedding band was no longer on her finger. I wondered how long it had been absent without my notice of the fact.

I saw her breast heave and she moved her face, like the sun, to shine on me. "Yes, Will I will marry you. I love you and would be honored to be your wife."

Almost collapsing on my shaky knees I dropped to the porch in front of her and reaching into my pocket took out a small box that I offered to her. With a shy grin she took it and carefully opened it with an excited expression. Aghast, I watched as she first laughed, then cried for a full five minutes. I thought perhaps she had lost her mind. I was bewildered.

With a strangled voice she finally stuttered. "This very garnet necklace was a gift from my husband which I sold a year ago because of my great need."

My blood boiled, it was the most important gift I would give in my life and it had already been given to my lover by another man.

Then shaking her head she leaned forward and put a hand on my shoulder. "Don't you see, this is makes your gift the more important? For, I so love the beauty and significance of this gift from you as a seal for our love and forthcoming bond. Still, the magic is that it comes with such innocence that I feel it is guidance from the past, from my former husband to confirm this new life that I approach. This beautiful necklace releases me from any fear or guilt I might have felt so that I can come to you, complete and free and new. When I gave it away with no hope of return it became a token of the past. Now, almost like magic I am given it back with freedom and permission to start a new life."

As I tried to calm myself I slowly began to think of my wedding gift with this strange new perspective.

Quickly rising to her feet, she looked down on me freely laughing with joy. "Now more than ever I accept your proposal. All I want is to be your wife. This wonderful and joyful gift is a bond between us."

This public embrace and kiss we shared tonight was without fear, we were both ready to face whatever the future bought. When we finally parted the panic of our fear of loss had departed. We agreed to make our plans later. Giggling like children with a secret, we parted. Our hearts were light and our joy was almost breaking from our chests.

In less than a month a major change occurred. I was reassigned to Colonel Farrar in Brookhaven. This duty had been planned for some time and the separation from my love and fear of being moved even farther away made us apprehensive. We planned to marry the moment I could return from Brookhaven.

The duty itself was similar to the work for which I was suited, I was to oversee illegal activities, just as I had in Natchez. To my relief it did not entail continual horseback duty although the damn paperwork was almost doubled. The assignment would, should the postwar duty be prolonged, put me in good position for advancement. Now that I was considering being the head of a family, the appeal of a pay raise was even more desirable.

Before I left Fort McPhearson a strong outbreak of Cholera began that would devastate the city by October. There were ever more tensions as carpetbaggers arrived to take advantage of desperation sales and use the Colored citizens as pawns to the profit of the adventurers.

Antonia Quitman Lowell, still living upstairs at Monmouth, wrote her husband, "I fear our once lovely South – such a desolated country as it is now left to us. Our hearts are broken by the ruin of our beloved country. Alas, we have now no country." She recounted the first arrival of the troops on the property of Monmouth, "'Twas on the night of February 7 when we were exposed to the fury of 60 thousand friends in the shape of Yankee soldiers. Much as I hated the race before, I feel the ten-fold bitterness of them now. I cannot grow familiar with the sight of them, the glimpse of that uniform fills me with loathing and horror and I feel, as I ever shall, that they are our bitter foes forever. With me there is no forgetting the past." [35] This lady had shared a common sentiment of many of the townspeople.

The military, freemen, citizens, the Freedman's bureau, two governments and numerous scoundrels kept an uneasy peace in the city of Natchez. Several times there were forays nearby by the troops. The woods were still full of criminals, Black families hiding to escape the Kraal, weary soldiers, displaced White families and deserters of both armies. The situation was only stable with the balance changing like a pendulum all the time. Now the city was living with an inflation of 5,000 percent.

One of the last days before I left for Brookhaven I was crossing the field when approached by Corporal Hunter. He saluted and asked for a moment. Having been gone so often, I inquired of his current assignment. With some regret I found he was no longer on duty at the stables, which was probably the government's loss. Yet, the man took pride in the new authority and supervision of other affairs at the fort.

With crisp salutes and straight posture he looked me in the eye and began, "Sir, I thank you that you requested my advance." With a shyer grin he continued, "Now that I'm a married man the salary is most welcome."

I returned his smile. "So you are a married man? Who is the new bride?"

"Yes sir," he beamed, "it be the lady who gave us the clothing when we went after O'Malley. Her name is Belle, and she is the most beautiful woman in the world. We are really married. It was by a man like us," he grinned with a cunning twinkle in his eye. "That chaplain from Pennsylvania, Sergeant Matthew Hunter married us. We Hunters have to keep together." He laughed out loud.

I now was more than aware that the ceremony and recognition of marriage was most important to my soldiers. After generations they would also be able to name their own children instead of accepting the masters naming their babies.

With joy and pride in my own voice I broke convention and bragged, "I am engaged also, and I also love the most beautiful woman in the world."

The new corporal went on. The army had finally agreed in March to pay the Colored soldiers their equal pay in rank to that of the White soldiers. The early raises brought the privates pay from $10 to $13 and now, as a corporal, there was even more.

I could sense the man's confidence and optimism. There had always been an unspoken pleasure and respect between us. Soon we would be separated forever. I reached for his hand, and we shook hands.

As we parted I slowly and sincerely said "Good luck Matthew," meaning this in the deepest sense. The tumultuous reconstruction was in the main a daunting and dangerous thing to the Colored community. I thought to myself , *what would become of the brave man and the young couple.*

In the all, these two months before my marriage were busy and without danger despite several incidents. For several years the occupation of Natchez and following Emancipation was interwoven with the establishment and implementation of the Freedman Boards and also the advancement of persons of Color into positions of more authority. The most memorable event was that of Peck. I was not directly involved but Edwin was. He was stationed near enough that we occasionally met. His report and those of written information fell within the jurisdiction of Colonel Farrar so I was well informed.

The Freedman's Bureau had been designed in the final months of Lincoln's administration, it supervised by the War Department, and attempted to reunite families, protect their rights and supervise Colored employment. There was an attempt to provide relief. From the emancipation in 1864 until now in Vicksburg, they were registering Black citizens, inquiring about parentage, color and marital situation. Such questioning allowed an understanding of the emancipated.

Two of fifths of the Black males had served in the Union army. Many had some White ancestry. About a quarter of the Negroes had been separated by force from one or more spouses. On many occasions mothers asked to be legally married. Clergy doing the interviews were also concerned with the sacredness of the couple. There were 4,527 new marriages of area persons.

The tragedy many of the men recounted was that many wives had been removed to a camp during the war or their enlistment and they knew not where. This condition had precipitated many desertions during the war, as the soldiers had left and sought their families.

In 1864, Brigadier General McDevlin had purposely sent the soldiers away, although children were thus separated from parents and wives from husbands. He had called the family "idle Negroes" and a serious threat to order and safety. Their complaints were also against A.W. Kelly, the military surgeon. They said that he rejected them with threats and said that they "appeared to think that the Colored man has a great many more rights than White men." This was probably part of the unexplained desertion in one company at McPhearson.

Now in the new limbo of peace, the Black communities struggled to offer for orphans, to provide a closer community and to protect others, many of whom were distant relatives. Many of the new citizens were reluctant to select surnames at the Freedman Bureau, and in 1866 many also applied to return to West Africa.

Major Howard, the director, and several of his family members were closely tied the Union Colored Troops Corp, and subsequently he hired many former officers of the UCT to implement the programs. The new relationships that were created between free Blacks and former owners were a very uneasy truce. This truce was one frequently lacking respect, cooperation or the trust of the White community.[41]

The Peck matter occurred in this strained atmosphere. Captain Warren Peck of the Freedman's Bureau was arrested in Hazlehurst in October. He was the superintendent of Freedmen and was in his own office. He was repeatedly insulted and threatened by a White citizen. He ordered him out of his office and when he did not comply he called on guards to remove the man. This angry citizen obtained a warrant and with a White, rebel posse arrested Peck and put him into jail.

I came into the matter then, for four companies of the Fifty-eighth arrived, released Captain Peck and put the jailer in jail in his place. The Governor of Mississippi was newly elected, as the incident had occurred under the prior governor. This new governor reported to the President. His description of the situation began, "The civil authority is thus defied and put in subordination to the military."

The subsequent result was that the commander of the Fifty-eighth was relieved and the jailer was released, by command of the Secretary of War, Edwin Stanton. This response was to the great disgust of the UCT, and especially to Edwin and myself who feared that this was a major step backward in the political arena giving White southern government far too much power over the emancipated people. [34]

This was typical of the type of disturbance in the state and especially around Brookfield, but seldom did it call for such a resolve from such a high position. The continual jockeying of power and politics began in a painful dance that would continue through reconstruction and into the next century. Black people were pawns and the several governments the players.

Early in November I was told I would be released back to Natchez so Edwin requested leave and accompanied me. On November 11, 1865 at Trinity Episcopal church in Natchez, Sarah Drucilla Scothorne, age 23, and Captain William Hugh Hunter, age 29, were married by G.B. Perry, who was the current rector. Our wedding and certificate was witnessed and signed by Edwin L. Hobart. Finally, I met Louisa and Joseph Spencer's young family. Our small wedding party ate at the fine hotel where we had celebrated Edwin's advancement.

Late in the afternoon we said goodbye and went to the rented carriage. There was excitement and anxiety in our hearts as we rode the short distance to "our" house. We hardly spoke, but sat proudly with our arms touching. In defensive pride, I publicly put my arm around Sarah's shoulders and squeezed her. We did not speak, too full of anticipation.

When we stopped at the front of the house. I alighted and helped my new wife down. Firmly taking her arm I led her to the porch, then stopped. Kissing the top of her head I paused and laughed. "Please wait in the rocking chair while I put the horse into the shed. It is the last time you will need to wait on the porch."

It was really with a sense of newness that I stabled the horse in "my" shed instead of my father's or the army's. Then I hurried back to the front of the house. Grabbing both Sarah Drucilla's hands, I pulled her to her feet and grabbing her waist pulled her to me and twirled her around and around until we were both dizzy and she was squealing to be released.

I set her down, still holding her waist with one hand as I used the other to open the door, then I swept her up in my arms and crossed the threshold. For long moments I kissed her as I slowly lowered her feet to the floor. We then clutched each other with breathless passion and kissed long and hard.

Catching her breath she gasped, "Let me show you your new house, you have come home." Virtually bouncing with joy and excitement, she grabbed my hand. With a sly wink she closed the door and locked it.

Then she toured me through the whole house, opening drawers and pantries in her urge to share her own joy. Finally, she approached the narrow staircase. Taking a deep breath she looked me in the eye and softly said, "Follow me." She led the way to the small, sunlit bedroom upstairs. The lonely, young widow was bringing her lover to her bed where we would await the magic moonlight of Natchez, together.

Chapter 18

# Kansas

Sarah Drucilla struggled to open the window on the north side of the small sitting room. The window seemed swollen and jammed so it took some effort. Finally, the casing gave and she pulled it to full open. She moved to the second window which opened with more ease. Carefully, she replaced the lace curtains over the panes and pushed the drapes back a bit farther. Then she went to the first window to similarly arrange the window coverings. She fanned her face with her fingers as she flexed her hand at the wrist. There was some relief in the cooling, morning breeze which came from the north. Early June heat on the Western Kansas prairie could be quite stifling.

Even though it had been weeks since it had rained, there was a real mugginess in the air. It was nearly nine in the morning and her guests would arrive in an hour. Turning, she swished across the floor, her petticoat and crisply ironed skirt rustled against a long, linen apron trimmed with tatting.

She began to hum under her breath and with a start realized she was humming *Dixie*. A pang of homesickness washed her as she entered the small hall of their home. She stopped to look into the entry mirror. It was fifteen years since she left Natchez, never to return to the beautiful, garden city where her heart still rested, or to see her loved ones again.

Memories of Dixie were long ago and far away in Kansas. The memories that she chose to remember were in terms of the warmth of her family, the beauty of flowers and trees, and a gracious life style. She seldom allowed herself to remember her first husband, that life seemed another world and so far away. The pain of the loss of her baby, Henry, flashed every now and then.

Louisa, her sister, had informed her for years of the true condition of her homeland. The carpetbaggers had destroyed any hope of the constructive rebuilding of a healthy, productive South. The anger of Southerners was still unresolved in most of the families of the region. The hate and bitterness ate like a cancer in their hearts.

The unemployed, mostly illiterate Coloreds, swarmed across the whole region. The situation left this beaten and bedraggled part of the nation in throes of despair. Something called the Black Codes were put into action. A new system called 'sharecropping' gave Negroes hard work on small patches of land that left little profit, and the Negroes always in debt to the land owner. Their movement was restricted almost as much as it had been in slave days. In elections the ballot boxes were regularly stuffed to guarantee the White minority held control, which was self justifying since illiterate Blacks could not vote.

William had a leave from December 6, 1865 to January 8, 1866. He had taken his bride to visit in Illinois. On this journey they had conceived—after only three months of marriage.

When they had arrived in December by steamer they had been met by William's father Henry and his brother James. Sarah looked at the trim, beautiful horses and the lovely carriage. She felt an excitement to be where poverty and desperation were not commonplace. The Hunters and her Grandfather were all at the Wysox farm when they arrived. Clay had not mustered out yet and was the only missing family member. It was almost overwhelming and she soon escaped to a lovely and cool upstairs room to take a short nap.

After a careful grooming, the bride went down to meet her new family. As she had passed into the house with its large, cheerful family, it had been almost like being in a whirlwind. The joy and hubbub had left her a bit incoherent, and with her slight nausea she was overcome. She hoped that they did not think she was not a bright person. Even the close embrace of her own weeping Grandfather made her a bit uncomfortable. She had not seen her father's father since she was around ten years of age.

Her mother-in-law Mary Hugh Hunter was kind and gentle. On the first day Mary presented the couple with a very old blue and white tea set that had been in the family for generations, suggesting that they might some day pass it on to their child.

Because of her pregnancy, her husband took her home to Illinois and left her with his parents. For her comfort and the baby's safety, they wanted her to be away from the beautiful but disease ridden, overcrowded city of Natchez.

In April of 1866, Will had reported to Vicksburg and at last had been mustered out. They had already sold her house, regrettably to a man who else was probably a carpetbagger. Yet, who in the city had any money? The couple then had moved into William's parent's home in Illinois and into a new life.

In the Illinois neighborhood there was no dearth of young people that she found charming. Many young families called on them. William took her riding in the carriage. Often from the carriage he showed her his pride of community, and shared the history of his youth. The land clearing on their own property was progressing and a late crop was planted on a small portion of the farm. In his free time William was busy preparing the house on his property to a better state, so that they could eventually move in after the baby was born

It was late June by the time the newlyweds settled. The man who had been renting Will's seventy-five acres already had his crops planted even before William planted the small, new patch.

It was decided that Will would temporarily act as a hotelkeeper in Mount Carroll, their lodging was provided by the hotel, thus they would be together all day. They then moved into Mount Carroll instead of living at the farm. Will found he had some skill as an innkeeper. He was a good manager, attractive in appearance, a sound bookkeeper and, when needed, found he could be quite firm with problems that might arise.

Their son, William Wallace Hunter was born at the hotel on September 25. Of the several things they considered in the naming was to honor his father. In memorial they recalled of the son President Lincoln who died that was named William Wallace and the commander William Wallace who had died at Shiloh. Their child was dark, healthy and the pride and joy of the newlyweds; they were exuberant and literally glowed.

Will's brother John lived in Iowa and glorified in the postwar boom which Iowa was seeing, especially along the Mississippi River. After two years, the young couple moved to Rockford, Illinois where they farmed until 1871. They sold the farm in Illinois in 1869 to pay for the move.

His brother Clay was now the surveyor in the county and perusing a strange endeavor. Clay was trying to build something he called a biplane. His father was aging and they hated to leave but wanderlust and occasional postwar depression would impel Will to move often.

His brother John had died in Madison County, Iowa in 1869. The death of this 40-year-old man left his wife Emily Alice a widow and his children Henry Frederic, Joan and Nellie who were almost all grown, fatherless. Henry Frederick went to live with his Grandpa Henry. This loss had weakened William's Iowa ties somewhat.

William and Sarah had farmed in Iowa with only moderate success and the physical maladies which Will bore from the war were disruptive to his farming labors. The rheumatism in his right arm and shoulder made farming quite difficult.

There was impatience and restlessness in Will that seemed related to the war. In the beginning of their marriage he read all the reports at hand on the war, and he yearned to meet any and all veterans to talk to. Now, after years, he finally did not retell of his adventures with the Colored troops. Although Northern veterans had risked all in this war, they had little interest or sympathy with the Black population, either those self-emancipated or those emancipated by the war. A few citizens, even in Mt. Carroll, were almost antagonistic toward William and his stories of the freedmen.

*My husband,* Sarah thought, *always had optimism for something new.*

So next they were transported to Spencer, Iowa. While in Spencer, he returned to innkeeping from 1872-1874. Their daughter Mae was born about that time. Briefly, Will and the family were in Northern Nebraska, then they moved to Kansas in 1876. The best opportunity there was in Minneapolis, Kansas where he was again an innkeeper from 1877 - 1879.

The family of four had arrived here in Hill City, Kansas in July of 1879. At the same time in Illinois, Sarah's father-in-law Henry sold part of his large land holdings in Wysox Township and moved to Elk Grove, Illinois. Thus the two Hunter families, junior and senior, made major life changes that same year. Since the Hunters were great letter writers there was regular contact, and once a year they rode the railroad with the children to Illinois to visit them.

Their son William Wallace was a lively thirteen-year-old when they had moved to Hill City. He had far too much enthusiasm and energy. He was always off with friends to create a new adventure, many of which ended in his discipline. Mae was sweet and dark as any of the mother's own Spencer lineage. She tended to be rather quiet and loved school.

As Sarah peered into the mirror this June morning, the girl was gone, replaced by a woman of thirty-nine. First she checked her hair, she saw a full, warm, chestnut cluster of curls on top of her head with only a random white hair making its appearance. She checked the nape of her neck for fly-a-ways and found it tidy. Pulling the apron over her head she turned from one side to the other and also inspected her dress. It's fabric pulled tautly across full breasts and the scooping neckline modestly ended far from revealing any cleavage. Turning sideways she saw the gathers at the back of the gown that created a bustle effect. From this view it was evident that in leaving girlhood for womanhood she had truly bloomed. Yet, she was pleased that her waist still had a stylish turn for a woman who had born three children.

Today's social tea would be a major success for her if she could subtly nudge the ladies who would be coming for tea this morning toward investing, or encouraging their husbands to do so. She and William had such exciting plans for Gettysburg, the small town they were helping develop. Their own property there was the east half, block 9. It was purchased in Sarah's name since the last of her personal money from the Natchez house had helped them secure it. If the town grew, as hoped, it would bring them security and success.

Gettysburg nested in a valley among the hills near Sand and Soloman Creeks. The town had been founded in 1880 by Joseph Gettys. He was a native of Pennsylvania and had also fought at Vicksburg which was a bond between he and William. Gettys named the town in Kansas Gettysburg just as his ancestor Samuel had named Gettysburg in Pennsylvania in 1765.

True to the independent nature on the Kansas prairie, the new city had immediately embroiled itself in a political battle to become the county seat. William was one of a number of men working on behalf of the town's attempt to achieve just that.

William and Sarah had high hopes for the town. Last year, Sarah's husband had been 'knee deep' in political strife on the county seat issue. Articles were published in the local press decrying his character. This was during his appeal to become Commissioner. Perhaps the press was the reason he lost the candidacy.

In an attempt to get the newspaper to move to the growing community of Gettysburg, William made promises to the editor that the newsman felt were not fulfilled. The editor hated William and took many column inches to vilify him publicly. To Sarah there was a parallel to the civic history of some of his ancestors like Henry, the founder of Hunter Hall Plantation.

The town's aspirations were revealed by the new school and other buildings being constructed of the plentiful Kansas limestone. There were scattered frame and sod homes and many outbuildings and sheds.

Their current modest home sat west of Hill City on a small farm where they planted winter wheat. It was now tall and would soon ripen. They had hopes of a good crop, like last year. Because of their commitment to Gettysburg, they often stayed in that burgeoning village. But William's active community life still kept him quite busy in Hill City. He felt to support Hill City and the county would also help them with the development of nearby Gettysburg.

Sarah had one poignant thought about their location. Just ten miles east down the road from Hill City was Nicodemus. William was a frequent visitor in Nicodemus for harness, custom made by a blacksmith, goods or some other service. Sarah had some curiosity if Will's innermost memories of his troops drew him there, or only neighborliness and need.

The Black families who had come to Kansas were a people seeking a home, and a hope. Nickodemus was one of the all-Black communities that had sprung up. There were several of these in prairie states like Kansas and Nebraska.

In 1873, Pap Singleton pioneered the town with three-hundred Black settlers and became the "Pied Piper" for the Black settlement of Kansas. This movement in the state had attracted over 20,000 by 1879. People like those who settled Nickodemus were called "exodusters."

The town of Nickodemus was founded by W.H. Smith with people mainly from Kentucky, these had not been Colored troops. Mr. Smith and W.R. Hill had each founded a city at the same time. The all-White city was named Hill City, so the proximity that William had chosen seemed natural for him. The census of Nickodemus Township was listed in 1880 as 258 Blacks and 58 Whites.[16]

Four million slaves who were freed were an important part of a total population of twenty-three million in the nation. With the pain of the past war and the anger of expatriates on both sides, the KKK was gaining strength across the country. The Klan was a real threat to Catholics, Jews, the Colored community and those who supported them. By 1877, Jim Crow laws were being put into place nationally to erode many of the freedoms that had been offered to former slaves and freedmen.

Some things were respectfully silent between Sarah and Will. Those of a "color" nature were one unspoken topic. Some stirring in her heart convinced the woman that her husband was drawn to this neighboring town for an unspoken need within.

All Black towns were not the only presence on the prairie of these dark people. Numerous men of color had also enlisted in the Indian Wars, and were called Buffalo soldiers because of their curly hair like that of the buffalo heads. The cowboy life attracted thousands and at the peak of this period almost half of the professional cowboys were Negroes. Many families went on to become independent farmers. In cities like Omaha and Kansas City, the unskilled labor force was often almost all Negro.

Where they lived, Kansas lays flat and open, a native prairie of tall, waving grasses; the vistas are open in a way no other part of the nation is. The tiny streams, the nearby railways and roadways of civilization which lead to the burgeoning West were attractive in their promise. Land was cheap and the incentives to homestead there were strong. Many a community was being developed in the late 1800s on the Kansas lands. The deficits of Kansas included the intense weather. This open plain drew thunderstorms, powerful winds, beating sun in the summer and tornadoes. Wind drove snows in the winter.

The three ladies she was expecting today were potential buyers for Gettysburg property. One was a prosperous widow, she was young enough to see the adventure of town building, and the other two were married to men who were always on the lookout for good opportunities. If she could entreat an enthusiasm in them about the development project, then give them time to ponder, Will would be in a much better position when he approached these potential Gettysburg landowners.

Moving down the hall she opened the kitchen screen door and saw Mary, a slender golden brown woman from Nickodemus. She worked for them by the week and was of great help. Today she was under a young tree, appreciating the small shade it gave. She was in a Boston rocker snapping beans which she had earlier picked from the kitchen garden.

Something about the scene reminded her of her first child, lying in the Natchez cemetery. *Does a Mother ever forget the pain*? These other beautiful and bright Hunter children never filled all the space in her heart. There was still hollowness left by Henry.

Sighing, Sarah turned and moved briskly back into the kitchen. She pumped some water into an enamel basin and washed her hands and face. She poured the water out the screen door and returned the basin to the counter. Taking a bowl of tiny tea cookies she began to carefully arrange them on a blue willow platter. Then she put out a tray with an antique teapot and four cups that were Hunter family antiques that had been of their wedding gift from Mary and Henry Hunter.

When the sweets looked just right she ate one that had been broken. Then she went back to the sitting room and put the cookie platter on a marble-topped side-table. Returning through the hall, she picked up the apron she had removed and hung it on a peg near the kitchen door. Then she reached into a crock near the door and moved fabric aside until she found a proper piece of flannel. This she tore into a sizable strip. Then she wiped the fabric hard against a candle, taking the rag back with her she pushed it along table surface, mantles and windowsills.

In Kansas there was always dust, *guess you would be able to dust three times a day*. Seeing a fly she lay a doily on top the plate of cookies on the side table. Then she went quickly for a swatter. Checking a watch that hung from her neck and lay between her bosoms she realized it would soon be time.

Next, she buffed the blue and white creamer and sugar bowl. Taking the crock of sweet cream which was still cool from the root cellar, she used a ladle to fill the creamer. She vigorously buffed four small ornate teaspoons. Finally she was ready, and so sat on the settee in front of the open window and awaited her guests.

It was late afternoon when she heard Will's horse clip clop up the path to the barn. She had been sitting in the kitchen and watching as Mary prepared a stew for supper. The children had arrived home, courtesy of a neighbor. They were doing schoolwork in their rooms, or at least she hoped they were.

She pushed through the screen door and stood on the porch watching her husband unsaddle the horse, brush the chestnut mare down then lead her into the barn. The slender man with broad shoulders had hung his pork pie hat on a gatepost while he worked. His dark hair caught the light, and the white at his temple was accented by the glint of sweat on his forehead.

He retrieved the hat on his way into the two-story frame house. It seemed that each time she watched him it was like the first time. She still saw him as remarkable. Her pulse raced and her mouth became moist. There was still a shyness and holding back although she yearned for him to reach out to her. She wanted to rush into his arms, surrounded by his strength, his firmness and the special fragrance of his body. As she waited she smiled; her anticipation was enhanced as she saw him glance several times toward the house looking for her. Demurely, she stood quietly until he finished and entered the house loosening his string tie and collar buttons.

As he reached the bottom of the three wooden, porch steps he looked up, directly into her eyes. His expression was transparent. It spoke of his approval of her appearance, his pleasure in returning to his home. Just under his expression was an unspoken passion for her. He to was ever aware of decorum and simply reached out for her hand as Sarah held the door open.

As they entered the kitchen he greeted the young woman working there. "Good day Mary," he nodded. The woman nodded and returned the smile. "I would like to visit privately with Sarah."

"Very well, Mister Hunter."

Moving toward the kitchen laughing, he nuzzled the back of her neck and with a giggle of pleasure he kissed her cheek. Then the couple went into the sitting room and closed the door. Taking Sarah's hand he led her to the settee and sprawling he pulled his voluptuous wife onto his lap. Snuggling and whispering he buried his face in her breasts and pretended to bite at them as she suppressed her soft squeals. "Mr. Hunter, what kind of business have you accomplished today?" She whispered with mock coyness, and not waiting for a reply she lowered her voice, "Now you must ask, Mrs. Hunter what kind of business have you accomplished today?" Then she pulled her head back to see his beaming expression.

"Yes my dear, what have you done this day?" Rolling off his lap she propped herself in the corner of the love seat, at her back were plump, maroon, velvet pillows. She gathered her breath, "I am so excited, I could not wait for you to return. My tea was lovely. All the women were attentive to my story of Gettysburg. The widow even asked the cost of various properties. Both the others inquired if you were willing to let some lots go. After our chitchat I began to tell them of our plans. For the next hour they forgot tea, and listened and asked questions. I even pulled out the maps and showed each of them specific boundaries. If they seem even more interested by the weekend, perhaps we could take a picnic to the sight. Their families and ours could go to Gettysburg for a picnic. We could go with carriages and make a party of it and show them how well the land lies."

Reaching for his wife, Will pulled her to him and placed his lips on her's for a long kiss.

In the dark that night they both sat rocking in front of a moonlit window in the upstairs bedroom. The lace curtains appeared pale blue in the night reflections. The full June moon filled the room so that they had not lit a lamp and each remembered the magic of Natchez moonlight that had enchanted them.

Will moved to a table and taking the tobacco thermador, filled his large, brown pipe and her tiny, white one. He returned to the chair beside her. He passed her the small, white, clay pipe and put his into his own mouth. He tugged at the bottom of the legs of his white union suit until he was more comfortable. Placing his feet apart, he leaned over to retrieve the wooden matches that he kept on the floor under his chair. He struck one and first lit Sarah's pipe then his own. They sat quietly smoking and rocking for almost an hour. Each was involved in their own reverie.

In a quiet voice that was quite calm he shared, "I feel very confident about our success this time."

"With luck," Sarah replied, "we could even gain more support for your battle in Hill City next month. It would be right that Hill City be the county seat now that Gettysburg has no chance, I am sure the voters know that."

"For now, my dear, we need to concentrate on our new dreams," Will softly remind her. "I also had a good day, I had an inquiry about the purchase of a farm north and west of Gettysburg. I do not know what kind of profit we might see, but if it is generous we could invest it in our own project. Soon we can begin to build our permanent home there. The house needs to be as lovely as those in Natchez."

Her cold pipe now lay in her lap, she placed it in a dish on the table. Standing at the bed she ran her hand over the quilt hanging on the bedpost. The body of the quilt was the one she had used to hide her "projects" for the quilt society. The bindings were of grey and blue uniform scraps.

Then she stood with her back to the window, "I dream of building our own house. In my mind I have designed and furnished the rooms a hundred times. The house would have a large library, sitting rooms, separate maid quarters, and there would be a larger room for both William Wallace and Mae. I yearn to be settled and permanent."

"Do you know what I dream of?" Will naively cocked his head forward.

"What my darling?" Was her coy answer.

He began very slowly, "Sitting here and seeing the moonlight through your gown revealing your legs, your sweet body and loosened breasts. I dream of pulling you to the bed and removing your gown, right now."

With a sultry voice she stepped closer, "No need to dream." Will lay his pipe in the dish beside hers and moved to her.

Then he began to loosen the neckline so the gown could fall at her feet.

Sarah had a summer cold for about a week. Yet, she expected to feel better soon. When school ended the family went to the small, temporary cabin in Gettysburg for a few days. William Wallace was happy and went off on the prairie exploring and Mae read.

Not feeling at all well, Sarah went to bed. On Monday, William went five miles away to Hill City on more of the county seat business. In late afternoon, he heard a pounding on his office door.

He found his sweaty, overheated teenage son, "Father, come now! When I returned from fishing mother had become very ill. She did not know who I was. I am afraid." William was shocked. Holding his son's shoulder he gasped, "I will go right now. You must find a doctor and bring him to the cabin immediately! Hurry!"

When Will arrived Sarah was alive but breathing with great difficulty, she did not even know he was there. Three hours later his son and the Doctor arrived and administered a great deal of morphine to relieve her. It was too late.

In June of 1881 William Hunter buried his 39-year-old wife in Hill City. Beside the grave stood his ashen children. His daughter had a swollen face and red eyes and the young man was trying to be an unfeeling stone. The whole of that service and burial was like a blur to the family.

The election for the county seat on the Twenty-fifth of July in 1881 had been a disaster. The opposition in Graham County hired nonresidents to vote. They did not take the oath of office. The votes were kept in public room with no lock. The election judge was absent a number of times. The 823 votes named Millbrook the winner and Hill City lost its bid to become the county seat.

Will was named realtor to represent the Hill City against N.J. Hardin; C. Fountain; Willis Ellsworth*; S.M.Smith; H. Masters and O.C. Nevins in court. His scheduled appearances, interviews and preparing documents began to take much of his time. The county was trying to find a hearing in court that proved the election was fraudulent.**

In July, when no one else could go to court, he had to write the documents and attend to the proceedings. In a fog of grief he appeared at the bench for over a month to plead the case as plaintiff or realtor representing Hill City. Hollow and worn he struggled to do his wounded best but Hill City lost. Millbrook had become the county seat of Graham County.[2]

Alone with his children the middle-aged man mourned and remembered his beloved wife who was taken so suddenly. About six months after her death he wrote this poem and sent it to *The New York Sun* where it was published:

PASS UNDER THE ROD

I saw a young bride, in her beauty and pride, bedecked in her bridal array.
And the bright flush of joy mantled high on her cheeks,
And the future looked shining and gay.
And with woman's devotion, she had laid her warm heart.
At the shrine of idolatrous love;

**Willis Ellsworth became active in Gettysburg. In November 1883 he ran for sheriff there. Two men disagreed about his candidacy and in true 'western' custom they pulled guns and each suffered serious wounds. Bounty was offered and a hanging rope purchased. One man was arrested for his own protection.*
*** The town of Millbrook was blown away in a storm and eventually Hill City became the county seat of Graham County and Gettysburg became a ghost town.*

She had anchored her hope to the perishing earth,
By the claim which her tenderness wove.
But I saw when those heartstrings were bleeding and torn,
And the chain had been severed in two.
She had changed her white robe for the sable of grief.
And her bloom, for the paleness of woe,'
but the Healer was there, pouring balm on her heart
and wiping the tears from her eyes;
and He bade her look up from this perishing earth,
And fasten her love in the skies.
There had whispered a voice, 'twas the voice of her God,
I love thee, I love thee.
Pass under the rod

I saw a young mother in tenderness bend,
o'er the couch of her slumbering boy.
And she kissed the soft lips as they murmured her name,
while the dreamer lay smiling in joy.
Oh, sweet as a rosebud encircled with dew,
When its' fragrance is flung to the air.
So fresh and so sweet, to that mother he seemed,
As he lay in innocence there.
But I saw when she gazed on that same lovely form,
Pale as marble, and silent, and cold:
But paler and colder, her beautiful boy.
And the tale of her sorrow was told.
But the Healer was there who had stricken her heart,
And taken her treasure away,
To allure her to heaven. He had placed it on high,
And the mourner will sweetly obey.
There had whispered a voice, 'twas the voice of her God,
I love thee, I love thee,
Pass under the rod.

I saw, too, a father and mother,
who leaned on the arm of their dear gifted son,
And the bright star of hope glittered bright to their gaze,
when they saw the proud place he had won;
And the fast coming evening of life promised fair,
And the future grew smooth to their feet.
And the starlight of love glittered bright in the end,
And the whispers of fancy were sweet.

But I saw them again, bending low o're a grave.
Where their hearts' dearest hopes had been laid,
And the star had gone down in the darkness of night
And the joy from their bosoms had fled
And the Healer was there and his arms opened wide,
And He showed them a start
As he led them with tendered care,
And He showed them a star in the bright upper world,
'Twas their star shining brightly there.
They had each heard a voice, 'twas the voice of their God
I love thee, I love thee
Pass under the rod,
*Captain William H. Hunter*[42].

## Chapter 19

# Lincoln

*How do I remember the days after the funeral?* The heat was unbearable, as was the howling, dry wind. That was a dreary time in Kansas, with those winds only adding to my pain. My major feeling was emptiness. The very idea that I could ever loose my beloved Sarah had just been impossible to imagine. I would sit for hours empty and lost.

The whole thing about the fight for the county seat that next month would pull me to my feet, but I was only a shadow man—not a whole one. The crop of wheat came ripe, it seemed almost overnight, and I had no energy or direction. If my neighbors had not come to my rescue, I am not sure I would have been able to carry on. They helped me harvest as the families of this prairie do, for they are a people of generous spirit.

My children needed me, so with compassion for them and the responsibility to minister to the two, I would reach out to them. Yet the hollowness of my heart, I fear, kept us far distant from each other, each of us were suffering in our own way.

William Wallace became more sullen and quiet. As with all boys his age, anger would erupt suddenly into fistfights. He would be punished for whipping a horse, or I would hear him crushing a toy he owned from his childish past. The battle with William Wallace about attending school was endless for many of his friends had left school and he also wanted to quit. He hated school.

My dear Mae would sit long hours reading or simply lay limp in my arms after supper while we rocked. I saw her cry but seldom, yet there was hollowness to her also, an empty expression in her eyes. I was grateful for the special attention Mary tenderly shared with Mae and hoped the women somehow could help each other heal better. I was unable to provide solace. The care and providing given by Mary was the only consistent and efficient means of keeping us alive and comfortable.

*How does grief resolve?* I do not know, it is just that after a very long time a lonely widower can finally feel like he can take a full breath once more. Around Christmas there was a church supper. Our small family had attended the program, for Mae was to perform as an angel in the tableau. William Wallace had resisted attendance at the small white frame church. Now, this Christmas pageant was quite distasteful to the teenager for "that was for babies and sissies." The play had wistful charm as the congregation and community again remembered the story of the birth of the Christ child. Then there was group singing.

When we repaired to the basement hall to have sandwiches and desserts after the performance I moved through the line visiting with neighbors. I took some chocolate cake with a huge dollop of whipped cream, a heavy white cup of steaming coffee and a ham sandwich then went to a long crowded table to eat. The room was almost entirely full; the jesting, eating and talk were robust and jovial. Gradually, in the next hour, most of the other celebrants left for other conversations or to take small ones home, until there were only three or four of us left at the table.

One of the ladies remaining at the table was the Stone girl, an unmarried young woman. I saw her brother Robert come to whisper into her ear, she looked up with a smile and nodded. I thought little of this as it came to pass. A bit later I gathered Mae and the plate that Mary had sent with cookies. These cookies were now only a couple crumbs. After I found our silver and dirty dishes, I started for the door stopping frequently to visit with neighbors and as I conversed I saw the Stone woman squeeze past some visitors and up the staircase to exit the church basement.

Finally, Mae and I were snugly bundled into coats, mittens and scarves. Much earlier, William Wallace had departed with his comrades. The young men were much bored with such events. We climbed the stairs, then passing through the doors into to the bitter cold we moved to where the carriages were waiting. I placed Mae and our bundle into our carriage and walked to the other side to climb up. As I did so I noticed not far away several men were examining a carriage wheel and Miss Stone was beside them. She stood, stamping her feet against the cold. When I joined them, I also squatted beside the other fellows to examine the wheel's hub.

Miss Stone was somewhat nonplused. She stared with distress at the wheel "Robert has gone and I do not know how I will contact him."

"Do not be concerned," I responded " I will see you home and Robert can see to this wheel tomorrow. I do not believe that it would be wise to travel with the large crack in the hub of the wheel," I spoke without looking up, glad to be of any service. Rising, I smiled and looked the small woman in the eye.

"Thank you," she responded with relieved gratitude.

We walked together around to the side of her carriage where she retrieved her own dishes; these I took from her. The pony that had pulled her vehicle I loosed and tethered to the back of my own carriage. I loaded her things onto the floorboard beside our own tea towel wrapped bundle and helped her up to sit beside Mae. Taking a buffalo robe I tucked it about the laps of the woman and girl. Smiling up and nodding, I went to the driver's side and mounted. Clicking to the horse we started down the road to the Stone house where she lived with her father and family.

"Miss Stone," as a courtesy I began, prepared to make light conversation.

She interrupted, "Mr. Hunter, do call me Annie."

I smiled and nodded, "Annie, did you enjoy the evening?"

With real enthusiasm she responded, "Oh most certainly, it is so good to be among the community. Oh my, how I love to see the children perform," pausing she looked down at Mae. "You did an excellent job, your performance was lovely." Laughing out loud she continued, "In the program, I dearly love the charming way the smallest of the children do their part. They say things that were never written for the play, go to wrong positions, all the while doing their best with excitement and pleasure. They are so innocent and guileless, just pure innocence"

I mumbled an agreement. Then in the moonlight we trotted down the sparkling, snowy roadway. The chill was making the snow squeak beneath the wheels, and the moon effected the entire scene to have a blue caste. I was filled with calm. We only rode along in quiet, and then I glanced over to see that Mae had fallen asleep against Annie's shoulder. A peace descended on me that I had not known since Sarah had died. It was a calm that felt like safety.

It was not far to the Stone house which they had built when they migrated from Kentucky. When we arrived, I helped the woman down, and lifting her things out, we walked together to the door and I handed her the dinnerware. She once again thanked me and entered the house. I untied her horse and led it to the barn where I secured it for the night. Finally, in the middle of the night with my sleeping daughter almost hidden under the heavy hide blanket and I found the road to our own farm.

That night when I stood at the dresser loosening my collar buttons, I mulled the events of the evening. *Annie, that is a nice name.*

Looking down I saw the saucer on the marble top of the dresser. There were two pipes lying there, for I had not moved them since the last night Sarah and I had made love. I knocked the ashes from each, and then carefully lay them in a drawer under some clean clothing. The loneliness was so painful, my children needed to continue with life. Perhaps, I too could find the courage to begin again. The emotion and security I had felt on the ride to the Stones with Annie had wakened my need for companionship.

The Gettysburg development was going slowly and my heart was not in the project anymore. Farming occupied me but only as a responsibility for my heart was not in it either and my physical conditions caused much discomfort. My son was not as cooperative as I wished he were on the farm. The political rejections and problems had all but defeated me.

My courtship of Annie E. Stone was decorous and lasted over a year. In the beginning it was hard to keep my balance. I would take such pleasure in her company then my grief and guilt would resurface. The tension and difficulty of my first courtship had been so dramatic. My romance with Annie was gentle and cheerful and pleasing.

Mae was quietly accepting of our friendship but William Wallace was more than a little disapproving of my relationship. Several times he was rude to Annie or made cutting remarks to me. He would not attend school any longer and was often unaccounted for, sometimes even for several days. Young men in their teenage years are often of this ilk.

After I proposed, but before we married, my son announced that he was leaving. The cattle drives to and from Hayes, Kansas, which was in our near vicinity, were a strong lure to boys and single men . He left home when he was seventeen to become a cowboy. This would take him from the Mexican border to Arizona, New Mexico and Colorado. When he passed through Kansas I saw him several times.

Sorrowfully, he was poor about letter writing and I was pleased when he eventually settled on thirty acres near North Platte, Nebraska he had received as a homestead there and then he added other land to this by purchase.

In June of 1883, my 76-year-old mother died just after her birthday. She was buried in Carroll County, Illinois. My father was ailing and becoming more vague. Henry Clay was experiencing serious emotional problems. The family supposed the foundry had exposed him to far too many chemicals. I could feel my ties to Illinois being severed, another part to the past that was being left behind.[34]

Annie and I were married January 8, 1883 in Millbrook, Kansas. When we married she was 29 years old and I was 46. The marriage to this dear lady was a great comfort to me. Her youth, sprightly appearance and energy inspired me to have the courage to move on with my life, leaving Kansas behind to make new beginnings. Soon after our marriage we sold out and moved to Nebraska. Our first stop was brief, I managed a hotel in Franklin, Nebraska.

At just about that time I felt a yearning to move on to find a new life and home, and I received a letter from John Cadwallader. We only corresponded a couple of times a year. I had written not long before to tell him of my new bride and leaving Kansas. At that time I also told him I was also thinking to escape memories of Sarah that this region inspired in me.

At the end of the letter, John with his dry wit, suggested that when I pulled the wagon out of the circle on the Kansas prairie I might consider heading for Lincoln, Nebraska. Then he went onto praise the prosperous, small city.

We moved to Lincoln in 1884. In 1890, I worked briefly at a hotel across from the railroad station. We had first moved to 2383 "0" Street and then to "Q" Street. I bought property in Lincoln from Robert Hunter and wife. We moved in 1897 to 27th and Randolph Streets.

We are now living in a small home at 29th and F Street. Buying or renting lodgings and moving about the city fed my restless nature. The resources to live with the necessities, although modest, were adequate because of the sale of the Kansas property and my pension. On occasion I also help on some farms, especially at harvest and planting but have not been forced to take full employment. Labor is difficult as old physical ailments I earned in the war continue to painfully trouble me.

This lifestyle gives me freedom to be active in the community even until today. Most of my days I move about the town speaking with friends, and often drop in at the state house to speak with legislatures of the unicameral about issues of concern to me. The draw of government seems to have crept upon me again.

With foolish egotism and good intentions, I had thrown my hat in the political ring in 1884 when I first arrived. Although a newcomer to the city, I ran for police judge on the platform "my reputation is my bank account I shall execute...my duties." Regretfully, the election counted me out with my own 636 votes to Frank R. Water's 2,796 and H.S. Whitmore's 1,574.

Some of the things that were dear to my heart I have been able to accomplish in the state. I sought and succeeded in changing the name of the "School Boys' Reformatory" in Kearney to a more charitable and optimistic one. They will be called "The Boys' Military and Training School" so that the young men will not carry the stain of reform school into adult life.

The state of Tennessee had sent Nebraska a fine piece of marble, for the purpose of creating a statue of this noble stone representing Abraham

Lincoln, the city namesake. I have worked tirelessly for the creation and installation of that statue in the Capital. Hopefully, it will someday come to fruition.

One of my most proud efforts was in 1897. In April 11, in the issue of the *State Journal* on page ten was a heart-wrenching story titled, *Negroes Need Relief,* the article summarized 13,400 Negroes at Vicksburg, without means—must have help. A flood of an unparalleled 50 feet 4 inches had rushed down river. Levies were destroyed, all the way to New Orleans. Many of the fleeing Negroes had lived on those flood plains. The disaster was devastating. I was been greatly haunted remembering the Kraal and the wandering, contraband Negroes.

I sought out and strongly perused the emergency support by the Nebraska House of Representatives for State of Mississippi. The need of Mississippi was desperate and immediate. Mayor Benbrook forwarded my letter to the paper that published the article and called me "the noble man we take this gentleman to be."

"HOUSE OF REPRESENTATIVES, LINCOLN NE., APRIL, 10, 1897.

To His Honor the Mayor of the City of Natchez Mississippi.

Dear Sir:

Deeply sympathizing with the unfortunate sufferers of the overflowed districts of the South, I desire to do my part to relieve their wants. Should you have need of food or clothing or both, in your vicinity you will do me the favor to inform me of that fact at once. Having spent many happy days in your city during the war, I can but feel great concern for the many whose names I now recall, and whose memory I cherish. For those and all others who need help I would feel that I had fallen far short of my duty to my fellow man should I fail to render all the assistance in my power. In this I am prompted by love for my deceased wife, who was born and raised in your beautiful city, and by the gratitude and kind remembrance of many of your generous-hearted people in that land of flowers and refined hospitality.

Kindly yours,

W.H. Hunter"[43]

Ever since my time in Kansas, I had been actively pursuing the U.S. Government for an increase in my pension because of my poor physical condition. During this time, I persisted to apply for a disability from the army. The many years I have been occupied with this pursuit, although to no avail at this point.

In my search for justice and aid I solicited testimony from many who knew me in my adult life or at war. Edwin Hobart wrote from Cedar Rapids, Iowa where he was a local freight agent for the Burlington Railroad. My brother, Henry Clay, testified. He was employed by the county in Savannah, Illinois. He had made a permanent home there.

Doctors and pharmacists or friends in Floyd County, Charles City, Spencer and Shelby, Iowa responded; telling of the continual duty I had in the saddle at Natchez or of their knowledge of my health condition. Letters supporting my request arrived from Salem, Minneapolis, Gettysburg and Millbrook, Kansas. Those from Lincoln also supported my claim. The source of all of these were either from previous homes or where old companions now lived.

My daughter Mae briefly worked in our fair capital city as a stenographer before her marriage to Edward Speer. Annie was ever at my side. I drank not at all, smoked only a little. It is said that I am known as a 'man about town.'[43] Hopefully, this refers to my involvement in political and social interests. I must admit that I did take some ribbing from friends and a pretense of jealousy from Annie.

The letters from family in Illinois now spoke of the children and grandchildren of my brothers and sisters. There was always news or gossip of families I knew in my youth from Wysox Township, Elk Grove and Mount Carroll and the families I knew in my youth.

The veterans of the War of the Rebellion had named Carroll County veteran's organization after Adam Nance who was now a hero and had returned to become a successful businessman in nearby Savannah. He then became a state political personage. In 1891, the city and veterans constructed a tall monument in front of the courthouses on the square, near the hotel where I had been a postwar innkeeper. Henry Clay had attended the dedication of the monument and recounted the battles of the Fifteenth Illinois Infantry at this most pretentious event. The monument named these battles. This statue stood on the court house lawn.

Now, as my life nears an end, I can but meditate on the many locals and adventures with which my life has been filled. I have had a fine family, bold comrades, and two wonderful women to love. I have sired and raised successful children.

Today as I am rocking I read the newspaper. One of several of my favorite poems that I have penned has been published. I read it with pride and am reminded of the war in the Philippines which is challenging our nation now.

Jan 17, 1899, *The Nebraska Post*

DEWEY AND BRAVE SCHLEY
*Dedicated to our Yankee monarchs of the sea,*
*by Captain W.H. Hunter of Lincoln, Neb.*

Neath the guns of proud old Moro
The mighty Oregon lay,
With brave Clark and his gallant crew
Waiting longing for the fray

And just as day was dawning,
While yet, it was not day
The Brooklyn signaled warning
The Spanish come from the bay

Fighting Bob on board the Iowa
Through hid trumpet loud did tell
Boys, we'll send those Spaniards
To the bottom or to hell.

Then o'er the waves went rushing
Like maddened bull to fray.
Went fighting Bobs to glory
As the Spanish left the Bay

On came the mighty Oregon,
Brave Clark and noble crew,
When Admiral Schley gave orders
For the work that Clark should do.

Crowd team on every engine,
That proud Spaniard overtake,
Then flew the mighty Oregon,
In the Colon's seething wake.

From the guns of the mighty Oregon
Like lightning went her shell,
While the Iowa and the Brooklyn
Sang the haughty dons' death knell.

Straining her mighty engines
The wide wild sea to reach.
When a shell from off the Oregon
Sent proud Colon on the beach

From her decks came back defiance
As her colors, they went down.

While amid the deafening uproar
A thousand souls were drowned

To Wainwright, Clark and Evans.
And all were in the fray.
Let praises sound forever
And horror brave old Schley

No matter what cheap jingoes
May say of this great fight
The glory give to gallant Schley,
For Sampson out of sight.

Now what about those islands?
Let truth, prompt all to say.
For they never would have been taken but
For Dewey and brave Schley

And when God shall gather jewels
For heavens best display
I know some niche in glory
Will be of Dewey and brave Schley.[43]

The *Nebraska Blizzard* had also published my tribute to Dewey's victory on December 30th, then another ode. Every time I read my published work I am even more inspired to spend more time writing *The Sinking of the Maine* had prompted another piece. Included within was deepest comfort and sentiment to the families.

"Beloved mothers of our nation will sing their sad refrain
For dear ones lying neath the waves,
Gone down with gallant Maine
But thousands more can well rejoice
And to their children tell how Dewey, Schley
And Shafter sent Spaniards down to Hell"

The incident at Manila Bay had raised every battle fire that I had so long ago forgotten. I was fired by patriotism when I penned this poem. It was with pride and satisfaction I read the paper, which had published it. As my health was keeping me home more, as did the Nebraska winters I was more and more writing poetry. I was considering creating a diary to leave for my descendants.

Five days later, I began that diary for my posterity opening with the following introduction,

"LINCOLN NEBRASKA JANUARY 22ND, 1899.

This record of songs and important matters and events begins with the above date, and is designed as an heirloom of the house of Hunter. Arch [first grandson of William Wallace] at the death of the writer, here of this book shall become the property of the oldest lineal descendent of yours.

Residence 27th and Randolph Street, Lincoln, Nebraska"

Thinking about the nature and value of the diary I added:

"To you dear reader these words are given
Steal this book and you'll never reach heaven
And this is why these words I tell
My friend to keep you out of hell
Yours, Capt W.H. Hunter"

The same day, on the next page I placed a greeting:

"As a matter of future reference, these lines art written.

The writer hereof was born in Union county, State of Indiana August 20, 1836, the year of the great fall of the stars and of which the writer was supposed to be one. I have thought upon that question. History nor the family appears to be entirely clear. My ancestry is somewhere between the war of the rebellion and the flood? I am suffered to be French on the male line and Irish and Scotch on the female line. I was raised to manhood in Carroll County, Illinois at Elkhorn Grove. Enlisted in Company K 15th in April 1861.

I have two discharges, one from Company K of the 15th Illinois Infantry as a private. One from the 58th U.S. Colored Volunteers as Captain these discharges are made a matter of record by the court auditor of Floyd County, Iowa."

I wrote late into the afternoon, remembering war comrades, this ode later became a song.

"IN MEMORY OF OUR HEROES

A tribute of memory dedicated to our Yankee heroes whose courage, loyalty and heroism on land and sea has caused gelded tyrants of despotic lands to tremble for the welfare and safety of their gold cursed blood stained brown while millions of their persecuted subjects shout with joy their new found liberty. As the shackles drop from serf and slave above the din and uproar of shouting.

Slaves and crumbling dynasties beyond the reach of tyrant's hands float in strength majesty and glory. That tricolored youth ordained emblem the starts and stripes of free America, bearing upon its gilded crests. Peace on earth, good will to man.

Gleaming from her fruitful folds that heaven born principle equal rights for all. Special privileges to none, the freeman's joy the tyrants woe. Our never lowering. Never failing ever cheering banner of liberty and justice. Made sacred by the blood of the brave, who's deeds and sacrifices are rounding out in a manner well worthy, the prayers and plaudits of a grateful, loyal, and illustrious nation. The most remarkable and glorious century of all past time and as a boon of right was justice is our gallant heroes living and dead let all one whose heads the shadows of the memorable 19th century will soon close, from for our defenders in memory's casket –basket. Their richest pearls."

I then penned another ode to their glory.[42]

I had been reading most of the evening, now I glanced over my shoulder. Annie, a tiny brunette woman with the beginnings of grey in her hair, was sitting near a lamp. She was rocking and her knitting needles were flying like the dance of a drunken spider.

"I want to share a document I have found, Annie." She nodded toward me and set her needles to rest.

"I read that the first Black men came in 1600 to Virginia as indentured servants and others soon began to come in huge numbers as slaves. Negroes were brought to this continent between 1442–1880. There were eventually over 200,000,000. Of those who survived, over half died in the Caribbean and South America in the 'seasoning' to prepare them for their new lives."

"It took up to six months to get a full ship of captives. They were entrapped in numerous ways like tempting them onto the ships with trade goods or bartering for captives or attacking small villages. Only 13 of each 100 of those captured survived the trip on ships. In water shortages, manacled people were thrown overboard in numbers that rose up to 500 at a time. Most of the people were between 16-30 years of age but many were children, or older people."[44]

"I wonder at the tragedy, it is beyond imagination. Yes, Annie, I painfully wonder of the condition today of the men who served under me. Many of those who won their freedom in the Revolution earned the dignity to pass on to their families. They became self-emancipators as soldiers to earn their freedom. My heart aches for the lack of the vote, for the indentureships of sharecropping which they still suffer. Did mine and other's efforts and intent in the war come to naught?"

"When I was downtown in Lincoln this week there were hundreds of Colored faces near the train depot and around the warehouses. They lounge and hope for work. A few have gone to farms as labor or have acquired small farms of their own. There are many in Western Nebraska as buffalo soldiers or cowboys. Most, controlled by the economy and lack of skill, simply lounge, waiting for work, sleeping on the ground at night or fed by the churches and begging. I never stop looking at the faces there to see if any of the men are soldiers I knew in Natchez."

"Women of Color are working in houses and factories but the men seem threatening to White employers except in lowly positions or manual labor. My heart breaks, and I feel concern for those I learned to respect during those years in Mississippi. It is so repulsive that no matter how these people defend or support their own needs it is not sufficient. My desires for them are as ineffective as their own."

"Annie, I was discussing this situation with William Bryant. He spoke of his many travels for the silver issue. He said the employment of Negroes seems to be even worse in the East and South, where the Blacks unable to get any foot hold. The little I was able to do after the flooding, for homelessness and sickness in Mississippi had no lasting hope, and were just a brief reprieve. In Natchez, I learned a respect for the African's courage, loyalty to family and the very manhood they had earned. It became my dream that they would become more than free."

Annie sat looking at Will considering the conversation. It was amazing to her. The book he was reading must have raised a passion, for she had never heard him speak at length on the subject before. He had been quite private about his service in the Colored corp.

"Thirty years and still Negroes are a lost tribe." Pensively, William became quiet. That night he said little more, he just rocked and stared into the gas fire. His mind was a million miles away, perhaps she thought later, he was preparing for the longest journey.

John Cadwallder and I would frequently meet at a café near the rail station in the Old Haymarket. Our discussion was usually of politics and the State of Nebraska. We were both active and living well enough. He was single and living in rented rooms, but quite comfortable and usually employed.

We occasionally see the several enlisted Colored veterans who live in the area. Their struggles are continual. These men were not stationed with us but we must assume our troops are in the same condition. Neither of us are willing to be closely involved in the veterans' groups in the city. The majority of those groups feel no real empathy with the Colored troops. This leaves both of us with a sense of personal rejection and even some feeling of failure.

Although I have been active locally and nationally in all aspects of veterans' needs and rights, I have kept some space between the veterans who are biased and negate the power or importance of the Colored troops in the great conflict.

One day I received this request that was being circulated among the veterans. Receiving the pledge, I signed. It was "an agreement to stand by President McKinley and the Congress of the United States in all lawful demands for a redress of wrongs committed against our government.[45] In my thought were also my own needs. 'Let congress pass that bill allowing old soldiers to keep their pensions and very man that is able to walk will go.'[46]

Immediately I walked to the state capital and sought out Representative Elmer Jacob Burkett, as I knew he was in Lincoln this week. The honorable Mr. Burkett was in his 60s he had been born in Iowa in Lincoln he had been a successful lawyer and as a Republican was serving in the House in Washington, D, C. He was a person with whom I hoped to find some support in the pension issue and now also the support of this war.

The task took most of the day because the honorable gentleman was being approached by all manner of people with concerns of a wide variety. I thus needed to wait some time but his interest and sincerity on both the war and the failure of various pensions were most reassuring.

The newspapers or letters from other officers of the Colored troops far too often brought Cadwallader and I news of the tragedies. There had been less than 2,000 White officers in the Civil War. An alarming number of us came to no good end. There was a higher rate of suicide than from other military branches. Many simply drank themselves to death. [16]

One day we looked into the other's eyes and admitted how despondent we both were. With the coffee growing cold we admitted, as though in a confessional, how our shame had grown over the last thirty-six years. After far too many years of insult for the role we took, we both had finally stopped telling anyone of our assignments to the Black troops.

After the omission of Black troops in the triumphal march at the end of the war in Washington, our illusions began to melt. The downhill-race of the treatment of these families and men of Color that we had learned to respect, and indeed, love, well, I guess you could say we suffered from depression and could understand our fellows self-destruction. The welled anger at our nation was a bitter brew. We were unsure of our acceptance. We felt fear and expectations of rejection. For us the history of the United States Colored Troops was a closed and locked door.

Negroes got voting rights, but it did not always work that way. Many communities will not allow them to own land or property and they are still thrown about—homeless, and thus nonvoters.

While in Lincoln, I had developed a respectful acquaintance with William Jennings Bryan. He was a staunch Methodist whose social life circulated within the members of his own congregation. His loyalty influenced my own faith practice within the Presbyterian Church.

Bryan was at the center of the Populist Party that sought social and economic reforms to curb the power of the wealthy and benefit agriculture. They worked with some labor unions. This party was a strong third party in the nation. He aspired for his party and also for himself, the Presidency.

Of special interest to my friend was the silver issue. He wanted to change the government from a base of gold to silver. In this cause, he traveled continually. At one point he had even attempted to buy Thomas Jefferson's home, Monticello. He thought it would make a fine symbolic base for the movement as Nebraska's own, William Jennings Bryan, ran for the Presidency.

All of these things he espoused alarmed big business and they rallied behind McKinley. In the 1896 election, Bryan had carried 176 electoral votes and made a strong showing in popular votes, but McKinley was elected.

"One of the strange humorous things that occurred to William. Bryan was the children's book, *The Wizard of OZ*. When this tale was spun the public accused the author, L. Frank Baum, who was deeply Populous Party, for parodying that party's leadership. Pals would tease Bryan that he was—in fact—the Cowardly Lion, all bark and no bite." [47]

Not long ago in January 1901 Bryan began to publish *The Commoner*, his own newspaper in Lincoln. The publication was much enriched by his political views and the strong reporting of the international news. I had hoped he would publish some of my poems, but since that was not his venue he did not.

My friendship and respect for his brilliance and his loyal friendship had inspired me to write an ode for him not very long ago. This was presented as his campaign ballad.

"POP SOLILOQUY

Standing on his promise we all can see how our country shall have liberty.

Fighting for our fine life by Byron made free

Chorus,
Standing on the promise of Bryan standing on the honesty Bryan's work bound to him forever by birnetarie cord
Overcoming duty by the flaming sword.
Stand on the promises of Bryan
Standing on his promises we cannot fall, Nebraska and the white house we're going to have it all
While we're standing on the promises of Bryan."

Whenever I would read Annie any of my work she was kind and interested. I realized that often the political or military nature might be of less interest to her, but she was always supportive. One of the occasions that I wrote something funny was as a thank you to the Fox family who had invited us over for dinner, only to have plans go awry.

Animatedly, I said, "I have written something, may I read it to you? Remember the Christmas dinner at the Fox's house?"

With a chuckle, Anna winked, "Yes, I know you have been writing something light hearted for you have been laughing to yourself for two days now."

I proceeded:

"Foxes have holes, the birds have nests
I have but kicks and knocks
But thank the lord, I'm happy
When I can dine with Fox

Of riches he is not much blessed
But gives his bounties free
And when ol Xmas comes around
You bet, Fox just suits me.

His latch strings on the outside
Where all his friends can pull
And those who fail to pull it-
Are simply badly fooled

There Foxes on the hill side
Their plans are always fixen
And when they don't have turkey
You're welcome to their chicken.
Alas for those who gather there
On this day of good luck

Turkey not chicken such the either

But oh yes, oh that duck
When old Fox wanted chicken
The Mrs. Fox but duck.

What home is blessed
Where women rule
Lord bring to them good luck

When about cared for wind or storm
On the world's hard kicks and knocks
All there I'll bear the joys to share
Of eating duck with Fox

The Foxes praises I will sing
on them I'm somewhat stuck
Tho nearly not so badly
As on that luscious duck

The Foxes may their lives be long
And filled with naught but luck
In stuffing of their purse with gold
As they stuffed that old duck

Perhaps we ought remember
That on this Christmas day
A friend there was among us
Who came from far away.

The home I'll long remember,
As long as that of Fox
For like the writer that one has
Her share of kicks and knocks

Unlike their generous Foxes
She could not play their part
But long in memory I will keep
The giver of that book mark"

"Do you think it might offend them?" asked Annie. "They are such dear people, some of my favorites, so kind, cheerful and gentle."

"I had thought dear, well, that this poem might be a thank you gift."

I looked to Annie for her opinion of the meal where Fox was forced to eat duck against his will. The strangers at their table had been so hilariously bewildered.

Annie nodded her head vigorously. “No, don't you dare give them that poem. No married couple chooses to remember disagreement between them, nor coming up short of food for unexpected guests.”

I took her advice.

In May of 1901, William Hunter's health seriously deteriorated. This condition demanded that a doctor attend him each day. From either his prostate or the piles he had suffered ever since the war.

By November, his condition had worsened until his death was eminent, the hemorrhoids had broken into his bowels.. William Jennings Bryan and Congressman Burkett sat, at his bedside, until the grim reaper released him from the terrible pain of the resulting kidney failure that even laudanum could not relieve.

On November 19, 1901 William died.

Because of his popularity in the community the service at the Second Presbyterian Church was well attended. Reverend Mr. Hindman officiated and offered an eloquent sermon. The reverend had, not so long ago, baptized him after William's strong faith conversion. The ladies of the Grand Army of the Republic Custer Circle rendered a beautiful flag service in commemoration of the fallen soldier

His burial was in the beautiful Wyuka Cemetery in Lincoln. He was laid in the cemetery in the Grand Army of the Republic circle. It had been dedicated the first day of December in 1860. The location of his rest is on the northeast outer border of the circle, beneath a headstone with name and service record in the Civil War. The circle is the final location of the Grand Army of the Republic veterans of the near area. The tall statue of a Union Soldier stands just to the south of his resting place.

William Bryan, Congressman Burkett, John Cadwallader and numerous Nebraska legislators all attended the burial. Where William lay, he joined several veterans of the Colored troops and would eventually be joined by others.[9]

William Wallace Hunter's family came to the funeral. William Wallace, his son, came from North Platte with his wife Dora Mae Welsh Hunter, they brought their four small sons; Edmond Hugh, age nine; Ray Mattson, age eight; Archie Oliver age five; and Charles Henry, who was two. They had lost a child, Francis Gordon, the year before. Walter Harold would be born the next year, and Drucilla Inez would be born in 1904.

Francis Gordon died at one year of age. Dora had died in July 1908, a month after Francis was born. When William Wallace married again it was to Joanna Rebecca Williams whose maiden name was Masters. They were the parents of Florence Rita who was born in 1914.

William's daughter, Mae was now Mrs. Edward M. Speer and they arrived from Normal, Illinois. His children had come to comfort their stepmother, Anna.

Captain W. H. Hunter's obituary read:

> "William Hughes Hunter was born at Liberty, Ind., August 20, 1836, and died at Lincoln, Neb., November 19, 1901, aged sixty-five years. Captain Hunter was educated in the common schools of Carroll county Ill., where his parents removed when he was only a year old. In 1869 he went with a party to Pike's peak, returning to Illinois to enlist among those who first responded to the call to arms in defense of his country. His service was rewarded by promotion by President Lincoln for meritorious conduct when he was commissioned captain in which position he served to the close of the war, and for one year after during the reconstruction period, not being mustered out until 1866. His record as a soldier was of the best and he will long be remembered as a brave and gallant officer, who never shirked a duty or turned his back to a foe.
>
> At the close of the war he was married to Sarah D. Scothorne, of Natchez, Mississippi, and to them two children were born. Returning north, Captain Hunter engaged in farming and hotel keeping in northern Iowa, and later removed to Graham county, Kansas where he was prominent in business and political circles. It was here his wife died in 1880. A few years later the captain removed to Lincoln, where he has since resided until his death. He was married to his surviving widow, Miss Anna Stone, in 1882. During his residence in Lincoln, Captain Hunter has been identified with many movements of a meritorious character, having devoted much hard work and time to raising funds and provisions for the western sufferers a few years ago and he will always be remembered as possessing a kindly heart, generous to a degree, and absolutely indifferent to self when there was suffering or distress to be relieved. His cheerful, genial nature endeared him to the hearts of a large circle of friends and neighbors, who turned out to pay a last tribute of respect to his memory. His was a brave and chivalrous spirit, not easily daunted, and while not free from faults, his life and example will prove of value to posterity. His last days were cheered by constant visits from old comrades and friends. Of the latter Congressman Burkett and Colonel Bryan were among the last to soothe his dying moments.

The funeral was held on Thursday afternoon from the Second Presbyterian church, Rev. M. Hindman preaching an eloquent sermon in tribute to his memory, while the ladies of Custer circle rendered the beautiful flag service in commemoration of the fallen soldier, and at the grave the soldiers of the Grand Army of the Republic paid a final tribute of respect, when the remains were tenderly laid away in the circle set apart for the burial of old soldiers.

Of his immediate family Captain Hunter leaves a wife, a son, W.W. Hunter of North Platte, and a daughter, Mrs. E.M. Speer of Normal, Ill.

Captain Hunter enlisted as a private in Company K, Fifteenth Illinois, and was promoted to the captaincy of Company K, Fifty-eighth Colored volunteers.

Captain Hunter experienced religion toward the close of his life and made a free and joyful profession of the same to all who came near. Doctor Hindman of the First Presbyterian church, baptizing him. Mr. Hunter believed in old fashioned religion that makes the soul happy and enjoyed it."[43]

As Annie later went through his possessions she read his diary. The book had been an attorney's date book before William had taken possession of it. He had made it his last testament. Previously Annie had been too respectful of his privacy to read this book. There was a tribute for her in the book. "I married the best woman God ever made, and thank God I got her still." [42]

Anna lived a solitary life for the next twenty-four years. Eventually she became a resident of the Soldiers and Sailors Home in Milford, Nebraska, a small town west of Lincoln. She died there October 13, 1923. Her step-grandson, Walter Hunter, living in Lincoln, at 2735 Sumner Street, was called to care for her affairs. In her will she listed her brother, Robert Stone, of Abilene, Kansas; John; James; and Mary A. Speer, age 57 of Hayes, Kansas. Annie had a sister in Des Moines, Iowa, who was a Reynolds, Dora Martin of Plainsville, Kansas and three other unknown sisters.

The final door of the passage of a generation closed.

# Chapter 20
# September

The quilt of past, present, and future is formed by ten fathers, and mothers, ten births and nine deaths, as the river of time flows eternally. Wars of unbelievable horror, waves of self-serving greed, and replacement of worship and culture by shopping and possessions. The nation has substituted all with machines, pills and frenzied buying. These are the overriding addictive hungers of our society.

People swarm at our borders to enter this verdant land while one people stand uneasily full of rights—yet void of rights or dignity. These are a people whose ancestors came here involuntarily but who helped build and protect the nation. Their attempts to build their own society or to fit well into the existing one wax and wane, usually because of fear or ignorance. These people too often remain standing on the fringe.

The country's opinions and values sway on a mysterious decade timer from conservative to liberal. Is this truly a better New World? We enter hospitals knowing more children will survive. Yet, outside the hospitals families and society put little real importance on children because they no longer equal labor or power or money. When the less than perfect measure themselves by intelligence, appearance and power most of us come up less than acceptable.

For over three hundred years in America, immigrant people were born and have died, leaving their own mark on life or they depart in silence, exiting like smoke, leaving no sign except the next generation or no linage at all. Some people made the world better; a few spread evil and some were not missed when they passed.

Who is left to judge? History, who has no conscience? An infinite God, surely. Yet perhaps, at that moment of death, each soul saw clearly who they were, what they had accomplished or had failed. The only existing mirrors have become descendants carrying genetic fragments and intuitive memory.

If there is meaning to life it may be today, only. The desire to create, give, share, support and understand is probably our best tribute to yesterday. We are not that far apart in this land, ten generations, nine deaths. Between these generations often is a point of light. Were we preceded by heroes? Seldom, they were but visible persons who were a part of history, and a genetic code marking today.

In fact, we may all be but what the past has made us.

The neighborhood is old and gracious, these homes are a contradiction. The residents are successful, young families who have escaped the rush to the new suburbs. In the suburbs new divisions waste so many resources and sit like ugly push-pins at every perimeter of Omaha. The houses are built uniformly and far too quickly. The "starter castles" in the region have been created in egotistic, wasteful imitations of past wealth and powerful people of other centuries.

The grurr sound of a growl pushed through the woman's pursed lips. "Thunk," a deep breath, a growl, "thunk." "Whew," then another gasp of air intake, and a final, "thunk." Finally, the sound of a dragging scrape of the box being pulled across concrete ended the woman's effort. Five more steps and Dru would have the heavy, cardboard box out of the basement and at the garage entrance. It had been awkward to move it from the basement to the garage. Three times when she paused, she could not release the box from her cramped grip for it would have slid back down the stairs. The dry, corrugated surface felt like sandpaper on the fingers of her clenched fists.

The woman was strong, yet she was sorry she had started this foolhardy task without help. She was now out of breath, her heart beating not only from exertion, but from a fear the box would roll back down to the basement taking her with it or that the heavy cardboard would tear apart as she drug it across the floor.

With relief she went through the garage access into the cool air conditioning of the house. As she rinsed her hands in the scalloped, lilac basin in her bathroom, Dru Davis looked into the mirror. With a sidelong grimace she blew through pursed lips at a tendril of hair hanging in her right eye. Reaching to wipe her hands on a plush, black towel she stepped directly in front of the mirror once more. With a tissue from an alabaster box she wiped some sweat from her forehead then fixed the loose hair back into the barrette which controlled the thick, glossy, chestnut hair at the nape of her neck.

Looking down she saw the half-moon shape of the gap in the button strip of her blouse. "Damn," somehow, like all large breasted women, there never seemed to be a way to make shirt buttons lie flat. Again, she vowed to never buy another front button shirt or dress. She always seemed to forget the vow after seeing a pretty one on a slender manikin in a store. Sighing, she simply unbuttoned the shirt, tied the two tails into a knot at the waist exposing the blue knit topper underneath. Since it was a warm September day, the informal look would be fine and after all she was only working in the garage.

Switching off the light and leaving the lovely, airy bathroom the young woman went down the hall. On her way through the kitchen she pulled the refrigerator open, removed a clear pitcher of iced tea and reached for a tall glass in a cabinet. Forcing the glass against the door dispenser she filled it with crushed ice, poured tea and returned the beverage pitcher to a cold shelf. Then she crossed the kitchen, went through the access entrance and passed once more into the garage.

Tomorrow morning at eight she would raise the outer doors and find the usual, early, shopping birds flocked there. Thank goodness this year she had shared the annual efforts of the garage sale with two neighbors. Since she had a three-car garage, the sale would be located at her house. The help to set up had made the event preparation much easier, as would sharing the boredom of sitting there three days and completing the Sunday afternoon clean up.

Dru nodded slightly as she looked over the space filled with used merchandise. The garage cavity held odds and ends of her life. Many had been spontaneously purchased, outgrown, fallen into disuse or replaced. Objects piled against the door were the larger tools, bikes and furniture that would be placed on the tarmac when they opened the doors tomorrow morning. The walls and rafters were hung with equipment, kites, bright pictures, empty frames and tow chains. Three long rows of makeshift trestles or card tables were paralleled from front to back with wide walkways between them.

It was almost four in the afternoon and soon she would need to make a supper salad and lay out hot dogs and hamburgers for her husband to grill. Slowly, she made a round of the merchandise on display checking to see if each item was priced. She picked up a slightly worn pair of child's sneakers which belonged to her daughter Sissy. Dru let go with a snort of disgust. The shoes cost forty dollars, were worn two months and now she had marked them for three dollars. The growth spurts of a ten-year-old were amazing and expensive.

Looking at a stack of bright, woven baskets she decided they looked unappealing and carefully scattered them among several tables. Turning the corner of the first trestle, she began up the second row and noticed an unmarked skillet, Dru retrieved a marker and label from the desk in the front corner, marked a price, and peeled and applied the tag to the panhandle. Here and there she straightened a pile of garments, knowing how futile that was for the first shopper would leave them a tangled mound of fabric.

On the third table, in one corner, were some china, figurines, antiques and crystal that the three women considered of higher value and placed near the desk where they could keep an eye on them. Dru overviewed this section, paused, backed up and then went on to the end. She started toward the kitchen door, stopped, looking over her shoulder, then she went back to the third table where she reexamined three saucers and two cups which she had contributed. She turned them over in examination, noted a small chip on the skirt of one teacup, and studied the china mark on the bottom. After a second she decided to take them with her and look up the china mark in an antique book before she priced them. She lovingly fingered a music box Carol had contributed and decided she might buy it for herself. It was always tempting to buy her friends' used goods so she took the small box also.

When she entered the kitchen, she sat the cups and saucers and music box on the wide ceramic windowsill above the sink. The sun showed a milky peach color through the china cups. Next she went to the refrigerator and began to clean vegetables for the salad.

Friday's events were as expected. Jill and Carol arrived half an hour early, as did the early birds. The women took turns going to the door to tell the shoppers that they would not be opening early even if the shopper was on the way to court or a funeral. This street was just off Happy Hollow Road in Omaha. Elegant, large homes of an earlier era were now remodeled to the best of design standards on the inside while still retaining the quality craftsmanship and fine wood details within. The neighborhood garage sales here were a favorite of bargain hunters for everything from used clothing to newer furnishings and antiques. Between trips to the door or checking the garage contents the three women laughed, chatted and pulled long chugs of fragrant, gourmet coffee from heavy ceramic mugs.

As the stated time neared they took positions like racehorses rearing at the starting gate. Lovely, shapely Dru and slender, blonde Carol stood at either side of the garage door to move articles onto the driveway. Darkly, statuesque Jill positioned herself at the checkout table with a box of newspaper and brown paper bags at her side. Like the rumble of an electronic dinosaur, Dru consecutively hit all three buttons to open the doors and twenty people rushed, breathless in anticipation, into the cool interior intent on seeking treasures.

The first day of the sale was always the most intense, paced by the pulse and pause of customers. Gradually the crowd thinned and trickled until the final scurry by a few shoppers in the late afternoon or by the last minute bargain hunters who dove inside just before they were closing for the day. Finally, with all but one door closed, the three women escorted the last bird to the door and rolled it shut behind her at 5:15 PM.

It had been as they had expected the day to progress. Too tired to be funny, Jill gasped, "Phew! I can only stay half an hour; my husband's company has a dinner at eight." Each of the hostesses began to move things about and tidy the tables.

Carol murmured almost to herself, "If I knew the shoes would be so popular I would have brought more. Think I'll take a box and bring more shoes tomorrow." Frankly, Dru was to tired to talk and also too darn hot. As the late afternoon sun had poured into the garage, it seemed to heat the space like a concrete lined oven. As soon as Jill and the other two were done they turned off the lights and gratefully limped away.

The next day there were less early birds and the flow was slower, but continual. They took down one table and moved it into the driveway to make the goods more visible, and that evening they carried the table back inside when they closed.

Sunday they did not open until 10:00 AM. With what small amount was left of the goods, they moved all the card tables outside, leaving only the larger items in the interior area. About 2:00 in the afternoon Jill began to tally, dividing the income and making notes on the few things that were knocked off and broken. They deducted a small set of books they thought was stolen by a clever shoplifter on Saturday. He probably quietly slid them into a box of goods, which he had previously paid for. They had to move sold items from column to column as each had bought the others' junk.

Sipping on more tall glasses of iced tea, which had been their subsistence for three days the other women stood above Jill reading the tally of the sale. Dru looked at her column with some pique. She saw that her husband's old tools, sports equipment and leftover building materials had brought most of the money she had profited. After all the work she had done, it would be infuriating if he made more than she. The last hour Jill and Dru were alone because Carol said she had an awful migraine and left. They listlessly began to move the leftovers inside the garage, and discussed finishing the sorting and cleaning on Monday when Carol was there to help. Since some of the goods were nice enough for donation, by Wednesday they could call for a truck to get them. Much would also have to be boxed or bagged for garbage removal. Without Carol, the job just couldn't be completed tonight for they were both so tired.

At four the doors were finally rolled down, "Come into the house, Jill. Relax and cool down before you go home to face supper." Jill laughed, "What supper? It is pizza night at my house. I've decided on two hours of soaking in my whirlpool." Dru confirmed their shared mood, "I sent my family away for supper and a movie so our dinner is nada!"

The friends moved into the kitchen and the comforting air-conditioning. Slowly they moved down the carpeted hallway, and into the plush softness of the formal study, which overlooked the backyard garden. Both kicked off shoes and curled their toes in ecstasy. On one wall a grey and blue crazy quilt hung that Dru's great-grandmother had made during the Civil War. There were lace panels at the bay window, which gave the view of the autumn garden flowers a glazed, watercolor appearance. Subtle tones of rose and grey in the room were both comforting and elegant.

Dru pushed her weary back into the corner of the couch against a mushy velour pillow and lay her throbbing legs the length of the couch. Jill leaned over and pulled a footstool in front of the soft, Chesterfield chair she was slumped into. Then she let her arms drop over the arms of the chair on either side and hang limply.

"Maybe, next year we shouldn't do this? I know we made around six hundred each and if the man in the pickup comes back for the riding lawn mower, you'll make more. But we can deduct the donations," she emphasized, "and have clean closets."

Dru allowed a long groan to flow over her slack jaw.

The weary women lounged for ten minutes, quietly commenting on people and experiences of the last couple days.

"Jill, you know what would be wonderful? Some good English tea."

"Mm, sounds good to me," the chair draped lady answered.

Dru rose and went toward the kitchen on bare feet.

While her friend was gone Jill studied the room. She was often here to visit, yet they talked so much and laughed so much here she was seldom alone in the room and had never before observed it closely. She stared at the quilt noting the randomly shaped colors. There were walls of bookcases and a small, spinet piano sat against one wall. Above the piano were photos, plaques, awards and framed mementos.

She went over to study a photograph of Dru in a wedding gown. Her friend looked much the same now, except she was fuller bodied. The young man by her was without a touch of grey at the temples that were his trademark now. He seemed very naive and fresh. Jill observed in a family group picture that her neighbor seemed to look more like her Mother than her Father. Next, she peered at the three children at various ages.

There was a baseball award so, after admitting to herself that she was snoopy, she checked the year and mentally decided that Dru's husband must be around thirty-eight. Some historic documents, and medals were shown to nice advantage in velvet-lined, shadow box frames and Jill found them interesting. One memento was a small, oval frame with a hair braid including dry, colorless flowers and a wedding band tied into the flowers with a faded, blue ribbon.

Moving away, Jill stopped a moment, then awkwardly fingered chopsticks on the piano cringing at an untuned key. Dru called from the nearby kitchen, "Ready for your recital?"

With a phony retort Jill boomed back in mock threat, "Lady, you just wait!" The tall woman then bent to again to study the collection of memorabilia on the wall.

In the kitchen Dru rinsed the shiny, copper teapot, then filled it with distilled water. Turning the blue gas flame up to high, she put the kettle on top until it was wrapped and caressed by the blue fingers of flame. The base of the pot cast dancing orange and yellow colors.

Tea was a real ceremony for her. As a bride an elegant, international neighbor had instructed her in the preparation of proper tea. Dru reached into the cupboard for a stylish, fluted, porcelain teapot and using hot tap water she filled it to warm the china container. Next she reached into the cupboard for some fine, white china cups which matched teapot.

Calling toward the library she inquired if Jill used anything in her tea. "Yes, sugar," came the reply from down the hall.

Dru, standing on tiptoe, reached for an antique sugar bowl with a bleeding blue border. She rifled behind a stack of china and came out with a seldom used box of sugar cubes. Going to the refrigerator she grabbed a lemon. After rolling it on the counter, she lay it on the cutting board and sliced the pungent fruit in half. The fragrance was clean and the fresh tingling in her nostrils made saliva rise behind her jaw. With two fingers she secured a sugar cube and lay it very lightly on the sliced lemon and put it aside on the board. This was repeated with a half dozen other cubes.

As the cubes were prepared, water begin to boil making a distant train whistle sound. She unscrewed a tightly lidded glass container and with a wooden scoop, *always a wooden scoop*. Dru reminded herself of the manner she had been taught by the older Englishwoman. She measured enough tea for four cups of tea. These crisp brown crumbles were dropped into a cunning, silver, tea caddie that was shaped like a cat and she snapped it shut.

As the whistle of the pot sounded she checked her watch, *a four minute steep, that is important*. Dru reached to turn the burner off and emptied the warming pot, then poured the steaming water into the porcelain container with the tea bell hooked over the lip. She secured the lid. Bending to a cabinet she reached for an antique tea tray she was fond of. Taking a cloth from the linen drawer she spread a fine, embroidered napkin on her tray and placed the tea cups on it.

Looking at the sugar cubes she reached toward the cupboard again. Just at the corner of her eye a bit of blue color which had been caught by the sun took her attention. Removing the cups and saucers from the windowsill she ran hot water over the old china and wiped them with a tea towel. She had forgotten that they matched the sugar bowl and was glad she had not sold them.

Laying the extra saucer out she placed the sugar cubes on it, then set the blue and white cups and saucers on the napkin. The original, white china was moved back to the counter. From an ornamental canister she took some Italian lace cookies and lay several on the edge of each saucer. After checking her watch, Dru removed the dripping, silver, cat caddie with a wooden spoon and peering into the pot she checked the color of the liquid. Next, she bypassed the everyday stainless and selected two demitasse spoons from the good silver. *They might be too small, but how pretty!*

As she returned to the library carrying the tea tray, Jill came to sit beside her on the couch facing the piano. The tray rested between them on a glass topped, low, teakwood coffee table. They mellowed to the warmth of friendship, accomplishment and tea.

With cups in their hands they sat back sighing. "What year did you get married?" Jill quizzed, feeling a bit devious about her curiosity. She had never been sure which of them were older. "Just after we graduated from The University of Nebraska in 1979."

Thinking of the family pictures Jill smiled, "Wasn't Sissy a chunk when she was a baby?"

"Yes, she was eight and a half pounds when she was born."

Jill next inquired, "Was that your ancestor who was in the Civil War, or your husband's? I saw the discharge paper on the wall and some medals."

Dru's answer was direct. "Mine, I was a Hunter before I was married, that was my great-great grandfather."

Dru turned toward Jill as she again leaned her back against the corner pillow of the sofa and pensively waited for Jill's full attention. There was a look of hesitance on her face, "Will you think I'm nuts if I tell you something that you can't tell anyone?"

With only a pause, Jill's face became solemn, "Of course, you can always trust me."

"Last week there was a free lecture in the evening in Lincoln on West campus at the Hillstead gallery. I have always loved historic fiber and the lecture featured quilts, both modern and traditional. I treated myself to a day off and went alone."

First I had coffee at the Mill, walked through the Sheldon museum, then I still had two hours to kill. It was a lovely, fall day and I didn't feel like being indoors. Sitting on a bench in front of the Sheldon sculpture garden, I watched the students for a while. I considered walking the outdoor sculpture garden but I had done that recently, I dismissed that thought also, then I remembered I had always promised myself to visit the cemetery in Lincoln where my great-great-grandfather was buried. When you mentioned him I remembered what happened that day."

Reaching for her friends arm and squeezing it, "Oh Jill I hate to tell you this. It is kind of spooky and I feel silly." Jill reached to hold her hand for support, curious about what her friend was going to say.

"Well, I asked directions and right in the heart of town I found Wyuka cemetery. My dad always said we had an ancestor in soldier's circle. Actually, I know very little about the man or anything so the visit was quite casual. When I stopped in the office for directions I gave William Hunter's name and described what I was looking for. The director decided I was looking for Grand Army of the Revolution Circle of Union Veterans of the Civil War. He pulled out a map, marked the location and the road for me to take to find it."

"First of all, no one else seemed to be in the cemetery and it was so quiet. A few autumn leaves were rich in color, lying all over the ground among the majority that were still green. I drove on the narrow, old-fashioned brick roads. I rolled down all the windows and that dusty kind of warm smell filled the car.

There were some beautiful monuments so I drove slowly, reading names and dates. Then I took one wrong turn that took me back to the office and the lovely stone chapel beside the office. So I started all over, this time looking carefully at the map that the office had provided.

I felt lazy and relaxed, occasionally I saw a name I knew from Nebraska history and stopped several times to gaze out the window to read dates. Suddenly, on my right, I saw a tall statue of a Union soldier on a pedestal. It was surrounded by rows of small, orderly, white headstones. I didn't see parking so just pulled over parallel, stopped the car and got out. Hearing something, I looked down the hill and there were thousands of wild geese walking among the tombstones. Wow, it was surreal! They were right in the middle of the city! Isn't that strange and eerie? It was as though the world had stopped and in instinct was still the ancestral meadow imprinted on their memory."

"Slowly I began to shuffle around the outside row of the circle headstones considering names, states and military units. After about thirty, there it was. First, I saw Lt. John W. Cadwallader US 52$^{nd}$, Col. Infantry, Co. E. It seemed to be a name I had read as a child in a diary. Not far away on another marker was the name of Capt. William H. Hunter, 58$^{th}$ Col., Co. K. I looked at it carefully—the man seemed to be very far away, from another world.

Over the top of his stone I raised my eyes to see the statue of the soldier grasping a gun. That seemed to be my symbolic ancestor. He was a part of history, a part of the romantic, dramatic, tragic war that formed what our nation is today. I felt, I guess, solemn and embarrassed to be so spoiled by my own easy life.

*What was the war like? What was this man like? What did he see, do, touch, smell? What part of him am I?* I really wanted to know him. My family saying had always been 'it is the past that has made us all.' I almost prayed I could know about him—that he could reach to me from the past, beyond the grave.

Jill looked puzzled, "What's the secret? This seems pretty normal to me."

"No, what happened next is what I wanted to share. I stood there a while; looked at some more headstones, studied the geese and just enjoyed the total peace, quiet and beginnings of autumn color. Finally, I got into the car and slowly wound back down a road. Suddenly a fox appeared on the side of the road and I stopped the car. He was a brilliant auburn and with the most full red and white tipped tail I have ever seen, even in a Mangelson photo."

The white of his tail was like snow against his burnt sienna fur. I stopped the car ten feet from him. This beautiful animal crossed to the center of the road, stopped, turned and faced me. He stood staring me in the eye, in the dead silence, almost as though he had a message. I half expected him to approach me and was afraid to breathe; I didn't want him to run away. He froze for long minutes, his beautiful, black eyes looking into mine. Then, without fear or hurry, he turned and slowly walked, across the road and down the hill to a creek that runs there. Then the fox changed directions and disappeared."

"What is weird, Jill, don't laugh, there was a chill down my back; I knew that fox was my great-great grandfather's spirit. It was mesmerizing and I just sat there overwhelmed for a long time."

Smiling warmly, Jill looked into her friend's eyes. "I believe you Drucilla, sometimes a person just knows things. I had a Granny that claimed to know lots of things like that and I believed her. She even saw a real ghost once, I'm sure of it and I'm not nuts."

Dru had begged for reassurance of her sanity. With a gentle chuckle Jill said, "I am sure you aren't insane, but I still wouldn't tell very many people that story."

Sitting back, Dru finished her tea, "Want another cup, I'm going to have one." "Thanks, a good idea." Dru took Jill's cup, sat it by hers and filled both from the porcelain pot. Then using the demitasse spoon she dropped a sugar cube into both of the ancient blue and white, Chinese cups and stirred them before returning the spoons to the saucer.

With visible pride in her voice Jill said, "My great-great grandfather fought with the Union in Mississippi in the Civil War, too."

An awkward, embarrassing, "Oh," escaped Dru's lips and was followed by a stilted pause. Embarrassed she said, "You must be proud, too." She hoped to fill the difficult moment.

In a murmur, Jill said, almost as a postscript, "His name was Buck Murphy and I was named after his mother."

Then Dru held the paper-thin saucer toward her friend who received it in the palm of her left hand. Studying the bleeding blue pattern, Jill reached to hold the warm cup. Pink nails, pale palm and long ebony fingers grasped the handleless cup and she raised it to her lips. With the warm draught, the two young women shared friendship and also the historic bond warming Jill as much as the tea.

At that moment Jill felt pride that her family had shared with her the legends, the lineage and their hopes. For these had been keystones they had held for so many generations.

"The time has come to realize that the interracial drama acted out on the American continent has not only created a new black man, it has created a new white man, too....One of the things that distinguishes Americans from other people is that no other people has ever been so deeply involved in the lives of black men, and vice versa....This world is white no longer, and it will never be white again."

James Baldwin
*Stranger in the Village*

*(front) William Wallace Hunter with his second wife, Serena Joanna Masters Williams and their daughter, Florence Hunter and (back) Carol Williams and Drusilla Hunter.*

*Drusilla Hunter, daughter of William Wallace Hunter.*

*Mae Hunter Speer, daughter of Captain Hunter.*

*Dora Welch Hunter, first wife of William Wallace Hunter.*

*Henry Hunter, Jr.'s farm, Liberty, Indiana, 1814.*

*Final home of William & Annie Hunter in Lincoln, Nebraska.*

## Photograph and Illustration Acknowledgment

- Monmouth Plantation, Natchez, premier bed and breakfast
- Greenwood Plantation, Mr. and Mrs. Bedgood Pinkneyville, Mississippi
- Wyuka Cemetery Historic Association Lincoln, Nebraska
- African American Civil War Monument and Museum, Washington, D.C.
- Hunter Family photo, Linda and Don Licking, North Platte, Nebraska
- Airlie Military Hospital
- Edwin Hobart Diary

## The Hunter lineage of Jack Sadle

1. Jack Durwood Sadle
   son of Louis P. Sadle & Drucilla Inez Hunter

2. Drucilla Inez Hunter
   daughter of William Wallace & Dora Mae Welch
   stepdaughter of Serena Masters Williams

3. William Wallace Hunter
   son of William Hugh & Sarah Drucilla (Spencer) Scothorne
   stepson of Anna E. Stone

4. William Hugh
   son of Henry C.W. & Mary F. Hughes

5. Henry C.W.
   son of Henry Jr. & Martha (Patsy) Smith
   stepson of Isabell Heavenridge

6. Henry Jr.
   son of Henry & Lucy Ruffin

7. Henry Hunter & wife Lucy Ruffin or Hart
   father unknown (possibly William) & mother unknown
   brother of William, wife Anne Norsworthy, of Virginia and later Kentucky.

# With Gratitude To...

·*Dale Gray*, whose silent dignity was a lesson as his classmates learned the realities of the rural Midwest in the 1950s.
·*Jack Sadle* for thousands of miles and thousands of hours of support.
·*Nora Tallmon*, for commitment, encouragement and editing beyond the call of duty.
·*Jacqueline & Stephen Andrews* for military expertise.
·*Jay Tallmon, Louis & Hunter Sadle & Jennifer Szatko* for technical or material support.
·*Lars Szatko* for illustration advise.
·*Drucilla Hunter Jones* shared with me a deep insight into her great grandfather.
·*Ser Seshs Ab Heter-Clifford M.Boxley*, for encouragement and emotional support.
·*Helen Brandon Rayne* for open, generously shared memories.
·*Pierrine C. Brandon Bedgood* contributed to authenticity and offered us hospitality.
·*Sandy Aguilar* supplied a professional reading, technical and emotional support.
·*Edith Shank & Jean Howarth,* teachers who helped me love Literature. ·*Julia Mae Monfort* for sharing insights into her Hunter ancestors and Woodville. · *Terry Winchell* for advise on the battle of Vicksburg.
·*Frank Smith African American Civil War Museum* in Washington for support.
·*Ellen Menetre's* hospitality allowed me to learn about Scothorne heritage.
·*Don Estes* who shared the drama of Fort McPhearson and the Natchez cemetery.
·*Sue Antes* for the magic of interlibrary loans.
·*Michael Eckholt* for computer support.
·*Lael Spath* was the angel on my shoulder.
·*Elizabeth Mattern Rhodes*, professional reader, for her editing advise.
·*Mimi Miller & the Historic Natchez Foundation.*
·*Lee W. Jackson Family* shared ancestors, Buck Murphy and Alexander Turner.
·*Eastern National Park & Deborah Cowart* in Natchez.
·*Kimmel Harding Nelson Center for the Arts of Nebraska City* for generosity.
·*Lee Heflebower & Wyuka Cemetery Historical Foundation Auxiliary* for burial records.
·*E. Edward Holbrook*, Wyuka Cemetary Historian.
·*Natchez Cemetery Association*, for their special piece of Natchez history.
·*Lani Riches* of Monmouth Plantation for review of the finished novel.
·*Bess Nicholason, Marnell Sanders, Sandra Daggeson, Marilyn Pushon & all Hunter* descendants who shared their genealogy.
·*Numerous county seats*, the National Archives in Washington, Carlisle Barracks in Pennsylvania, Carroll County Illinois Genealogical Society, Graham County Museum in Kansas, Savannah Illinois Historic Society, Vicksburg Mississippi Museum, Nebraska Historical Society, Liberty Indiana Library, Natchez City Library, Adams County Courthouse in Natchez, Mississippi, and Omaha Library and Genealogy. Each are depositories of our nations' history. We appreciated the helpful staff we found there who patiently aided us.
· *The City of Natchez*, so full of history, hospitality and beauty.
· *The City of Syracuse, Nebraska & the Syracuse Foundation* for reaching out to help my husband and I in a time of need.

# Amy Sadle

Amy Brandon is the daughter of a grocer from Iowa. She lived in several small towns in Iowa and eventually graduated from high school in Atlantic, Iowa and left to attend the University of Iowa.

She later married Jack Sadle a Navy Seabee. His 20-year career took them to Kauai, Virginia, Cuba and Rhode Island where she attended the University of Rhode Island. The family, which includes five children, moved to Newfoundland, Denver and Scottsbluff, Columbus and Syracuse, Nebraska.

Art is her lifelong passion and one she works at full-time. At 12-years-old she began private instruction. In her life changes she studied with over a hundred nationally recognized instructors.

Creating and learning continually, she competes nationally and internationally with watercolor and woodcut as her strong preferences. She has received many best of shows, grants and purchase awards. Her creations are in private collections and she has displayed in many nationally recognized museums and galleries.

Collections that include her work are the Statue of Liberty Museum, the University of Nebraska, McCook College, the Nebraska Indian Commission, Tulsa Library, DesMoines Art Center, other institutions and numerous churches. Her biographies are in *Who's Who in American Art, International Biography Center* in Europe among others.

### Amy Sadle's literary background

With early recognition by National Scholastic Art Completions and as a prizewinning yearbook illustrator Amy was encouraged. She later illustrated the University of Iowa student handbook.

When Amy studied with Fritz Eichenberg at the University of Rhode Island, he emphasized the bond between literature and the artist. With this incentive and the assistance of the group, Amy wrote and illustrated a history of Newfoundland for the Women's Institute in Placentia. This book, *Home of Wooden Boats and Iron Men* sold out and received the Tweedsmuir award for "Best Regional History in Canada."

She wrote a series on the Stations of the Cross for the Catholic Grand Island Diocese in Nebraska, and illustrated a childrens' book for a friend. As her career grew she was featured on public TV specials, collaborated with magazines like *American Artist, Pallet Talk* and others. Two of the four books she wrote were seriously considered for publication during this period.

As the director and one of the founding boardmembers of Impact, she worked with Editor Dora Hagge to create *Impact, the Art of Nebraska Women.* This book was well-reviewed nationally, was a best seller and received the Addy for design and the best printing award regionally.

*Thank you for reading Hunter Hall.*

To order a book for a gift or for another personal copy, send a check or credit card information for $19.99, 6.5% Nebraska sales tax and $3 a book for shipping to:

Amy Sadle, P.O. Box H, Syracuse, NE 68446 *or*
e-mail otoeartcouncil@mailcity.com

For prompt delivery include your full name and address. If you would like an autographed copy please include a suggested message and name.
Wholesale rates are available.

*If you are considering visiting the sites mentioned in this book below are some that the author recommends.*

**Natchez**

•Fall Pilgrimage Tours, 1-800-647-6742. This tour includes many of the plantations mentioned in the book

•The Natchez Visitor Center, 1-800-647-6724.

•The Natchez Museum of Afro-American History and Culture, 1-601-445-0728.

•Historic Natchez City Cemetery.

•Grand Village of the Natchez (Indian), 1-601-446-6502.

•Forks-Of-The-Roads (Former Slave Market) Historic Site.

**Vicksburg**

•Vicksburg Battlefield and National Park, 1-601-636-0583.

**Woodville**

•Rosemont Plantation, Jefferson Davis home, 601-888-6809.

**Wilkinson**

•Wilkinson County Museum, 1-601-888-3998.

**Washington, D.C.**

•The African American Civil War Memorial & Museum, 1-202-667-2667.

• Congressional Cemetery.

## References


1. History of the Clans.
2. The Americans: The Colonial Experience. Daniel J. Boorstin.
3. Army Memoirs. Lucius W. Barber.
4. The Life of Billy Yank: The Common Soldier of the Union. Bell Irvin Wiley, 1971.
5. The Civil War: Strange and Fascinating Facts. Burke Davis.
6. Siege of Vicksburg. Richard Wheeler.
7. Men of Color. William A. Gladstone.
8. A Goodly Heritage: History of Carroll County, Illinois. H.F. Kitt & Co., 1878.
9. The Besieged City. Shelby Foote, audio.
10. Adjutant Generals Report on Fifteenth Illinois. U.S. Government.
11. Prominent Citizens of Carroll County.
12. Francis Lord Civil War Collectors Encyclopedia.
13. A Treasury of Mississippi River Folklore: Stories, Ballads, Traditions and Folkways of the Mid-American River Country. B. A. Botkin.
14. With Malice Toward Some: The Military Occupation of Vicksburg, 1864-1865. Gordan A. Cotton and Ralph C. Mason, 1991.
15. Official Records of the War of the Rebellion. U.S. Government.
16. Forged in Battle: The Civil War Alliance of Black Soldiers and White Officers. Joseph T. Glatthaar.
17. *Natchez Courier.*
18. Righteous Rebel. Catherine Cloud Templeton.
19. Spanish Passports in the Mississippi Valley. Adams County Courthouse.
20. Brandon genealogy.
21. A Gentleman of Old Natchez. Benjamin L.C. Snyder.
22. One Hundred Years With Old Trinity Church, Natchez, MS. Chas. Stietenroth, 1985.
23. Lee W. Jackson Family legends
24. G.W. Reese diary. Lewistown, Illinois.
25. John A. Quitman and Slavery. Journal of Southern History, 1980.
26. William Scothorne's original documents.
27. Hosier genealogy. Indiana Hunter Geneaology.
28. Ellen Shields, 1903. Document, Natchez Public Library.
29. The Black Experience in Natchez: 1720-1880. Ronald L.F. Davis, Ph.D, 1994.
30. The Serpent and the Rainbow. Wade Davis.
31. Tumult and Silence at Second Creek. Jordan D. Winthrop.
32. The Burning of Bowling Green. Stella Pitts
33. Bedgood Family, Oral History.
34. The Hobart Diary. Edwin Hobart.
35. Natchez National Park. Historic Documents.
36. The Civil War Diary of Bishop William Henry Elder. Reverend R.O. Gerow.

38. The Sable Arm. Dudley Taylor Cornish and Herman Hathaway.
39. *The Smithsonian Magazine.*
40. *The Civil War Times Illustrated.*
41. The Black Family in Slavery and Freedom: 1750-1925. Herbert G. Gutman.
42. The William Hunter diary.
43. *The Nebraska Post.*
44. Frank Tannenbaum: Slave Citizen. Joseph Maier and Richard W. Weatherhead.
45. Wyuka Cemetery Historical Association.
46. *The Omaha World Herald. Henry Littlefield, September 9, 1998.*
47. Carroll County Civil War Monument Rededication. Pamphlet.
48. Natchez Cemetery Society. Pamphlet.
49. Negro in the U.S. 1790-1915. U.S. Government.
50. The History of the Grand Army of the Republic. Robert B. Bath.
51. Going Home to Nicodemus: The Story of an African American Frontier Town and the Pioneers Who Settled It. Daniel Chu and Bill Shaw.
52. *Ancestral File,* Internet
53. Like Men of War: Black Troops in the Civil War, 1862-1865. Noah Andre Trudeau.
54. Quitman and his Slaves: Reconciling Slave Resistance with Proslavery Defense. Robert E. May. *Journal of Southeastern History*, May-Nov. 1980.

# Author's Notes

## Chapter 1

In 1374, Hunters received land from Robert II. The clan was then given to William Hunter. It served under Rollo in France at the battle in Paris and then came to the islands as the official Huntsmen for the Duke of Normandy. That is how the family came to be called Hunter and may be the oldest clan of all. The tartan is the green and black field. The red threads running through are for warriors. White threads running through are for the French. "In 1296, Hunters were in charge of the Royal Forests and were long soldiers in Ayershire. They had fought Sloden in 1513 under Laird John the 14th and under Sir Aylmer-Weston in the Boar War." *History of the Clans*(1)

## Chapter 6

Illinois troops 1863 at Fort McPhearson-There were the 4th Illinois Calvary, five companies of 5th Illinois Calvary, Battery K of 2nd Illinois Light Artillery, 28th and 29th Illinois, 30th Missouri, 8th New Hampshire, and the 26th and 83rd Ohio were also serving. The Colored Troops were 6th U.S. Heavy Artillery, Mississippi Volunteer 58th, 63rd, 64th, 70th and 71st Colored Troops. At surrender twenty officers and soldiers of the Confederacy had been captured as they tried to escape. The Post Office and mail matter had been possessed, as was the Court House and telegraph office. One hundred and fifty wagons of ordnance were confiscated, 312 Austrian muskets, eleven boxes of ammunition and 268,000 rounds were destroyed. Using infantry made up of citizens captured, 5,000 Texas cattle from a nearby location, four miles outside the city, were brought in. The disarming of the citizens supplied large quantities of weapons of all descriptions. Horses were seized for the Army's use. *Official Records of the War of the Rebellion*(15)

## Chapter 8

These emigrating settlers were among those who had been given property. They had been invited to migrate in an attempt to balance the population against the English. Historically, the area along the Mississippi had changed political control by France, England and Spain at various times. They were also selected to develop the district. Immigrants were even more of an asset if they had specific skills and trades. *Gentleman of Natchez*(21)

The Munson's also became a part of the neighborhood and settled adjoining our family. The next year, 1793, Henry and Mr. Robert Munson were called to court on an issue of a fight between Lewis Alston and Frederick Kimball. Eventually old Henry Hunter sold them some of his land. *Adams County Courthouse*

Brandon had been English born and reared in Ireland. He arrived on this continent in time to fight the English in the Revolution. Gerard C., Matthew and William were his sons. Gerard C. later became the first native born governor. The two families often took like positions in political arenas or signed the same petitions. In addition to the close bond as neighbors and personal relationships, Henry Hunter respected George Brandon who was to become a leading citizen in the new state that would be born in 1802. *Bedgood Family Legend*(33)

William had married Nancy Smith in 1778, she was the daughter of Zachariah and Frances Smith. Your grandfather Henry Junior had married her sister Martha, who was called Patsy, she was Henry's mother. When she died he married Isabel Heavenridge in 1807. Thomas, Joseph and Narswothy were married later; Narswothy to Mary Davis, daughter of Micajah and Mary Davis, but that was in 1808, after Henry's birth in 1804. It was in 1809 that Field Pleasant married Martha Kitchen. Elizabeth married John Bell, and sister Mary married David Andrews. William married Nancy Jessup in 1819. *Hunter Geneaology*(42)

Henry and son William were Narsworthy's executors. His brother-in-law, John Bell, oversaw his estate in 1907, in Mississippi. As he had no family, the estate was divided by male relatives. *Adams County records*

**Chapter 10**

"The rebels forty strong attacked twenty-five men of the 6th Mississippi. Of the men of the 6th who were killed or mortally wounded were four. Captured were seven, six of whom escaped. The seventh was shot through the head. Then the Rebels beat him to death with their muskets. The enemy lost their commanders, one sergeant, and four men killed or mortally wounded."

*Official Records of the War of the Rebellion*(15)

**Chapter 11**

Fatalities were John Schaffer, Burton Turner, Charles Wheelock, Chauncy Wooden, John Puterbaugh, Thomas King, George Kridler, James Heisroot, Hollis Hurd, John Clouser, Robert Bradley, James Hiesrodt and William Carter.

*Carroll County Civil War Monument Rededication*(47)

By 1812 there were in Natchez "four tailor shops, three blacksmiths, and four saddlers. Of the skilled laborers were six carpenters, five cabinetmakers, one coach and sign painter, three hatters, and two tinners. In service for the public were four boot and shoe makers, one trunkmaker, one bookbinder, one wagonmaker, one chairmaker. One nail factory, three barbers, four brickyards, one butcher, four bakers, one brushmaker, three gold and silversmiths, one confectioner and distiller, one horesemill (corn), one plasterer, and twelve watercarts."

Professionals flourished with "eight physicians, seven lawyers, three English schools, one incorporated mechanics' society, one Free Mason lodge, four magistrates, three printing offices, with weekly papers, two porterhouses, six public inns, five warehouses, one reading room and coffee-house, twenty-four drygoods stores, four groceries, two wholesale stores, seventeen catalenes, one commission store, and one bank of Mississippi, capital $500,000...Under the 'Hill' were two blacksmith shops, one tavern and thirteen catalenes. Old Natchez Region in 1799 the Natchez territory was organized into two counties Adams and Pickering. Of the entire region 635 people lived along the Buffalo River and Byou Sara." *Gentleman of Natchez*(21)

Official report of the war of Rebellion "On Sunday, December 6th, General W.Q. Gresham, with the 12th Wisconsin, 32nd Illinois, one battery of artillery and one of the Marine Brigades, with parts of the 4th Illinois Cavalry and 5th Iowa Cavalry, and some Marines, landed and moved out on the Washington and Woodville road as far as Kingston, where they met Wirt Adams with his cavalry. A skirmish ensued which resulted in the killing of one and wounding of two men. The expedition returned to Natchez, where the 12th Wisconsin, 32nd Illinois and 4th Illinois Cavalry remained until January 23rd, 1864, when they returned to Vicksburg, the 4th Cavalry remaining at Natchez. On December 31st, 1863, Colonel Farrar of the 30th Missouri Mounted Infantry, captured Colonel Connor, chief of staff to General Bragg, near Natchez. He was escorted through the city by a squad of mounted Negroes, which greatly mortified the feelings of the citizens." *Official Records of the War of the Rebellion*(15)

**Chapter 12**
Matching family names have been used from the church she may have attended but where she was certainly twice married. *Amy Sadle*

**Chapter 15**
"Under Tuttle there had been continual confusion at Fort McPhearson. Once he sent a Captain and a company of men to a private plantation. These were instructed to be under command of the civilian lessee. Such command of troops by civilians was without precedence.

Corruption on the base was appalling. Certain civilians were given free run to arrive at the fort and depart with provisions as they chose. Especially prevalent was the fact that many of these civilians were attractive young women. They also carried papers denying inspection of property being removed. Many in possession of such passes had not even taken the oath of allegiance, required of all wishing interaction or freedom with the occupying forces. In one period of eight weeks, $118,000 goods were carried away. Troops were assigned fatigue duty cleaning streets. Such duty was especially demoralizing for former slaves.

When, in February, Tuttle was accused to illegally moving cotton. He escaped unscathed in that event his arrogance was undaunted. In March he was again found moving a large quantity of cotton. Finally, March 7, Brigadier General Tuttle was relieved of duty and assigned to the Seventeenth Army Corps.

In July Adjutant-General Thomas reported that in the prior command, that of Tuttle, there had been great abuses, swindling, oppression, and blackmailing was said to be common. Colonel B.G. Farrar, then commanding the base, reported everything connected the proper administration of military affairs in the recent past having been entirely neglected. Lack of discipline was evident.

A large proportion of troops were quartered in the city and under no restrictions whatever but allowed to roam at will throughout the city at all hours of the day and night. The natural consequence was that assaults, robberies and incendiary fires were matters of almost daily occurrence.

Colonel Farrar reported, 'When I took command I sought to rectify military order immediately. Important general orders had never been seen or heard by the officers and troops, this I immediately rectified. Reports were that there had been found witnesses and affidavits to having paid Tuttle many thousands of dollars. Persons and property had been abused under frivolous pretenses or arbitrary exercise of will. He was accused as he withdrew funds in large amounts of money for vague and extravagant expenses from the government offices. It is believed that Brigadier General Tuttle carried this money away with him and has not rendered any account of it to the proper authorities. It was suggested proof be gathered." *Official Records of the War of the Rebellion*(15)

"About the town was a man of great character, yet one who refused to yield to the Union orders or take the Oath of Allegiance. This was to cause his being sent beyond the lines away to Vidalia, Louisiana at one point. He was expelled on pain of imprisonment for some time when he refused Special Order # 31, to pray for the President of the Untied States during church services. In a time of great danger he moved about the countryside ministering to all, White and Black, rich and poor, Union and Confederate. He even visited the soldiers in Union hospitals and the kraal offering last rights, baptisms, marriages, communion, sacraments, and comfort to all. He visited the marine hospital at the fort to comfort the ill and dying. At homes in the path of the war he was told stories of courage. One was of a Catholic Union soldier rescuing and returning a stolen chalice from Jackson where the church was ransacked and burnt. One tale was that of a freed slave finding food for his former owner when the planter's crops and animals were stolen or slaughtered. His personal witness was one of human compassion and duty rather than rebellion. Yet his stubborn courage was undaunted, and he became a poor public evidence of disregard to the occupying force. The command eventually yielded and allowed him to return. Bishop Elder stood to his values in all conditions. In one case he gave a wounded soldier, a paroled prisoner of the defeat of the Vicksburg battle, his own horse to ride while he walked." *The Civil War Diary of Bishop William Henry Elder*(36)

## Chapter 16

Edwin Hobart, April 12, 1845,Carthage, Hancock Ill. Died July 17, 1935, Denver, Colorado. Parents, Joshua Chase Hobart and Sophia Calkins-Estabrooke. *Internet, Ancestral File*(52)

## Chapter 17

Anderson and Hunter are fictional but the other men are soldiers of the Fifty-eighth. Turner and Murphy legends are shared by the family of Lee W. Jackson. Parents of Buck Murphy are Jack and Lucy Pendelton. Father of Alexander Turner was the owner at the Hedges in Wilkinson, County. *Lee W. Jackson Family legends*(23)

"Davis, a gracious man, had served the south well and stalwartly answered the call for his impossible task. He was to languish writing his accounts of the war for two years in the prison at Fort Monroe. In October, the *Natchez Democrat* made a plea that to win the respect of other countries he be released. The paper reported there was no precedent in history (rightly). The paper questioned that General Lee was pardoned although called by the same authority as Davis." *The Sable Arm*(38)

"Major General Tecumseh Sherman's march to the sea with thousands of troops including Colored soldiers, which he had first objected to. Begun in late 1854 to further disable the south, moving thousands of troops from Atlanta to Savannah they left a swath of 20 miles of devastated scorched earth. 'It was said that a crow when it flies over will have to carry its own ration.' The Colored troops soon adapted to the destruction yet in several instance the Black scavengers were seen to leave rebel ladies some meat. Thousands of homeless men women and children of color followed in their wake. 15th Ill had joined Sherman in the Carolinas in January and were under his command until the surrender....Because of proximity they were present in the grand victory march in Washington on May 24 and the 14th Illinois who had rescued at Shilo them marched at their side. From there they moved across Kentucky to Fort Leavenworth, Ks. They marched across the hot dry prairie to Fort Kearney ,NE July 1-14 and served there until September 1. Then they all returned to Leavenworth to muster out on Sept 16, 1865. By the end of the war the 15th Illinois had lost 6 officers and 81 enlisted in battle. Five officers and 135 enlisted had died of disease. The casualties were a total of 227. This brave company of soldiers from

Carroll county Illinois had marched 4,299 miles. They had ridden by railway another 2,403, and by steamer another 4,310 miles in four years and four months. Of the 1,963 who had enlisted in the regiment 640 were present at muster out."

*Civil War Times Illustrated, April 1989*(40)

**Chapter 19**

William Wallace's farm was Northwest of North Platte, Nebraska in 1889. He married Dora May Welch on Christmas Day in 1890. He had met her while working on the Van Broklund Ranch near Wellfleet. He became active in many activities of the area, especially on the school board of what was always referred to as the Hunter School. *Amy Sadle*

Henry Clay was eventually placed in a mental hospital, the ward of his wife Angeline.

*Carroll County records*

*Excerpts from the William Hunter Diary follow:*

"CHEERS FOR THE LIVING

Tears for the dead
To the Union of the blue and the grey
This song is kindly dedicated by the
author, Capt. W.H. Hunter Lincoln,
Nebraska. Long live our Yankee
heroes In memory and in song
Their deeds of valor for the right
Gainst tyranny and wrong
Fair islands of old ocean
Would never have been free
Except their blood was freely shed
On land and on the sea

*Chorus*
Three cheers, three cheers for gallant
Schley, brave Dewey and their men
The haughty don will never reign
Ore those fair isles again
And may our gallant heroes in
In memory ever dull
While stories of their courage
We all delight to tell

Farewell brave daring Lawton
Thy warfare now is ore
The bugles notes or saber's clash
To hear, no, never, more

The tazalos of the jungles
The red men of the velt
No longer dread, brave Lawton
His sword is now at rest

Long years he marched, ore desert
Or rode through mountain file
Alas. That he should end his life
Mid Luzons' mountains wild

Also the mysteries of this world
No one can ever know
Why God should low brave Lawton
to fall
To fall by hidden foe

We cannot understand the plans
Of he who rules on high
Why cowards revel in this world
And brave men they must die

Speak kindly of brave Lawton
On others cast your blame
He died obeying orders
Fighting for gold and fame

To fill the shylocks' coffers
With pale and ill got gain
While sights and tears are flowing
From loved ones of the slain

Brave Lawton we will ever thy
deeds rejoice to tell
Through now as sadly bid you
True friend brave heart farewell

On the day before Christmas William wrote another poem inspired by the Battle in the Philippines.

Brave Stottsenberg, tho sometimes rash
And wry oft seemed unkind
But when the battle's strife was on
We bravely led the line

And when the fight was hottest
And some perchance might run
With neither horse nor saber w
We nobly fought with gun

Our hero with his loved one's
Not many miles away
Perhaps were thinking of the home
They'd left in lands far, far away

When suddenly there came a sound
Brave Stottsenberg knew well
Alas for home and love ones dear
That sound was his death knell

Like whirlwind went brave Stottsenberg
Through swamp and jungle wild
Like Sheridan's, tho not so long
It was a fearful rider

We quickly saw the danger
His gallant men was in
A charge from bugle sounded
Then sounded the battles dim

Brave Stottsenberg advancing
To meet the deadly foe
When by the deadly mauler
Our hero was lured low.

From ambush, cowards have slain him
While brave men round him stood
With hearts now filled with sadness
Watched the ebbing of his blood

God's ways are strange but stranger still
Are the ways on this old earth
It rulers plan for millions war
To few they ere bring mirth

Beware ye rulers of the land
To avenges be not led
Brave Stottsenberg and Lawton's blood
May fall on your proud heads

Brave Stottsenberg thy gallant deeds
We've long delight to tell
And our hearts now sadly bid you
Brave Stottsenberg farewell

William added a dedication "to the loved ones of the gallant Stottsenberg these line kindly dedicated by the writer, Capt. W.H. Hunter, Lincoln, Nebraska."(42)

Joshua B. Doren, died in Lincoln in 1895. Doren had served as a soldier with the 114th USCT Company G and was a first sergeant. His unit formed in 1864 in Kentucky. Among other things he occupied Richmond, Virginia. *The Sable Arm*(38)

John W. Cadwallader, William's good friend, was buried ten years after him in 1911. Samuel Parker 113th Heavy Artillery had been seventeen when the war began. He came out of Arkansas, late in the war, through a consolidation with the 112th USCT. He was buried in 1923.

William's final companion, Archy Pullen, was laid to rest in 1937. Archy was a drummer in Company C of the USCT. His regiment was formed from the Iowa Colored and his duty had covered Arkansas and Tennessee. As soon as the 60th returned to Iowa they agreed to meet and push for the right to vote. About 700 men gathered at Davenport in 1865. They organized, signed a petition for suffrage for themselves and all black men in Iowa. In addition of pressing for the vote, they also resolved that all Negroes abstain from alcohol. They applauded the present governor of Iowa, William Stone, who was elected with a platform offering people of color in Iowa the vote. Suffrage was granted in 1869 by the United States Constitution.

Robert Woods of Company H of the 3rd USCT, had served in Louisiana. He was with the 3rd from Pennsylvania. He was interred in 1892.

In 1894, Fleming Harrison was honored by his burial in Grand Army of the Republic Circle. He served with Company H of the 15th USCT, organized in Nashville, Tennessee in 1863. His duty included the infamous Milikins Bend in Louisiana

Other colored troops, where they mustered and where they lay within Wyuka Cemetery:

Pvt. Alexander West 10th USCT, co. B Virginia
Pvt. Charles Wells 17 USCT, co. D Tennessee
Pvt. Andrew Nettles USCT, co. E Tennessee
Captain Peter Karburg 51st co. G. Louisiana
John Somerfield 56th USCT, co. G Infantry Missouri
John Auman 135th USCT, co. K Infantry North Carolina
Pvt. Fleming C. Harrison 1st U.S. Colored, Co. H Mississippi
Captain William Benjamin Coffey, 5th Colored Troop Infantry co. F, Ohio and the 79th New. (42 & 45)

Coffey fought at Jamestown where slaves first arrived. Tribute from his unit below.*

All prisoners of the 51st were butchered in Alabama in 1865 at Fort Blakely.

Another Nebraska related veteran, William Owen Van Vaxen Goodlow, 16th USCT, Co. E Tennessee, who served with Pullen rests elsewhere.

*Luther Givehand*

*"There is a brighter day coming for the colored man and he must sacrifice home comforts and his blood if necessary, to speed the coming of that glorious day,"
Feb. 4, 1864, Sergeant Milton Holland of the 5th

*Like Men of War*(53)

Some readers may find it of interest that there were so many mysterious circumstances that occurred during the creation of this book. Amy would like to share these as she experienced them.

"My mother-in-law, Drucilla Sadle, took pride in her grandfather's participation in the Civil War. I saw the poetry he wrote about his wife and his obituary listing of his service record. In a shadow box were her grandmother's small clay pipe, his medals and a few other momentos. It was rumored he had left a diary and that he had arrested his wife as a spy. We had visited his grave in Lincoln, but thought 'US. Col.' was some military unit. I found interest in these things but put no serious effort into finding more information, and so knew very little.

My husband and I spent years traveling and completing both the Sadle and my Brandon genealogies. Two of our adult daughters were told by dentists that they each had 'Native American tooth enamel' ( vertical ridges and serration on the front teeth). With interest Jack and I assumed that since neither of us had seen a source of this history in our genealogies we would stop in Natchez and investigate his great grandmother Sarah Drucilla Scothorne.

On that particular trip we stopped at Vicksburg and found William was a private, not a captain? This did not become clear until we discovered that he had enlisted as an officer of the colored troops. Next we stopped at the library and found Sarah was, in fact, a widow and her maiden name was Spencer. Six trips to Natchez and six years ensued as we widened the circle to many trips to Illinois, Indiana, Washington, D.C., Pennsylvania and Kansas.

Thousands of pieces were like a puzzle-only bits here and there. I eventually decided I would write a brief love story for our family use. The task began to grow to record the occupation and slavery. Because of my personal convictions, I began a prayer communication with my respected, deceased mother-in-law. It was mostly because I knew she would have enjoyed the information we were gathering.

Then began the following strange and powerful events.

1. After visiting William's tombstone I met the fox I describe in the last chapter.

2. Seeking a means of allowing the lovers to first meet, I invented an assignment. Four years later I found it was, in fact, his job to ride to both home plantations.

3. From the diary of Edwin Hobart I knew they shared an adventure so I created him as a best friend so that William could share his feelings about the war. Years later, I realized Edwin was their witness at the wedding. His assignment would have made it impossible for him to be present without great effort.

4. It was five years before I stumbled on information about the probable relationship of Sarah to a Cherokee great-grandmother. I had been walking through a large library and a tiny green pamplet caught my eye.

5. Near the end of the writing I had found no authentic, family stories for the Colored soldiers who served under William, and I had been praying about it. On a casual business call to Washington I connected with not one, but two true incidents.

6. A year and a half before I completed the manuscript, one thing that could not be circumstance happened. Because I am dyslexic I write things down. During the many times I had visited the cemetery in Lincoln I sought Colored troops in the small GAR circle, wondering if postwar bonds might have existed between men and officers. I had found none.

That June I feel I got a call from the grave, "You forgot my friends." At the location where I usually enter, I saw a stone marked USCT (United States Colored Troops). I went to the car to find a pen and pad. The stone was marked JOHN CADWALLER, 42ND USCT and I had never seen it before. Two weeks later, in Omaha I went to examine the Colored troops source index. The 42nd USCT served in Natchez. This man would have been William's roomate at McPhearson for the officers were housed together. The spelling on the pad of the name was different so I assumed he had changed his name to John W. CadwallADer. When possible I returned to the Lincoln cemetery. The stone *was not there.* After looking some time, I found it several rows away where I never go. It read JOHN W. CADWALLADER. There were also several colored enlisted troops there that I had overlooked in my many visits.

These were the many events that were encouraging. Others were not frightening to me, because of my sense of protection by my higher power, but they were quite dramatic. After the copyright and into final rewrites in June 2002 events occurred that I cannot explain other than as obstacles to the creation of the book.

1. My editor is quite professional, she could not find any of the novel in her files. That same day I called about a chapter I was mailing to a reader. When I returned my computer was jammed I worked some time, going "in and out." Then I remembered the editor's concurrent problem. The hair on the back of my neck rose. I got holy water and blessed my desk and computer area. It suddenly blinked back on.

2. Holy water must repair lots of problems, later three people could not attach a finished chapter on disk to an e-mail, until the holy water was applied and it went through immediately,

3. Two family members were told they probably had cancer. Because it was on the same day, in my opinion, "it was the hassle." I held tough and of course all was finally well.

4. The editor lives near a large city yet had no electrical power on a weekend she had assigned to work on the book. Of course, we both became suspicious of every interruption to our work and schedule, which might well have been accidental.

5. Then on September 12, 2002, at 5:30 am. our home, my husband's business and my art gallery burned. We had a 95 percent loss. In my opinion, this was no accident When the family was finally allowed inside I found an open cardboard box that sat in the middle of the room with over 300 loose footnotes which had not yet been entered into the text were unburned. The irreplaceable footnotes suffered only a few waterspots even though the firemen soaked the building for hours. The first five complete chapters were in white folders in the middle of studio table, with no smoke on them. My computer was melted, but the data was salvaged, as were the disks.

6. My editor's computer was destroyed by lightning, but her documents were saved.

7. The week I selected a printer to create the book my telephones were disabled, disks failed, word programs would not respond and my computer died.

I am witnessing and describing what I have observed in the challenging but also momentous birth of this novel." *Amy Sadle*